Baghdad at Night

By

Dallas Pearce

To Karl:

I hope you enjoy the book!
All the bg!

Baghdad at Night

By Dallas Pearce

Synergy Books Publishing
www.synergy-books.com
PO Box 911232
St. George, UT 84791

ISBN: 978-1-936434-70-1
(Paperback Edition)

Synergy Books Publishing, USA

Introduction

When I signed my life away at the ripe old age of eighteen, I had no idea what I was getting myself into. I had some idea, mind you, when I walked into the Army recruiter's office and pushed the button. I had been watching the news reports for years, I had read a lot of books on war, and I had seen all of the films.

I wanted to boldly go forth and change the world. I suppose everybody does that in their own way, for better or worse, regardless of whether or not they're sweating behind the butt-stock of a rifle in a foreign land.

I didn't always enjoy my time as a soldier. Some of it filled me with a sense of duty, and a deep, resounding pride that will last me a lifetime. Other times it just flat out sucked. As I've always said, you get what you pay for; they paid me, so that's really saying something.

I don't believe I succeeded in my young quest to create world peace through the majesty of small-arms combat, but I do believe I learned a thing or two about living.

I regret nothing about my military service; it will forever remain a source of deep personal pride for me. It gives me great pleasure to have finally finished my story, and I find it even more exciting that you've decided to take this journey with me.

There's not much more to say about this book. It's a part of my life, and in its own way, these pages and the type upon them have been my guide and counselor. Now that this tale is in print, after these few short years, maybe I can finally move on to a different subject.

I've always loved military literature. My all-time favorite is *All Quiet on the Western Front* by Erich Maria Remarque. In the decade since I first read that book, I have encountered nothing like it.

Most military literature that I come across puts the reader into a position of poring over a tactical map or envisioning large scale military maneuvers. Novels, as well as cinema depicting the modern war are more concerned with showing us non-stop action, explosions, and incredible amalgams, instead of showing us what goes on inside of a soldier. Regretfully, I feel that modern media has reduced the man in uniform to nothing more than a boiler-plate plastic action figure become flesh.

Reader be warned. If you're looking for an accurate and tactically sound recount of troop movements and tactics in central Baghdad during 'the surge,' you are going to be sorely disappointed. Also, if you are looking for a tale about a man in a sleeveless shirt diving out of a fifth-story window to waste thirty terrorists in the street before he hits the ground, you are also going to be very dissatisfied with what follows. My story is none of the above; I hope you'll enjoy spending some quality time with me, and I hope I can show you what modern combat is really like.

Naturally, when thinking about writing this book I gave a lot of thought to operational security considerations. Though the characters in this story are based on real people, their features, names, and attributes have been changed. In this book there are also a lot of references to locations, military routes, and radio call-signs, all of which were randomly generated for the purpose of realism. My names are fake, my routes are invented, and the layouts and actual locations of the places I describe have been turned around and juxtaposed with one another; I've even changed the cardinal directions. Much to my detriment, is my lack of knowledge of the Arabic language. If in the creation of a fake name I have accidentally said something silly, you'll have to forgive me for that.

I wake up in Baghdad every morning, and I still go to sleep there every night. Thoughts of my time spent in Baghdad will never leave me, so I might as well ask you to come along for the ride. I've never liked long introductions myself, so let's go fire up the truck.

All the Way,
Sgt. Dallas Pearce

Contents

I thank God for my life, and my mother for believing that I could do this.
I thank my brother for inspiring me, and my father for always being there for me.
I dedicate this book to Chapel, who was always with me, helping me to keep my sanity, and teaching me to say, *"Two Weeks."*

Chapter One: Stagnant

No wind in your hair as you lay gazing at the sky,
Your vibrant eyes reflect the sun,
As the day goes flying by.
Your lips part to tell a story I've not heard,
Glossy pink as

The breeze plays in your hair,
And now you lie thinking:
'The hot gray clouds are stagnant today,'
Beautiful as you are -

A world away you lie upon the stones,
Alone with all your lonely thoughts.
Lonely though so beautiful you've become,
As the day goes flying by above,
Your vibrant eyes reflect the glowing sun.

Against the gray my static mind
Sifts through all my wasted time,
But I can only see the sun shine in your eyes.

There's a feeling printed in my sky today -
There always is lately.

It's almost like nobody else can see,
As the day goes flying by above,
Your crystal eyes become
A signal mirror shining for my soul.

Lying on the gray rocks in my head,
Nothing going on,
And no wind plays in your hair today.
The most beautiful thing I've ever seen
Is this thought of you,
Living in my mind.

That's how I get by lately.

Getting out of the truck is always liberating, save for all the shit that needs to be carried. I glance at the gray and cloudless sky as helicopters fly overhead, low enough to kick up dust all around our halting convoy. I'm put off that I can look directly at the subdued white sun without feeling pain from the brightness of it. It appears as though God put a neat hole-punch in the mute January gray; smaller than I'm used to, the tiny ball is a very dull, neutral white.

"Chinstrap, Fuck-Face!"

That would be Chapel, my best friend, and incidentally my Truck Commander for the last eight hours. Assault pack on my right shoulder, rifle clutched in my right fist, I reach up with my left hand to secure my helmet to my head. The time to joke is over, and the moment to move has once again arrived.

The Humvees break from their lazy-W positions and slowly trundle to their parking places nestled against a fortified wall of HESCO barriers. I feel a bit naked now that I've dismounted. This is a new neighborhood, and none of us know what to expect. I fall in with my fellow soldiers, and start the journey toward our new home for the next eight days: an Iraqi police station in the very heart of Sahad, Baghdad.

"Check that shit out. Wow," my buddy Freddy says to me. I follow his pointing finger to my right, and my eyes rest on what appears to be a miniature wrecking yard. Dismantled, rusted, and previously detonated cars haphazardly litter the small yard, bordered by twelve-foot-high sectional concrete barriers.

Nothing seems to have moved here for a while. A sparse scattering of small weeds and snack food garbage bend and flutter in the light January breeze, scattered around blown out wrecks of vehicles and random industrial looking garbage. A paint can here, or an old tool box there, lie among the other detritus that thickly populates the narrow alleyways between the destroyed vehicles. I keep grinding my vision across the wrecks until I see the objects of Freddy's attention.

"Hajji-Kittens!"

Out of the twisted metal and garbage, four baby cats emerge and look confusedly on at the twenty-five of us as we trudge by.

"They probably don't speak fucking English either," I say over my shoulder, smirking to myself. Freddy nods and waves to the critters as we pass the fledgling family, saying, "*Salom Alikom!*" But the cats don't reply.

Making our way through a makeshift courtyard of sorts that is formed by towering concrete barriers, we enter the main foyer of the musty, blue brick building that is to be our home for the coming days. Then I see the stairs, always a pleasure. But these are not stairs in the American sense of the word. Uneven hand-shaped concrete leads to the second floor of the station, like a very lumpy handicapped ramp. The foyer of the police station seems to be in slightly better shape, although the housekeeping could be better.

Iraqi policemen with sleepy eyes and apathetic expressions stare blankly at us as we begin our journey to the second level of the building. At once I'm overwhelmed with the stench of old dirt and body odor as we move deeper into the structure.

Except for the cracked plastic paint buckets that serve as trashcans, a couple of shoddy wooden benches, and some very nice standing marble ashtrays that were no doubt stolen from the 1970s, the foyer is completely bare. Just to the right of the stairs I can see a small jail cell, although I can't tell if it's occupied. It's too dark to see much deeper into the building as my eyes have not yet adjusted to the dim light, the only sources of which emanate from the main entryway and a square shaped hole in the roof at the top of the staircase ahead of us.

We climb the wacky pseudo-stairs with little incident and emerge onto an outdoor patio; the flooring is nothing but simple slabs of concrete that serve as the roof for the chamber below.

Half a dozen policemen stand and smoke with their uniforms disheveled, and their eyes jealously eyeing our rifles. Two Iraqi men in filthy off-white undershirts move slowly and nonchalantly away from the doorway that our Lieutenant is leading us toward.

From my second-story position I can see a decent swatch of the city from either side of the odd rooftop, or social gathering area, as we make our way across the breezeway, relatively naked to the city except for the small reassurance provided by the concrete barriers that separate the police station from the residential streets below. I can hear more helicopters clipping through the sky above, but I don't have time to search for them and see what they are before we sweep into our new home.

Just inside, we find the open bay that will house the twenty-five of us for the next eight days. Scouts and Delta Company; we're one big happy family.

We scouts stick together in our billeting arrangements. For now, there are only six of us attached to D Co, as our whole platoon has been butchered into small squad-sized attachments and placed with each of the

4

companies: Alpha, Bravo, Charlie, and Delta. Counterproductive, I think, as we have always trained as a platoon. It's disconcerting to have our cohesive element separated and spread paper thin across the entire battalion.

Delta company is a fun company. We call it AT-4, or heavy weapons platoon. There's a bit of comfort in being attached to the company that rocks .50 calibers, MK-19s, and anti-tank rocket systems when they drive.

Together the six of us, Freddy, Duke, Cole, SGT Dick, SSGT Cloud, and myself make our way down the long aisle in the center of the dusty, dirt-filled bay to a row of cots at the end of the chamber.

I select the rearmost cot, far back in a darkened corner. That's my own personal sleeping style; out of sight, out of mind. Fewer men in body armor trip over me that way.

Putting down equipment is always a pleasure. Helmet first, it gets the pillow position. Assault pack goes at the foot of the cot. Not too heavy now, it contains mostly necessities like water, MREs, socks, underwear, a spare uniform, night vision shit, and some other minutia. Rifle, lover, girlfriend, whatever you want to call her, she comes next. Right on the cot. She sleeps with me.

Body armor next, and then I'm free. I sit on the edge of my new cot and stare at the dirt speckled floor between my boots. Beads of sweat drip off my nose, and I wipe my face with my already salt-starched sleeve. It's going to be a long week.

After SSGT Cloud finishes making his own gear deposit, he leaves our group to consult with the platoon sergeant, no doubt drawing up our schedules for tower guard and foot patrol shifts. In the meantime, the rest of us are free to go piss, drink water, maybe grab a snack, and take in our new pad.

Freddy is a bit older than me, twenty-three maybe. I think he's an all right guy. I've only been with the scout platoon since October, so it's still a new crowd for me.

"How's your mom, Freddy?"

"My mom's a whore."

He smiles and chuckles to himself while I take a drink from my canteen, suddenly laughing, choking, and sputtering on the gush of tragically wasted water that now rains onto my boots.

"I asked how she was doing, not what she was, Silly."

I thought he'd say that. That's the running joke. Has been for months, and it never seems to get old. One just doesn't expect to hear someone talk about his mother that way, although Freddy doesn't seem to care.

We dress down to our undershirts now. It's only January in Baghdad, but this morning it's already sixty-five degrees outside, which is a fairly toasty temperature for walking around in full kit.

Freddy reaches his arms into the air above him and arches his back, stretching away the cramps slouching in a military truck brings. He's been driving lately, which is an involved task that doesn't allow much in the way of comfort.

As he lifts his arms aloft, his boa reveals itself. It's probably one of the biggest, and most unique and amusing pieces of tattoo work I've ever seen. The tail end of the beast, almost two inches wide, starts at his right wrist. The body of the beast, ever widening, climbs his skinny arm all the way to his shoulder where the snake's broad, open-mouthed head always hides under the short sleeves of a tan army-issue undershirt.

One cot past Freddy, Cole is already asleep, naked from the waist up with his tactical blanket, or woobie, laid out beneath him on his cot. Beyond his sleeping body, SGT Dick can't be seen. Probably off pissing. Or flogging the dolphin or some shit. That guy's a fuck.

I recline on my green army cot and think about the morning. Uneventful, but nerve racking as always, our long and pointless mounted patrol took us across the same six miles of central Baghdad again, and again, and again. Cultural tours are exotic experiences and are even somewhat enjoyable at times. However, the fact that we are required to drive for eight hour blocks of time is a bit disconcerting, when thoughts of IEDs enter our heads. Everyone is always looking for them. Drivers, truck commanders, dismounts, gunners, everybody is always on the watch for roadside bombs. So along with dirty Arabian streets, Muslim children begging for soccer balls and chocolate, falafel stands and cigarette vendors, every large piece of garbage, every cardboard box, and every vehicle, unoccupied or otherwise, has the potential to explode at any second.

Apparently there are new artists in the country, whose specialty is making powerful explosively formed projectiles covered in neat little paper and foam facades, made to look exactly like stones or chunks of concrete. Yeah. Good luck finding those.

Baghdad hasn't had a functioning trash service since the 1970s, a period of time that some of the old men refer to as 'the Golden Age' of

Baghdad. Instead of dealing with public garbage like a normal, modern civilization, Iraqis simply discard their garbage into the street. This is a city of six million people. Six million people throw their garbage into the street for two thousand years, and our job is to find bombs in all the junk. Sure; we'll get right on that.

Our new home doesn't have a window, and the space was never fitted with electrical outlets or lighting. The only illumination that enters the open bay streams in through the cheap piece of bent wood on weathered hinges that begs to be recognized as the door. Other than that, a half dozen or so red flashlight beams dart hither and yon about the darkened space as soldiers, still mostly settling in, dig deep into their assault packs for books, water, toilet paper, or food.

I'm tempted to reach into my pack and pull out my copy of the *Canterbury Tales*, purchased in the warm, coffee-scented safety of Barnes and Noble, my personal ashram, less than a month ago. But my brain says no. This morning happened at around two a.m. Add on an eight hour drive of super-alertness, and you have us here and now, at 1000 hours. Dallas is sleepy. So instead of bending down to grab the book from my assault pack, I simply lay down, helmet serving as my impromptu pillow, and shut my eyes.

My world goes blissfully dark in my own little corner. I can hear the rest of the newly made barracks bay growing quiet as conversations dim one by one, going out like snuffed candles. I hear a gas-powered electric generator somewhere near and below, and smell my own sweat mingled with the scent of the old concrete building, which is composed primarily of mustiness and green smells: my new friends. I think about Emily briefly before blessed darkness overtakes my world.

I feel myself sink a little deeper into my green canvass bed, and then I don't think about anything.

I didn't dream. I wake from the darkness with Freddy roughly shaking my shoulder.

"Go time, brother man."

"Fuck."

It's a random draw when we get to work at a site like this. There are three squads on rotation in D Co, broken down into three working shifts. Who does what on arrival is decided by a formal pow wow between squad leaders, the platoon SGT, and our Lieutenant. One squad will work the

7

Command Post. This is also their eight hour block of down time. Individual soldiers work the CP while others sleep. It's quite rare to sleep all the way through a down shift; invariably, your number comes up more often than not, so sleep patterns are disorderly, if nothing else. Second, one group will stand tower guard for an eight hour block, while a third squad patrols the local environs on foot. That makes for eight hours up and sitting, eight hours up and walking, one hour working as a radio operator, and if we're lucky, about seven hours of time to sleep, eat, shave, read, or whatever.

Scouts are unlucky today, as usual. As an attachment, we normally get volunteered first. Those are the rules.

"How long have I been out, Freddy?"

"Fifteen, maybe."

"That doesn't seem very fair, now does it?" Freddy gives me the internationally accepted facial expression for 'Duh,' and replies, "You were expecting a good rest?"

I think for a moment. "Truth be told, no."

"Good."

And then we're moving. Blouses on, armor next, then rifles are slung, and helmets donned. Water supply, check.

"Where are we headed?"

Freddy thumbs the air behind him and above, "To the towers."

"Ugh, I say. Ugh."

"All right, Popeye, let's go."

Normally a tower shift wouldn't be so monotonous or demanding. It's only eight hours to sit and watch things, after all. You could watch grass grow, if there was any to be found. Most of the other squads have ten or more people in them, but for us scouts, as there are only six of us, with only five that do actual work, we often get spread rather thin. So while many of the others work their towers with buddies that they can talk to, we scouts get split and go it alone. More often than not, our mission changes. 'The War on Terror' frequently escalates, at the individual level, to 'The War on Boredom.'

"We know where we're headed yet?"

"Yeah, D, you're going southwest."

"Catch you later, road homey."

Freddy nods to me, "Peace."

I make my way out of the darkened barracks into the bright midmorning sun of central Baghdad. Here on the previously visited patio area, there are wall lockers that the IPs use for all their personal durka shit. I can't see too far into the city from this vantage point, but I can make out enough to remind myself of where I am, and that it's time to wake up.

Switching on my radio, I do a quick coms check with the CP to make sure my mic is up and running as I climb the flimsy, clanking aluminum stairs that lead the way up to tower one.

This isn't a military base of any kind. Nobody has yet solved the mystery as to why there are concrete fortifications on the roof, although I think they're probably leftovers from the older conflicts this city has seen. Or, they may have been hastily built during Mr. Hussein's futile attempt to repel 'the Great Satan.' In any case, they do the trick for us. Hell, if they weren't here we'd probably be filling sandbags by now.

As soon as I'm up in my tower, I take a look around. Generally, the slits in most of the towers' fortifications are open and without covering. But, for the time being, tower one is blessed with having a bit of old camo-netting draped across the view ports. That's good for my soul. The netting makes me feel more hidden, and less like I'm about to get my face blown off by a sniper, which is exactly the kind of person that I'm supposed to be looking for.

The big news coming down from command lately focuses on the unsettling fact that many foreign fighters from Iran, Syria, and Assistan have been employed specifically to target and kill American soldiers in the city. This means paid professionals, as opposed to the usual Kalashnikov wielding rabble. Experienced soldier-types with discipline and good long-guns for sniping.

Neat! Someone left me binoculars.

I call downstairs with my radio to tell them that I'm set. I look at my wristwatch: just about 1000. So, 1800 will be a good time. And here I am. I sit. I listen. I look around. And I wait for something, anything. Nothing.

I try to vary my routine as much as possible, though options are limited when one's sole occupation is to sit in a concrete box for eight hours. Like jail, I warrant. Anyhow, I scan my sector from left to right, over and over again, for as long as I can. I try to remain vigilant and disciplined by not looking at my watch.

When I finally do break down and check it, I find that forty-five minutes have passed. Swell. So I start to play my super-human tower guard game again, this time spicing it up a little bit: I move my eyes right to left, instead of left to right. I'm not complaining about the quiet. Any situation to the contrary involves blood and death, fear, courage, and the like. I'm tired, and though Baghdad is generally a wicked animal, this morning it seems a bit serene.

I can hear a wild dog barking in the distance to the south. Underneath my tower, just outside the concrete barrier that surrounds the compound, groups of children are playing soccer, which is what you can easily consider to be the national Iraqi pastime, aside from selling goat falafels, of course. Soccer, or football, takes precedence over even some of the more important Muslim activities, such as prayer time. Beyond, from my fourth-story position, I can see into the private backyard worlds of local people, who for the most part seem to be minding their own business.

Against the landscape of what would otherwise be a peaceful late winter morning, I can see the signs that betray why nobody ever books a vacation at this locale; nobody other than my kind, anyhow. Beneath the brightly glowing sun, under the shade of hundreds of backyard palm trees, I can see the makeshift mud and hodge-podge brick fences that surround local dwellings. Every fence is topped with a deterrent of some sort. A rare few have intricate mechanisms like barbed, or what you would consider to be razor wire, or concertina, but generally the common people can't afford such extravagance. Instead, broken glass is seated atop almost every fence, secured into position by mortar of some kind. Many Arabs choose to be a little festive about this defensive measure, like Americans with their Christmas lights. No, no, one wouldn't deck out his whole home around the holiday season with nothing but white lights. I believe it's the same mentality for aesthetic pizzazz and festive variety that leads most Arabs to use assorted pieces of multi-colored glass. So rather than mundane landscapes of clear jaggedness, there is green beer bottle glass and glass that's been painted red or blue. A common theme is to paint all of the backyard glass in patriotic colors, those being red, white, and green. Sometimes even gold. *Allah Hu'l Ahkbar.*

Among the glinting blades of sharp backyard fences and foreboding glass daggers, miscellaneous wires stretch over the whole cityscape for as far as the eye can see. Having generally no civic power supply, or a governing body that would regulate their employment, wires are strewn haphazardly, seemingly at their own volition and whim.

I count them: there are fifty-five backyards that I can see into. I can also view a local road from my vantage point, though I cannot pronounce its name, *Al'Safahak-fa' Al'Saifahdurk'hula'l* or something, but I can watch the cars as they lazily trundle by on this warm winter morning.

There is not much that goes on in public in Baghdad after noon or so. Most street vendors, the primary way people make their living in this town, close up at about noon to beat the heat. That, and I've never heard of anyone accusing Iraqis of having an outstanding work ethic. That is, unless they're trying to blow something up.

I remain diligent. I remain vigilant. SGT Pearce, as I am commonly addressed, completes a successful radio check every hour. There have been three so far. Which means that I'm almost halfway done.

I lie to myself consciously. I say, "Pearce, you're halfway done now." I smile. I feel good about this new news.

At times like these, I can't stop my thoughts. I can't stop drifting. It would be the same way with you. Unless somebody out in that great urban unknown discharges a firearm at you, there's not a whole lot going on that can steal your attention. So I count, I think, and I sing to myself. Anything to stay awake.

She's there in my mind, clearly. Like a stained glass window that hangs before my eyes, threatening to cover the urban landscape. I can't remember her face if I try to think of it in static form, so I have to envision an instance, a context in which I can see her. So I tell her a joke and she laughs. Then I can see her smile. Or I listen as she talks to me. If I think about the words she's saying, I can make out her voice. Army life is great for cultivating wonderful powers of concentration and imagination.

Four years is a long time to hold down a long distance relationship. I try to make it fun and good. We do, after all, see each other every three months or so. She goes to college in New York, and I'm stationed at Ft. Bragg, NC, so it's not too big of a deal to schedule a train ride or a plane ticket. Anything, just to be able to see her.

For the last three years, our relationship has gradually unfolded itself, first in hotel rooms, and then my apartment, which I've since left. These visitations are punctuated every once in a while by a good dinner or a night out on the town. Generally, there's not a whole lot of personal growth that can happen between two people once every three months, though talking over the telephone helps a bit. I think to myself about the recent times we've spent together, and I get the number forty-seven. I've seen her on forty-seven days since I left her four years ago.

That's the kind of monotonous shit I think about when I have three hours left to go in the box.

I love her more than anything, but I'm used to going without. At that, I'm a seasoned veteran.

Suddenly, the monotony of my personal reverie is broken when a flash of red movement catches my eye. Startled out of my thoughts, having certainly gone too deep, I quickly snap my gaze down and to the left, focusing my eyes on the source.

It's a little girl, waving a red paper heart high over her head in the bright afternoon sun. I didn't even know that the heart was a symbol in this country; I always equated that to be a western sort of thing. Here's one for Baghdad, I suppose.

She's probably about two hundred meters away from me, but I can still make out her smiling face. She's making an obvious display of waving this paper heart at my tower. I know she can't see me; the camo-netting assures me of that, but still, in a way, I find it disconcerting. This is not the sort of environment I usually expect eight-year-old girlish cuteness to come from.

Even so, whether she's looking at me or not matters little. She's movement that I can watch. Anything moving is much more entertaining than watching rocks or an empty street. There's no landscaping in this city, and therefore no irrigation, tragically resulting in no grass to watch grow.

In my own way, I'm very thankful to this little Arab girl. She's like company. She's talking to me. She's young, and happy, and alive. Though her happy state cannot last in this terrible city, I don't think about its inevitable end this morning.

I join her in her dance. She makes me happy. She reminds me that no matter where we are, the sun shines on all of us, whether we're baking in a concrete box or not.

I've run out of water. *Fuck.* Two hours left. I can see the bottom of the reddening sun now as it starts to descend into my view from the heavens above. It's blinding, so I take the time to switch out the lenses on my army-issue Oakley M-frames from clear to gray, and then continue my observations. My new friend has left me alone again with my thoughts, and I already miss her. She's been gone for a while now; my throat is dry, and I no longer feel like singing.

I stare again at the enemy city. The heathen city. The city filled with the bane of all Christendom, the unfaithful, and laugh. Whoever thought being a crusader would be this much fun?

After two more radio checks, it's over. Triumphantly, for me that is, I hear armor and gear laden boot-steps fast approaching my position from down the shoddy stairs, and I get that same giddy feeling I've been getting since grade school -- the one that tells me I've just finished my homework, or a project, or something.

It's Moore and Forrester. I don't really know anything about either of them, other than their names, and that they were silly enough to become airborne infantryman, just like me. I quickly say howdy, thank them for liberating me from the cruel clutches of tower one, and then I continue on my merry way down the stairs. I'm so looking forward to a nap. It's stupid to feel a sense of freedom here though, as I know what's waiting downstairs.

Cole gets to the barracks area before I do, and so promptly delivers me the news when I arrive.

"Fuck."

"Yeah, foot patrol is on after tower."

"Thanks Cole; I needed that."

There's no undressing. No sleep. No napping. Nothing. I just get to piss and fill my canteen again. Yay.

The scout squad, just the six of us, get to spend the next eight hours walking around town, smelling the smells, seeing the sights, and trying to communicate as best we can with locals, in an attempt to gather pertinent information about our new neighborhood. Command has assisted us further by not providing us with an interpreter this week. Maybe that's a secret training measure to motivate us into learning hajji-speak at an incredible rate. Who knows?

Along our foot-patrol route, everyone seems to be generally happy. No, there's no violence here, they say. No explosions, yada yada bullshit. Sure, just none that they want to tell us about. Thank goodness, some Iraqis in this town speak a smattering of Engrish. If they didn't, we'd be totally fudged.

It's still our first month, and this is still one of our first patrols. We're still taking it all in at face value, seeing what it looks like, and getting a feel for it; just experiencing the general reality of this new planet. Anything that a tourist in a new locale would do, we're doing it. Only we

13

don't take as many pictures, we brought our own maps, we don't have local currency, and we're not having any fun. But at least we're packing heat. Oh, are we ever.

The neighborhood in Sahad seems decent enough. There is less trash here than in most places, although there is still plenty to speak of. I can actually see the gutter in some rare instances, and the front yards of individual houses seem to be policed nicely. Some even appear to be manicured in a way, as best the owners can, by keeping the sewage-weeds in check, tiled entryways shiny, and the common palm trees rather healthy looking.

No contact with the enemy has yet been reported by any of our fellow squads. As we walk along in the setting sun throughout the quiet evening, under the harmless fronds of tropical-esque trees, we keep a constant lookout.

I can smell locals cooking dinner. The setting sun casts a beautiful red glow against the stone houses as we walk by, and I can see a single velvet cloud, a stratus I think, high above. It slowly grinds across the sky carrying a blue-pink color that feels like home. We relax a little. The war's pretty chill today. Just a groovy little war. That's all. Nothing major, Sir.

I'm walking close to Freddy in formation. At this point in the war, he's my best buddy in the squad. From up ahead, Duke addresses everyone.

"About chow time, isn't it?"

I smile to myself.

Yea. That's what I was thinking, Lard-O.

All of us concur; we've been awake and working for upwards of twenty hours now, and nobody seems to have given much thought to anything other than drinking water. Our thoughts all begin drifting towards warm food, now that the cursed mention of it has been made. The sun is setting and the temperature is rapidly descending into the forties. It's been a long day and we're all covered in sweat, so we all feel the sudden chill coming on.

"Carl's Junior six dollar bacon cheeseburger, with extra cheese and guacamole sauce, with fries and a large ice-cold Coke."

I can't help it; the wonderful thought is audibly ejected from my mouth, and the majority of my squad gives grunting, or cussing acknowledgements that such a thing would be fantastic right about now.

"Shut the fuck up, Pearce, and keep your cruel, unattainable thoughts

14

to yourself. *Fuck*, dude."

Dick seems generally displeased that I smashed his lust for an MRE in a single sentence.

"Warm day today," I arbitrarily mention to no one in particular.

SSGT Cloud rounds on us over his left shoulder and makes his comment, "Used to be."

As a group, we all agree. As we're walking and scanning, scanning and walking, I reach into my left cargo pocket and pull out my neck-gaiter, which is a wonderfully warm, seldom forgotten, and very comfortable piece of clothing. As one, we duck into an open yard in front of what appears to be a fairly affluent house, at least in comparison to the rest of the neighborhood. I judge the owners to be very wealthy, by multi-colored Monopoly money standards. Something about the marble pillars that support the house's Persian façade just says '*Ritz!*'

Crouching, with my voice hushed, I feel the need to comment to the guys in reference to the owner of the unusually fine property.

"Man, this motherfucker's dirt-rich." Everyone laughs a bit, but properly, whisper-laughing, as we kneel and take off our helmets.

I take this time out to slip my neck-gaiter over my head, and immediately feel the assuring dry warmth begin to surround my head and neck, telling me that I won't be uncomfortably cold for much longer. Quickly, everyone in our small party digs their night vision crap out of pockets or tactical pouches, and affixes the devices, or nods as we call them, to our helmets. America loves the nighttime.

Everyone's gear checks out, and we proceed into the darkness that's slowly unfurling over Sahad, central Baghdad. Everywhere we patrol, I can smell the low rot of garbage, and overtones of a local ginger-like spice that seems to float on the air wherever anyone's cooking anything.

We pass home after home, our destination not really known. We walk a bit, take a left turn, then we try to talk to a local. Walk a bit, take a left turn, try to talk to a local. Repeat. Repeat. Each time taking slightly different turns, and viewing and passing by slightly different local streets, people, and cars, all of which are parked.

The soccer children have gone home for the day; Baghdad goes to bed early, except for the occasional group of people hanging out on the street in front of their small homes, engaging in behavior that you can sort of refer to as a barbeque, or tailgating. Cole strongly disagrees, as he's from Louisiana.

Unmistakable though, is the smell of pot that issues up from every one of these little truckless tailgate parties. Unmistakable also, are the laughs and bloodshot eyes of the locals that we try to speak with. Most of the attempted communication is ineffective at best. The locals speak only one or two words of English, and as none of us have been 'in country' for very long, we've not really learned to speak Arabic either. I never intend to, save for what is absolutely necessary for basic communication and general inner-city wartime survival skills. Funny how that happens, by the way; outlaw alcohol, and everyone smokes hashish. Weird.

As we move on, to our left we pass a small house with handprint of blood smeared on the entryway. I'm not the only one of our group that finds this alarming, so we document it. We knock on the door aiming to pose the question, but there's no answer, so we hang up our Sherlock hats and press on down the street.

Our journey brings us to a friendly, smiling, late-night neighborhood food vendor. He's a man who appears to be in his late forties, casually tending to a metal counter on wheels that stands directly in front of what we assume is his home. We don't know exactly what he's cooking, but it smells all right. We're all starving at this point, so springing at the chance to sample some exotic homemade cuisine seems like a great idea.

The local falafel buns are made of what we call foot bread: a sort of Mexican-esque flat bread that we believe to be kneaded by the bare feet of the local women who bake it. Within the bread lies some sort of meat, a mixture of somewhat recognizable vegetables, and a strange yellow paste that reminds everyone of mustard, although it does not seem to have a particular odor, or taste.

We buy twelve of them for a dollar, God bless America. By decree of the clock, in three hours' time, we'll be able to go back to our barracks and eat them.

The squad is starting to feel comfortable with our new neighborhood. For the third time, we approach the Entry Control Point of our new home, and SSGT Cloud wishes to speak to us.

We make our way passed the four Iraqi policemen who stand guard at the vehicle gate. Already, we're trying to pick up some of the local courtesies.

"Salam Alikom."

"Alikom Salam!" The IP that speaks flashes us a hearty, though chipped and yellowed grin. Although they are insufficiently trained and somewhat lackadaisical in their duties, it's important to remember that our allies here fight the same fight we do, and most likely have families that

they care for nearby. Their fight is our fight, and vice versa. A little mutual understanding serves as a reminder of our humanity, as well as that there is no real division of us and them, but rather, we're all people who desire the same thing: a lasting peace. Mechanical and to the point, our greetings are not without some feeling. It is after all grounding, if not gratifying, to learn local customs in a new land. It serves to remind us of where we are. Importantly as well, it makes us feel, as well as seem to others, a bit more friendly. It's always important to have some good sentiment among allies, especially when we are invaders in their country.

Just inside the safety of the concrete walls, SSGT Cloud gathers us all around in a sort of quasi-football huddle. We all crouch down together and get ready to have a listen.

SSGT Cloud is a man of small stature and very Hispanic. I've never asked him whether he hails from Mexico, Puerto Rico, Colombia, Cuba, or wherever. Some people find that disrespectful. I think it's Mexico though. His English is heavily accented, although easily understandable. Under his calm, casual façade, everyone understands that he knows his subject matter. Everyone that is, but SGT Dick; he never understands much of anything. Cloud is regarded by the rest of us as a true soldier. Although hardly autocratic and less than domineering, he has a manner that exudes confidence and subtly demands respect. His nose is also without peer: he can smell anything. Primarily my cigarette habit, which he loathes.

"All right you guys. Notepads."

Without a hitch, all together, we hardy soldiers deploy our pens and writing materials. Programming comes in handy every now and again.

"We're here." He points to a hastily drawn X on the ground and proceeds to draw the streets that surround the police station, or Joint Service Station; our current location, the JSS.

"This will be a good exercise. The way I see it, the neighborhood is really quiet tonight. There's little chance that we're going to be spotted if we break into groups of two. It'll be a good opportunity for us to get a better feel for the locale. Also, we may have a chance to see some stuff that otherwise we wouldn't in a group of six. Everyone comfortable with that?"

We look around at each other, feeling for the group sentiment, and we read each other very well. Everyone seems excited at the prospect of venturing out into a foreign neighborhood, in a dangerous city to play ninja. That is a scout's job, after all. SSGT Cloud sees that we all approve and is satisfied.

With no further commentary about how we feel about what we are going to do, Cloud proceeds to give us our approximate zones of patrol, relying more on generality and cardinal directions than the hastily drawn boxes and lines in the dirt beneath us.

"Good. Time?"

From SGT Dick, "0130."

"All right."

As we move back to our feet, we flip our nods down over our faces. Being as we're the cool folks of the common rabble, we get the monocular type unit. It's much handier than the older, more cumbersome model that covers both eyes, allowing us to see in the dark, as well as not completely robbing the wearer of his peripheral vision and depth perception. Even better, the slimmer, more ergonomic unit is lighter and more comfortably and conveniently stored in pouches. The tradeoff however is a bit of foolery that goes on in the brain before the operator is totally used to the monocular effect. The wearer's eye that remains in darkness keeps transmitting as usual, while the viewpoint for the eye utilizing the optic is projected to the brain as being a good three inches forward of normal. At first, it's a weird kind of cross-eyed, but everyone eventually adapts to it, as if seeing into the darkness with an electronic telescope hanging from half of the user's face was a totally natural experience.

Cloud closes out his briefing.

"Me and Cole will walk together. Freddy, you go with Pearce. SGT Dick can accompany Duke. Meet up here at the ECP at 0245. We'll talk about what we see then. Listen up, I'm not gonna lie, if anything hot happens, send it up on coms and di-di-mao back to this location immediately. Nobody dies in our first month. Clear?"

"Roger, Sergeant."

Cloud gives a nod of approval at our apparent understanding, and turns on his heels toward the gate. I don't think I've ever seen a more light-footed man, other than Baryshnikov. He just has one of those walks, like a man in a 1940s film that just got that big promotion.

Freddy and I break off from the rest just outside the gate. We space out from one another and move to the darker side of the street, hidden from the light of the desert moon in the shadows of the concrete barriers.

Orange light burns from foreign made floodlights atop the JSS, threatening to betray us to observers with their bright slivers of rusty light that slip through the seams of the sectional concrete wall. A few dozen

18

meters more and we're away from the JSS, walking away from our buddies, assistance, and help of any kind. It's a funny feeling to walk alone, as two friends, into a terrorist occupied neighborhood in arguably one of the most dangerous cities on the planet.

Through my green digital eye, I look to my right and make monocular eye contact with Freddy. He's tall, six-foot-two maybe, with a care-free east coast swagger and a genuine goofy smile; just an all-around good guy. In good keeping with his monochromatic appearance, he shoots me a broad grin and exclaims, albeit very quietly, "Man, I love being a turtle."

I stifle a good laugh because the comment fits the situation so well. Green light. Shell-like armor and backpack. Sneaking in the shadows. Very accurate indeed.

Everybody comes back alive from our first solo patrol in Sahad, with a complete set of fingers and toes to boot. We meet up in the main courtyard at 0245 on the dot, lock and clear our weapons, and take the gleeful trudge upstairs to rest at long last. There's not much to say in the way of an after action review, as the night remained uneventful for us all.

After we deposit our gear on our bunks, Cloud happily distributes our easily won falafels. It's a game of catch played at rather short distance, but we all seem to manage without destroying any of the goopy little curiosities.

Cole takes one of the little breaded creatures and holds it in his Louisiana fist, just inches from his face. He looks like a prospector appraising a lump of rare ore.

"You think these are safe?" His question is aimed at nobody in particular, but I key onto it rather quickly.

"Well, the last time I checked, this city didn't appear to have any sanitation standards. The meat probably wasn't refrigerated, if you get me."

SGT Dick pipes in, "Shut the fuck up, Pearce. Everyone's hungry; don't ruin it."

"Roger, Sergeant." I half-smile and nod, but unable to stop myself in my new, however truthful jest, I continue, "But, you do know what night soil is?"

"I do!"

Cloud laugh-speaks around a mouthful of what we think is meat of some kind. "Pretty good too. Not bad at all."

Duke takes his first bite. In his usual pompous and sing-song tone, he states the question, "So, tell us D, what is night soil?"

"Should I tell him, Sergeant Cloud?"

Taking a moment to remind myself that I'm also terribly hungry, and am already tiring of MREs, I begin unwrapping my pseudo-sandwich from a thick blue layer of cellophane, the neighborhood equivalent of a to-go bag, and wait for a reply.

Cloud laughs a bit and responds through another mouthful, even more accented, "Go ahead. It doesn't bother me." He washes his first falafel down with a long draw on his CamelBak hose. "Growing up in my city, people grew crops the same way. I grew up eating market food. You pasty virgins be careful though."

"Pearce, out with it. What's night soil?"

Duke slows his chewing a bit as he eagerly awaits my response. Freddy and Cole even listen to the new cleric.

"Well you see, being as the dirt in this country is for all intents and purposes barren and radioactive, and Miracle-Gro isn't readily available, people fertilize their little backyard gardens with, you know, whatever's on hand."

Cole resumes his munching. "Like fish heads and stuff?"

"No, Pocahontas. Like feces and stuff. Shit. Doo-doo. Excrement. Human type, quantity one each. There's no bleach in this country either. A lot of the locals have never heard of bacteria, and disease and sickness are still largely attributed to demons and sinister, malicious spiritual forces."

Cole puts down his surviving falafel, now half eaten.

"Fuck you, asshole," followed by an uncomfortable verbal pause. "You ruined my first multi-cultural dining experience."

I laugh out loud, "There's no Panda-Express where you come from?"

"Fuck you."

"Damn it!"

This time Duke sounds off, informing me of his disapproval.

The squad is suddenly thrown into educated upheaval.

Sergeant Dick says, "Man, that's the most fucked-up thing you could have said. Do pushups."

Cloud speaks again. "Nope. You asked him. He speaks only the truth. You ever think about the specific reason they tell us not to buy food from locals? It's because you boxed-food, video game generation

20

virgins can't stomach real food. It's just how things are done outside of your Louisiana Lysol bubble."

I can't help it, though I'm already breathing heavily with the world quickly moving up and down, as I'm already pushing, though not so much because I have to; the ruse just seems funnier this way.

"Sergeant, if I may?"

"Speak up, D."

"I don't think that they have Lysol in Louisiana."

From the back, "Fuck you."

"Keep pushing."

"Roger." I reply, hitching now with pain and laughter as I do so. Twenty. Thirty. Forty.

Cloud laughs to himself, in on his own joke now, and lets my prospective torture slip under his radar this time.

So I just keep pushing. It's very difficult now, because I'm already tired, and now laughing much too hard. After I'm good and smoked, I'll eat a bit myself. The food smells great, in all of its lukewarm glory. Besides, I can always do a holistic parasite detox if I ever get back to the states.

Stalling out from exhaustion, my body rigid as I work my muscles, I start to get hungry as I watch the others eat. Up, down. Up, down. Up, down.

After eighty pushups or so, I'm spent. I'm not the best pusher-upper in the world, and coupled with the fact that I haven't slept or eaten for over twenty-four hours, I feel pretty weak-sauce.

After being satisfied that I have been sufficiently racked, SGT Dick allows me to come to my feet. Although we are both Sergeants, E-5 style bucks, he outranks me due to time in grade.

Catching my breath, I succumb to temptation and eat one falafel. Thank God, I don't eat two.

Pain. Twisting, searing pain. I grab my red photon light and look at my watch for the time: 0600. Three hours since the risky foreign meal. I was told to expect this. It happens to everyone the first time; that's why they tell us not to do it.

I'm covered in sweat. My stomach twists again and I feel bitter bile start to kick up in the back of my throat.

Trashcan.

I think there was one just outside the barracks door.

In less than a second I'm on my feet, red light cutting a dim path before me through the darkness to where a sliver of dusky light breaks through a crack in the barrack's shitty wooden door. Conveniently, I was sleeping with my boots on.

I heave once, but manage to keep it down.

I hate throwing up. I always have. I hate the taste, the burning, the uncontrollable heaving and the abject helplessness of it. Almost to the door now, and I heave again, but somehow keep the horrid, burning liquid inside of me.

I don't give much thought to being quiet at this point. The only squad that's down and resting is my scout squad, and they're all the way at the back of the barracks.

I noisily fling open the door and dash into the mute pre-dawn light, where I'm met with jubilant success. I see the trashcan I thought I remembered, mere feet from the door. I reach for the rim; it's a new can, and thank God, it's been emptied recently, bearing a new plastic liner.

I hurl away. Thank God twice, because I only ate one of the little demons.

After my episode, I walk sleepily and disorderly towards a bunch of lockers that have been pushed together to form a U shaped theatre, complete with shitty wooden chairs. It's the designated smoking area.

I light up and take a moment to reflect on what just happened, and I laugh a little. I know the crucible isn't yet over; with food-poisoning, if that's what you can call it here, there's bound to be at least one more show-time, maybe two.

The smoke tastes good. It doesn't fully cleanse my burning mouth and nose of the taste of puke and goat meat, but it helps a bit in its own fashion. When the cigarette dies, I wiggle the last of the tobacco leaves away from the filter, and then flip the useless butt into the nearby trashcan, my new friend. As if on cue, I'm suddenly helpless once again before my new altar, gripping the sides of the rim tightly as I begin to retch once more. I know this can and I will be spending a lot of quality time together over the next five hours or so. Grudgingly I assume the position, and feel a fresh wave of hot bile start to rise in my gullet.

"What's up, my puking expatriate?"

"Hey, Freddy. Kind of busy." The words slur out of my mouth, as if uttered by a helpless drunk. "About to-"

"Catch you at a bad time? Hah. You're the lucky one. At least

Islam's not coming out your ass right now."

I laugh at that -- a full and hearty belly-laugh. It's a big mistake with dire consequences, as I laugh-puke a great wad of yellow pseudo-mustard into my nose, and gag again.

"Can I get you anything?"

"*Wasser, bitte.*"

"You got it, Freud."

"Donkey's mane."

Four hours and four evacuations later I feel fine, if a bit shaky. Cole got it the worst of us I think; he's still in the port-a-shitter downstairs. Poor guy. I have no excuse; I told me so. He can't blame me for it though: I told him so too. Deep inside, that sort of thing makes me happy.

1200 hours. Tower guard again. Cole saunters in and joins in the mass-dressing with us.

"Welcome back," I comment to him as he reaches our group.

"Fuck you, D."

"Right. I'll do that; I might need to do a little yoga first though."

Chuckles all around. Routine is up. Blouse. Vest. Kit. Brain bucket. Gat. Agua. Got it all.

"Same positions as last time?"

Freddy, always in the know about our latest posting information, answers back, "Yep."

"Roger. Catch you after."

"Same bat time, same bat channel."

"You like the comics. Don't deny it Freddy. You really do."

"True that, homey. Proud of it too."

Freddy flashes me a hearty grin, as the truthful wrinkles of a genuine smile lightly crinkle the skin under his eyes.

"Later man."

"Late."

It's the same stair climb. The same concrete box. The same weather. The same view. Someone has removed the stool that so conveniently served me yesterday. That can only mean one thing: somebody got caught nodding off, the fuck. Now I have to pay for it by standing for eight hours in sixty pounds of shit. Thanks Fuck-O, whoever you are.

The absence of a stool greatly complicates my shift. I stand 5'11" tall. Add my Advanced Combat Helmet, or ACH, and I magically become 6'1". Arabs are generally tiny, and the concrete block I'm standing in has a ceiling that I feel must be about 5'8". I'm fucked. I Can't sit; the view ports would be way above my line of sight. Can't lean up against the wall to look out either: that's a sure way to silhouette myself as an easy rifle target.

So I begin my duties standing and slouching, in a very uncomfortable manner in the rear corner of the room. I can see out just fine from here. My wrist-watch tells me that I only have seven hours and forty-eight minutes left to go. Good. That's progress.

I start softly singing a mixture of Josh Groban and James Blunt songs to idly pass the time, as I resume the scanning patterns I developed yesterday. After about an hour, I don't feel like singing anymore.

Power lines and an empty street. Hastily made plaster coatings on small square concrete hovels. Miles of trash and litter. Every once in a while, American or UK armed forces give me a rare treat, providing me with the opportunity to view helicopters clipping their merry way across the dusty horizon. I appreciate them, as they're something interesting to look at. Blackhawks, Kiowas, Chinooks, and Apaches all populate the foreign sky. All the tribes seem to be active today. I even manage to catch a glimpse of some 'little birds,' the special forces motorcycles of the sky.

Every once in a while, neat little chocolate-chip colored helicopters fly by. They're mid-sized, look a bit like Russian Hinds and carry armament, but I don't know where they hail from, or even what their nomenclature is. English or Aussie most likely. Hell, we've even seen some Georgian Humvees since we arrived in country, so I wouldn't be surprised if the different birds were from Lower-Slaboobistan.

There's really no such place called Lower-Slaboobistan; I just make up silly words sometimes, that's all.

After three hours or so, Emily descends over my world again. It's late July, and we're pool-hopping with our friends in our sleepy little Nevada town. Being proactive, we've stolen the hot-tub first and are enjoying one another's company. It's my junior year of high school, and we're all young and free. Our other friends are in the pool, splashing around playing some game where girls perch on the boys' shoulders, trying to knock each other off into the water. I like that game, even more so because of Emily. It pays to have a skinny girlfriend, as less chiropractic visits ensue.

24

We kiss in the warm water and giggle. I can feel her warm, nearly naked body against mine. She floats just above me, exciting me, holding onto my waist as she kisses my neck. I can feel her smooth legs against mine; her feet gently brush my feet. We kiss, and moan, and laugh, half floating, half lying in the small circular pool. I can feel a bubbly jet inflating the legs of my swimming trunks with air, and I can smell the clean blue smell of new chlorine. I won't take her top off though. Not yet; this is, after all, just a daydream. I can't afford to abuse myself too much. Discipline.

I cut my thought of better times short and stare at the horizon once again. Not too much has changed in twenty-four hours. From my gray concrete Lego block, I can see two fully garbed-out Muslim women in burkas hanging laundry on a yellow extension cord in a nearby backyard. It looks like some kind of a twisted, post-apocalyptic Kansas.

Just beneath me in the courtyard, two IPs are smoking cigarettes and drinking chai, and they inspire me. I need a smoke too.

Smoking on guard is only taboo in super-spy locations like listening posts or observation posts, and never, ever at night. Fire gives you away. Here in my castellated tower, in the broad daylight, I deem it not only safe, but also appropriate to smoke.

Cigarettes are a pleasure, and a boon at times like this. Not only is satisfying an addiction a triumph in its own right, but smoking also offers me a sort of diversion. It's very entertaining: I can French inhale, blow smoke rings, or just about any other stupid thing that a guy can do with a roll of burning paper hanging out of his face. Currently, I'm trying to master the very obscure art of using the tongue as a tool to fold the lit cigarette into my mouth, close said mouth, and then redeploy the burning smoke back to where it belongs. Trying to do this I manage to burn myself twice, the casualties of the foolish game being the inside of my right cheek, and the roof of my mouth. Smoke break's over; this is a stupid game anyway. I think I'll give up on this one for a while. I also fear that for at least a few days, I have unwillingly given up my ability to taste.

There we are again. It's midnight in our Nevada desert. We're laid out underneath the stars on cool golf course grass, trying to find constellations in the night sky above us. I point out Orion. Although not very impressive astronomy, it's one of the only constellations I know. She has her head on my shoulder, and we talk a while. I don't know what about; I can't make out the words. I don't have time to translate either.

25

Sharp, sporadic automatic weapon's fire erupts from somewhere to the south, followed by shorter reports from what I think is a pistol, so I call it up to the CP.

"CP, this is Tower One, over."

"Tower One this is CP. What is it? Over."

"I have shots fired. I'd say about 250 meters to the south. Sounds like rifles and pistols, over."

"Copy." Followed by a brief silence.

"Tower Three, this is CP; you hear those shots? Over."

"CP this is Tower Three. Roger that. I got 'em from the same location. Over." That would be Cole, long lost since the last radio checks.

"Roger that, towers. Keep us posted."

We send up our replies and close out the conversation.

A few more reports issue up from the belly of the city, but nothing is ever visible. That's one of the key problems with urban terrain: you can't see through it. You also can't accurately hear shit either, because the sound bounces around too much. Lower to the ground, gunfire is often heard issuing from a completely different direction than it's actually coming from. The audio wave shit just bounces off everything.

After a few more minutes, the gunfire becomes completely absent. Nobody much cared about it anyway, as none of us were directly involved. Even the soldiers on foot patrol, being miles away to the north, are unable to respond to the source of the disturbance.

The CP also has communications with other US battalions operating nearby. No hits on them either, so life goes on. Everything is golden.

I miss the girl with the red paper heart. She made me feel cheerful yesterday. Now, her backyard is empty, save for a few empty soda bottles and a rusty old motor-scooter, lying on its side in a pile of garbage.

Our guard shift and foot patrol go smoothly. No enemy contact for us yet.

As we turn in our radios at the CP, SSGT Cloud moves deeper into the barracks to wake the other squad leader for the next shift. We quietly gather together as a group around our row of bunks, removing our helmets, and putting on our headlamps. No longer reserved only for coal miners, headlamps are an ergonomic necessity for barracks living in modern warfare.

26

0300, and it's dark as a midnight forest in our little home. I secretly wish I had a space heater, or a small fireplace, as it must be below 45 degrees in our little home. I suppose I should be thankful for my cot at least. Elevation offers some protection against evil terrorist spiders, and other maledict no-see-ums of the underworld.

After downloading his crap, Duke approaches my bunk with the stripped down main course of an MRE balanced neatly on his upturned palm, looking every bit the part of a maitre d'. He's also a bit of a narcissist. A fat narcissist.

"Good evening, Mr. Pearce; I would propose a trade." He clicks his heels together in a very smart, Englishman-like gesture, bows at the waist, and holds forth his morning offering.

"What, pray tell, dost thou intend to barter?" Off-hand, as if I speak like this every day.

With little warning, the mush laden food packet becomes a laser-beam in the fantastic red light of my headlamp. I'm tired and slow, unable to defend my dingus from the malicious cock-missile. *Silly pain.*

"Goddamn you fellow scouts and your irrepressible affectation with assaulting my jewels!"

I catch my breath, then quickly ascertain that I still have two balls, and realize with great relief, that MRE no. 2, Pork Rib Meal, did not render me any serious damage.

"Funny way to talk in Bangkok, Pearce."

"Agreed. I suppose you want my chili-mac?"

"Perceptive of you."

"Done deal."

And that's how breakfast commerce is done here in God's army. I've never understood why some regard the chili macaroni meal as such a delicacy. I'd take mushroom steak, pork rib, or Hell, even the tuna meal over the chili-mac. It gives me heartburn. Sins of the father.

"Cheese for peanut butter anyone?"

A nod from Freddy, a small game of condiment packet catch, and everyone is satisfied. I'm pretty excited; I saved a jewel from yesterday: a chocolate brownie. They're rare, second only to lemon poppy seed pound cake. Add some peanut butter to the flat little motherfucker, and you've got yourself a bangin' good breakfast item. Goes perfect with green-plastic flavored canteen water too.

Most of the guys are still using the just-add-water chemical heaters to warm their food, but I don't see the point this morning. I rarely cook my food in the wintertime. Usually I scuttle as many of the chemical heaters away as I can, saving them for later. In the woods, training for example, while others are wet and shivering half to death in their damp sleeping bags, I'm usually toasty warm. Sacrificing two warm meals during the day leads to a lot of warmth in a sleeping bag at night. Tricks like that make me feel like a real winner sometimes. Good way to dry your socks out too.

Lying in my bunk, I'm very contented with the peanut butter, chocolate chemical, and pork rib slurry in my stomach. Although not exactly the prescribed breakfast of champions, I don't have to worry about it giving me parasites. I wonder if I contracted any falafel-dwellers yesterday, come to think of it.

I desperately want to read a bit, but the brick in my stomach is weighing down my eyelids. I think better of it, and promise myself a bit of reading tomorrow. Five more days of these stupid tower shifts, and then it's back to the Forward Operating Base for some cushy living, laundry time, better food, and at long last, a shower.

As I drift to sleep, the roadside diner scene from Mel Brook's Spaceballs starts looping through my head, and it makes me feel slightly ill. *Hello my baby, hello my honey, hello my rag time gal.* Parasites.

I roll over on my side, and address the rest of my squad mates with our new nightly sign-off: "Goodnight Never-Land."

"Goodnight, Never-Land." All reply in turn.

It also seems a good nighttime phrase, at 0430 in the morning, for lost boys like us.

0600, and my number's up in the CP. Bleary eyed, I grab my rifle and don my blouse. One hour on the radio is not a bad gig. I had to piss anyway. Radio checks with the towers and foot patrol go smoothly. I even get the chance to small talk with the LT a little. And the real perk: I get to read Chaucer for a bit, in between the much needed radio babble.

0705. Back in bed again, sighing all the way to Sleepy Town.

I wake an hour early, at 1100. I can't fathom why. I trundle my morning self out to the little wall locker smoking area and light up. I've got pants, boots, a T-shirt, and my rifle, so I'm good to go. Although the large patio area affords a good view of the city, solid concrete walls serve

28

as the edges of the building, instead of the token metal rails you find anyplace else. With sniper threats minimized, so long as soldiers don't lean over the balconies like cardboard cut-out dumb-dumbs, the smoking area remains a no-hard-hat zone, which is great for my morning comfort level. I finish my first cigarette of the day before anything else. You know that you've finally reached fully addicted status when the first cigarette of the day always takes precedence over the morning piss. Rather than venture all the way down to the port-a-johns, I've been frequenting the Hajji bathroom. The urinals only, mind. Hajji bathrooms are no place to take a number two.

As I enter the tiled facility, I marvel at the filth of it as I ponder the word 'Hajji.' Or Hadji, like I think of it sometimes. *Sim Sim Salabim!* Most people think the word Hajji is derogatory, akin to saying a bad, foul, and offensive word, like rag-head, or towel-jockey, or even dirt-nigger. But it's not. Quite the contrary, Hajji is actually the formal, politically correct way to address a Muslim who has successfully completed the pilgrimage to Mecca, called the Hajj. I didn't know that before, having picked up the simple knowledge just last week.

The little urinal looks familiar enough. It even has a flushing handle to speak of, and an ample supply of almost clear water that can be summoned to whisk my urine away to other portals. The shitting places though, are unspeakable. I say 'shitting places,' because the amenities in this little yellow room can't possibly be referred to as toilets.

The stalls have dividing walls, of course, but no doors. There's no porcelain to be found either. Instead, just mucky, dark holes in the floor. From the cracked appearance of the tiles around the shit-holes, it's clear that the original purpose of this room was not originally as a lavatory.

Many people think that westerner's aversion to shaking hands with Arabs is racially based, or prejudiced; it's not: it's just the simple fear of Hepatitis B.

To the left of the shit-splattered chasm sits a water spout, and a complementary watering can that comes complete with a blue leafy design. The methodology here, apparently, is that you try to shit down the small hole, invariably miss, and then scrape the misguided shit-missiles down the poop shoot with your loafer, or whatever the fuck you happen to be wearing. Sandals, or even Arab toes, whatever. Anyhow, when the main mission is over, you simply reach over to the water spout, fill the watering can, complements of the house, and proceed to wash your ass with nothing but the left hand Allah gave you. Maybe wave to a passerby, who knows. Like I said, no doors.

As I leak, jiggle, and button up from my morning relief I observe an Iraqi man engaged in the tail end of this behavior. Thankfully, he's already over to the wash basin, so presumably, the worst is over. However, instead of seeing him washing his poopy hands, I witness something which I perceive to be very odd.

He bends down, removes his shit sodden shoes, and places them under the running water directly in the middle of the sink. After briskly scrubbing some of his very visible crap off of his patent leather shoes, he places his bare feet inside them, bids me a happy morning greeting, and exits the bathroom. Mind, no attention was paid to washing his hands.

That's why we don't shake hands with Arabs. I think about the falafel again, and shudder.

Back in the barracks, Freddy is already up and at 'em as well.

"Top O' the morning to ya. Where the fuck you been?"

"I was busy meeting the Arab with the cleanest shoes."

"What?"

I chuckle a bit. "Tell you later."

Chapter Two: Tomb of Dreams

There is a place that waits for me
Of melodies and endless calm,
A place adrift and free from time,
Far off and distant from this tomb.

It shines and gleams, my world of dreams,
With light and endless dancing.
I behold a world with infinite eyes,
Where nothing is what it seems.

It captures me and captivates
My doleful mind to wanting,
My soul by these things infatuated,
To awake at last, a prisoner to my parting.

My body aches, its pain undaunted
By the thoughts of future pleasures.
It's much too much and all too real,
Overloaded today with too much to feel.

There is a place that waits for me,
Away from pain and war machines,
Where quiet woods and serene lakes
Wait in peace for souls to take.

Someday I may wake to see
A land that rests now far from these,
But until that day I'll simply march
And feel my soul's unease.

Two days left in Sahad. Two days until we get to go back to the FOB. Our patrol shift ended just over an hour ago. I've eaten, and I've settled in for a spot of reading. I'm not on the CP roster for tonight, so I'm free to take my time.

I feel the time pass slowly as I turn the pages, reading methodically. I love the middle English of the Canterbury Tales, but as I'm generally a contemporary guy, I have to take the time to reread the modern translations as I go. After about a half hour of this pleasurable chore, I look at my watch.

It's 0400, which means I get to enjoy six unbroken, blissful hours of continuous sleep. I might even get the chance to hit that fabled REM cycle.

Time to be responsible. I put my prized book back into the dark confines of my assault pack, and lay back onto my woobie, which I've folded into a makeshift pillow.

My mind begins to drift. It would be wonderful to go fishing at Mead this time of year. I'm thinking about a warm lakeside cook-fire, a tent in nature's clean air, and a peaceful retreat by the lakeside when quiet sleep takes me.

We've been riding all morning it seems. I'm covered in sweat and flagging a bit. I manage to keep pace with Mike, but I'm not enjoying myself as much as I should be.

I think my bike seat is too low. My pedal strokes are labored, each one taking all of my effort. As I gaze forward up the mountain path, I'm disheartened. It seems to stretch on forever.

I try to enjoy the ride more by thinking about how clean and fresh the high altitude air smells. Speckled sunlight drips through the trees, and I can hear dozens of birds chattering away. Thankfully, before much time passes, we reach the crest of the path, on top of the last rise, and I can see the lake again. About a mile wide, with crisp blue water reflecting the soft cumulus clouds above, the lake looks like mirrored glass.

I breathe a sigh of relief and lean back, letting the momentum of relaxing descent take me and the bike. With gravity taking charge, my personal effort is over; with any luck, we can just coast back to our campsite.

Leisurely descending from the hill, we snake our bikes along the path, taking in the view as we come ever closer to being level with the wooded horizon on the far side of the lake.

We coast across a small, man-made wooden bridge that stretches over a small creek, and begin to pedal again as we near our campsite, at long last.

Coming to a stop next to our tents, placed only yards from the lake's rim, we tip our bikes over on their sides and reach for our water bottles.

"I thought this trip was supposed to be fun." I shoot Mike a scornful look. He just smiles back at me.

"This is fun," he begins, "it was only eighteen miles after all. Not too far on a bike."

"I think my seat's too low."

I'm sweating from head to toe and still breathing hard. The Skoal in my mouth probably isn't good for this sort of mid-morning athleticism, but I didn't want to get ashes in my eyes or start a forest fire. Smokey wouldn't like that very much.

"You might be right."

He swaggers over to my resting bike and rights it. He looks fresh, not breathing with any difficulty. The only signs he bears of any exertion at all are two very small, unpronounced rings of sweat on his T-shirt underarms. Other than that, he might as well have just gotten ready for the day. He's nothing like the mess I am.

"Yeah man, it's all the way down. That means climbing the hills you've been having a hell of a time. You can't use your body weight like this."

"Good to know. Noted. Right. I'll remember that for next time."

I've never been much of a bike rider. I think the last time I rode like this I was twelve. Embarrassing and tragic, I shattered my left wrist by going down a hill too fast, and having a whoops at the bottom. I haven't really been on anything with pedals since.

On to the fun part. The breeze is cool and feels fantastic on my wet body. There's cold beer in the cooler and fresh steaks that I'm about to roast over a wood fire. It's too early in the day yet for fishing. They don't bite here until well into the evening, so until then, we can focus on the finer points of camping. Man-food and beer.

I hear something strange in the wood-line, though I can't make it out. It sounds--

"*Get the fuck up!* Christ, how long does it take, D?"

I exhume my head from the comfy folds of my woobie and check the time: 0822.

"What the fuck's going on?"

"We just got called up, didn't you hear it?"

Freddy is looking down at me, bent over at the waist, with an impatient expression on his face.

I'm puzzled. "Hear what? I was worlds away."

"The blast of the century, Beethoven. A bus just blew the market to Hell."

"Shit. Any numbers yet?"

"Nothing's been confirmed yet. The dismounted patrol is on its way down to the market now. There's a lot of shooting going on though."

Everyone hurriedly straps on their battle-rattle, from head to toe. As we get kitted up as fast as we can, Cloud comes quickly marching down the dark aisle towards us from the CP. He starts with what Freddy just told me, then continues on with a few more specifics.

"All right, listen up: it *was* a bus. Nobody knows how many civilians, if any, were onboard, but the thing went off, like, ten meters from an Iraqi Army checkpoint, right in the middle of the Sahad market. Our guys are en route, and they should be there any minute. We've got to move quick, and that's all we have to go on. Also, there are 1st ID troops in the area, so we should expect to see some of them as well."

Cloud continues, "I'm not gonna lie. There's a lot of gunfire down there right now, but nobody seems to know who's popping off. We'll move through some of the mulhallas towards the market traffic circle. When we get close, we'll find our way to a rooftop that has a good vantage point over the square."

SGT Dick steps forward, "Any specific building in mind?"

"Not yet. We'll just have to address that when we get there."

As a group, it's evident that we're all displeased with having been roused from our slumber early; however, there's an almost palpable tingle in the air. I tend to be the least excited member of the group about this sort of thing. Call it a bi-product of being intelligent.

As always, at the first mention of danger, Duke looks pale and like he's about to shit himself, but he plays it off by trying to act collected. Heroic even.

He smiles, and though his gear resists him, he stretches though all of his crap, arms as high over his head as he can get them, with his chubby

35

hands bunched into cute little fists.

"Everyone ready for this?" He asks the question rhetorically, but he takes a good second to make eye contact with me.

We don't like each other all that much. Suffice it to say, we don't *believe* in each other. Our differences of opinion have never led to out and out fighting, but our personality types mesh like water and oil. Most likely, it's a product of having shared the same squad in a different unit. I liked our platoon sergeant in another place, in the land of Long Ago, and Duke did not. Consequentially, we used to have a lot of disagreements on how to go about our daily tasks. He also has a very disconcerting habit of sucking up to his superiors with the goal of personal gain. That's probably why I mentally refer to him as cock-breath all the time.

That's my logical reasoning anyway. I really just think that he's a brat: a spoiled only child, narcissistic and filled to the brim with entitlement, what I hold to be one of humanity's least desirable qualities. That, and he's generally just a fuck. A more pusillanimous person I've not seen. Further, it's a miracle that he hasn't got himself booted right out the airborne for it yet. That, or face a medical board for being too damn fat. That sort of behavior is not tolerated. Hence the ass-kissing; he covers himself rather well. All of this, and further, he incessantly brags about his sexual exploits, which can only mean one thing: he's probably a virgin.

I like Freddy. He's sensible. In an enthusiastic and rather non-condescending tone, I heartily ask, "You ready-ready Freddy?"

"Freddy as I'll ever be!" His reply comes out in his familiar, optimistic sing-song Philly tone. At times like these, his tonal quality makes me think we're not in that much danger at all. It's an inflection that says, 'fine by me; not a care in the world. Too easy, man.'

Like a six-piece tactical nylon worm, we hurriedly make our way down the stairs and across the compound's main yard. Although the market is over a mile away, we can clearly make out the sounds of automatic weapons fire, sporadic and wild. We're all looking for the smoke that indicates a burning wreckage, but from our current location we can neither see nor smell it.

Taking a moment at the gate, Cole, acting as our Radio Telephone Operator for this particular excursion, radios in to get a good coms check with the CP, while the rest of us lock and load our weapons, and make sure that all of our gear, pouches, and grenades are tied down right proper. There's a pretty fair chance of a decent run in our near future.

Satisfied that the squad is ready to move out, Cloud waves us forward. All together, we fall into our standard squad-column patrol formation, space out from one another, and wheel through the ECP out onto the main road, one at a time. Left. Right. Left. Right.

Rather than walking parallel to the main roads, as we do sometimes at night, we duck into the secluded, haphazard alleyways that snake between the nearby dwellings. Mulhallahs they're called. Every one of them seems to have a unique character. Rather than being a public street, the narrow pathways seem to take on the character of the individual houses that flank them, as well as the people who live within. With never a straightaway, and never level for any distance, the ancient cobbled stones of the paths are somewhat uncomfortable to walk on. In most places, the mortar that used to hold the ancient stones together has eroded away, leaving a treacherous gauntlet of sunken, disjointed stone flooring that threatens to twist an ankle with every step.

The locals never seem to have any difficulty walking around. We attribute this not only to their familiarity with the shifting terrain, but also to the clothes that they wear. A dress and some flip-flops hardly weighs them down, in contrast to our cumbersome boots and additional sixty to eighty pounds of crap per man. The additional weight we carry makes the old pathways much more treacherous. I feel as if I could walk normally over the smooth stones if I were in tennis-shoes and shorty-shorts.

Laundry hangs from lines stretched over the narrow breezeway, while urine and dirty water pool in ditches to one side of the narrow path. As most of these homes have no running water, lavatory protocol consists of simply emptying buckets of filth right in front of the house, medieval style. Not a very hygienic situation, as the Mulhallahs are on average about four feet wide, if that.

What they do lack in aesthetic value, they make up for in shade. It's always nice and cool along these narrow residential roads.

We move like this for about a half of a mile, waving to civilians and trying as best we can to be friendly. Offers of chai tea and cigarettes are constantly extended to us as we briskly pass by. Of course, there is some forgiveness on the faces of our hosts as we refuse their hospitality, as they too can hear the gunfire, and doubtless know why we're headed towards it in such a hurry.

The mulhalla ends, cut short by a modern-seeming two-lane highway that crosses our path. Cloud sends his hand signals back to the rest of the squad, and we start moving to our pre-determined locations, getting ready to run the dangerous crossing like a football play. A street is a very open, very deadly place to cross in any environment, let alone an urban one where every window serves as a potential sniper hide.

I take up a covering position to the right side of the alleyway, while Dick and Duke go left. Freddy falls in behind me, picking up security to our six o' clock. Cole and Cloud each take a corner, and look out from the protection of our alley, assessing what lies in either direction further up the road.

Having determined that the path is clear, Cloud waves us forward. We cross two at a time, covering each other as we move. Two men advance, while two men protect them. Simple, and to the point.

Cole and Cloud cross swiftly, half jogging while aiming down their rifles as they make their way across the street. Once in place on the far side of the road, they pick up new sectors of fire to cover our crossing, ensuring that no unwanted surprise goes unnoticed. Nobody ever moves alone. A man can only look one way at a time, which is a damning circumstance when operating in an urban warzone. Three hundred and sixty degrees of security is the lifeblood of any unit; that goes double for one as small as ours.

Getting the signal that the crossing is clear, Duke and Dick stand up and begin moving across the street, while Freddy and I cover the rear; Cole and Cloud's focus remains down either side of the road, covering the crossing soldiers' advance.

Straight ahead, I can clearly see the demographic change. Rather than continuing into more residential areas, our path straight ahead is a wider, paved street flanked by large buildings, signifying that we are about to move into a large, commercial area. Usually bustling at this time of morning, the path ahead seems eerily quiet.

After the others are set, having moved deeper into the far street, both hanging together on the right side of the road, they pick up security to the twelve o' clock, our direction of travel, taking positions on their knees a good five meters passed where Cloud and Cole still sit and wait.

Freddy and I, not needing a signal at this point, pick up and move together quickly. I continue pulling security to the three o' clock as we move across the street, while Freddy jogs, half-backwards, still securing the mulhalla to our rear.

The gunfire has quieted for the time being. On the far side of the crossing we enter the wide road, and take cover along the pillar-flanked sidewalk under the eaves and facades of three and four story commercial buildings, whose original purposes have most certainly long since been forgotten.

Large, tangled power lines droop sadly over the empty street, as men and children timidly stand in doorways, trying as best they can to listen to the events of the day. War scores more 'look at me' points than a rubberneck-causing traffic accident on I-95.

"All right, people, spread it out."

Cloud calls up our position on his small, portable radio. A communications purist, he doesn't use a handset, but rather prefers to speak directly into the radio brick, looking every bit the part of a tactical real estate agent who just stumbled out of the eighties.

Staggering and proper spacing are important, especially when dealing with an enemy that primarily fights with explosives. If everyone is clustered into a tight group during a detonation of any kind, the amount of damage done to a squad can be calamitous. To avoid such unfortunate eventualities, we leave about three meters between us, on average. It's a good, textbook behavior that ensures that the entire squad doesn't get greased in a single explosion, or one good burst of automatic weapons fire.

Concrete pillars line the street, acting as supports for balconies above that run along the facades of the square stone buildings. Keeping our spacing we move quickly, but conceal ourselves as best we can behind the strong, regular lines of cover provided by the pillars.

I hold my weapon at the low ready, thumb on my fire selector lever, trying as best I can to focus on everything I can see. The squad moves forward naturally, bouncing rapidly and smoothly from one covered position to the next. I can feel the tension in my shoulders and the fresh moisture of sweat beading on my neck.

On this deserted street, I can't help but notice the unique feel of the cheap automobiles. Many of the cars bear familiar makes, although the models are new to me. That is, when they are written in English at all. The vehicles project the same neglected and forgotten feel as the rest of the street, complete with dents, chipped paint, broken headlights, and rust, with scrawled Arabic license plates mirroring the foreign signage the populates nearly every store front. They seem smaller, thinner, and lighter than American-made automobiles; many of them can be purchased for the equivalent of 200 US dollars, brand spanking new. Talk about a cheap deal.

Making our way past the parked cars, I feel out of place. The automobiles are similar here of course, but they're different enough that I don't forget where I am when I see them. Many Japanese budget vehicles look familiar: a Toyota here and a Mitsubishi over there. Interspersed with the parked, dirty four-door cars are open-air bus-like vehicles, that always look to me as if they've been squished from front to back. None of the guys know exactly what they're called; however, the general appellation we use for them is 'bongo' trucks. Like a standard hippy van, but shrunken, and lighter, with nothing but tarps or plastic sheeting suspended on poles to cover the passenger compartment.

Down a narrow alley to our right, shooting starts once again. The rapid bursts rip the still morning air, and as one we take cover, orienting ourselves toward the source. It sounds like it's right on top of us. Though the reports aren't loud enough to deafen me, their proximity is alarming, echoing off the concrete walls and pillars that surround us.

Cloud shouts now, *"Move! Keep your spacing! Watch for friendlies!"*

And just like that, we're running towards contact, button hooking into the alley where the sound is originating from. Duke is in the lead, rapidly sprinting deeper into the mulhalla, with Cloud bending protocol a bit, lagging just a few feet behind him. I run to the left of the new, blurring alley, with Freddy's reassuring presence properly spaced behind me and to the right.

I'm excited, though hot fear grips my balls. Stinging sweat assails my right eye, but there is no time to brush it away. I blink hard as I run, clearing the irritating distraction as best I can, as I run down a familiar seeming sidewalk.

I can feel my gear fighting against gravity as I run. Grenades, medical kit, and ammunition bounce in the pouches on my chest. My heart pounds in my temples from fear, excitement, and the sudden exertion. Running, keeping pace with the rest of the squad, I feel completely alert and alive as I run with the palpable fear burning in my stomach. My rifle feels light in my arms, held at the low ready, my left hand securely gripping the heat shield that covers the barrel, my right hand on the grip, index finger extended straight above the trigger well; my thumb is on my fire selection lever, currently set to 'safe.'

The world becomes surreal as we increase our speed. My buddies, the sewage, the garbage of the alleyway, and the cracks in the sidewalk all become blurs as we pick up our pace. With adrenalin kicked in at full force, I can no longer feel my body as I run in formation with the others, ever nearer to the source of the gunfire; the sounds of which now pummel us loudly, bouncing and reverberating off both sides of the alleyway.

We come to a halt, taking cover at the end of the short side-street. Nobody has spoken, which means that along our hundred meter murder-dash, nobody saw shit.

Everyone is breathing heavily. I can feel my heart ready to burst out of my chest, and the sound of drums pounding in my ears.

"We're here. Round the corner, look for cover, and keep spread."

"Rodger, Sergeant."

Cole and Duke move first, and the rest of us follow shortly. Around the corner, it's a mad house. We've reached the market square.

It's a traffic jam. A goat rope. A dunder-fuck, whatever you prefer to call it. Dozens of cars lie in gridlock, completely blocking the four-way street. We don't have a good view of the main spectacle from our current location, but we can make out the smoke. Thick, black, and oily, it snakes up into the midmorning sky. The scent burns my nose, filled with the essence of roasting tires, blood, transmission fluid, and the smells of burning flesh and hair.

The sound of the close gunfire is immediately revealed to us, as a group of Iraqi policemen, only five meters away from us in the middle of the road, are discharging their AK-47s into the sky, for reasons known only to them. Traffic signals, maybe.

We scatter, and take up positions of cover among the concrete pillars that flank the street, and the automobiles trapped within. The Iraqi truck crews mindlessly continue firing their Ak-47s into space. Why, who the fuck knows. Maybe it was a satellite attack.

"All right, follow me!"

The squad forms a column, falling in behind SSGT Cloud. Quickly, we come to the main door of a commercial building adjacent to the traffic circle and hastily enter.

"You smell that?"

"Yeah. What are we, thirty meters maybe?"

"God, the fucking stink!"

"It's called Sex-Panther. Stings the nostrils."

"Shut the fuck up, Pearce."

An elderly Iraqi man greets us, standing behind a marble counter with an old-fashioned service bell on it. From the look of it, we've stumbled into the small, disheveled foyer of what was once probably a fairly nice hotel.

41

Pointing to the roof, Dick asks the man, "Up? Up?"

"Yes, Mista." The old man points down a short hallway to our left. *"Shukran."*

"Ma a' Salem a."

I don't really speak any *Arabee* yet, but I get the gist: thanks, and goodbye.

Moving together, rifles ready for anything, we stack on each other closely and snake together through the short hallway until we reach a flight of narrow stairs. Freddy and I pull rear security while the others advance up the stairway with their weapons aimed high, butt-stocks of their rifles short-stocked, placed above their shoulders to make the weapon shorter, minimizing the potential for flagging. This is primarily a measure to keep potential enemies from seeing the barrel of a rifle round a corner before the infantryman behind it can kill him, thus ensuring that an enemy has less time to take aim at the soldier behind the firearm. We move slowly, carefully, and quietly.

The lobby vanishes from my sight as I round the corner on the first landing. The rest of the squad has already reached the second floor, and I hear them announce that it is "Clear."

As Freddy and I pass the hallways that lead onto the other floors, we can't help but notice how deserted the place seems. With nothing but dusty concrete floors and long hallways leading to most assuredly dirty and unfurnished rooms, it's apparent that business hasn't been good for over a decade. Uninvited, Cole Porter kicks down a door in my head, and starts to sing*: "It's dilemma, it's de-ritz, it's deluxe, it's DeLovely!"*

I stack up with the rest of the squad at the top of the narrow stairway, where our path dead-ends at a single doorway, secured with a simple chain and padlock.

"Duke, Hooligans."

Duke performs an awkward about-face at the very top of the stairs, and Cloud relieves his assault pack of the cumbersome weight of military-grade bolt-cutters.

A sharp crack announces to the rest of us that little Arabian padlocks can't stop the American war-machine. We scouts are always running our own little 'Lock and Awe' campaign. Though I'm still looking down the stairs, covering the rear of the squad, my eyes don't welcome the harsh sunlight that suddenly floods the interior of the stair well.

Sergeant Dick stops in the doorway, a noted fuck-up, and turns to the rest of the squad, "Stay low." I feel for him, I really do. Poor guy, he wants to be *special*, so fucking bad. I try to like him, I really do. But, in my heart of hearts, I know that if he had his way, we'd be rappelling into the center of the traffic circle by now. The man is a walking liability, and I find it slightly shameful.

We advance out onto the roof and into the bright mid-morning sun, and immediately, the awful burnt smells return. As we take to our knees and halt on the roof, Cloud notifies the CP that we're now in position directly over the market square.

After a brief chat, he stows his radio.

"All right, listen up. The other dismounts are on a rooftop about a hundred meters from our position, across the circle from us to the west."

Cloud continues, "Freddy, you take rear on the stairwell. Dick and Cole will take the southeast corner. Pearce and Duke, take the southwest. Remember to stay low, don't silhouette yourselves. Call out anything that doesn't belong, clear?"

"Roger Sergeant."

I move to the southwest corner of the building with Duke. Right away, we can see the gray turtle-heads of our buddies across the way. When they see us, they give us a brief wave, *Hey Ya'll.*

Our roof is bordered by a concrete and makeshift stucco wall that stands about three feet high; it's the perfect cover too for roof-dwellers like us. From our corner, we can see the main body of the intersection and what's left of the market scattered around it below.

There are hundreds of people and dozens of stranded cars, all making a tumultuous noise. Third-world police and ambulance sirens, women and children screaming, men crying, tires screeching, and every minute or so, a burst of automatic weapons fire is sent up into the air. Off to the south side of the intersection, I can clearly see the still burning remains of what obviously used to be a passenger bus, probably big enough to hold eighty or so people. And from the look of the fire, it was almost full.

I can see bodies cooking in the shimmering BBQ haze that radiates from inside the twisted metal hulk. Corpses, burnt and naked, jut from the windows of the doomed transport.

For a good twenty meters around the wreckage, it's clear that nearby vehicles were flung airborne by the blast, and now they lie burning, turned over on their sides and flattened roofs, leaving a clearing of sorts amidst the debris, save for clearly visible body parts, shoes, and splatter patterns left behind by whizzing chunks of burning gore.

Remembering the task at hand, I focus my attention on scanning the

43

surrounding market. A man stands over half of a body already covered in a bloody yellow sheet, screaming Allah gibberish at the sky with his hands held high above his head, as if trying to catch raindrops that won't seem to fall.

All around the square, civilians and military personnel alike stand in slack-jawed wonder, watching the spectacle unfold among burning, overturned cars and the bloody, splintered wrecks of dead fruit stands and wooden shopping carts. Iraqi ambulances try to maneuver closer to the burning wreckage, while two trucks are stuck in the gridlock, nearly free of the circle's traffic jam with their truck beds full of even more twisted bodies, every one of them rigid and scorched.

"Fuck, man. They don't even look real, do they."

"No, like mannequins or some shit."

I notice similar rubber-necking from our friends across the way. Some things are just stupefying. The only way not to pay close attention is to forcibly avert my eyes, and attempt to focus on something else, like looking for those responsible for the blast.

Dozens of Iraqi policemen can be seen at the far side of the market, intentionally staying out of the mess. Their aversion to taking any action that would directly involve them with the situation is painfully obvious. They look stupidly on like the rest of us, low-grade cigarettes hanging out of their mouths, and soda cans dangling from their fists. They look ever so much like fans at a concert, just waiting for the line to start moving.

Other than the general chaos of a country destroyed, there's not much else to see. Wounded men, women, and children, all sit and wail, holding burns or bloody wounds, waiting for someone, anyone, to come help them.

In the middle of the square two children with paint buckets slowly walk around the still-burning hulks of cars in the middle of the circle, stopping now and again to pick up bits of human remains. I witness a few of the children's finds: a finger, a shoe with a jut of flesh and bone still protruding, a burnt severed head, and several unrecognizable pieces of human gut-works are dropped from their naked, bloody hands, one by one, into the dirty plastic buckets. The children don't overtly seem to mind the grim task, engaging in the morbid work with a measure of energetic enthusiasm, stopping every now and then to show each other their gory collections.

If this were the modern world, mass casualty incident procedures would come into place. Emergency Medical Technicians would be running around the scene, administering water and small comforts to the walking wounded, while the more serious cases would be given triage tags, and separated according to the severity of their injuries. Not in this country though. Iraq doesn't have systems for shit like that.

As we gaze on, for what eventually becomes hours, little aid is rendered to the remaining wounded. Instead, they collect themselves one by one, form small groups, and simply help each other walk off the scene, presumably to another location to scavenge for medical care. Some, no doubt, will simply go home, lacking any other options.

We wish desperately that we could do something to assuage the chaos below, and help some of the wounded. Even so, there are limits to what the six of us could accomplish in all the turmoil. We understand that we would be more of a hindrance than a help. American soldiers wondering around in the cacophony would simply add to the spectacle. Further, in this country, we're bullet magnets. If we drew fire in the circle, it's a sure bet that even more innocents would be killed.

Language barriers aside, we also have no control or authority over local forces. As far as our ability to dispense medical care, each soldier carries one small first aid kit, which contains only the bare necessities required to keep himself alive in the event of massive hemorrhaging. Though the heart is willing, the mission is different. All of that aside, we're not here to render humanitarian aid, although we do have time to fit some of that in on the side. Primarily, helping their own civilians is the host country's failing responsibility to its people. Our job is to look for, and ultimately kill the bombers. Most assuredly, in this case, the bomber has already done our work for us. At least we don't have to worry about this particular individual doing it again.

Radio checks go up. Nothing hostile can be seen. Thankfully, the Iraqi army has stopped acting like children, and have become disinterested with firing their weapons in the sky above us. Or, maybe they just ran out of ammunition, which is a much more likely scenario. The bullets always have to come down somewhere, so there's an element of relaxation present, now that they've decided to stop popping off.

As a few hours pass, the market finally becomes deserted, and the last Iraqi police flick away their cigarettes as they leave the scene. The throngs of spectators, the wounded, and the dead are all long gone. Heavy quiet falls over the market as the sun sinks in the sky.

What remains, other than the still smoldering bus-wreck and the other burning automobiles, are the usual pieces of garbage and detritus that commonly remain after any day at the market. Smashed fruits and

45

vegetables, as well as prepackaged food garbage litter almost every inch of the street, failing to totally cover the evidence of the events of the day, which still stain the dirty circle in rusty splats and drag-lines. I can see a child's shoe, abandoned and alone in the middle of the quiet, smoldering market.

A dozen or so deserted automobiles that were heavily damaged in the blast remain in the center of the circle, appearing determined to stop traffic again tomorrow.

As another hour or so passes, and the sun sinks low in the western sky, Cloud's radio crackles. Magically, it's time to move again.

Our slow walk back to the JSS is alert, but quiet. Nobody has much to say about what we witnessed today. It was our first market bombing; nobody much knew what to expect, and nothing could have adequately briefed us for the chaos that we saw. That, and even if we were fully prepared, there's not too much that can be said about it anyway.

Baghdad has serious issues. The police and army seem incapable of doing anything but look on as people die violently in their own city. In their own *Wal-Mart* for fuck's sake.

I feel sorry about the dozens of people killed, and the dozens more that will probably die in the absence of any real medical care. Iraqis die every hour of every day because of their apathetic servicemen, who seem more focused on cigarettes and cell-phone porno than they are in doing actual work.

Standing in the open bay, our squad scrutinizes our former living area, looking for anything we may have left behind, including everything from high value equipment, to MRE garbage. It's almost time to get moving again. After five minutes or so of paranoiac searching, I feel as if I've collected everything. I can only look at the same ten square feet of concrete for so long before I feel as if I've been completely thorough.

SSGT Cloud addresses us all.

"All right. Sensitive items."

A 'sensitive item' is anything that an individual soldier has to sign for. This encompasses every piece of our kit that an average person would consider to be fucking expensive. The rifle is one such item, and the optic on it, another. Also, every man has a IR laser targeting system: a PEQ-2 black plastic brick that is mounted to the forward grip of each rifle, sitting just behind the barrel. And, of course, night vision optics:

46

they're very expensive.

Cloud and Dick approach each of us individually, and physically lay their hands on all of our items. Word of mouth isn't very reliable as far as army inventory is concerned. A hands-on approach is always recommended.

"Okay. Good to go. Move out to the trucks."

Our squad is naturally the last to slowly shuffle out of the barracks into the blue, pre-dawn light, as we chose to live in the ass-end of the bay.

Feeling unwelcome in the presence of my own squad, I drift a bit further to the rear. We're all dog-tired but a bit happy today. It's summer vacation after all; semester break. It's a national holiday for us. We get to go back to the FOB today, after a cute eight-hour drive, that is.

As we descend down the main foyer stairs into the lobby, we pass A Co as they enter the JSS to relieve us.

Eight days of tower guard for them.

"How's it going, Freddy?"

"Going just great. I'm sure glad I'm not them." I smile at that.

"Well, don't get too used to not being them; we'll be them again in four days."

Not contented to let the conversation end on a down note, Freddy continues, "Four beautiful days."

"Forgetting something?" Freddy contemplates his boots as we walk passed the miniature wrecking yard. "I don't believe so. What's on your mind?"

"Cloud says that we have two mounted patrols in our FOB block."

"Shit, I thought there would only be one."

It's bad of me, I suppose, to delight in the slight disappointment of a buddy; however, we don't generally expect much else. We're quite used to getting shit on, as we are an 'attachment,' and have to answer to the command of Delta Co. I haven't even seen the scout platoon sergeant or LT for over two weeks.

"Did you hear that?" Freddy looks puzzled.

"Hear what?"

"Your bubble bursting."

As we near the designated parking area, our line of soldiers separates, dividing itself into groups of five that move toward their assigned trucks, now walking somewhat faster than only moments before.

We're riding, or I should say, I'm riding in the second truck; Freddy's driving the thing.

Our Humvees are as new as army equipment gets, with hardly a scratch on the fresh beige paint. From what I've been told, the new armor plating they bear makes them unbelievably heavy. A ton more. As such, they're creatures of inertia; they don't like to accelerate, and they don't like to stop once they get moving. That makes these particular trucks a bit more dangerous for the gunner. The extra armor on the chassis, and the addition of thick plating to the gunner's turret on the roof makes them top-heavy. Rolling a Hummer usually results in death or serious injury to whoever was unfortunate enough to be hanging out of the turret.

The weather is cold this morning. At 0400, the sky is midnight dark, and I can feel a damp, chilly breeze trying to snake its way into my body armor, which is still damp from yesterday's patrol.

Radio checks come up good, and the trucks' engines are all fired up.

"We rolling second?"

I ask the question to nobody in particular, as SGT Dick stomps up to the truck, somehow looking a bit childish. He's tired this morning, and he's also short. His small frame is unfortunately a permanent condition, leaving me always to imagine that his height is responsible for his brash Napoleon complex. I can't hate him for it though. That would be unfair. I dislike him for a myriad of other reasons. Nay, a plethora, Jeffe.

"Yep. Get in."

We get the word to lock and load, and proceed to do just that. With my right hand, I point my boom-stick at the nearest concrete barrier while simultaneously fishing a magazine out of my left cargo pocket. All of my other magazines make their home in the ammo pouches on my stomach, but I keep one handy in a pocket for speed and convenience. Entering and exiting living quarters of any kind is constantly marked by locking and loading, locking and clearing; locking and loading, locking and clearing. Quick magazine access is essential: it helps to combat the redundancy. After everyone's weapons are hot, we enter the truck.

The heavy Humvee doors open silently. The trucks are still new, and very well maintained. One would expect that a four hundred pound door would squeal a bit at being opened, but it's not so this morning.

I claim the rear seat on the passenger side of the truck, and am reminded that the vehicles are much less accommodating on the inside than they appear to be on the outside. A lot of expense was apparently spared for the thin, cheap seat cushions, as well as a lack of covering on any of the interior vents. Who knows, maybe they did away with such things to lighten the load, after bogging the truck down with thousands of pounds of necessary steel. On second thought, I'm not complaining.

To my left sits a pile of green metal .50 caliber ammunition crates, fixed into place with white nylon ratchet straps, where they wait, itching for their chance at combat just like the rest of us.

Cole kicks me in the shoulder, so I look up at his downturned face. "What's up, besides you?" I say.

"Hose, if you please."

"You got it, gunner-dude."

Standing in the gunner's turret gets cold; really cold when wind-chill is a factor. So, being as we're a bunch of inventive infantry types, we're always searching for tricks to live a bit more comfortably.

I hand Cole up the black plastic hose, about two inches in diameter, which is shoddily connected to one of the rear heating vents with an artful use of duct-tape and somebody's old brown undershirt, which is wrapped around the end of the hose and secured into place by the tape, forming a tight fitting plug that effectively jams the vent's flow into the hose. This prevents me, of course, from enjoying much heat, but I don't mind. At least I'm out of the wind.

"Thanks, man."

"No problem, although I wasn't really busy with anything else. Small sacrifice."

Unceremoniously, he opens up his crotch buttons and inserts the tube through his fly, snaking it in a little further before fastening his britches once again.

"Cole, you never told me you were black!"

"Nope. Hung like an elevator button."

Our snide chuckles die down as our lieutenant addresses the platoon over the radio.

"All trucks check in. One up."

There's a brief silence, followed by another beep.

Dick keys his microphone, "Two up." The other trucks respond in order.

"Three up."

"Four up."

"Five up."

And then we're rolling, leaving the JSS behind, for four blissful days. We're not excited about doing laundry yet though, as an eight-hour patrol still stands between us and such creature comforts.

On the way into the JSS, I was lucky enough to be placed in truck three. Currently, truck three usually has Chapel in the TC's seat. There's an odd friendship if ever there was. He's a career man, complete with a wife, kids, and a house; he's the responsible type. That puts him in a different class altogether from the manner of soldiers I usually work closely with.

I'm kind of an artsy kid. I enjoy playing my guitar and spinning poetry from time to time. Chapel likes his Harley, Jack Daniels, and Camel Wides, those sort of things. Add on a ten-year age gap, and I'd say we have a pretty remarkable friendship.

Chapel takes a lot of flak from his superiors in D Co, with a lot of negativity generated from his previous duty assignment: S & T.

Supply and Transport platoon. S & T is a parachute inventory, ammunition sifting, truck driving nightmare. It's not the environment that one would assume to be the favorite posting of a career infantryman. Usually, the folks that can be found in S & T are posted there as a result of some sort of booboo, like drunk driving, drug charges, assaulting superiors, or similar transgressions. It's shit-bag land: the happy horse-shit place 'undesirables' are sent to waste away what's left of their dying careers.

I served in S & T for eight months. Chapel served longer. His crime? Breaking both of his ankles on a jump. Mine? I volunteered to be a scout. The joke was on me, as unbeknownst to me, I really had volunteered to sift empty brass and drive three-ton transport trucks. The army is that way sometimes, which is precisely why the majority of veteran soldiers will warn the young and foolhardy to never volunteer for anything. Tough shit on that one; it's a volunteer army nowadays. Being airborne is a voluntary certification, and the army always seems to love its own particular brand of dry, life-changing humor.

The 82nd Airborne Division has a ridiculously unforgiving sentiment, culturally speaking, towards soldiers who become injured in training. But that's a story of injustice for another time. Long story short, Chapel broke free of S & T and drives on with D Co. He's as fine a soldier as I've ever seen. If not for his long distance running capabilities, then surely for his personal integrity, stamina, and personal discipline.

And that's how our friendship began. He, my gruff, stern-faced, hand-rolled cigarette-smoking superior, and I, his gopher. You know, go for this, and go for that.

I finally ended up where I wanted to be after my cruel 'bitch-boy' volunteer prank. I just had to wait for the real scout platoon tryouts to come along, much like the reindeer at Christmas. As a result of this success, I'm blessed by getting to sit next to Cole, his fake black plastic tube-wiener swaying gently beside my face as our convoy commences its exodus from Sahad. Taking the city in at face value, I gaze out the window once again, looking for landmarks, insurgents, and explosives.

There's never much to see on the other side of the ballistic glass. Or, you could say that there's too much to see. Everything viewed in the living painting outside my window is broken. Busted vehicles, broken glass, screaming children, and always the bustling, crying markets where hajjis ply their wares. *Sugared dates and figs! Sugared dates and pistachios!*

We, speaking of the civilized world, have become accustomed to looking at a reality that is governed by order. Tables are round, glass is squared and whole, sidewalks and structures are composed of regular straight lines, and roads are generally smooth ribbons of black that gently take us to where we need to be. Our electrical wires are hidden, our toilets flush, and pulling your own cart to market went out of style in the 18th century.

Not so here. Everything is rough. Everything is jagged. Everywhere, nothing is whole. Rather, as the cityscape passes slowly by my window, I'm awed at how ripped it is, seeming barely to hold together. Life in the states is a tuxedo; life in Iraq is the old T-shirt that you check your oil with.

I've heard it said that there are no straight lines in nature, but rather, symmetry and straight lines are crafts of human kind: marvels of the civilized world. Truly, by this rule, Baghdad is itself composed of beastly nature, with no straight lines in sight.

Old concrete buildings lean, and electric cables which no longer supply power have become serviceable once again as laundry lines. As our truck passes an empty lot, I can see an old woman, all alone, briskly washing her leathery feet with water spouting from a pump that appears to have grown out of the muddy ground of the deserted lot, seemingly of its own volition, and everywhere, the garbage.

Many of the old-style concrete and yellow-brick buildings in the city were built in an architectural style that would not accommodate central supports. The buildings that exist instead of modern high-rises are square structures, however many stories tall, with great hollow spaces in the center. Back when the city was used for a bit of industry, the hollow

51

buildings can be envisioned with cranes on their roofs, busily hauling goods and furniture from the ground level to the floors above. Nowadays, the only cranes that can be seen are empty skeletons with their cables looted, spirited away to be used for some other practical purpose.

Many of the people who live in these great hollow buildings are squatters, and survive by occupying whatever unclaimed space they can. More often than would be expected, people erect their own houses out of anything that they can find: scraps of sheet metal, plywood, particle board, plastic, and you-name-it. Having gathered their construction supplies, they build little shanty huts against the exterior walls of the larger structures to escape the filth and smells within. Which leads me back to the garbage problem.

Occupants living on the upper floors of the buildings, with no solution for their own waste, simply throw the detritus over the open balconies into the hollow interiors below. Once such a building becomes uninhabitable due to flies, odor, and disease, it is simply burnt to the ground. That's how Arabs in Baghdad do the garbage.

Two hours into our aimless drive, I begin to get sore. Sitting in a car with a five-pound hat on will do that to just about anybody. But I'm not in a car. I'm in a military Humvee, with the space allotted to me shared by ammunition crates and Cole's fake dick-tube. My kneepads create pressure between my legs and the TC's seat, while my lumpy body armor necessitates sitting straight up. No rest for the wicked. The icing on the cake is my rifle, wedged between my legs in the only place it will fit. Sardines, nothing.

"Everybody awake back there?"

"That's a big Roger. I was just thinking about how these ergonomic seats make my ass happy."

"Shut the fuck up, Pearce."

Yeah, my bad for complaining. The TC's seat, in an exercise of abject cruelty, somehow manages to feel smaller and more cramped than the back seat. This is attributed to the presence of multiple computer screens, radios, and other commandy-type stuff.

As our drive continues ever onward, I stare out the window, trying my best to look forward at the terrain ahead, although a ninety degree angle is the best I can manage. Scan for bombs. Scanning for bombs.

I've had to piss for upwards of an hour, so I feel inclined to pose the question, "Hey Sergeant Dick, do we have any stops on the horizon?"

"Nope. Everything that's been planned for us we're already doing."

Shit. It's time to impart the fabled adaptability and versatility frequently boasted by the American paratrooper.

"Anybody got an extra spitter?"

Cole from above, "Why D? Got Cope?"

"Nope. Muthafuckin' Skoal."

"Spitter for a pinch? Pretty, pretty please?"

I crane my already sore neck to tilt and look upward at Cole's grinning Louisiana face. I guess he's been out of dip for a while. Oh well, the bastard should have asked sooner.

"Sure, homey."

I flip him up the can, and as if by magic a mostly empty water bottle rockets from the turret, narrowly missing, by some act of the devil, Cole's wide, phallic wind-tunnel, and cracks me right in the very real, very loaded dick.

I can't hold back a laugh though; I'm in luck, as I've got my Kevlar cock-flap deployed.

"Hey, Cole, what's the capital of Thailand?"

The question is followed by a brief pause.

Before Louisiana can put two and two together I give him a good, solid, however friendly tap to his elevator button.

"Thirteen please. Going up!"

"Ah!" His knees buckle a bit from the impact.

"Motherfucker!"

"Back at you, love!"

It's a healthy relationship. So healthy, in fact, that rather than the normal quip to shut up and 'pay-the-fuck attention,' SGT Dick decides to play into the fun.

"You've never heard that joke before? *Inconceivable!* That's an older trick in the book than getting your *Swartz* twisted!"

Laughs all around, followed by deep silence. If there were no movies, blokes like us would simply have nothing to talk about at times like these.

Just like that, thirty seconds of jocular conversation dies, and we're all in Baghdad again, rolling around in a generally circular fashion, waiting to get blown up on our fine midmorning suicide drive.

Thank the maker for plastic bottles and a little bit of lower back flexibility, which together enable me to efficiently piss into Cole's donated bottle. After I button up, I put the piss in my pocket. Normally people throw piss out the window, but it's bad for public relations in residential neighborhoods like this. Iraqi children think that the only things to come out of Humvees are candy and soccer balls. The truth of the day, however, is more akin to bullets and piss. So I put the piss in my pocket, to save some silly child the torment of drinking my yellow-surprise sports cocktail.

The patrol winds on aimlessly. Currently, our post in Sahad is roughly 10 miles away from the FOB. Consequentially, filling up the space in an eight-hour drive requires a lot of backtracking. Though the repeating streets, buildings, and sprawling markets remain the same, the faces that pass change throughout the day. Here is a man selling falafels, next, a middle aged woman in a burka carries a cumbersome sack of some sort. Hours later, a pack of wild dogs occupies the space occupied by a vendor mere hours before. Round and round we go.

The day seems eternal long before the bright sunlight crests at noon, but hours after it does at long last, our armored convoy takes a joyful, final turn towards the south, and we start the short, anticipatory drive 'home.'

"How does that make you feel Freddy?"

He tells the truth, "Like a living orgasm. You?"

"I feel like a dirty fuck who's desperately in need of a shower."

Cole calls down from the turret, "I desperately need to shit!"

Fully aware of the dire situation plaguing Cole's bowls, I reply, "You didn't have to tell me dude; I've been 'spider-sensing' that for over an hour."

"My condolences."

"None taken."

"What?"

"Never you mind."

My concerted effort at good-humored slapstick goes unnoticed. It's been a long day for us, and we're all just eager to get back.

The stretch of road that we're currently driving on is unfamiliar to me. Although we've spent a great deal of time traversing central Baghdad in the last few weeks, the area just outside the FOB is not in our platoon's designated patrol routes. As we've only gone out and come back a small number of times, we lack an intimate knowledge of the area of town closest to our own base.

Outside of my thick ballistic window I view the weird advertisements that serve as Arabian attempts to attract business to otherwise unremarkable store-fronts. Pictures of cellular phones, food and drink items, as well as other assorted household goods flap and bend in a slight breeze, printed on weathered strips of cloth or painted on rusty sheet metal signage. Characters stolen from western civilization grace the advertisements, as if Baghdad desperately wants to participate in the corporate business dealings of the western world.

The likenesses of Mickey Mouse and Goofy are displayed, contentedly munching on unrecognizable foodstuffs. The Micheline Man, rendered in green paint, is also present, although it would appear that his vocation has changed from peddling tires to the more unrefined task of hitting an old television set with a monkey wrench. And finally, Popeye the sailor man, in good keeping with tradition, is swilling down a can of green vegetables.

The oddities are so brazen, that I can't stop myself from commenting.

"I wonder if we should report these copyright violations?"

"Yeah, dude!" We've picked up speed now, having just turned onto a main highway, and Cole needs to shout to be heard over the rushing wind. "They're pretty fucked up. They got the Stay-Puffed Marshmallow man wrong though. They painted him green!"

"I think it was the Micheline Man."

"Whatever. Same shit anyway. How many of these bastards do you think have cable?"

"All of them, from the look of it."

The bad caricatures march in an endless conga-line, forever out of place in the dead, gray-brown world. Mickey Mouse in this locale makes me feel strange, reminding me of Disneyland and being very, very young. Interesting, that such images would be used by a people who proclaim to fervently hate the west.

Our truck begins to slow as we pull onto the glorious dirt road the leads to the FOB's entry control point.

A high stone wall surrounds the base, which was built, as we understand, by Iraqi soldiers preparing for the glorious defeat of America during the initial invasion. As evidenced by every major news network throughout the modern world during the 'Shock and Awe' campaign, it's clear that America can't be kept at bay with a fence. At regular intervals around the perimeter, guard towers stand to provide the occupying soldiers with clear fields of fire that cover all of the areas immediately surrounding the base, in an attempt to deter bomb placement, raids, and other such nasty things.

Our truck comes to a halt just inside the main gate while all of our IDs are evaluated, as if we could be anyone other than who we claim to be.

After the super-human National Guard fucks on gate duty declare us to be non-threatening, we proceed inside.

It feels like home. A strange thing to say, as this is a decrepit outpost in the middle of Babylon. But, it's home just the same. The familiar dirt road takes us past several outbuildings that flank and service the ECP. Most noticeably is the interpreter's shack, where Iraqi nationals wish to assist in the American war effort by living alongside American troops receive decent pay, and help us communicate with local persons in our attempt to paint a fucking rainbow over the entire world.

Protocols still need following, however. There is no such thing as simply parking the car. Two more hours of chores await, the first of which is a trip down to the motor pool to perform preventative maintenance checks and services, or PMCSs on our vehicles, as well as to empty them of garbage, such as bottles of piss and the like.

Next comes fuelling. Oddly enough, many brave souls from India have been contracted to man the fuel point. I don't suppose you could pay me to do that. American military bases in this town are 'impact areas,' that is to say, places that undergo a lot of exploding from day to day. This is sure to become exponentially more stressful while hanging around thousand-gallon tanks of explosive liquid for twelve hours a day. Doubtless, the fuel point is one of the primary bulls-eyes for local enemy mortar crews. Count me out, even at a hundred dollars a day.

At long last the trucks are fueled, and we happily park the God-damned death machines. Stay doggie, stay.

The FOB hasn't changed much since we last left it. Everywhere, hard packed dirt serves as the roadway, and every day, large tank-wielding trucks roll slowly over the surface and spray the barren earth in an attempt to keep the roads packed hard, and deter the eternal dust.

We've been led to believe that this particular forward operating base used to serve as one of Saddam's primary security bureaus. Since Baghdad's fall some years ago, the fortifications that once surrounded the sparse smattering of concrete structures have been somewhat modernized and improved.

Old concrete buildings that were poorly constructed in the mid-seventies allow US forces to occupy the installation in relative safety. Our barracks, for example, is an eight-story concrete building, which looks every bit the part of a giant's Lego block. Soldiers generally are only allowed to house themselves on the first three floors, as any floors higher than the wall surrounding the outpost are the frequent targets of rocket attacks.

Aside from the rows of uniform concrete buildings where the entire battalion makes its bed, there are other structures within the FOB that have been requisitioned and modified to suit the needs of American soldiers, such as the old, cracked building that now serves as our gymnasium.

Not all third-world wonders of architecture are created alike however, and some necessary structures have been newly erected on the post by American private contractors. One such example is the chow hall, which resembles a sort of gigantic aluminum tent rather than a brick structure of any kind.

As our flimsy chow-hall is the primary target during many of the morning mortar attacks, I usually swoop in quick, pile a 'to-go' plate as high as I can with the usual breakfast fixings, and trot quickly back to the barracks where I am free to enjoy breakfast at my leisure, sans the fear of spontaneously detonating.

Some pockets of open space on the FOB have naturally become improvised parking lots, which service the droves of American Humvees, heavy transports, and even some Strykers and Bradley Fighting Vehicles.

Then there are the abandoned structures: blown-out, gutted concrete wrecks which stand as quiet monuments to the destructive power of American J-Dam and Tomahawk missiles. Though most of the destroyed buildings still stand, they slant inward on themselves at wacky angles, as giant blasts efficiently cored out their middles long ago. These buildings are of no use to us, as they are too dangerous and structurally unsound to be used as barracks, or anything else for that matter. They do serve one purpose though: they remind us that we're not here to fuck around. No no no. We're here to break things.

Unloading the trucks goes smoothly as usual. Giggles and jeers abound as armor, assault packs, weapons, and ammunition are stored in their proper places, relieving us of our burdens.

Our home is rather simple and bare. We scouts live on the second floor, and although we used to have windows, we've plugged them all up with sandbags for added protection against incoming mortar and rocket fire. Although there's not a lot of airflow inside as there is no ventilation system to speak of, small slivers of sunlight still flow into our small bay through the cracks left between our green mesh sandbags and the crumbling brick mortar. I can see dust motes lazily dancing in the bright slivers of light, and just like me, they seem to be in high spirits today.

About twelve feet wide and ten feet deep, our little room away from the rest of the world houses all six of us. The three second-hand-special bunk beds that we sleep on are a God-send for a multitude of reasons, the first of which is that they allow us to better use the small space we live in, as they provide us with individual living areas of sorts. Second, they're beds. They're awesome, plain and simple. Much as hunger is the best sauce, sleep deprivation is the best Tempur-Pedic. Lastly, our bunks provide a wonderful storage solution for all of our personal effects, and each man's bunk looks every bit like a wagon in a gypsy camp.

Our bunks are decorated with pictures from home, valuable electronics, (our video cameras, which we are not allowed to take out on patrol), other personal belongings, as well as our body armor, weapons, and helmets. We just strap all the shit on there. Not only does this make for convenient storage space, but simply stated, the more junk a soldier has hanging off his bunk, the more privacy he is afforded. Privacy is a limited resource hereabouts.

Our floor is composed of some kind of cheap Arabian slate. Oddly enough, no matter how often it is swept, there is always a sheen of dirt that covers the floor. This is why Arabs can't have nice things. No matter how many times a soldier attempts to clean anything in the middle east, it somehow gets dirtier every single day, as if by genie magic. This rule applies to everything from religion to economics, politics to business, all the way down to our stupid, dirty little floor. I'll probably have to sweep it again later. Sergeant, nothing. I live in a scout area, scouts clean their own area, and my squad generally dislikes me. Do the math.

Dick, as is his custom, promptly blasts his stereo, which is really just an mp3 player hooked up to some very cheap, however very loud speakers. Our track of choice upon getting home is usually Zombie by the Cranberries. As the motion of unloading tones down, all of us settle into our groove and the usual routine: some radio-rocking and weapons cleaning.

I have it easier than most in this regard. This week I'm lucky enough not to be in charge of any additional weapon systems, as I've been active as a dismount. Basically, I'm one of the guys who just sits in the back seat with his rifle, waiting to be told that there is an emergency, which signals me to get out of the truck. That's me. The perk? I only have to clean my M-4.

As a standard weapon system which hasn't been recently fired, the rifle is easy to clean. A satisfactory cleaning can generally be accomplished in less than an hour, provided of course, that I didn't do anything stupid on walkabout, like fall into a massive shit-puddle.

"Happy to be back, Freddy?"

"You know it!"

Cole sits, shirtless as usual, on his top bunk, scrubbing his rifle's guts with an old toothbrush. Smiling, he puts the brush down and shoots Freddy a glance. "Hey, Freddy, what's black, and white, and red all over?"

"Um, gee. Let me think on that a minute."

Stupid joke. However, it's a somewhat entertaining one, as the punch-line is always different, nearly every time. The pause grows longer, with nothing but active little toothbrush sounds to fill it.

"I know," Dick exclaims, "It's a zebra bleeding out."

I say, "You know, Sarge, that the random reply is supposed to be funny and inventive, as opposed to thoughtless, morbid, and disturbing."

"Shut the fuck up, D."

"I only speak the truth."

Duke, from the back: "It's Freddy's mom. Has to be."

Freddy laughs out loud. "I knew it! I had the inkling that that's what you were eluding to."

Nobody feels particularly witty at the moment, and it shows. What has the potential to become a very lively, comical, and entertaining diatribe dies abruptly with an unthoughtful potty-reference, and is snuffed out.

Brush brush brush. Dental pick here. Brush some more. This comes apart, and that goes back together. A little oil here and there.

In your head, in your head, zombie, zombie.

I love the song just like everybody else. It has a very fitting, somewhat telling ambiance about it. I reckon we've only listened to it about forty times or so by now, and somehow it's nowhere near old yet.

One by one, we present our cleaned weapons to SSGT Cloud, who in turn checks each to verify that all of our sensitive items remain in place. CCOs, ACOGs, PEQ-2s and 4s, nods, and radios are all accounted for.

Just like that, we're on a day off. Glory, Glory Hallelujah.

Having been dismissed into the quasi-freedom of our little desert paradise by my squad leader, I take the short trip down a narrow hallway to a smaller back room with four inhabitants, one of which is Chapel.

"Done with your gat cleaning, ye olde pirate bastard?"

"Yar."

"Awesome."

"Laundry chow?"

"Laundry chow."

Just like that, we've communicated all that needs to be said and done. Simply. My buddy and me.

"Smoke?"

"Smokey-smoke."

"Well hurry then, D. Get moving; we don't have all day."

"Sorry Chapps, but yeah. Yeah, we do."

He replies to me, in his gravelly baritone, "Fucking schweet."

Body armor off, we set out into the great Arabian unknown with nothing but our rifles, two magazines apiece, our eye protection, and our boonies, which are big floppy army sun hats; they're really just whiz.

Most army types are forced into wearing the standard soft cap overseas, and as our maroon paratrooper berets are not allowed in combat theatres, there are really only two uniform options: the soft cap and the boonie. As we are an airborne battalion, we like to dress cool, like we're special. And we are. And that's awesome.

Just outside our flimsy wooden barracks door, the sun is doing its hole-punch trick in the rapidly fading late-winter sky. Just over the wall, which closely flanks two sides of our building, the bustling sounds of Baghdad can be heard. Wild dogs bark. Police sirens wail, and somewhere not too far away, someone discharges an AK-47. Love the Baghdad.

The FOB is not as big as one would expect. Couple of square miles maybe, if that. Accounting for over half of that are empty swaths of open ground to the southeast, which provide helicopter landing areas and a sort of out-of-the-way refuse dump where old garbage is put to the torch.

Our barracks rests to the far west, flanked by a KBR 'double-wide' that serves us as a four-stall public bathroom, which by our estimate services about 400 soldiers. Two hundred of us, and roughly as many 1st Infantry Division legs from across the way. Leg is the derogatory, un-politically correct way of referring to someone as non-airborne. Na-nana Na-na.

Leaving the small sheltered courtyard which houses our barracks, we cross a small dirt street where we only have three choices. To the right is a small trailer surrounded by twelve-foot-high jersey barriers that houses the AAFES phones we use to do our ET stuff. To our left a bit and down the road, situated in front of another series of barracks buildings that are clones of our own, sits the laundry mat. Heading southeast towards the center of the FOB will take us through the motor pool, passed the gym, and hallelujah, eventually to the chow hall. Farther down the little dirt road and passed the laundry mat are even more concrete structures requisitioned for barracks. Just a little farther beyond is our command post.

Laundry is a first-come, first-serve process, as well as a simple one. Stand in line, fill out the ID ticket, tie it to your bag, and wait in line. Depositing and picking up are quick hand-offs, as the employees are very efficient. Also, they are very well paid from what we understand. Probably not as well as the fuel point guys though.

After successfully handing off our bags of moldy shirts, dirty underpants, and Godforsaken socks, we're free to roam.

"Nothing like another day in paradise."

I shoot Chapps a hearty smile as I put on my eye-pro.

He snugly smooshes his starched boonie -- yeah, he starched his hat -- deeply onto his brow, and throws me a hearty thumbs-up.

"Time for some burger-chow."

"Indeed. What day is it?"

"Fuck if I know; why, you have an important obligation?"

I say, "Not unless it's Friday. I hear they're doing surf and turf on Friday soon."

"I wouldn't recommend that." Chapel lights up a Camel Wide as we near the chow hall. Wouldn't seem right not to join in, so I pull a Marlboro Menthol out of my left shoulder pocket and fire it up.

"Last time I ate seafood around here was in Fallujah, and it made my ass throw up for a week."

"I'll keep that in mind; I'll remember you said that; later, you can say you told me so. But, if free lobster tail is available, I have to try it. Maybe just once. I've already had the squits for a week, so I risk nothing."

The cool menthol-laced American smoke feels good in my mouth and lungs. I ran out of real smokes when we were out on the town, and had to resort to smoking locally available brands: Single B class French-made *Miamis* and *Royale's*. Yucky times.

Chapel gazes fifty meters away to one of the old concrete wreaks, to the building we commonly refer to as the 'J-DAM' building. "It's amazing that fuckin' thing is still standing." He says.

"Yes. I concur, doctor. What does J-DAM stand for, by the way?"

"Just Damned is my best guess."

"Fitting, and most likely absolutely true."

What was once clearly a rectangular structure is now a mushroom-topped trapezoidal thing. Although the first three stories of the structure maintained their shape after the missile strike, the fourth and fifth floors buckled outward. Somehow, the outside of the structure did not collapse, which is more than can be said of the inside. Through the broken windows at the bottom of the structure, all that can be seen is broken levels of shattered concrete and twisted wires. Jagged, broken steel beams and crumbled concrete tell their own story about the kind of force that struck them.

"You can see where it hit, on the top level," Chapel says to me.

I look toward the top of the broken building and confirm with a nod that what Chapel says is true. Through the sixth floor, light dimly floods through the roof. Almost completely obscured by the rubble from our view below, sunlight near the top of the structure betrays the gaping wound that likely caused an early Armageddon for everyone inside.

We put out our smokes and cross the street towards the entrance of the chow hall, which is easily the largest structure that KBR has built on the FOB. Roughly one-fourth the size of a football field the D-Fac, or dining facility, serves every soldier on the fob, of which there are thousands. Our IDs are quickly scrutinized by the POG 'guarding' the main entrance.

Luckily, chow-time is almost over, and the line is sparsely populated and moves rather quickly. On a busy day at the beginning of a scheduled meal time, five-hundred soldiers pack their way into this place and chow down at the dozens and dozens of cheap plastic tables.

Chapel and I generally don't stay and eat at the D-Fac. Being as it's the only place on the FOB where hundreds of un-armored soldiers congregate, it's the FOB's primary target for mortar attacks. Usually we get about two a day, signaled by 'incoming' sirens and explosions. For whatever reason, the last three days have supposedly been quiet on the incoming side of things, so me and Chapel decide to sit in and eat, rather than take our food back to the barracks in flimsy Styrofoam to-go boxes.

"No smurf and turf: someone lied to you, D."

I'm not very disappointed at the news anyhow, because it's Kuwaiti chicken cordon bleu day.

"Yeah, but we get our favorite anyhow."

As we eat out of MRE bags eight out of every twelve days, eating in the chow hall is a rare treat, regardless of the daily fare. Surprisingly, the little chicken pockets on the menu today are consistently delicious, and right on par with any dish that can be found at a casual American all-you-can-eat buffet.

We quickly roll through the remainder of the line, scooting along in front of the aluminum and glass cafeteria counter, scooping up anything good that we can find. Today's celebration revolves around instant mashed potatoes, rolls, and some sort of local vegetable dish that appears to be a funny combination of green and purple, but does not smell all that bad.

Leaving the main line, we move toward the center of the facility with our loaded trays to the drink fridges. Inside is mostly what you'd find at any stateside cafeteria: Coke, Pepsi, 7-up, milk, and orange juice. A few local exceptions do present themselves though, such as locally distributed strawberry-cream Fanta, complete with Arabic nutrition facts. Two drinks per man, and we're on our way.

There's not a lot of time to talk when we have real food in front of us. In the semi-silence of the chow hall, we sit and devastate our food while glancing at one of two televisions that broadcast Fox news, CNN, and reports from the AAFES network at regular intervals.

Tonight's news suggests that our war effort is going well, video games create violence, and somehow, coffee and chocolate are more nutritionally beneficial than once thought.

Chapel swallows the last of his chicken and chuckles. "I love that they can learn so much about the state of things from the Green Zone. Must have some remote-viewers at CNN."

"Agreed." A bit of a pause. "It's funny; I almost felt like this crap educated me a little while ago. It's almost accurate reporting I guess. It just lacks a certain, um, pizazz, maybe?"

"It lacks accuracy, context, common-sense, and genitals."

"Well put," I say.

The news report abruptly ends, as does our meal. Before grabbing our empty trays, we both stoop to ground level and pick up our rifles, which we always lay neatly beside our chairs under the table, ejection ports up with the dust-covers closed. Safety switches are checked, the weapons are slung, then with trays in hand, off we go. Exiting the chow-hall is a simple enough affair. Just as there is only one entrance line leading into the land of food-stuffs, there is but one way out, also roped off so as to neatly corral us passed the tables and bins where we separate and discard our dirty utensils, plates, and empty drink garbage.

Just outside the hall we briefly pause and don the proper Baghdad evening excursion attire: boonies and ballistic lens sunglasses.

The dusty gray evening light is fading as we make our way past another parked convoy, returning the same way we came on a path sheltered by the battered hulk of the J-DAM building and a wall of concrete T-barriers. I can't help but glance at the wreckage one more time as we stroll by, not saying much of anything.

Wires, broken glass, and other detritus are visible just beyond the makeshift barrier of concertina wire, set in place to discourage any third-world urban exploration. I can't imagine what such a spelunker would hope to find in there. Tetanus, maybe.

Suddenly Chapel tenses and stops. I'm curious about the nature of the brief pause, so I start to ask him what's ailing him, but before the quip can leave my lips he shouts

"Incoming!"

I don't remember moving. I'm just aware of gravel grinding beneath my sliding body, and the thump of my rifle against my shoulder-blades as I hit the hard, uneven ground. Coming to a stop at the base of a barrier, I gaze straight ahead. Inches from my face, I see the soles of my buddy's boots through the light film of dust on my eye protection.

Like magic or clockwork, the sirens start. Dim at first, the air horns quickly hit a crescendo and climb into the evening air. The resonation from the sirens doubles over and buffets us from all sides, reflected from dozens of directions by the stone surfaces which shelter and surround us.

I shout forward at the size-twelves in front of my face, *"Good call Chapps!"*

He laughs at me, in a friendly way. "Ain't my first rodeo you smurfing smur-"

The world explodes thirty meters to our front. The blast is deafening, and takes the wind from my lungs. As in training I press my face to the barren earth and leave my mouth open a bit. In the event of a closer blast, leaving the mouth open equalizes the pressure in your head somewhat with the pressure of the hateful outside world. The end result being that, in the event of unlucky disaster, I may still be able to keep my ear drums, eyeballs, and that sort of thing.

The echo from the first blast reverberates across broken concrete, the gravel, and the brim of my hat as a sudden, violent shockwave rips the air over our heads. I hear the pitter-patter of gravel rain striking the ground around us, and I am suddenly pissed-off at the ringing in my ears. More noise from Chapel.

"Woohoo! Dumb fucks missed the chow hall by a hundred meters. Fucking shithe-"

Boom. A second blast rips reality once more, this time mere meters behind us. How far, I cannot tell, but the terror and force of it is so shocking that I feel every muscle in my ass tighten, and my boot bedecked toes try vainly to dig themselves deeper into the hard-packed earth.

Incoming. Incoming. Incoming.

An emotionless, urgent, and very electronic male voice has been embedded into the audio warning system as an orchestral accompaniment to the World War II air raid chorus. It drones on, echoing throughout the FOB, sounding very much like that old iconic navy message: *Battlestations, Battlestations!*

Incoming situations always inspire fear first, and giggles second. First comes the shocking rush. Instantaneously, the situation rears its head as if proclaiming 'Worst fears realized, we're not in Vegas anymore!' It happens almost every day. Sometimes close, sometimes far away, but it can always, always be clearly heard. When exploding hammers fall from the sky, they grab everyone's attention. The elephant under the table shows itself, and then detonates.

My mind is always a bit behind actual reality when the world is ripping itself apart. The uneasy tension is so palpable, so deliciously horrific, that it makes my hands shake. It's like a prank at a bonfire, times a thousand. The giddy uncertainty of where the explosive bastards will land can drive a man up the wall: sometimes more, sometimes less.

"I say this shit every day, and nobody ever listens to me! Chapps, every god-damned fucking day, I say that we should just fucking-"

BOOM!

"Just fucking eat in the barracks, but no, everyone says, hey D, don't be a pussy! Just relax and eat in the fucking ch-"

BOOM!

"In the fucking D-Fac! To-go plates are not for pussies; they're for common sense!"

I'm giggling at this point, but not Chapel: he's cackling instead. The blasts have stopped for the time being, and it seems as though we have survived. I can feel the tension slipping from my body, and in the midst of the blaring sirens, I'm not afraid. At times like these, we're ecstatic. Seize the day and all that shit.

"Hey, Pearce!"

As abruptly as they switched on, the sirens disappear, and Chapel lowers his voice a bit, although just a little. He still has to speak up over the chimes in his own head; mine too, for that matter.

"You know that stupid shit people say about horseshoes and hand grenades?"

He makes his voice high and breathy, much like Rick Moranis in Ghostbusters, foretelling of the impending comedy of the punch-line.

"I know people say a lot of shit. I know a lot of it probably doesn't apply to this particular situation worth a fiddler's fuck, but I know I'm rather going to enjoy your input."

"Well, whoever the fuck said that never had a mortar fall onto their breakfast table."

Without another word, we both know that the coast is clear. Shakily, I get to my feet, and then in a display of gusto, I brush my shoulders off. Chapel takes a moment to wipe and reposition his Oakleys and then methodically begins to re-do the ranger-roll in the top of his boonie cap.

I laugh with Chapel as we start moving again, faster this time, as a head count needs to be done back at the barracks to ensure that nobody from Delta Company has gone wounded or missing in the mortar strike. If that happens to be the case, we'll be back out here in a jiffy, hollering and running as fast as we can, trying to hunt down the rest of our buddy-dudes. A genuine smile lands on my face, and I feel a bit of wit coming on.

"I didn't think that would bother you people."

"You people? Who do you mean? Pirates?"

"No. I mean country folks who oftentimes get flash-fried while deep grease frying the thanksgiving turkey. If I had to die, a tragic victim of my own culinary folly, I think I would prefer the quick and painless blast of a mortar over the avian-napalm-Joan D' Arc trick any day of the week."

"To chair, my friend. To chair."

"We'd better pick it up a bit. They're probably all frothed up back at the Bs."

With that, we start jogging through the fading light. More tension leaves my body as we approach the further safety of concrete buildings, leaving the FOB's primary impact bull's-eye farther behind us.

"That's the closest I've been Chapps."

"It's pushin' it for me, but I think I still have you beat, noob."

"Most assuredly. Where was it? Afghanimastan?"

"Nope. Falluger."

"Ah."

The rest of our evening jog goes quickly and quietly. Once back to the second floor, Chapel peels off to report to his platoon sergeant, as I go my separate way into the scout's living space to find Dick or Cloud.

"Look who just shows up unannounced! Took your time, didn't you Pearce?"

The scouts all appear to be accounted for, except for Cole.

"I did make a concession in the interest of time. I jogged. Where's Cole?"

Duke pipes up from his bunk, "He's poopsterbating."

It's a relief that everyone is accounted for. On the one hand, none of my buddies are dead or injured. Second, we can continue to chill out for a while, as opposed to forming a happy band and going on an expedition to find missing persons. Of course, that's never really too much of a chore anyhow. There's only so many places that they can be.

"Pearce, run down to the CQ and tell them that the scouts are up."

"Roger."

Before I make the short trip downstairs to the CQ desk, I take a moment to lose my headgear, rifle, eye-pro, and blouse. It feels liberating to walk about freely in a T-shirt, which is something that nobody takes for granted. The modern war is a long-sleeved war, and it's very uncomfortable, generally speaking.

I quickly leave the bay, take one right turn, and lightly hop down the steps three at a time before coming to a less than graceful stop at the bottom.

"Howdy, Mason, what's the word?"

"Everything sounds good at battalion. Everyone's up but A Co, but they should be accounted for in a minute. Some of them are still doing motor pool shit."

"Cool. Hey, call the CP and tell them that the scouts are up."

"Sure."

I hang out for a minute while Mason radios in. No infantryman gets away with not being a glorified receptionist every now and then. My shift will be later tonight, at around two in the morning. I don't mind, as tomorrow is a bona-fide re-fit day. I'll have all the time I want to sleep a little extra, and maybe get in a little bit of PSP time. Love the PSP.

Stateside, CQ duty is generally a bullshit job, requiring 24-hour shifts. No leaving the post, no sleeping, no games, no books, nothing. It's a discipline run, composed primarily of trying to stay awake and keep your stripes throughout the night. It's different here, and blissfully so. Each squad takes a six hour block of CQ throughout the day, leaving only one hour per man, which is definitely one of the true perks of being deployed; that, and an un-taxable paycheck.

"Well, I'll leave you alone to attend to all this radio excitement. Have fun, desk homie."

"You know me: I'm McLoving the fucking McDesk."

"Oh, come on now. I know you love the desk. It was scavenged from the wasteland with loving care, with you in mind. Your desk, your destiny."

I turn to climb the stairs once more, but Mason holds me captive a bit longer.

"Hey, D, have you eaten yet?"

"Yep. Ears are still ringin' too. They're making a really loud tuna melt today."

"On second thought, can you grab me a mer?" Which so happens to be bored, lazy speak for MRE.

"One mer coming right up. Any preferences?"

"Just no egg shit, Sergent."

"Gotcha."

Up the stairs I go, heading to my right this time as I reach the top of the landing, now venturing into the other half of the barracks. It's not a scout friendly area. Usually, when a scout enters this side, or on the converse, when a D Co trooper enters our domain, a good old fashioned friendly mugging ensues.

Amidst the tightly packed bunks, my fellow D Co soldiers are listening to music and opening mail; not the paper kind, but the good kind, primarily composed of big square cardboard chunks with goodies inside, as well as playing games on handheld devices. As far as soldiers are usually concerned, we're very spoiled, which is why we enjoy our time back at the FOB: eight days of suck, topped off with four days of bliss. Granted, not all FOB days are re-fit days. Our last two days here, we will conduct eight-hour mounted patrols, but for now, everyone is on holiday.

Simmons, a new private I don't really know, calls me out from the shelter of his mosquito netted bunk.

"Looking a little lonely there scout."

68

I hastily reply, "Looking a little light on stripes and body weight there, private."

SSGT Brass, reclining in the shadows of his bunk, adds his two cents.

"Ya'll don't start that stupid shit right now. I just ate. I'm settled in. I'm relaxing. I really don't feel like scrappin' right now, and if any one of you dumb motherfuckers mentions it again, there's gonna be some pushin."

Brass is North Carolina's finest, born and raised, and speaks with a sing-song southern drawl around the enormous wad of Copenhagen lodged squarely in the center of his bottom lip. I like Brass, as he never gives me too much shit, and his personality is not unlike my own.

"Your desk pilot is hungry Sarge; thought I'd go for the assist."

"Simmons! You hear that? A scout sergeant is doing a chow run for your battle buddy. Get the fuck out of here, Pearce, and Simmons, get the God-damned MRE. After you're done, get back here to do some push-ups."

Slowly, PVT Simmons rises from his bunk under a continuous shower of profanity from Brass that primarily calls attention to the fact that he is not moving nearly fast enough.

Shrugging, I smartly turn on my heels and take the ten steps or so forward that bring me back into the relative safety of the scout den. Okay. Me time now.

Before I get fully settled in for a fobbit evening I like to take the opportunity to call home. Chapel usually shares this routine with me, so I make my way through the scout bay to the smaller room beyond where Chapps and three other D Co paratroopers make their home.

"Hey Chapel, phone time?"

"Not today brother. Media blackout. Internet's down too."

"The mortar strike?"

"I'm guessing so. One of the 1st Infantry Division guys."

"I tell you, Chapps, they're out to get us."

"It's important to remember that boredom is a weapon. They figure if they keep taking the internet away from us, we'll have no choice but to surrender."

I turn to leave, but Chapel stops me on the way out.

"Hey D, Family Guy marathon later if you're up."

"Wouldn't miss it."

Back on my bunk, I take inventory of my sensitive items, remove my boots, and fire up my PSP. All around the barracks soldiers are happily clicking away at handheld games and jamming out to personal MP3 players, everyone that is, with the exception of Dick. Apparently SGT Cock-Face thinks that everyone in Baghdad wants to hear Zombie one more time. It's a shame that others support the notion as well. I, for one, am growing tired of the tune. Thank God for headphones.

Freddy and Dick are busying themselves with opening packages from home, the first that they have received this deployment. I've not yet received any mail from home, but I'm waiting on the day. Mail is our only source of supply outside of military kit, which is solely MREs, water, ammunition, and gun-lube. There has been a rumor circulating that we may have a Post Exchange by the holidays, but the last time I checked it wasn't even February yet.

I wanted very much to make a phone call, and am somewhat pissed that I can't do so. It's been over two weeks since I've spoken to Emily. When I think about her, a lonely pit forms in my stomach, so I focus all my attention on the killing of my digital enemies; I turn real life off for a while. I feel guilty too, for being a brat.

Media blackouts aren't a product of malfunctioning generators, downed power-lines, bad reception, or sun-spots. Media goes dark whenever somebody stationed at the FOB is killed. This is done primarily as a protective measure for the families of soldiers, providing that they hear of the deaths of their loved ones through the majesty of a flat-rate letter, as opposed to an ineloquent e-mail surprise. Personally, I don't have an opinion. Dead in government mail is every bit as dead as on Facebook. Oh well, protocols.

Blissfully, DJ Dick switches tracks to something much more palatable for me. A sentimental Norah Jones number, "Painter Song", which has always been one of my favorites; Emily's too. I stare up at the plain blue bottom of the top bunk which serves as my ceiling, and fix my gaze on a photo of Emily that I taped there. She's on a white bench at a park somewhere in the summer sunshine. I can see the shine of her beautiful red hair in the afternoon sun, and the white teeth in her happy smile. There's a green bandage around her left bicep, no doubt from donating blood or plasma. She's always doing stuff like that. A world away, she smiles at me and I smile back. *I love you.*

I tune in on the song and let it take me away for a blissful minute, to my old Honda out in the Nevada desert somewhere, with me and Emily cuddling together as we gaze up at the bright midnight stars.

If I were a painter, I would paint my reverie,

If that's the only way for you to be with me,
We'd be there together,
Just like we used to be.

With no place to go, and nothing to do, the weight of the day starts to drag my eyelids down. As much as I want to fight the feeling and try to have a little fun, after a paltry fifteen minutes or so I switch off my Playstation Portable and submit to the fatigue. The darkness washes over me, and once again I'm free of my life for a little while. I slip away to the sounds of a soft jazzy clarinet, and a groovy string bass, thinking of Emily all the while.

I'd climb inside the swirling skies to be with you.
I'd climb inside the sky to be with you.

Waking up in a military aircraft is always startling when I'm about to throw myself out of it. The time has once again come for my prescribed monthly battle-ready vitamin.

The paratroopers who are still enjoying the surrealistic sleep that this morning offers -- obviously the more experienced ones, while some of the new cherries are clutching their one-size-too-small airsick bags in their white-knuckled hands -- are waking slowly, raising their helmeted heads one-by-one, because even without a word, we know it's time.

Seated across from me in the narrow aisle, Freddy opens his eyes and gives a brief speech, mostly in profanity, about exactly how much he loves his job today. Then looking across at me, he stretches as best he can in his little seat with his parachutes, main and reserve strapped tightly around his body, front and back.

He smiles, yawns, and announces to everyone who would listen, "Man I love being a Turtle!"

Most can't hear him over the drone of the C-17's engines, but I silently praise and approve of his early morning bravado by rapping my helmet a few times with my fist, which is my personal, universal signal for, 'Here we go again; by the way it's early as Hell.'

The shout we've been waiting for echoes from the rear of the aircraft, "Ten Minutes!"

All at once everyone is awake, and we shout this wonderful information in unison, three times, to make sure everyone is up, collected, and gets the message. In ten minutes, this plane will have dropped its payload.

71

It's a dark and chaotic sight. Being 0530, not a scrap of light enters through the small, high windows of the aircraft. Instead, our entire world is lit by red-lights. The aircraft interior appears more like what one would imagine the spaceships of the future to look like, with nothing but stark gray metal walls, computer hardware, scattered emergency gear hither and yon, and everywhere, bundles of industrial wires and multi-colored signal lights. There's only one light in the aircraft that we care about. It's in the rear of the craft by the jump doors, and for all intents and purposes, it looks just like an everyday traffic light, with the exception of meaning: the green light means jump out of the aircraft, while a red light means there's a problem, and if you jump out of the aircraft you will most certainly die; yellow is quick and inconsequential.

Another shout from the jumpmaster at the rear of the aircraft, "Outboard Personnel, stand up!"

Maintaining the usual pattern, we all echo the message back. Slowly, encumbered by all of our shit, the outboard personnel stand and help each other to their feet. It's a goofy process, as nobody can move properly. Mornin' Sunshines.

My T-10 Charlie parachute cuts into my shoulders; my rifle digs sharply into my left armpit, and my heavy rucksack hangs awkwardly, dangling just in front of my knees. I'm a heavy bitch today.

It's about go time now, the moment my mind really starts running. From the moment I stand up, I remind myself that everything I do now until the moment I'm under canopy influences, with potentially severe consequences, the lives of everyone around me. If someone were to have a reserve parachute accident, that is, clumsily snagging the handle on anyone or anything around them, that said parachute runs the risk of shooting forth, catching air, and snaking towards the jump doors, which are now open. If a chute like that catches wind and flies, whoever is wearing it becomes red residue, along with everyone ahead of him in line. There hasn't been a tragedy of that magnitude in recent years, but the chance is always present, with a hundred and sixty lost boys pressed against each other, each one wearing a spring loaded reserve chute instead of a belt buckle.

Barring death of that nature, a good static-line hand off is the key to keeping your limbs intact, and the head of the man behind you firmly attached to his shoulders. A bad hand off can mean a stray static line, which results in mortal wounds. I will do my best this morning, as I always do.

72

As I take my feet, I look forward to exiting the aircraft. I won't have to wait anymore, and standing with all this garbage on hurts in an explicit way. That, and I've had to piss for upwards of three hours. Sicily drop zone is now 1,000 feet below us, and with that, all the acreage one guy who has to pee could ever dream of.

We receive and repeat our commands.

"Check static lines!" And, "Sound-off for equipment check!" The aircraft comes alive and vibrates with the course shouting.

Every man runs his fingers along the parachutes and lines of the man in front of him to insure that everything is in its proper place. We're hooked up, each man's static line ascending from his pack-tray to the cable above that runs the length of the cargo bay.

Thirty second warning. I feel my guts tighten; my legs shake from the weight they're bearing as well as from the anticipation of what's to come. I remind myself to live this moment, and as always, I tell myself that this might just be the last time I fly. I smile to myself; scared to death, as we all are, I start the mad chuckle which always comes up from a strange place in me at times like this: a laugh, a sound, that try as I might, can never be mustered on its own.

Green Light.

Brothers in arms, a living worm of fear and sweat; a cattle call of turtles in tactical nylon, start shuffling our slow rush to the jump door. I'm thirty souls back, so I see my brothers sucked out into the dark void of the pre-dawn sky one by one. Almost. Almost.

I make eye contact with the jumpmaster as I button-hook by him. I give him a strong static line hand-off as my mind automatically impels my body toward the door. I take a single step toward the doorway to the void, and jump.

It's fear; it's rapture; it's being eaten by a god. The hot engine wind pressurizes and deafens my ears as I'm blinded by the tempest of this dark foggy morning. I hold position as best I can as I feel my body being violently ripped sideways, and down. I've always equated the feeling to riding a dragon on rocket skates. I feel the positive G-forces of a strong parachute opening start to crush my chest and my thighs.

It's over in an instant, and startlingly quiet. There's no noise discipline on this jump; it's not tactical, it's administrative, and, as a result, shouts of joy and relief can be heard at every level of this new morning sky.

I look above me to make certain everything with my rig is kosher, and when I bring my eyes back to the horizon I can see the first bright warm rays of the sun breaking through the tops of distant trees. A calm, fresh green wind plays on my face as I make sure I'm not going to crash into any of my buddies.

In another instant, it's over. It's a soft landing, always a fortunate occurrence, as doubtless someone else will break their legs today, which is fairly common.

I roll over in the wet morning grass and

"Wake up, D."

"Hey, Freddy."

"Your CQ time has arrived, buddy."

"Oh fucking happy day."

Chapter Three: Phantasms

Ah! What worlds that dance and churn
Beneath my very eyelids,
An endless waste aghast of face,
A freakish fragile hybrid.

With sands that swim on raging winds
Bereft of any feeling,
I close my eyes and grit my teeth
In vain against my reeling.

This is the place from ages past that has
Spent its days in war,
An endless feast on tired flesh never sated,
Still craving more.

The blood runs free in rivulets,
Across the ancient stones,
And burning barrels light the night,
Illumine rust on tortured bones.

This world is never seen save by
Those here thus encumbered
With many rounds and heart fires dim,
A sign that man is blinded.

With laws and creeds and hallowed writ,
Their lights go out in driving grit,
Who chose this life, these sorry men,
Whose fates were sealed in shit.

I gaze outside my window, as the broken glass and grit of Baghdad slide roughly over my tired eyes. Six hours into this mounted patrol, and only two hours left to go, hopefully. One can never fully know the real truth of the daily plan until well after the fact.

Our trucks are crewed in the same manner as on our last outing, although we've been told this is going to be subject to change in the coming weeks. This voyage is our last trip to the Sahad JSS, and as such, we are all looking forward to never seeing the inside of the towers ever again.

Tower guard is normally a duty reserved for shit-bags and ne'er do wells. Occasionally leg units will have tower guard shifts as part of their normal duties, but it usually isn't so with the airborne. Those of us that get landed with tower shifts back at the FOB are normally the victims of article fifteens, counseling statements, and the like. For the layman, that means a soldier who has landed himself in some sort of sticky doo-doo.

It always seems an unjust punishment to be locked away in a tower, so all of us are looking forward to some quality time at a new post out in the city where we can spend more of our time patrolling, and less time starting at nothing.

Feeling sleepy, I decide to strike up a conversation rather than risking the chance of falling asleep in the truck.

"Hey Cole, you got any Cope man?"

"I have mine. You bring any?"

"I certainly did. I just have Skoal right now though, and I'm not really digging the idea of sour apples."

Cole passes me the can, and thinking about how it would be absolute bullshit to survive the war and die of throat cancer or have my face fall off, I start packing the can like any good baseball player would.

I generally hate dipping. I hate the necessity of having to spit every couple of minutes. More so, I hate having the shit stuck in my teeth for extended periods of time. But at a time like this, that's just groovy by me. Cloud has me slated to work the gun or drive on our coming patrols, so at least there should be a change of scenery for me in the coming weeks. This, of course, will come at a price, as I will no longer be able to jump out of the truck and stretch my legs every time the LT wants to look at dirt, or attempt to talk to the locals.

"Hey, Cole, catch!"

I deftly flip the can of long-cut back to the gunner and rest a little easier in the knowledge that I'm not about to nod off on accident.

Freddy pipes up from the driver's seat.

"Are we there yet?"

Dick, from the front seat, immediately but in a somewhat jocular fashion, responds, "Don't start that shit again."

"Aw, come on Sarge, tell me."

"Shut up, Freddy."

I can't help myself, so I decide to join in on the fun.

"Are we there yet?"

"Honestly, motherfuckers, this joke has more than run its course."

That is most likely absolutely true. On our last adventure that old phrase was uttered by all of us no less than a hundred times.

Cole, from the gun, "Are we there yet?"

"God damn it."

After a brief pause, Dick reaches for the ASIP radio handset.

"Delta four-five, this is Delta four-one, over."

"Go ahead, four-one."

"Roger, four-five. Are we there yet? Over."

"That's a negative Delta four-one. We are not there yet. Over."

A moment passes, and the questioning begins anew.

"Delta four-five, this is Delta four-one. Break. Are we there now? Over."

"Delta four-one, that is still a negative; we are not there yet. How copy? Over."

"Roger, that's a good copy. I read as 'we are not there yet.' Over."

"Delta four-five, out."

A moment after the nonsensical conversation ceases the radio crackles again, but this time it's a very pissed off First Sergeant telling us to keep our bullshit off the net. Although we understand and agree with that, it's also pretty clear that we're not in any manner of trouble at all, and that our First Sergeant, conducting his end of the conversation from the JSS of our destination, still possesses some manner of humor.

I look out my window once more, looking for roadside bombs as is my custom. Although I'm still nestled in my own little corner in the rear of the vehicle, I can still get a pretty good angle on about thirty meters or so of the road ahead.

At the moment, Freddy is driving us counter-flow, that is, on the wrong side of the road. It's our primary defense mechanism against roadside bombs. That is, unless we account for times when things explode that were meant for traffic heading the other way. Either way we can be screwed royally by a well-placed, well-hidden bomb. Like Forrest Gump said, shit happens.

I gaze lazily out the window and watch the faces of people pass: the young and the old; men, women, and children go about their daily routine, which generally amounts to a pure quest for survival in this crazy pretend city.

A bit farther up the road we see a familiar man; we've seen him three times already today, driving in circles past his shoddy vendor's stand. He stands above a dead donkey, wailing with his empty hands outstretched towards the tan sky, crying out to Allah, or the Easter bunny, or Peter Pan, or some other shit, obviously expressing his discontentment with being mortal today.

"He does have a lot of shit in the cart."

"What does it look like to you, D?"

"Fuck if I know. I'll bet you money it's hajji shit though. Toenail clippings maybe, or Durka-Durka puffs. Ass-cheese or some shit. Maybe there's even a GECK in there, by the will of God. Who the fuck knows?"

"A GECK?"

"Yeah, you know, a GECK: a Garden of Eden Creation Kit."

Cole can't seem to wrap his head around what I'm saying.

"Were the fuck did that come from?"

"Fallout One, or Two; can't remember which one. Anybody play the old Fallouts?"

For once in his entire life, career, day, moment, whatever the fuck, Dick speaks to me with acknowledgment, under the guise that he thinks I'm an actual human being.

"Hell yeah I played Fallout, way back, and I think it was number one. In Two, you were looking for some kind of water chip, right?"

"I don't think I ever played number two. But the point is, these fucking people need a GECK. Open it up in the middle of the fucking city. We could all do with some shade this time of year. Teaching these people how to farm and bath couldn't hurt anybody."

"Hey, D, be nice."

"Sure, just for you, Cole, I'll modify my behavior and language, as well as my outlook on life in the big city."

One hour left to go. My eyes return to the road ahead. To the right hand side and about forty meters to our front is the turn that will lead us to our destination, a place we've all collectively termed, 'mud-village,' which denotes that our patrol has gone full-circle, and will soon begin anew.

"One more hour to go!"

Freddy from behind the wheel responds, "You know it!"

We don't simply drive in circles, mind. That would be suicide. It's bad enough that we drive around in the same 'hoods for eight hours at a time anyway. Our route varies slightly every time, taking new streets, or new mulhallas when we can, stopping as we go to speak to locals at different locations. While the drive essentially remains a gigantic, near pointless circle, the route itself is always different. Which is why we're moving to a new sector soon: we can only drive so many ways in one area before we start repeating ourselves. That, and the purpose of our being in Sahad is a bit dead. There haven't been any fights worth noting; at least none that our squad has been directly involved in. As far as combat goes, it's a quiet neighborhood. However, as I'm rather fond of all my fingers and toes, I don't much seem to mind. Nice easy war we're having lately.

As we gently grind into our turn, the world explodes.

My ears immediately start ringing, and grow dimmer. I can feel the base from the blast in my chest, and a cloud of billowing dirt obscures the world on the other side of the windshield.

The explosion rocks the earth around our truck, and the convoy immediately halts.

I never saw the other friendly convoy, but I can see their silhouettes now through the grime on the windshield, and the lingering haze of dirt in the street. Four American trucks had been taking the corner on the far side of the road, at the same time as us. We were the lucky ones, while the other convoy was unfortunate enough to be on the detonating side.

The LT crackles over the radio and asks if all trucks are up. One by blessed one, we all answer back.

"One up."

Dick calls back to us over the hellish ringing in his ears, "Everybody good?"

I look to Freddy as he responds that he's fine, and Cole speaks up from the turret, "My ears are ringing, but I'm up."

Duke, bless his chubby, lazy little heart, is just waking up from the worst alarm clock ever in the seat just to my left, also working dismount for this patrol.

"What the *fuck!* I think I was on the beach somewhere."

Around the splattered and crumbling wad of just-smooshed long-cut in my mouth, I manage to laugh-sputter-cough, "Morning, Sunshine."

SGT Dick responds to the radio call.

"Two up."

After only a slight pause, we get the collective word that trucks three, four, and five are also good to go.

The net hisses one more time, and the disembodied voice of our LT commands us to pull the trucks into a Lazy-W formation, and that all ground personnel are to dismount.

"Here we go, boyos."

Our trucks creep forward into a careful line, on the one hand ensuring that all vehicles have space to park in the proper positions, and on the other, checking to make sure nobody lost a tire in the explosion.

I place my right hand on the door-handle as I confirm with my left hand that my rifle is still firmly clipped to my rack. The truck stops, and I pump the handle.

"See you later, Freddy."

"Come on back now, y'hear."

I quickly button-hook out of the truck, lifting my rifle to the ready and scanning the area behind me while taking cover behind the open door. When I deem myself to be moderately safe, which is always a quick operation, I slam the heavy door behind me and take up my designated position on a knee at the front right side of the truck.

In a combat theatre getting into a vehicle, and subsequently dismounting are two of the most dangerous actions an infantry soldier can perform. Snipers and other combatants will target the door for all the obvious reasons. Not only is the man leaving the vehicle exposed and unable to properly defend himself, but any bullet that finds its way into an armored vehicle is not going to stop. They'll simply bounce around inside for a while until they find a cozy home in someone's flesh. Quickly closing the door behind me is a great service to my buddies, who are essentially trapped inside the vehicle at the mercy of the fates.

Not everybody on the ground has a radio, including me. That will most likely change if and when we get to our destination today, as my squad likes to land me with all the heavy shit. I sort of ask for that as a product of my nature. I rarely complain about shit. In Army Land, that's just asking for it.

Rather than relying on coms to assemble, all dismounts present simply get up and fall in together in a squad-column formation.

Everybody has a sector; everybody has a field of fire; everybody has a zone; everybody is a combatant. We fall into place, pulling security and scanning for threats. Together, we immediately begin to move across the street towards the damaged American convoy.

Duke and I are at the rear of the patrol, with three meters separating us from the next pair of staggered soldiers, Moore from D Co, and our very own SSGT Cloud. Five more soldiers lead us up the street accompanied by our LT, who just so happens to be the only soldier out of formation, as well as the only soldier without his hands on his weapon. Instead, he's having a conversation on the M-bitter radio which I cannot hear, most likely communicating information with the JSS, requesting additional support, or making sure a medevac is en-route.

After having crossed to the other side of the street, our squad takes up positions and starts pulling security and waiting for what orders come next, as well as looking for any clues that would hint towards the origin of the explosion.

Other soldiers from the 1st ID, Big Red One, have been out of their trucks for a moment already while they pull security, assess the damage, and make medevac radio calls of their own.

They were rolling with four trucks, three of which appear to be fine; it appears that the lead truck got the brunt of the blast. Down the street to my left about ten meters away, the truck looks sad and dead. Two 1st ID soldiers stare numbly and blankly into the hulk of the wreckage through more than one smoking hole, the largest of which is bigger than a basketball.

I look at Duke. "EFP, say?"

"Had to be. Weird, big fucking holes."

To the right of the vehicle bleeding to death in its own gasoline and red transmission fluid lie two wounded soldiers who are already receiving aid from their comrades. Doubtless there are three more that no longer need any aid, still trapped inside the wreckage of their vehicle.

Cloud calls to us from the front, "Okay. It's buttoned up here. Medevac is on the way. Prepare to move out; watch your spacing. Let's go get that motherfucker."

Nowadays, cell phone transmissions are the most popular way to detonate roadside bombs, followed by Wiley Coyote style command wire detonation, which means only one thing: it can be inferred that the bastard who set off the bomb was watching when the device detonated, and is very likely still in the neighborhood.

The intersection was busy, but it doesn't seem like any Arabs were caught in the blast. Somebody else surely should have been.

"The whole fucking neighborhood must have been in on it. Nobody else got hit."

Duke says to me, "Ditto, D, that's what I was just thinking."

One about face and a hand-signal later we're moving out, away from the intersection and toward the neighboring mulhallas on the side of the road where the blast originated.

Just ahead of us is an open field bordered by a warped chain-link fence. No chance of any baddies hiding in there, so our attention turns to a row of houses and apartment blocks that border the road. Many of the apartments have balconies that give clear vantage points to the blast site, but as far as we can tell, there is no sign that the terrorist, insurgent, or generalized fuck-wit was operating from any one of them.

We look for the tell-tale signs of command wire detonation, such as strung wire from the site of the blast, but we do not see any. Trying to play detective with the balconies is a much different story. Hundreds of electrical wires spring forth from the balconies and hang every which way, like crazy vines in an Alice in Wonderland tale. Any one of them could be another life-line to Kuwaiti television, or the actual detonation cord to the bomb. Take your pick.

As we move forward Duke examines nearby traffic and stupefied pedestrians while I slowly turn to the rear, then to the front, over and over again, surveying a line of sight back and to the left of the formation, as well as my own stretch of the local traffic. Ours is a fast advance, but it's methodical and thorough nonetheless.

"Hey, Duke, do you think that these bastards can get a hold of detonation cord?"

"Dunno. We know they have Semtex. But det cord? Did they have that in the '70s?"

"I don't know either; surely some form of it maybe. High grade and modern? Probably not."

Arab lands have never made their own ordinance. If they have, it was obviously so dysfunctional as to never be openly used, or mass marketed to the rest of the world. Instead, terror organizations and local militaries primarily rely on bought or scavenged weapons and other hand-me-downs from the soviet era. AK-47s rule the day in Iraq, along with Dishka .50 calibers and old soviet-era explosives, primarily Semtex, which is comparable to, but not quite the equal of our modern day C4. RPGs too. They have a lot of those.

"If they have it, it's most likely a slower burn. But who knows?"

"We'll never know unless we find some anyhow."

"Yup."

Our patrol comes to a stop at the first of the neighborhood houses. Unfortunately, we do not have a trained interpreter with us on this particular foray. Instead, it looks like our LT is doing a very legal, very called for bribe with one of the local English-speaking passersby. A very lucky find indeed.

"I'm so very fucking distrustful of volunteers."

Duke doesn't respond to me, but I can read his sweating face all the same, and it's a look of agreement.

As our slow march picks up once more, I start to feel the heat as well. The sun has just sunk behind the shelter of the surrounding buildings, but the sky is still plenty bright, and the late afternoon heat, though not oppressive, covers everything.

Through the next two hours, our search for the Mad Bomber becomes tired, impotent, and lame. Door after flimsy door, interrogation after interrogation, we yield no new news, and find no crazy Arab reeking of insanity and gunpowder. Instead, door after boring door, we find the tired, hopeless faces of people with little or nothing to live for. Scared of us and insulted by our unwelcome intrusions, they offer us whatever information they can, some of it genuine, and some of it suspect.

Tired, we return to our trucks after the space of two hours, having apprehended no bomber, having taken no fire, and having quelled no insurgency. I scan my sector, looking into the peering eyes of some spectators, and crank my door handle open.

"Welcome back."

"I'm quite welcome. And, we're quite back. In one piece no less. No worse for wear. How are the others?"

"First ID?"

"Yep. Those ones."

"Not too good. Two made it, we think. The other bodies got taken away in the truck by the wrecker."

"T-88?"

"Yep. You missed it?"

I do the no no. The not-allowed, and the unthinkable. I take my helmet off.

"Yeah, we were too busy trying to find Muhammad San Diego to take notice. Went all the way back, three mulhallas over."

"Find anything?"

"Not a thing."

"What a fucking day, man," Freddy replies to me.

The others are already in the truck. The radio crackles once again, and just like that we're on the way to pull into the JSS for our final eight-day rotation.

"Who's on tower first?"

Dick replies from the front seat, "You still a scout?"

"I believe so Sergeant."

"Then you're on towers, Einstein."

"But who's on first?"

"Shut the fuck up, Pearce."

"Gets you every time."

I download my shit quickly and take an immediate rest on the bed I know and love, the little olive drab green cot in the back corner; my home, my home, my home away from home.

Blessedly, we're not on tower first. D Co is up for that. Instead, we're taking the first foot patrol shift, so we simply get to kick it for a while until the sun goes down.

"How'd we get out of first shift this time?"

Cloud, just barely putting his gear down after the initial arrival briefing replies, "Sergeant Fritz didn't want to pull tower shift at 0400, so we get to instead."

"If they don't get us coming, they get us going. Shit, I hate the *naturlich* course of things."

Duke replies, "The what? Sorry, I don't speak *Deutsch*."

Cole can't resist himself, "Sorry, Pearce, I don't speak douche either, say again?"

"Never you mind with all that bayou gumbo crap."

Everyone has a good chuckle, and each of us lies down in his own space to rest up a bit from the solemn events of the day.

I can't help but feel somewhat guilty; I've not been keeping up on my reading. It's been a few days since I've picked up the *Canterbury Tales*, but I'm so fatigued that I quickly decide against it. By my calculations, it will be about three hours until full dark, which is our most preferred time to prowl around town on foot.

I deftly arrange my woobie under my head, where it resumes it's faithful service as my impromptu pillow. *Boom.* My ears are still ringing from the excitement of the day. *Boom.* So sudden, fast, and cold. Three dead, two wounded, just like that. And that's the way it was.

It just as well could have been us traversing the other side of the street, or the Mad Arab could simply have placed his little toy on our side of the route. Any way you look at it, travel is always a terrible game of motorized Russian Roulette, complete with authentic Semtex. It *could* have been us. Hell, scouts take duty on lead truck seven times out of ten, far more than any other element in the platoon. Just another way we routinely get shafted. Pick a number.

My mind wanders back home for a bit, and that's quite cruel. Although our time in country is barely approaching two months, the days are already growing longer. The occasional mortar, small arms fire, or roadside bomb seem to make the prospective future stretch on forever without end.

The timing feels proper, so I roll away from the prying eyes of my militant society for a little bit and face the wall, bowing my head ever so slightly to say a sincere and silent prayer; for myself and those around me, as well as for the two survivors of the blast. I take the time to thank God as well, not only for my survival though yet another day, but also for the privileged and safe life I have lived so far.

War is a lot like church: it strong-arms you into praying and forces you to dwell on and evaluate instances and circumstances in your life that, had you not endured them, would have most likely flown under the radar.

I close my quiet time out with a silent Methodist rendition of the Lord's prayer, and smile a secret smile to myself in my darkened corner. If God was going to see me dead this month, he probably would have made it so already. As always, I beg forgiveness for my sins, things I've both done, and not done, and then quickly sub-vocalize a quick amen. As if by some strange magic, I feel instantly better about the events of the day. A little tired, and a little sad, but as far as an armed combatant goes, I feel right as rain.

I make it a point to think about Emily before I let sleep take me away. She gives me something beautiful to look forward to; something to fight for, and maybe even to die for. She gives me hopes and dreams for the future, and she gives me the comfort of memories from good days gone by. There's an assurance that accompanies thoughts of death that comes from knowing that I may have already experienced the most beautiful

86

moments of my life. I smile to myself as I take a dark comfort in that.

I close my eyes gently, patiently beginning the slow wait of the exhausted. I try to focus my mind precisely on the moment when sleep takes me, but as with us all, I can never quite grasp it. Still, the world goes black again.

SSGT Cloud wakes me first, telling me to rustle up the others. I knuckle my eyes to clear the sleep away and take a quick glance at my watch: 2200. It's the perfect time to go sneaking around central Baghdad. Freddy is already up, so I move between Duke and Cole to shake them awake, one at a time. Dick is a light sleeper, so he rouses himself easily amidst the others, who seem less tolerant about the violation of their naptime. Through the waking process we attempt to be as quiet as possible, so as not to disturb the rest of still sleeping D Co, or at least those lucky few that have the first down shift.

Quickly, and without a word, we grab our weapons, radios, optics, and armor, heading outside to where Cloud can give us our mini-briefing, as well as where we can get into our battle-rattle without making a huge ruckus inside the barracks.

Out on the roof of the JSS, the hajji locker-room, we gather around our squad leader.

"All right, listen up. Change of plans. I know you would all like to walk around the neighborhood in circles, but there's other shit going on tonight. There is an engineering company from the 1st ID securing an intersection about two miles east of here. We don't know exactly what they're doing, or how long they're going to be doing it. Some of Delta Company's guys are coming with us, and we'll be moving in three trucks to the site."

A look of confusion lights on all of our faces; we don't normally drive once we're in our neighborhood, let alone for a paltry distance of two miles. Dick speaks up.

"Why the trucks?"

"Because. The LT is going with us, and he doesn't feel like walking, for whatever reason. There has been some light contact in the area tonight, some of it just a half an hour ago. I think the LT just wants to have the heavy guns up and assist with pulling security in the center of the square. Meanwhile, we're going to dismount about a click out to the west, and approach the intersection on foot. We're going to set up and over-watch the whole damn thing until it's finished. It might be a really long shift, or it might be short one."

We all nod acknowledgement to what was said, and what is expected of us. With a little bit of enthusiasm I strike up a smoke, my last chance to have one in quite some time, and begin the short but arduous process of throwing all my shit on. Moments later, bedecked in weaponry, armor, and in full possession of the ASIP radio, I look around at the others. Everyone looks ready to go.

I do a quick radio check with the command post, as well as the D Co soldiers that are already waiting for us down in the running trucks.

"Coms up?"

"Good to go, Sergeant."

I sort of like being the RTO. I don't much enjoy the extra weight, but I do welcome the extra chore that communication brings. Having the radio means that there's more soldierly stuff for me to do, and less time spent just staring at concrete and waiting.

I fall in with the rest of the guys in a slow and steady gaggle as we make our way down the crude stairs to take our places in the dismount seats of the three trucks.

I crank the handle, pull the door open, and plop down heavily on the uncomfy canvass seat.

"Mornin', dudes."

"Mornin'. How we doin' today?"

"Same shit, different planet."

"I hear you."

From the front seat I hear the distinctive, gravelly voice of my good friend.

"All comfy back there smurf-stick?"

"Yar howdy that. Truck commandering tonight, I see."

"Nah. We're moving out last, so my job is minimal today. I'm just going to sit here and meditate for a while, and take over the middle-east vicariously, through the power of imagination."

"Sounds good to me. More Empire. Just so long as that shit gets done."

"I'll do my best."

The final radio checks are sent in, and like so many times before, our convoy, somewhat shortened on this occasion, boldly trundles out of the ECP, headlights off, gone full black, with the drivers relying solely on night-vision equipment to navigate. Baghdad has turned a freakish

Kermit the Frog green, and lazes its rough imagery into my left eye through my monocular. Now that's a town of a different color. Chapel decides to spend the next six minutes of his life talking to me again. He'd better make it quick though; we don't have long to chat.

"You hear about Route Africa?"

"Did they clean it up or something? Can't imagine anything like that over there."

"Nope. Nothing of the sort. The battalion commander chewed into Sergeant Major this morning over the name. Said we can't call it that anymore."

"Why? I though it seemed rather proper. Davidson, who just so happens to be black, named it himself. Further, it's descriptive. Killians? Don't know it. Hoffner? Never heard of it. Route Africa? Oh yeah, that's the one in the middle of town with all the black people. See? Simple. Good nomenclature, that."

"I know, I know. So Smag re-named it. Take a guess."

"Uh. Black People Street, maybe? Creole way? Queens Boulevard? What?"

Chapel starts to laugh, and has to compose himself before he has the calm to say the punch-line.

"Martin Luther King Boulevard!"

With that, the rest of us in the truck burst out in a fit of unprofessional, undisciplined laughter. It's just too good. *It just be too right.*

Before further commentary can be made, our truck rolls to a stop in a somewhat shorter than average lazy W position, and LT's call to dismount instructs us to do just that over the net.

"Well, Chapps, every city has one."

"They do indeed. Be safe, brother."

"Likewise."

Dismounting goes smoothly, with nary an Arab in sight. Our humble scout squad assembles in the shadows and cover provided by a row of concrete pillars in front of a series of local store fronts. We're in the very center of the developed part of the city now.

Up and down the road as far as the eye can see, old industrial buildings and what may have once been tenement apartments flank the street. About a hundred meters to our front, one lonely streetlamp, a surviving vestige of the land that was, gives off a faint ruddy light. In my right eye there's a bit of color, but in my left it appears as a lonely bit of stale green illumination.

I do another radio check with the command post to inform them that all of the dismounts have left the trucks. Naturally, we begin to move with Cloud in a small squad column at about a three meter spread.

We don't say a word. Every man breaths as quietly as possible while scanning both his field of fire, and the ground just in front of his boots. Stealth rules these situations. Effectually, we are in the center of a city of six million people, the majority of which who want to kill us. Gunfire could come at any time from any one of the hundreds of windows which overlook the darkened street from above our position. I listen but hear nothing in the still night, save for a pack of howling dogs somewhere up ahead in the distance.

The main streets pose the most danger, so we quickly turn into the first mulhalla we come to on the right-hand side of the road. Mulhallas offer us much more cover and concealment than the wider, more public roadways. The small alleyway is tight, roughly four feet across from door to door. As we walk deeper into the narrow alley I see many different kinds of doors built into the naked, old, and ugly stone of the buildings on either side of the mulhalla. Some of them are great metal things, looking every bit like they were transported here from some steam-punk dwarven world or an old sunken battleship. Other doorways are composed of simple wrought-iron grating complete with padlocks, stretching over darkened maws in the side of the cold, ancient stones.

To my front Duke takes a misstep and splashes, quite audibly, in the rivulet of human shit, piss, and garbage that flows down the center of our path.

He quickly rights himself, cussing very softly, as we all take a brief pause to listen. Cloud holds up his left fist, a sign for us to halt.

Freddy and I are at the rear of the formation once again, but even across the space of a hundred and fifty darkened midnight meters, I can see the form of a middle-eastern man in a gray man-dress walking down the center of the mulhalla directly towards us.

We hold our positions and wait for him to draw near. The night is dark, but not so much that a man passing us in the narrow alleyway would fail to notice our presence. This old man's visual acuity aside, it's quite likely that he would literally stumble upon us in the darkness.

Cloud motions to us in the typical infantry 'follow me' fashion, and we pick up pace again and follow.

Inevitably, the man sees us as we draw closer. Dick, at the front of

90

the formation, proffers a friendly greeting.

"*Salom Alikom.*"

The elderly man is taken aback, appearing very surprised to be surrounded by so many armed American turtles on his midnight stroll. After only a brief pause, he utters the words "*Alikom Salam,*" and continues on his merry hajji way, wither-he-whilst, behind us, and into the darkness beyond.

A bit further down the mulhalla, we begin to hear the unmistakable sounds of army machinery. Just over a small structure to our front we can see the illumination of construction grade floodlights illuminating what is most likely the intersection of our destination.

We take cover under the eaves of the structure directly to our front and bring it in to Cloud to hear what lies in store for us next.

I never would have had the bright idea myself, but it looks like we're climbing the side of a building adjacent to what looks like a tall, abandoned industrial structure. At three stories, our target building looks to be a dangerous climb, even by recreational standards.

"Okay, listen up. I'm not gonna lie; it's a tough fucking climb. We get onto the roof of this three story motherfucker, and then down into the courtyard of the neighboring building.

Dick points at the lumbering eight-story behemoth next door, "That one?"

"Yeah, that one. We should be able to see everything from up there. Keep noise and light discipline; nobody will see us enter or exit, unless one of you guys makes a huge racket while falling off the building."

Duke quietly, in a whisper, elbows me in the stomach and says, "You ready to get your climb on, D? Not scared of heights today, huh?"

"I'm just happy to be carrying the radio."

Which I am not happy about at all. I have spare batteries to boot, and if I remember correctly, I left my grappling hook in my other pants. I usually reserve my own introspective levels of pissed off hatred for Dick and Duke when they do stupid shit. Rarely do I feel this level of disgust and disdain for SSGT Cloud. Every once in a while he can't seem to help himself: Dick's bead on the world is contagious to the ego; everybody wants to be special. Everyone it seems, but me.

What I see is a squad enamored with Tom Clancy videogames and misdirected testosterone. The guys want so badly to do something cool. I, for one, though not overly cautious, do see the merit in living out the rest of my days enjoying the full function of my lower extremities.

"What's wrong, D?"

My turn to give a corn-pone 'pinion.

"Sergeant, Freddy has the Hooligan tools, and there's a gate right in the middle of the fucking wall. We can see into the courtyard from here. Cracking the lock would be a lot less noisy than Duke Nukem here doing a double-axle back-flip onto the concrete from halfway up the side of a crumbling wreck."

"I know that. I also know that we're going for a climb. Not the best idea, but that's what we're doing. We're training. We're going to have a lot of climbs like this coming up, so you better get used to scrawling up the sides of tall-ass hajji buildings."

Walking up to the gate next to the wall and grating which we will shortly climb, I can't help myself. Pulling security and taking a position next to the gate that I so badly want to crack, I quietly reach out and turn the rusty handle, swinging it unopposed and quite unlocked, out into the alleyway just a few inches, so that my team can see.

"Can it, D."

"Roger, sergeant. Just sayin'."

"You ain't sayin' shit tonight, unless it's on the radio from now on."

Commando Cloud is going first. Unceremoniously, he swings his weapon around his body so that it rests on his back, where it doesn't interfere with his hands as he takes hold of the metal grating; he wedges his left boot into a depression in the cracked wall, and hoists himself up, beginning his climb.

"You really should keep it to yourself, Pearce." Freddy says to me.

I strain to keep my voice quiet as I start to feel suddenly vehemently angry. I can feel the heat rise in my face and in the pissed-off quality of my voice, so rare to show itself.

"You know what, Freddy, I was asked for my humble opinion, and I gave it. Not my problem if every-fucking-body else likes to think that we're at some kind of fucked-up family fun center for the developmentally disabled. Good fucking times. I'm laughing if Cloud takes a bullet in his swinging, clambering ass."

It's Cole's turn to climb, but before he does he leans in toward me, and in a hushed whisper, gives me a piece of his mind.

"Rare I know, but I'm with you on this one, buddy. This is some stupid, unnecessary bullshit."

From just behind us Dick gives his two-cents, "Shut it."

Freddy's turn comes to pass, and without a word he grabs the wrought-iron grating and begins to pull himself up the wall.

A few blocks away, automatic weapons fire rings out through the quiet night, and I feel my stomach tighten a little.

It's taking much too long. A good ten minutes have passed since we dismounted and Dick, Freddy, and myself have yet to start the climb. The squad is also making a metric fuck-ton of noise, battle-rattle and weapons clicking and clanking against the chipped stone and bent metal above.

Blissfully, the wait is over and it's my turn to make the climb. I feel good knowing that Dick and Freddy aren't paying much attention below me, and those above are most likely not pulling security, but instead are probably cracking jokes at us, talking to themselves about how very fucking special they are for making a pointless rock-climb part of a combat engineer over-watch mission in central Hell.

I have a good idea as to how I'm going to negotiate the wall, after having watched the others ascend. The first six feet are not too tricky, as a stretch of decorative metalwork provides great footing and handholds. Why is there metal grating going up the outside of a perimeter barrier? I have not a clue. Probably to keep people from climbing the wall. Dumb shits.

After my metal handholds are gone the rise becomes a bit more difficult. The next six feet offer almost nothing in the way of handholds, traction, or purchase of any kind. Couple that with sixty pounds of dead weight and it creates a stupid, leg shaking situation for me. It's impossible to see detail on the surface of the wall through my monocular, so I flip it up with my left hand and amazingly, I still can't see shit.

I smile to myself a bit, as I think about how glad I am that Emily can't see me doing this stupid crap. If she gets a flat-rate letter on my behalf, let her think I died in a great battle, or a glorious explosion; anything but knowing the truth about the lemming tumble I took from the third story of a decaying building.

Feeling upwards along the wall with my left hand, I feel a crack that's just large enough for me to stuff the first three fingers of my hand into. After getting a good grip, standing on my tippiy-toes as best I can on some sort of half-inch ledge I cannot see, I reach as high as I can with my right hand.

At first I don't feel anything, and begin to feel stumped and inadequate compared to the rest of the climbers up top. This gives me sinking fear, as I am all too aware of my position, over twenty feet above war-zone concrete, shaking, with no place to escape to. My breathing quickens and I feel a slight tremble start in my legs. I have to piss. I keep reaching higher, as much as my shaking body can stretch, and then I feel it: the squared top of a badly placed brick. My own personal Jesus rock. Hallelujah.

After hoisting myself up with all my might, I can see my next station in reach. Only about four feet up this time, a balcony juts crazily out of the wall. Grabbing it is easy, although hoisting my cumbersome body onto the metal platform proves awkward, uncoordinated, and noisy. I also take note that the other guys weren't just being sloppy, other than the unnecessary climb of course, and that no matter how it is negotiated, the balcony is one noisy bitch, teetering to and fro while hanging from an assortment of flimsy, noisy bolts.

Still thinking negative, horrifying thoughts as I stand up on the shaking metal, I think about how easy it would be to stand on the inside of the balcony doorway, and blast a stupid American tourist with my AK-47, right from the comfort of my own home. After all, they come by, tempting as they are, one by helpless one, defenseless. I heard them coming.

I stop thinking about it.

The rest of the climb goes smoothly, and near the top the wall gives way to the uneven masonry of a little rooftop casita that was never finished. Sighing a heavy sigh of relief, I crouch inside next to Cloud and look over the edge, waiting for the others.

After another five minutes Freddy and Dick join us at the top and blessedly, our squad is no longer unnecessarily hanging like conveniently separated bullet piñatas for all to see.

"Enjoy your hike, Dick?" I can't help myself.

"Shut the fuck up, Dallas."

"Roger."

After our brief conversation, I radio the CP and let them know that our squad is almost in position.

"Delta One-Two, say again, what do you mean almost, over?"

"Delta One-Seven, yeah, break. That means we took an alternate route. Lots of tourist traps out here, over."

I sign off and rejoin the squad, who are presently bitching about not being able to see anything from this particular rooftop.

From our vantage point on the third floor we cannot quite see over a freshly erected wall of eighteen-foot-tall concrete barriers that have recently gone up in the square.

"Separating two neighborhoods again?"

"Looks like it."

Many westerners would be surprised to hear about how the cultural dynamic of an Arabian city works on the street level. One neighborhood will be Shiite, the next Sunni, then Shiite, and so on. Many neighborhoods can't seem to figure out the whole Muslim peace and fellowship thing, so instead of peacefully coexisting, they're happy to try to kill each other from across the street, day in and day out. I myself am a bit fuzzy on the nature of the age-old feud, although I believe it has something to do with the legitimacy of Muhammad's true lineage or some shit like that. It reminds me of the stupid dialogue between Christians and Mormons that we're all subject to from time to time, only here the arguments are settled with automatic weapon discharges, rather than the conventional suburban door-slamming.

To make travel safer through some districts of the city, Uncle Sam sometimes decides to erect high concrete walls between warring factions of the dirt people, which also happens to be why we're out on furlough in Sahad on this fine evening.

I take the time to saunter along the top of the roof to where Cole is crouching, double tasking. He's looking towards the square, pulling security as best he can while at the same time filling his lip with fresh Copenhagen. It seems like a great idea to me.

"Hey, Cole, you got a pinch man?"

"Not usually, but tonight, I make an *exceptione'* for you man. That is, if you like peaches. I'm all out of Black."

"Why the conversion?"

He unceremoniously flips me the can, and even in the low lume of the dark night I can see his smooth Louisiana smile.

"Because I ate it all, dumb-shit. This is my reserve can, you know. The one I can't let anyone see me with."

I can't pack the can. That would be much louder than our foolish whispering, and we've already been noisy enough tonight. Rather than packing, I fully employ the abilities bestowed upon me by my fingerless leather gloves, and simply smash a pinch between my fingers with enough force to get the shreds to set. I place it into my lip gently and quietly pop the can closed.

"Don't worry, your queer-flavored secret is safe with me. I'm an apple fan myself. Don't tell."

"Gotcha."

The smooth taste of American tobacco and fresh peach syrup fills my mouth immediately and makes me start to salivate like crazy. Quietly spitting to myself on somebody else's private property is not the very best diversion in the world, but it comes in a close eighth place; it's right there in between walking around my old apartment in my birthday suit and going to Starbucks.

Sergeants Cloud and Dick, having decided amongst themselves that the time is ripe for finding a decent route down from the rooftop and into the courtyard below, stand up and start moving together across the maze of broken masonry and haphazard electrical wires. I watch them for a moment until they hurdle a low wall, vanishing from sight. Only a few minutes pass before they return.

Just about when I start to become tired of looking at motionless concrete through my nods, I notice Cloud and Dick making their way slowly along the rooftop back to our position. It's slow going for them as they duck under worthless barriers of barbed wire, and over stupid makeshift dividers topped with broken glass, or the occasional broken AC unit. Every few strides one of them quickly sidesteps before committing to their footwork, doubtlessly dodging the occasional pile of human crap. It's quite obvious that this particular rooftop, as well as almost every other rooftop we've visited, is host to squatters throughout most of the week. Tonight the military presence, floodlights, and heavy machinery probably scared them off.

Looking towards Cloud, I can see our destination looming into the night sky about five stories above us, high, dark, and green, standing in staunch opposition to the display of light and activity spilling up over the barriers. To my right side is an almost beautiful display of light, real orange, yellow, and red; we've been on mission for over a half an hour, and yet the site is still hidden from view. It won't be too long until we get to see what all the illumination and engine noise are about.

"All right guys, we found a ladder that will take us down nicely. We have to go one at a time though, because it's missing some bolts and looks really rickety."

Separate. One at a time. The stuff of twelve-year-old fantasy and wasted Hollywood machismo. Any infantryman worth his sand knows that the value of an infantry squad is its ability to work as one cohesive unit, and always, always, to be ready and able to lay a large volume of fire down on an enemy at a moment's notice. One at a time. Worse, unnecessary and avoidable one at a time, and rickety too, like the rest of the evening so far I suppose. If it were my squad, which it will never be, we would have been in position over twenty minutes ago, providing much needed security and solid over-watch to the mostly defenseless engineers below. Instead, we're still climbing in a hajji wonderland, for no reason.

No hand and arm signals this time, and with no real organization or formation, we simply head out, with our weapons at the ready and our footsteps soft, across the desolate concrete wasteland, complete with shit.

Mostly, as always at night, my focus is on keeping my footsteps well aimed and quiet, pulling security, and making sure my head doesn't get caught on anything. These seem like silly concerns until sections of our travel leave us ducking, bobbing, and weaving through dozens of poorly strung electrical lines, as if we were competitors on some sort of boring, shitty version of American Gladiator.

Coming to another low wall, it's purpose unknown, I stop walking to plan a strategy. The low wall, only about three feet tall, is adorned on top with a layer of particularly diseased and menacing-looking glass.

Carefully, I find a place to grip the abomination with my bare fingers, and gingerly hoist myself up into a low crouching position on the top of the wall before not-so-quietly hopping down to the other side, where I'm generally safe, and also completely un-gored by some paranoid Arab's pointless waste of time and broken soda bottles.

As we come to the edge of the rooftop we can see the small courtyard below us. Although the place looks to be a repository of sorts for now dead industrial machines and car engine parts, the dull moonlight gives away large patches of gray which signal smooth, quiet places for us to move through the yard to a shoddy vestibule of sorts at the foot of our target building, complete with its very own guard-shack, or latrine. It's difficult to tell from this distance.

Following the same order that we fell into before, each of us takes his turn at descending the 'ladder,' which has somehow transcended the word 'rickety.' It's apocalyptic. It's junk. It's not a ladder; it's an assortment of badly glued, stapled, nailed, and welded metal poles and furniture scraps. Damn these stupid people. By stupid people, I mean both Arabs, and my fine leadership. Follow them into Hell, I would. That, or the pavement, either one. One before the other, for glory and shit.

The longest distance between two points is time, and nowhere is that more certain or profound than when one is dealing with plain cruel gravity. Gravity is a stubborn bitch. She never offers any condolence or reprieve; she's always there, just doing her thing, clearly not giving a shit about the fucked-up situations she puts soldiers like me through. Airborne.

Basic training comes to mind every so often, although years have gone by since. One of my favorite moments in particular, was rappelling. Many people say boldly to themselves, 'I love rappelling. Rappelling is fun!' But they don't repel like army infantry basic trainees rappel.

Rather than being issued a proper harness, every soldier-in-training simply sits through a fifteen minute class learning how to construct a 'Swiss-Seat' harness, which is really just a rope knotted around the pelvis. The thin piece of rope, hand-tied in haste, is the only thing that keeps a man from falling to his doom when some angry, impotent, hung-over drill sergeant kicks him over the edge of the hundred-foot training wall at Fort Benning.

Suddenly it's my turn to descend the rickety abomination; as I lower myself carefully out over the abyss, gently applying my first bit of my weight onto whatever the Hell is beneath me, I feel the same feeling I felt way back then: the sickening, tightening sensation in my generalized ass, nuts, and nether-region area.

At times like these I thank God for gloves, as well as the one-at-a-time sensibility. Although, as I descend, I can't help but feel horribly leery about the situation. For one, I've just stabbed my knee onto some sort of pointy projection, undoubtedly drawing blood, and two, my tetanus shot is about to come due. Surely this particular conveyance was intended for children, or a single, malnourished, half-naked man. The designer obviously never thought that his magnum opus of crafts-arab-ship would see use by fully loaded metal people who stand six feet tall.

At about twelve feet from sea level I feel myself start to relax about the height situation, and I begin to scan the ground around me for various hazards such as crazed terrorists, landmines, goat shit, and such.

Having not seen any, I reach the ground safely and take a knee over by Duke while starting to do my part as I watch for strange happenings.

The night is cool, but still I feel the first trickles of sweat start to bead at the back of my short-cropped hair, under my armpits, and at my wrists. I never really have much bad to say about my family, although I must admit, much to our detriment, we are a sweaty people.

Waiting for the last two soldiers to make their rollercoaster from hell journey, I take the time to draw my little handkerchief and wipe the grime and fog from my optic's lens cups. Afterwards, I don my personal clear-lens eye protection. I Love the Oakleys; they're definitely one of the few perks of this job. That, and free travel.

The others are with us now, but we don't move just yet. Instead, we sit and listen patiently for any sign that our presence here has been noticed. We allow three minutes or so to pass in this way as we listen for other human activity while drinking much needed sips of water from canteens and Camel-Baks.

I'm a canteen man myself; can't fuck with a good design. Me and Camel-Baks don't generally see eye to eye, as they are very fragile when full of fluid and I like to fall down a lot.

Many a Camel-Bak has met an uncertain and expensive doom while resting upon my shoulders. I can't be enthusiastic about being soaked and without water again any time soon, and neither can my wallet at ninety bucks a pop. A literal pop, mind you. And a squish. Cicero. Nevermind.

Right beside me, Freddy turns ever so slightly to the right and unlimbers his cock. As he pisses he shakes his dick rapidly from left to right, so as to make the sound very, very quiet, like raindrops, and not like an elephant pissing. The scenario strikes me in just the right way, and I too realize that I'm quite tired of holding my own liquid any longer than absolutely necessary this evening.

Courteously, I pick a worthy target to the front of the squad, away from my buddies about five meters ahead of where we're all stationed. Wet abuse awaits a dusty pile of shredded tires, as I intend to give them a little shower.

Checking behind me to make sure my squad doesn't mistake me for a pissing terrorist, I undo my buttons and proceed to do my thing, stealth side to side jiggle-thing mode in full effect.

Not very smart of me, my new latrine leaves me well ahead of the squad, offering me a more complete view of the courtyard.

As I let fly, I look over my left shoulder and see my squad peering alertly into the darkness, finishing their listening post duties, as well as taking other pre-recon jiggles and drinking from their Camel-Baks.

Halfway through my glorious evacuation I look over my right shoulder into the black night and beyond, scanning the yard of tires, garbage, and other automotive relics for any sign of threats or local foul-play.

I can't help but smirk and utter a slightly disparaging statement under my breath, as I see, on ground level, the gate that I easily opened not fifteen paces from where I'm currently draining the lizard.

The retards call me a pussy for not wanting to play stupid games with them; I say they're hopeless inept wrecks from the X-Box generation, so bent on wanting to play hero that they can't see the forest for the trees. Or the objective for the gate, for that matter. Sure, Pearce is a pussy for not wanting to climb, but I'm still at war. My compatriots, my brothers in arms, are not at war. They're busily playing at a game in which they can inflate themselves beyond the confines of their sexual disappointments and shitty cars. Me, I'm a motorcyclist by preference.

We could have straight strutted though the fucking door a half an hour ago, and I'm not the only one who recognizes that, thank God. Score one point, or three, for Pearce on this one.

A flashlight with an unknown operator, out of the blue, shines on my back as I'm hurriedly fastening my buttons.

Forgetting my pants, I swivel around on the balls of my feet and raise my M-4 to eye level, aiming directly at the source of the light as I say the only Arabic that I comfortably grasp.

"*La noor.*" No light.

A reply comes back at me in Arabic that I recognize but do not fully understand, although I get the gist of it. *Yes, sorry.* With that, the light immediately switches off, and my squad mates are already on their feet, looking for any other interlopers on our nightly recon while aiming at the very unassuming, very frightened elderly man standing before us.

Dick, the one among us with the fastest and best grasp of Arabic, proceeds to speak in short sentences to the man in his native tongue.

"*It's okay. What's your name?*"

"*I am Muhammad. Mista, don't shoot.*"

"*No shoot. Why are you here?*"

The reply comes back, and not even Dick with his two months of linguistic practice can decode it. He tries again, simply this time.

"*Why. You. Here?*" The statement is accompanied by internationally understandable hand and arm signals that are boisterously delivered with appropriate levels of both gusto and bravado.

"*Mista, Security.*"

"*They pay you?*"

"*Yes Mista, this is my home.*"

Throughout the conversation, each of us hardcore soldiers has been slowly lowering his weapon, and by the end of the exchange we are quite at ease, not aiming weapons at worried old men, but rather passively standing and listening to the meet and greet with our weapons hanging casually at our sides.

Without a word, Duke proceeds to slip inside the small concrete square box that serves as both this man's home and guard post.

"Got an AK in here."

"Bring it out. Anything else?"

"Nothing amazing."

Dick's conversation drones on as Freddy, myself, and Cole continue to scrutinize the shadows for any signs of additional movement. Meanwhile, SGT Cloud has slipped into the darkness behind me, essentially doing my job, communicating with the CP about our current status, as well as explaining exactly what the fuck we are doing, time now, and stating in a matter of fact fashion the 'totally acceptable' reasons why we are quite fucking late for a combat over-watch mission. 'Rock-climbing like a tourist' is not in his dialogue chain, but somehow I find space in my lonely, wilted little heart to forgive him. He is, after all, a good squad leader, even if at times he acquiesces to the elementary requests and thrill-seeking impetus of man-children.

While the short dialogue concludes, Duke clumsily, because Americans don't train with AKs very often, locks, clears, and field strips the prophet's weapon. Keeping the ammunition hostage, he hands the dismantled rifle to Muhammad as a sensible gesture to prove to the man that we don't intend to steal from him, and that he's not in trouble. There will be plenty of time for such discipline if he does anything stupid.

"You have to come with us."

"Yes Mista, OK."

Apparently, OK in Arabia sounds the same as OK everywhere else.

Cloud once again takes point as the squad, now well rested, bladders emptied, and with a clear mission finally in mind, falls in behind him to proceed along the somewhat arduous journey to the top of our vantage building.

Muhammad doesn't seem at all nervous. After all, this is a middle-eastern mercenary. Despite his age and apparent frailty, he is obviously a man who has made his living behind the butt-stock of a rifle since long before any of us, with the exception of Cloud maybe, were born. Muhammad is definitely a hardy man, especially living in a non-heated concrete box through the heart of winter.

We pass through the last length of the yard, which is mostly empty save for the aforementioned trash and 'save-it-for-later' brand carburetors, transmissions, fuel drums, and scraps of garbage ranging from rotten foodstuffs to a vast assortment of easily recognizable post-apocalyptic scavenge. War never changes. Find the GECK and all that shit.

One by one, we enter the doorway to the main structure, which is an unassuming and borderless rectangular cutaway in the flat, smooth façade with no door, or any other covering to speak of. Bent nails infer that a drapery of some sort may have once been hung over the entrance, but as of now, no trace of the cloth remains.

Just inside, we are met with a well-formed staircase that climbs the entirety of the square structure, attached to the inside of the outer walls, running their length and making predictable ninety-degree turns throughout the entire journey to the top. Through my eye of green, I can see the great empty chamber which covers the entire ground floor as we begin our ascent up the long staircase. Recently swept and completely barren, the clean expanse of square concrete in the center of the building comes as a complete surprise. Most structures like this that we have seen have been virtually destroyed by squatters, the lower levels having been packed with human refuse and great piles of garbage. I suppose a little bit of cheap security really goes a long way to protect personal property in this town.

I pick up a position in the center of the formation, which is the usual position for an RTO. Radio Telephone Operators never go first, as they are an essential part of the element, usually being solely responsible for communication with the outside world. Abiding by the same universal law, neither do they pull up the rear, for if the rear man were to fall the element would be cut off from communications, which is the key lifeline for an infantry unit's survival.

Being somewhat sheltered from the echoing concrete of the outside world, small conversations spring up in our midst during the long ascent.

Dick continues to pry casual, but highly cultural and potentially invaluable information from Muhammad, while Duke and Cole proceed to bitch about the length and intensity of the climb. I'm quite happy, as I reflect upon how our squad may have been a little bit more prepared for a battle-gear laden, Ghostbuster-esque hike if we hadn't taken the K-2 detour of the century.

"Tell me when we get to twenty. I'm gonna throw up."

I share the thought with Freddy, who easily picks up the Ghostbuster

102

vibe, so we go back and forth with a dialogue from the film as we climb the stairs while having a nerdy laugh amongst ourselves.

Our whimsical chat ends abruptly as we near the seventh floor.

I can't help but be a bit lost in my own thoughts while reflecting on just how dangerous a stairway this is to have in any building, even an industrial one. Throughout our climb, the left is a great pit that grows deeper and deeper the farther upward we climb. No handrails, no safety guards of any kind, the pit that impales the center of the building is bordered only by jagged rebar that juts out of the concrete that serves as our path. I'm amazed that the stairway holds its own weight, let alone that of the entire squad, as nothing supports the naked bottom of the concrete that holds our weight. Escher would be very impressed, I'm sure, by the unsupported staircase jutting directly out of the wall, seemingly of its own volition.

To our right are a series of shallow rooms that branch off the landings at regular intervals. Various junk inhabits the small rooms, most of it quite decrepit, as well as a few things that could still hold some value. The treasures include many items, mostly handmade looking furniture, often wedged up against old and forgotten-looking electrical appliances: a washing machine here, or an old lamp there. From my best estimate, the owner of the building has figured out how to eek out a meager living by providing some of the neighborhood residents with a local storage unit of sorts. Unlike civilization, instead of electric gates, thick padlocks, and electronic surveillance, you get Muhammad here in Baghdad. Muhammad will watch over the building day and night, and shoot anyone who decides to come in and fuck with your stuff without permission. Fast, effective capitalism from the Muslim world.

I wonder who really holds the deed to this place. Does the middle east even have a system for deeds and title? Property ownership? Good questions, these and many more I ponder as we near the top.

No door awaits us at our destination, rather, our path simply ends on the open rooftop. The large building, probably covering an entire city block, provides us with a huge empty swath of plain smooth roof to survey, with little about it being remarkable. Together with Muhammad we crouch-walk towards the side of the building that overlooks the work site. Our destination is a large set of improvised concrete and metal sheeting that looks like it used to serve the building as a shed of some sorts. It could have been anything.

"What do you think they used this for, D?"

103

"Don't know; a shitter or a chicken coop. Hell, maybe they even used to store the lawnmower in here. Otherwise, I've not a clue."

The small structure stands about seven feet tall, which is high enough to comfortably stand in, and is roughly twenty feet long and ten feet deep; it's more than enough space to comfortably house us all. Through loopholes, square cutouts that may have served as windows, and gaps between the siding and the floor, we can see down into the square perfectly.

Random gunfire sounds into the night from somewhere not too far off, but we can't make out any of the flashes.

Cloud points toward the origin of the noise and begins to speak.

"All that sounds like it's about two blocks over. Be cognizant of it, but don't call it in. For now, it has nothing much to do with us. Keep light on the radio traffic. Also, watch out for friendlies. We have a squad from the first ID across the way, about a block down from the site, doing exactly the same thing we are. If you're going to do something, call it in first. Got it?"

We all respond that everything is crystal clear. Scrutinizing a 'clean enough' patch of floor next to a window slit, I set down my assault pack, or radio bag as this evening would have it, and take a seat with one hand on the grip of my rifle, and the other manipulating my radio handset.

"Delta One-Four, this is Delta One-Two, over."

After some brief beeps, pops, and clicks, Forrester's voice sounds in my ear.

"Delta One-Two, this is Delta One-Four, over."

"Roger. Shadow element is in the OP over-watching the engineers, over."

"That's a good copy, over."

"Delta One-Four, out."

Having completed all of the necessary radio checks for this hour, it's now my job to watch and listen to the events of the night with the others. Being finished with my radio duties, I gaze around our temporary home and watch the behavior of my peers.

Cloud and Dick are striking up a conversation as best they can with Muhammad, trying their best to get a better feel for what kinds of people are currently living in and around the building, as well as how quiet or noisy the local gunfight-O-meter usually is. I can't catch much of it because I'm still very much lacking in the Arabic language department.

Cole, having adjusted his kneepads, is taking a knee right beside me and doing his best to peer through a crack in the aluminum siding and down into the center of the square. Behind us, Duke is busily setting up the M-24, just in case.

My field of vision is hardly obstructed by either the structure we're in, or the building we're on. I'm greeted with an open view, and feel as if I can see for what must be over fifty miles, past the edges of the forsaken city, and beyond into the reaches of the Arabian wasteland to the east. There's a cool breeze blowing tonight, and it feels fresh and fantastic on my damp face. Even better, it seems that the slight adjustment in our altitude has taken us mostly away from the dank smells of old sewage and wet garbage.

"Hey, Freddy, got the time man?"

"1230."

"Top O' the Marnin' to ya."

"And the rest of the day-O to you, brother-lad."

Below us, the sounds of heavy machinery are finally met with visible forms that snake their way to and fro in the middle of the site as they load and carry a seemingly endless supply of the eighteen-foot-tall barriers that are being continuously brought into the square by flatbed trucks, some of which look quite local, one after the other, after the other.

It looks like patient work due to the amount of time involved, but it doesn't look very labor intensive in the sweaty sense of the word. Most of the chore is being done by forklifts, gators, and heavy trucks with cranes, leaving little for the boots on the ground to do other than watch and point at things with their index fingers.

Across the intersection and beyond the fake horizon of another empty concrete husk like the one we're sitting on, bursts of gunfire erupt again, sounding somewhat closer than the last time they announced themselves.

I say, "Two hundred meters, maybe?"

"Can't tell, D. Sounds right, but who knows."

"Yep."

The night is once again bright and green in one eye, and orange, yellow, and black in the other. Somewhere near the foot of the building I can hear wild dogs having themselves a bit of a territorial dispute. The noise is terrible, but just far enough away for distance to really take the edge off.

Outside the brilliantly lit plaza where the crews continue their labor, the night is dead and black save for the orange flickering silhouettes of small structures and people alike that are illuminated by trashcan fires. I count twelve little blazes in all, some on rooftops, and some hidden in mulhallas and alleyways, scattered throughout the night at random.

In the morning and afternoon the town is bustling, filled with the sounds of a thousand hawking vendors, and the endless parade of donkeys, mules, and cars alike, that proceed below unhindered by either traffic signals, or traffic laws.

In the dead quiet of this night, save for the eerie yelps of the hungry dogs below, and the droning gasoline generators powering the floodlights beneath us, there is no sound.

My radio beeps and hisses in my left ear, where I've secured the handset to my face by smashing it into my helmet's chin strap, and I'm briefly content to listen to a bit of the play-by-play traffic regarding what the entire battalion is doing around the sector. Most of it catalogs activity much like our current enterprise, whereas some of it is relegated to day-to-day business chatter about the supply levels at the JSSs, such as food, water, battery supplies, etc. Occasionally, a suspected bomb somewhere along one of our routes is called in, but other than that, tonight the transmissions are mostly mounted patrol chatter, with five-truck convoys announcing their coming or going from this FOB or that JSS; it's just the standard fare.

I feel my eyelids start to get heavy, as there is little or nothing interesting to look at during the present moment, so I try to divert my attention as best I can to something exciting. I need something hopeful; something to lighten the mood and give me a bit of much needed energy. The Skoal was supposed to have done that, but the pinch in my lip is now dry, the juices have all gone, and nothing remains but the lump of dead leafy fiberglass in my lip. So unceremoniously, I withdraw the dead pinch from my mouth with nothing but my tongue, and hawk it into my own little corner. Normally that sort of thing is a dangerous measure; a lack of discipline that could potentially alert an enemy that we've been here, but tonight nobody gives a flying fiddler's fuck, because this is most assuredly the last time any one of us will be on the roof of this building, and beyond that, we're bugging out of this neighborhood for good in a few days. Hopefully, we will never return. Even more so, the engineers below aren't exactly stealthy: of course enemy elements know that we're snooping around. Besides, Muhammad is sitting here right next to us.

I think of Emily for a bit, then decide that I don't want to torture myself quite so much on this particular night, so I elect to think about something else. My mind leads me away to thoughts of home and family, but those too seem to have an adverse effect on me, tempting me to go away with them into a sweet dream, rather than staying alert and vigilant here, on my Baghdad rooftop.

As I look out onto the blasted cityscape I realize that I still have a good notepad in my left shoulder pocket, so without much thought I withdraw the implements and begin to write. I've been writing in the dark a lot lately, which is part of my job as an RTO; I've become rather adept at the process.

I've also been trying my hand at a bit of poetry, as some form of silly militant expression. Together, the wish to stay awake, coupled with the urge to maybe create something while I sit and observe take me over in a pleasant fashion, and while I rest my eyes, one biological and one electronic on the fiery landscape below me, my pen starts to move.

All the world seems as if it were a painting; a calm breeze is on my face and the sounds of the wild dogs below me seem to pick up a certain rhythm; the green darkness and my memories, together with the pen in my hand keep me rooted and awake, but by the same token, they take me far away to an altogether different place. I think I'll call this one 'Baghdad at Night.'

By 0500 the gunfire stops, with us having taken no direct part in it, as it drifted farther and farther away from the square throughout the night. At 0600, as the sun begins to tentatively peek its little eye over the top of the eastern horizon, we're giving Muhammad's assembled AK and ammunition back to him before beginning our two mile trek back to the JSS.

"Why is it that we're walking again, Freddy?"

"Because the LT forgot about us and ordered the trucks back without us. That's why."

"Freddy, why is the sun up?"

"Fuck you, that's why. God hates us today."

I say, with a cheery inflection, "Just as I suspected: we're so valuable that they have to pretend that we don't exist, just to feel better about leaving us behind in hostile territory, and also to feel better about themselves."

Freddy is also trying to have a good time, jesting with me as we start our suicidal morning jaunt. "You got it, man. That's just what I was thinking. They probably thought, 'those scouts are so badass that they don't need a ride home, especially if the sun comes up and the whole damned city knows where they are.'"

"That's just what I was thinking. After all, it's time to show them that just the six of us can fight the six million terrorists in this city with two-hundred rounds of ammo each. I think you'd get another ARCOM for that."

"Shut the fuck up, guys."

Duke decides to step in and be babysitter for the sake of noise discipline. Under normal circumstances, that would be sensible; however, the sun is already up, and we're walking through what can almost be considered a crowd at a relatively fast clip, into the bright light of the new morning.

Yeah. Keep down on the noise, dumb-fuck. They won't be able to see us that way.

If there is a negative element waiting for us between our current location and the JSS this morning, you can bet your sweet money that we're going to find it, and in so doing, find ourselves in rather deep and considerably sticky shit.

Not panicking, not running, we simply walk around and say hello to all around us like a bunch of real cool guys. A bunch of cool guys who were not left behind and abandoned in the center of a hostile neighborhood, in the very center of the most dangerous city for American soldiers on the planet, two miles from the nearest friendly support, and all just before sunrise.

The squad sort of blames me; I am the RTO after all. But they don't *really* blame me, because I gave everyone the complete fucking message when the trucks started to pull out during the small hours. This morning's quaint danger dash is really Dick-Brain's child, as he volunteered over the radio that us scouts would be more than happy to walk back to the JSS alone, just after sunrise. *Hooah!* We could be at the epicenter of a neighborhood Jihad, two miles away from support, and not even know it.

As the neighborhood crowds come out into the morning sun to shop, mingle, drink tea, and wash themselves by the side of the street, we pick up the pace, just enough to look like we're absolutely in control of the situation, but still very, very much in a hurry.

As we walk down the center of a rather large mulhalla, my sniper-bait squad and I can smell the not-half-bad aroma of roasting meat, as well as a myriad of different types of breakfast falafels. The sweet aromas make my mouth water, but when I think about the last time I indulged in local cuisine my stomach sours and starts doing back flips.

I can't help myself sometimes, so I say, "Anybody want to do a McArab's run this morning?"

Freddy quickly replies, "I was thinking about it, D, but I'm pretty sure you had better stay out of that sort of thing next time."

"I concur, doctor."

Walking across the sidewalks by day is a simple enough affair, even if there always seems to be more shit to step in when I can see it. It's not so bad in the sunlight though; at least I can make a concerted effort to avoid the stuff.

Curbs are simple obstacles that can be surmounted by day without having to stare directly at them and judge monocular distance. Open sewer grates in the sidewalk -- yes these idiots have a lot of those -- pose less of a pitfall hazard, and present more of a simple, minor annoyance to step around when direct sunlight is readily available to serve us.

While the presence of so many potentially hostile people all around us can be a bit unnerving at times, this morning the crowd seems especially friendly, hospitable, and permitting.

Small groups of children follow our party as we traverse the narrow mulhalla, begging for candy and soccer balls. Luckily, the squad was packing some good loads of candy in our assault packs when we departed from the FOB for this trip, so as the cute little street urchins follow us around we spoil the crap out of them, making sure each and every child gets at least one of everything. Candy is never in short supply, thanks to regular mail drops from home. Sometimes candy delivery is so effective that it's downright cavity inducing, and a good Wednesday on the FOB can put most any six-year-old's Halloween fantasies to shame.

As I give a palm full of Jolly Ranchers to three five-year-oldish looking girls I miss Halloween. I've missed the last three of them.

Out of almost every store front, different men emerge to offer us tea and snacks. They don't persist in their offers however, as they can clearly see we are in quite a bit of a rush. Not only the impending threat of ambush impels us forward; there are other motivating factors as well. None of us have really slept in over twenty hours.

"You think they'll put us on tower first when we get back?"

"Probably, D. Never fails. They've already adjusted the schedule for us, but I think at least we may have a good two hours to flop down beforehand."

"Yar-Howdy."

"I still don't get that word, Pearce."

"Neither do I."

Before long, the clamorous noise from crowds of people and Arab prayer chants emanating from one of the local mosques fade away behind us as we approach the mostly deserted and quiet Mulhalla which parallels the main street that crosses in front of our police station. The JSS is our one way ticket to not being maliciously blown up or sniped this morning, so I for one am going to be decidedly happy to reach it. That, plus the added perk of maybe, just maybe being able to take a nap.

"You know, fellas, this is one of the last times we'll ever have to enter this gate."

Freddy replies, "Amen to that. Farewell, Mr. Tower-guard-duty. You, sir, can eat a dick."

"A most unpleasant image, Freddy."

"Why thank you, brother; I do the very best I can."

"Turtle Power."

"Werd."

And just like that, we're back on home turf. As we pass by two of the Iraqi policemen manning the entry control point, we take off our helmets. It's highly unlikely that if anyone were to kill us this morning, they wouldn't have tried a good half an hour ago.

Nearing the lobby and main entryway to our casa, and our own personal stairway to heaven, we stop briefly to make sure all of our radios are powered down, and that the squad's sensitive items are accounted for.

Cloud addresses us before we are dismissed to wander about according to our own devices.

"All right. The next ten hours are going to be pretty tiring. We're on towers next, so get rested up. It's 0620; we're on towers at 0800."

"Raga."

After our talk, it's time for this morning's final stair climb. Button hooking into the darkened bay, we quietly proceed past our sleeping platoon fellows to our own cots at the back of the barracks. As quietly as I can, I download my gear and lie heavily on my bunk. I feel too tired to even take my boots off, so I simply burrow my face into my woobie, my love, my tactical blanket, and feel exhaustion and relaxation sweep over me from head to toe. The feeling is delicious. I'm just starting to really enjoy myself when the blackness swallows me whole.

The next three days pan out as expected, with endless tower shifts and walkabouts that are punctuated by eight-hour reprieves. Each one of us does his duty just fine. Delightfully, as no dumb-fuck has fallen asleep on shift for some time, I have my sainted stool back as an added perk.

MREs, the feel of a wet, sweat-starched uniform, and the dusty desert sky mark the early spring days where we say goodbye to our first JSS.

On the fourth day, while us scouts were enjoying a short slumber, Zimmerman got his left arm ripped off at the elbow by a sniper while working in tower one. He's lucky we suppose; at least he didn't lose his head.

None of us heard the shot, but we witnessed the aftermath of IV bags, scissors, screaming, tourniquets, and blood. It serves as a good reminder to the rest of the platoon that vigilance is not only proper decorum: it's essential for our survival.

Radio checks in and sensitive items packed, we roll out from the JSS for the last time, back toward the FOB. Next time we leave the comfort of our FOB we'll be headed off on a new adventure, although where to, we do not yet know.

The drive goes as expected, with minimal stopping this time, and blessedly, there are no dramatic explosions to punctuate the day.

As I gaze out the rear passenger side window to my right, we drive by the old cathedral in the center of town. The cathedral, built sometime during one of the first crusades, still stands beautiful and untouched in the center of the Muslim wasteland. Even more surprising is that the locals have not harmed the structure, but instead revere it as a part of sacred local history.

As we weave through traffic just in front of the mighty, ancient structure, I can't help but marvel at the beautiful arches on the façade, and the fine stonework that has lasted so long, through centuries of time. Wood panels fill the arched windows that would give us a glimpse into the upper levels of the structure. They do not appear to be temporary, particle-board wrecks like those found elsewhere in the city, but rather, they are made of a dark, polished looking wood, and evince a well preserved, if not overly secretive decorum.

Mind, there's no great artistry here; no grand bar-relief or gold gilded filigree. Just the naked, surviving beauty of simplistic, yet very advanced craftsmanship that has survived for as long as the builders intended. It's looks at me as if to say, 'We were crusaders too, but we did it first, and we did it better than thee.'

The amazing old monolith fades out of sight as the traffic circle that the grand church sits upon drifts away behind us, and is lost in the din of crowded streets, donkey traffic, and falafel stands.

Back at the FOB it's the same old song and dance. The trucks need to be inspected, then topped off with fuel. The weapon systems need to be cleaned, and then all of us happy, though tired ground-pounders need to ingest hot dinner chow. After the army chores are done, it's seven in the evening, and all of us fed, happy soldiers are relaxing in our bunks, our home away from home, once again.

The scouts are celebrating today, as we've pooled about fifty dollars together and bought ourselves an old Arabian television set from one of the local vendors on the FOB. Duke also took it upon himself to purchase one of the local-region X-box 360s. That's always a gamble, as they are not built to last, or with the same quality as the American or European models. We also all thought it was a foolish move, because no doubt the software is region specific, meaning that there will be no use for it when Duke gets home. Three points for sacrifice to the community, I suppose.

While Duke, Dick, and Cole are giddily setting up the new squad toy, I settle into a game of liar's dice with Chapel and Andrews.

It's a very simplistic game, played with five dice and one cup per man. It's generally a guessing game wherein the players make wagers pertaining to what value of dice, and in what quantity are present in the game. Each player knows the value and number of his own dice, but shelters them under his cup, keeping them secret from the eyes of the other players. I guess you could say it's a piratical, old-fashioned version of Bullshit, with dice as the medium. If you lose a bet or a call out, you lose a die. Whoever survives the game with a die left wins. The losers simply sit the match out when they run out of dice. The bet for this match is meager, though valuable: ten packets of instant coffee; not army crap, but good Folgers fare mailed in from the states, complete with a smattering of sugar and powdered creamer packets.

Andrews is one of those: a real good kid who picked the wrong vocation. Weighing in at around a hundred pounds, with a quivering voice, and little to no real-world experience, he's one of my favorites.

112

Without Chapel and me, it's safe to say the he probably would have lost his mind by now. Everybody needs someone to talk to, and everybody needs to have friends. Even if you can only ever seem to collect three or so, like me.

Andrews is never allowed to leave the FOB. Instead, he spends his days in relative safety, guarding the barracks and talking to the CP on the radio, as well as doing some of the other odd jobs that are fundamental necessities around the Bs, such as carrying bottled water or MREs into the building. Every once in a while he'll have something more exciting to do, like run papers to the command post, or occasionally run items or orders back and forth between the CP and the motor pool. He's functionally retarded and innocent, and thus far too incompetent to perform a tower guard shift, but me and Chapel love him anyway. Like I said, he probably couldn't pull me out of a firefight, but everybody needs a friend, and everybody, especially Andrews, needs someone to talk to.

Near our floor-based and by now very intense game of dice, one of Chapel's three roommates, Waldo, is busily performing his own rendition of 'Operation DVD,' but he is having a little bit of a problem with local power plug conversion.

Happy with my cup, and beginning my run, I turn to Chapel, "Three threes, ye old bastard."

Chapel smirks at me and nods, then turning to Andrews, "Four threes, pipsqueak."

Apprehension showing on his face, Andrews looks tentative about making a real commitment.

"Five threes," and the pressure is on me again.

"Bullshit, Andrews-Man."

With that, the round is over and everyone lifts their cups, revealing all the dice, and the counting begins.

"Motherfucker," I say.

On this particular hand, there happen to be six threes, which means I'm completely defeated after my little ruse, and have lost a die.

I say, "I'll get you next time my pretty, and your Inspector Gadget too."

"What?"

Chapel pipes in, "Don't tell me that you're too young for a combination double-feature allusion to both the Wizard of Oz, and Inspector Gadget."

"I know what the Wizard of Oz is."

"Good Andrews, good."

I start to chuckle a bit.

Chapel continues, "Because, if you didn't we'd have to tie you up and force you to watch it. Then we'd have to eat you."

Laughs all around. Time for round two.

I'm up again, and this time, after shaking my dice cup, plopping it down, and peering under the edge so that only I can see, I believe I have a winner; I start the bidding high. "Three sixes."

Going around the opposite way this time, it's all Andrews.

"Four Sixes."

Then to Chapel.

"Five Sixes."

Then it's back to me. I'm about to raise, but before I can place my bid, a loud electric pop cracks the air in the room, the power in the building flickers, and all can hear a resounding

"Fuck! Fucking Fuck-shit! Motherfucker!"

It sounds like a man in pain, and I can smell a bit of O-zone in the stale and dusty air.

Waldo dances about the room waving his right wrist around as if it were on fire, continuing to yelp a series of colorful, yet appropriate curses as he does so. As soon as the dancing ceases I ask, "What the *fuck*, dude?"

"I don't know. I just plugged in the adapter."

"The hajji lied to you, and it's obviously faulty; that, or you've just survived an assassination attempt. I have a working spare. You okay?"

"Yeah, man, where at?"

"Top drawer of my filing cabinet."

Chapps looks at me with a silly expression and says, "Where did you find a filing cabinet?"

"After chow we took a scout-scapade underneath the abandoned JDAM building to see what we could scavenge from the wasteland and we found the cabinets. Thought they'd make good dressers. Just had to clean them out a little bit; there were lots of spiders in them."

"Any still down there?"

"Tons. Might want to get you one before they're all gone. Sorry, didn't think about telling you before."

"Schweet. I'll run and grab one tomorrow."

Waldo quickly comes back into the room bearing my spare adapter. "Thanks, D."

114

"No problem. Where was I, you jerks. Ach, I remember. Eight Sixes."

Andrews, with absolutely no lack of conviction this time, calls my bluff.

"Bullcrap."

We lift the cups. Andrews only has one six, while Chapel has two of them. I have five. Five of them. All sixes. Fucking amazing.

"Dallas, if you weren't a good buddy of mine and it was 1450 AD, I would run you through for that."

"I know, right? I couldn't believe it myself. You know it's legit too, since I'm not that much of a magical man." After a brief pause, "Otherwise, I'd be rich, shit a Dodge Viper out of my ass, and grow my cock."

"To chair, my friend, to chair."

After the game concludes itself, I crawl into my bunk to enjoy some digital game time and a full night's sleep before our slated 're-fit' day. Good old FOB life. Gotta love it.

"Hey, D, you playing?"

"What are we playin', Freddy?"

"Hajji pirate copies of Call of Duty."

"I'll sit this one out thanks. Sleepy."

"You're just afraid of losing."

I look at him askance and say with bravado, "Pirate dice champion, bitch!"

"Whatever."

Before long not just the scouts are enjoying their own little digital paradise, but the rest of the platoon comes in one by one to watch, or get spanked in brutally quick split-screen matches. The last time I saw combat conducted this way was on the N64 back in the day, with Goldeneye 007. Good times, and a little bit of sweet nostalgia.

I'm content to while away the rest of the night with my Playstation Portable and an odd, but very complicated and involving Japanese role playing game called Spectral Souls, which pretty much has me enthralled whenever I have free time to burn with it, whenever I am not totally exhausted. I even skimp on a little bit of sleep every once in a while to play; that's really saying something.

After a while, as they always seem to do, my eyelids get heavy and I no longer wish to remain concentrated on a digital toy, so I save my game and flip off the machine. Rolling over on my side, I grab my mp3 player and slip in my headphones. Amber sounds like a particularly good night-night song this evening, so I go with it and feel myself drift away to the sound of 311.

Whoa, amber is the color of your energy,
Whoa, shades of gold displayed naturally.

I flip on my flashlight for one second in the dark, just to get a good glimpse of my favorite picture of Emily, taped above my head on the underside of the top bunk, before I slip off into the darkness.

I'm with her there, in my dreams. We catch up; we visit. She holds my hand tightly and tells me how much she loves me. We fade away into the night as we walk down our own little yellow brick road, trying to find our way home.

Chapter Four: Rapture Lost

I felt you here last night, my love,
Enraptured under the stars above,
Entwined with your ethereal kiss,
My heart rested as a dove.

I held you in the bubbling water,
Our words becoming frost
As we talked the night away,
But I remember, this is lost.

So from my dreaming I come alive
And let out a doleful moan,
Another day has come to pass
In which I remain alone.

So I will return to you and the midnight blue
And the warm water in which I held you,
As the softest of smiles lights on my face,
I close my eyes to find your embrace.

Chapel has collected his filing cabinet, and my laundry chores are now complete. It's time for some phone calls. Hopefully nobody has gone and gotten themselves killed today, as it's been over three weeks since we've been on the FOB without a media blackout.

Cloud speaks to me as I leave, knowing that he doesn't really have to.

"Make sure you sign out when you go."

"Roger, Sergeant."

Chapel and I trundle down the barracks stairs to spill out of the front door into the warm afternoon sun with a whole day of nothing but life chores, rest, and recreation ahead of us. I haven't been able to get in touch with Emily for over three weeks now, except by reading the occasional letter from her. Although effectively bringing me up to speed, the interaction is still nowhere near as satisfying as actually being able to hear her voice. Although it is neat when she sprays her perfume on letters. A little bit of sensory excitation never hurt anyone; at least I don't think so.

The phones are located inside an impromptu rectangular shell that is not unlike any single-wide that can be found at any trailer park back in the states. Rows of phones on each wall, operated solely by calling cards, each possess their own little shelf that serves as a desk of sorts, as well as little elementary school chairs. They even come with their own particle-board dividers, which offer some semblance of privacy.

Luckily there is no line this afternoon, so I bid Chapps farewell and make my way to a lonely looking phone in the back of the trailer away from the other chatters. Following the prompts on the calling card is a simple enough process, but it seems to take forever, one beeping connection and long number entry after another.

I'm quite pleased with myself today, as I completed my first call without any typographical errors. While the automated dispatch runs my signal through satellites, power lines, ground wires, and radio waves, I wonder what time it is back in Nevada. Was it thirteen hours difference? I can't seem to remember, but I am pretty sure that I'm calling in the dead of night. That's one of the perks that comes with being deployed far away from home: nobody cares what time you call, so long as you do every once in a while.

First on the list is my mother, but her phone doesn't even ring; it simply takes me straight to voicemail, so I leave the standard message: 'I love you; things are going good. We're being really safe. Everyone says hi. Tell my bother I love him.'

On to the next call; this time my father picks up.

"Hey dad, how are ya?"

"Taylor?"

"No dad, it's Dallas, in the land of far away."

He sounds at once elated and surprised, with sleepiness immediately leaving his voice.

"How are things over there?"

"They're going good, dad; real smooth so far. Just the day-in, day-out grind thing so far. How's everyone at home?"

"Everyone's doing great. Ginger says hi."

"Tell her I say hi back."

Which is funny, because Ginger is the family dog, and has been for quite a while. My parents have been divorced since the dawn of time, so at my father's house it's Ginger, and at my mother's place it's Kona. Kona is my definite favorite, although she's becoming a bit smelly and cantankerous in her old age.

"How's Taylor doing anyhow?"

"He's doing well. He's got another physical therapy appointment this week, and they're sure it's going to make him feel a bit better this time. He just had another closing this week too."

"Awesome. Glad to hear he's doing a bit better anyhow."

"Can you tell me anything new about what you guys are doing? I've been getting a lot of news on Yahoo lately, but I haven't seen anything about you guys. It' mostly bad news anyhow."

I hear my father's voice drop a little bit, and I can imagine him perfectly, standing in the kitchen in his underwear, trying not to worry while staring at his feet on the cold kitchen floor.

"Things are about the same as they were last time we talked, dad. It's pretty quiet so far. As quiet as a war gets I suppose, but we should be moving on to a new neighborhood soon. I don't know where yet though, and even if I did I wouldn't be able to tell you."

"I know you can't tell. I'd sure just like to know is all."

There's a brief pause as we think of something else to say. He breaks the silence first.

"They give you an idea yet of when you're going to be home again?"

"Not a clue. Rumor has it that we won't be needed around here anymore come Christmas time, but that's all just he-said-he-said. There's rumors that cover from August of this year to 2014 pretty good. I don't know. Less than a year maybe. Who can know?"

"Well, are you having a good time at least?"

"I'm having a cultural experience. No further comment on that one."

We both have a bit of a laugh. Our conversation concludes with token comments about the weather, and other small talk about what we've been eating, and what movies and things I need to catch up on when I get back home.

"I love you, dad. I'll call you again when I get the chance."

"All right. Love you too. Stay safe."

"As safe as I can be. Also, don't worry anymore if I can't call you again for some time. We've been having a lot of outages with the phone lines."

"I won't worry. I won't. Love you."

"You too, dad. Love you. Buh-bye."

"Bye now."

With that call finished, I quickly place the handset down and disconnect. My entire family has the nasty habit of staying on the line interminably while wasting valuable call minutes, of which I only have about fifteen left, as well as creating really long awkward pauses in the hopes that I'm going to say something else. I'll be happy to tell them everything someday, but there's simply not enough good time over the phone. That, and it's simply illegal. Loose lips sink ships and all that shit.

For my next magic trick, I make the one call that I'm really excited for. I hope Emily picks up this time. I tried calling her about three weeks ago, and I was only able to leave her a voicemail. Quite a long and comprehensive one, I might add, but still just a recorded message. That's not the same.

Following the instructions on my card once again, I place another call to the states, this time to New York.

Emily is currently attending an all-girls college upstate, where her mind is slowly being poisoned by liberal feminism. I don't mind so much, as long as she continues to write once in a while. It should be her cup of tea after all; she does happen to be an English major. As she's never going to have a land-line installed in her dormitory, my call attempt is dependent on her cell-phone battery level. As I punch in the last number on my card, I hope she remembered to plug her charger in before retiring for the evening.

The phone rings once. Twice. I have butterflies in my stomach. I want nothing else in all the world but to talk to her today. Three rings. Four. Finally, she picks up.

"Hello?"

"Hey, babe, it's me."

"Good! I've been wondering why you haven't called. I've been worried about you."

Her voice is beautiful. It sounds silky, like she's singing, even though she's speaking to me in a low whisper so as not to wake her roommate.

"How's school so far?"

"Good. I think I'll be able to get my GPA up a little bit more this semester. It's my last chance. I'm so excited to be almost finished." She sounds sleepy, like she's not fully awake.

"One year is never a long time. I'm glad you're excited about it."

"What's going on over there? I think I saw you on the news the other day, but I can't be sure; the camera was too far away to see anybody's faces."

"I'm sure it wasn't us, love. There aren't any reporters where we are."

"Ah. What I saw was in someplace called the Green Zone."

"Yep. That's west of the Tigris. I'm far to the east, on the bad side of town. No media coverage is allowed over here."

"Is it bad so far?"

"Not too bad. Not too scary. Just a lot of patrols in the springtime is all. Summer's going to be a hot one though."

There's another long silence; there always is. It's difficult to keep the conversation going, even with someone you love, when you're simply not allowed to talk about what's on your mind. The real world, for operational security reasons, is not permitted over the airwaves. Conversations are endlessly dragged-out small talk. A lot of talk about emotions and feelings, but not too much else.

"I love you."

"I love you too."

"I'll keep an eye out for more of your mail. I have to go get some stuff done today. We're leaving again in a little while, but I'll try to call you in a week or so."

"All right. I just sent you off another little package last week, so be on the lookout for it."

We say a long goodbye. Maybe two whole minutes of goodbye,

with a lot of 'I love yous' thrown in for good measure. She tells me to be safe and come home soon one last time, then does me the mercy of letting her phone be the first to click away.

I sit hunched over the small desk for a moment, staring at the grain of the wood under my elbows with my tightly slung rifle digging into the very center of my back.

I don't want to get up yet. I want to talk to someone else, but I'll have to wait until I get another phone card. As there's no place to purchase them on the FOB, I have to rely on mail from home to be granted the opportunity to make any future calls. I'm not worried about it though. I'm sure I'll get another one soon. Besides, there's always e-mail. I'll see if I have time for a late-night computer run later.

It's almost time for Chapel and me to head back, so while he finishes up his long phone call with his wife, I step outside to take a quick smoke break before the short walk back to the barracks. Walking and smoking is still very much against the law in army land, so I have to take my little nicotine break from a stationary position before we start moving.

It's good to call home. It reminds me that nothing lasts forever, and that my time here in this stupid place is numbered along with everything else. I'll be home soon. Nothing lasts forever; not even the bad things.

Chapel emerges from the phone trailer and wastes no time walking over to me, firing up a Camel wide as he does so.

"Have a good talk, D?"

"Two good ones. Couldn't get through to my mom or brother though."

"Have to catch 'em next time. I couldn't get a hold of anyone back home. Chatted a good long time with the missus though."

"How's she doing?"

"Good. She got used to this sort of thing a good long time ago. To tell you the truth, I think she enjoys my little vacations every once in a while. She gets some time to herself that way."

"Huh."

Without further ado I squish my cigarette into one of the standing bins that have been erected for just the purpose, and start walking back to the barracks with Chapel.

Bad news awaits us when we get there.

As soon as I climb the stairs to the top of the scout landing, Dick tells me quickly to turn around and go back downstairs.

"Why?"

"We all have to go meet with SSGT Rams. We have a platoon meeting. Something happened."

Staff Sergeant Rams is our real platoon sergeant: the leader of the unit that we should all be working together as right now. Scouts and nobody else. Funny that we would waste all that time training as a cohesive group, only to go to war just to be split up and attached to different squads in four different companies.

"We got everybody?"

"Yeah, the others are already over there."

"You know what it's about?"

"No fucking clue, D."

"Is this an all-squads type thing, or just us? We in trouble?"

"I'll say it one more time man: I don't have a fucking clue."

Quickly Cole, Dick, and I make our way down the half mile dirt path towards Rams's barracks room, the usual place where all of us sophisticated scouts congregate. We take the path less traveled on the small road that leads behind the barracks, sheltered by the safety of the large concrete fence that borders the FOB. We're constantly cognizant about these sorts of things because it's nearing sundown, which really means that it's nearing mortar-strike time.

After passing behind four long buildings, each identical to our own, we move through an alleyway to the front of the fifth barracks building. Just inside the flimsy wooden door, then through an empty doorjamb on the right, we are greeted by SSGT Rams and the rest of the scout platoon, about twenty five soldiers in all. It's good to see them, as even a month seems like a great deal of time not to be in their company.

It appears that we are the last to show up, but it also seems like we are not very late. The faces of most of our brothers are red and lightly perspiring, implying that they also just ran over here as fast as they got the word.

Rams stands up to address us all. "All right, at ease guys. Everyone relax and take a seat."

Both his eyes and his voice seem heavy, as though he's about to inform us of something he'd rather not.

Suddenly I come to the realization that four of our soldiers are not present: our four-man sniper element led by SGT Rock.

"How have everyone's patrols been going?"

124

Slowly, the other squad leaders and a few of us underlings respond in turn.

"Good, Sergeant."

"Really good, Sergeant."

Cloud speaks up, "No complaints from Delta. I'm not gonna lie, most of our duties with D Co have been boring as all Hell. Charlie still out?"

Rams takes a seat in an old officy-looking chair no doubt recently stolen from the CP and takes a deep sigh, heaving his shoulders and leaning forward over his knees before he begins to speak.

"The reason I told all of you to come here today concerns Rock and the others who are attached to Charlie company."

Without looking down, and without emoting, he continues to address us all, who have by now taken seats around him as if it were children's story time at the local library, or an in-close personal request hour with Santa Clause.

"Two days ago Charlie Company had some heavy contact in Moudan, along with a large detachment of soldiers from the First ID and some Redwater corporation guys. The action was good. All total there's reported to be over a hundred Al' Qaida and other insurgents dead, with allied casualties numbering in the low twenties, the majority of which were Iraqi Army. Expect a funeral before you leave the FOB again though, because PVT Henry was killed first off in the fighting, taken clean by who we think was an Iranian sniper. No way to tell for sure. Dead men don't talk."

There's a brief silence while everyone takes in what was just said, each man looking around the room to read the concerned faces of every other soldier.

"We feel like we're getting a handle on that particular neighborhood, which is where you're going next, Delta."

I feel a bit sad at the mention of that, and also a bit nervous. I also feel a pinch of adrenaline and hatred for the people causing the fighting, and I think I'm in the right frame of mind at the moment, as I'm feeling very enthusiastic about killing me one of them. From the looks on the faces of the others, I'm not the only trooper that feels the violent sentiment.

The somewhat shocking news about one of our new privates doesn't seem to really draw an emotional response from anyone. None of our platoon seemed to have known him, so the news comes as less of a tragedy, and more like the news we sometimes hear about a relative we didn't know who has just passed away because of a freak aneurism in Ohio. We're concerned, sure, but nobody really seems to mind.

"That's not all, however. Colin and Curtis are in the ICU in the Green Zone with Rock. He was attempting to help another soldier to his feet after being wounded in the opening moments of the fighting. Before he was able to move that soldier out of harm's way, he took a bullet in his lower spine."

That hits us very, very hard.

If there was one soldier you could point at and say, 'he'll make it through the war just fine,' that would be Sergeant Rock. If you could take one person in your mind, and put them on a podium that said, 'most motivated, fit, and knowledgeable foot soldier in division,' that would be Rock also. Not huge, and not with farm boy retard-strength, he's simply the most powerful man any of us have ever met, simply through the virtue of his own work ethic and sweat. Greater than his physical measure, he is always taking his career to the next step. Army Sniper School, Ranger School, Air Assault, you name it, he has it. Definitely a career soldier, Rock loves his job, and never had any other desire or motivation other than to fight for the division.

"Right now he's fighting for his life in the ICU, and I'm sure he wouldn't mind a prayer from all of us. It seems unjust that he would get taken down while trying to help someone else to their feet, but as we know, nobody can really call the shots."

Smiling, with the hint of tears coming to his eyes, he continues, "How many of us really thought that he would just hang back and take cover anyway?"

The statement draws a bit of laughter from us all, as we all know that would not have been Rock's style. Just last month we caught him moving his lips and squeezing his right trigger finger in a rhythm while sleeping, as if he never stopped trying to kill the enemy, even while sound asleep.

"That's all there is to say. I'll let you have word when I know something new. Otherwise, keep him in your thoughts. The funeral for our other man is at noon tomorrow in the old theatre. You can all go if you like. Dismissed."

We never make it to the funeral. Instead, D Co gets tasked with the very first trip out to our new JSS, one day before we planned.

Packing for the newly slated twelve-day jaunt comes accompanied by the Cranberries, and their hit 'Zombie' as usual.

We load the trucks and roll out like clockwork, the same as every time before.

The warm afternoon sun is starting to blaze halfway through the month of April, and it follows us everywhere we go, threatening to cook us with its radiance at all hours of the day.

My truck has been all scouts this afternoon, save for SSGT Brass, who is acting as the designated TC today.

"You about ready to be done with this drive-about boys?" He says it a bit like Crocodile Dundee, but it comes out in a sort of southern whiskey mash, but that doesn't prevent me from replying.

"Oiy cud gow fer a bit of a walkabout me-self, mate. Neu scenery would be a great playsha sure, I wadger."

I feel like my fake Aussie comes out a bit better, and I blame it on a bit of the eccentric, lonely self-taught Russian sessions I've had. Granted, one dialect does not randomly spawn itself from another, but rather, I believe that one can get a good grasp of the accents of world language simply by learning how to manipulate the mouth in new and exotic ways. Besides, a woman always helps with that. Haven't practiced in a while though.

As I gaze out my window in slightly a different fashion than Cole Porter ever imagined, I see the usual debris and detritus that marks the grand culmination of two thousand years lived in the cradle of civilization.

Empty soda bottles, human shit, half-eaten falafels, and many other forms of paper garbage decorate the streets as we drive by a new part of town.

Over several freeway overpasses, three miles of mulhallas, and down Martin Luther King Boulevard, we finally find ourselves nearing our final destination. Our new place in the world, our new JSS, which happens to be an old luxury hotel in the middle of central east Baghdad. I personally can't wait to see the new digs for myself.

That, and any new accommodation has to be better than our old lodgings. Although the fact that this place used to be a hotel leaves me somewhat skeptical.

I have seen many modern Arabian conveniences that leave much to be desired, such as a telephone, a toilet, and a restaurant. The word 'hotel,' pleasant and inviting though it may be, leaves me with plenty of mental leeway for a bit of healthy skepticism.

"Just about five more minutes, and we should finally be there."

The truck breathes a collective sigh of relief at the news. After spending close to eight hours on our mounted patrol rotation while getting acquainted with our new part of town, we're all sore and aching from being smashed into the Humvees like sardines in full body armor. I, for one, am happy that it's soon to be over. I couldn't seem to get my dick out of my pants and into an empty plastic bottle this afternoon. Too many stops and whatnot. As a result, I've had to piss for upwards of three hours, and am very relieved to be about to be relieved, if you take my meaning.

We trundle down a very wide, very busy street to a market square that will serve as the very center of our new area of operations. Crawling at a speed of less than two miles per hour, we keep our eyes peeled for anything. Command has informed us that there has never been a western presence of any kind maintained in this district of town before, as it has traditionally been far too dangerous. Lucky for us, we get to break the place in.

Engineers arrived yesterday with an escort of 10th Mountain infantry support types, in an effort to build meager and hasty fortifications around the hotel, which is slated to be our home for the next twelve days. As we near the emptying square -- nothing too ominous there; it's nearing three in the afternoon, a time when business is concluded, and all the good little hajjis go home -- I catch a glimpse of the engineers' handiwork off to my right, as best I can through the narrow angle that I can see from out of my tightly shut ballistic window.

It's easier to see the big picture as Freddy pilots our Humvee slowly to the right, and into a driveway of sorts that is flanked by newly filled HESCO barriers. After a short drive down the mostly straight ECP, our convoy spills into an open courtyard in front of the thirteen-story structure that we assume is our new pad. Not close enough to share a wall with the hotel but still within the impromptu fortifications, a small Iraqi police station stands, not unlike the structure that was our previous JSS.

Brass addresses us all from the front seat, "Time to stretch and piss, yeah?"

"You got that right, Sergeant."

I'm giddy with the excitement of it, and I can't help but chuckle to myself a bit as our truck rumbles to a safe stop inside the impromptu compound, undetonated and in one piece once again. I'm thankful for that.

"Everybody out. Grab your shit. Link up and conduct your sensitive item checks inside. Ain't nothing been secured around here yet, git me?"

Duke responds quickly, and in a rather soldierly fashion, "Roger, Sergeant."

I open my truck door and lift my aching body gingerly out of the Humvee, in much the same way as the other twenty or so that are getting out. The gunners are staying put for the time being for all the obvious reasons, while the still trucks underneath them have all assumed the staple lazy W position.

I get no immediate sense of security from the barriers; their only real purpose is to prevent an explosively charged vehicle from ramming the lower levels of the compound, or to serve as basic cover for infantry soldiers in the event of contact in the courtyard. From my position of cover, while I collect my assault pack and other gear from the truck, I can plainly see dozens of passersby going about their daily routines in the square, not fifty meters from where I stand. All around our little compound, four and five-story buildings stare blankly at us with literally hundreds of dark, mysterious windows, some with glass, and some without, that could serve as eyes to anyone. Nearly surrounded by the nearby structures, the only relief from tactical claustrophobia is the market square, the center of which is only about a hundred meters to the northeast. Though a wall of buildings present themselves at the far side of the open square, effectively blocking our view of what lies beyond, the JSS has a good view of the wide commercial thoroughfare that serves as the central traffic bloodline to the market.

I sling my pack onto my shoulder and grab the gun case which houses my designated sniper's system for this particular jaunt: the Barrett 107 .50 caliber long rifle. It's a good friend of mine. Although sometimes it hurts me.

Crack.

A single, too-close-to-tell-where-the-fuck-it-came-from type shot rings through the afternoon air, and we're in contact. Welcome to the neighborhood.

"Where the fuck is it!"

Brass shouts to no one in particular, as he shoulders his weapon and takes a knee by the front right side of the truck.

Similar shouts erupt all around me as paratroopers drop their bags, shoulder their weapons, and take up fighting positions behind HESCO barriers, still open armored doors, and the armored bodies of the trucks.

"It sounds like it-"

Crack.

Another crash rips the afternoon air, and I can hear the hiss of the very angry sounding bullet as it cuts through reality just above us.

From my position behind the Humvee on one knee, I slowly pie out of cover with both eyes open behind my optic while trying as best I can to still the new shaking in my legs. I try to quickly scan every window overlooking the market square.

Freddy, crouching beside me, quickly looks to where I'm aiming and says, "Are you sure it came from the front? I can't tell-"

Crack.

He continues, "Okay yeah, front side, eleven o' clockish and high, I think."

Freddy is playing the same game I am, and is apparently turning up just as much evidence as me. If we were dealing with a stupid sniper, we'd have killed him by now, but we're obviously being shot at by someone who knows just what he's doing, taking pot shots at us from the back wall of one of the apartments above. Though the attacker's marksmanship needs a bit of work, his positioning is sound. With no sure way to see him, and no way to get a glimpse of a muzzle flash in the bright afternoon sun, we continue aiming at where we think he may be, keeping as much of our bodies in cover as possible, and wait.

Beginning to lose patience and wanting to be involved, five IPs to our left, not bothering to grab any cover of their own begin discharging their AK-47s at every window overlooking the square, of which there must be hundreds. They appear jubilant, boldly and stupidly standing in the very center of the courtyard as they tempt luck and fate.

"That's bad business."

Freddy takes the time to look over at me and reply, "Yep."

America isn't allowed to conduct reconnaissance and suppression by blindly firing into civilian housing units, however the Iraqi Police, as per their usual behavior, appear to be hundreds of years behind in regards to how counter insurgencies are run these days. They've probably never heard of the Geneva Conventions either. Worse yet, they're actually laughing at us.

An IP moves closer to Freddy after having discharged all of his ammunition, laughs, and holds his hands up to the sky, as if to say, 'Stupid

130

fools! Look! I'm out here! I'm okay.' That's Arab culture for you. Cover and concealment are not necessary things when fighting with modern weaponry. It's best just to stand out in the open and be brave. *Right.*

Crack.

Freddy's bold new Iraqi friend is smiling when his face comes apart, split with violent force through the middle. A jagged puff of blood and gray matter glint beautifully for a moment in the mid-morning sun as the sniper's bullet tears free from the confines of his skull. Ushering forth now freakish laughter, he is still trying to smile through his destroyed face when his sputtering, twitching body hits the dirt.

Crack.

Looking once again towards the square I think I see a small flash from one of the third story buildings on the far side of the market. I open my mouth to consult Freddy, wanting a second opinion on positive target identification before I open fire, but before I do, pained screaming erupts from one of the faceless man's poker buddies. Although I glance quickly at the wailing man, I cannot see a wound.

This interval, two of our gunners apparently see the origin of the fire.

The afternoon air is dashed to pieces by the horrid and vengeful sound of Browning .50 caliber machine guns springing to life. Brass can't help himself.

"Wahoo! Get you some, motherfuckers!"

I try to shout intelligibly to Freddy over the awful drumming of the guns, *"What do you think of that, Freddy?"*

I can't hear myself think over the rhythmic thunder from the guns, but just as suddenly as they erupted, the guns are still.

Freddy, having obviously heard my shouting through the gun-cadence, replies in a very calm, quiet, and thoughtful fashion, "I think this was pretty damn frightening, and pretty damn cool at the same time."

I reply, "Cool? Maybe not so much. Definitely not, I'd say. Well, cool for Cole anyhow."

I shout a friendly hello to Cole, still up in the turret watching the window he just blew to the 13th circle of hell. I can barely hear my words through the fresh ringing in my head, and my enunciation sounds mushy. "How you doing up there, buddy?"

"High as a kite. I swallowed my dip."

Our platoon sergeant allows a few moments of quiet to pass, how long I don't know, before giving the all clear.

Slowly, but with weapons still at the ready, we clumsily pick up our bags and proceed to move cautiously out into the uneasy open space, free from the cover of the trucks.

There is a bit of confusion, as common protocol would suggest that an infantry team should be entering the sniper's hide and clearing the building, thus making sure that the guilty party is currently in a generalized state of dead-ness. However, instead of forming a team and boldly charging into the target building, we proceed as ordered into the safety of the hotel and the blessed coolness of naked concrete that has not yet been heated by the warm spring sun.

As we approach the simple green door that leads into the hotel, it does not appear that any Americans were hit in the sudden assault. To my right, still pooling warm blood into the dirt, I can see our two Iraqi Police friends, now lying still and humbled in the fresh quiet.

Entering the rickety door with the others and letting my eyes adjust to the dark, dusty light, I say to nobody in particular, "How many friendlies down?"

Duke sidles up beside me and gives his two cents as we proceed to climb yet another naked concrete stairwell, located just past a small entryway that has already been furnished with a plywood desk, and fitted with wiring for a field telephone. Rather than an official lobby, the entrance appears to be a simple, slightly wider than average hallway. Into the lap of luxury we go. Hotel. Sure.

"Three, we think. IPs are already taking the bodies away. None of ours. The only ones to get hit were the trigger-happy ones standing in the open."

"Smart cookies, these allies of ours."

"You got that right," Freddy says just behind me.

On the second floor of the hotel, each squad rejoins his respective group, with each man scouting out a place in the empty concrete bay where he can drop his shit. Sticking together, each small element of soldiers looks to bunk up together as usual, in an effort to maintain a sense of squad cohesiveness.

Cloud and Dick never rejoined the rest of the scouts, and are no doubt already in the talk, eavesdropping on the conversation between our platoon sergeant and lieutenant which will dictate who's on watch, or whatever it is that we're doing here, and who's down, or patrolling the new neighborhood on foot.

The bay is large, covering maybe half of the surface area of the hotel's second floor, and for the time being it is very well lit, as there are open, mostly glassless windows on each side that allow the bright afternoon sunshine to flood in from every angle.

"What do you think this place used to be, D?"

"A latrine, maybe?"

"This room, jackass, not the entire country."

"Ah. A banquet hall of sorts, maybe? An empty, dark, low roofed, powerless banquet hall without furniture?"

"Nah. It's been this way longer than that. Maybe the Iraqi army prepped it years ago."

That makes an awful sort of sense. As the tallest building for blocks around, our new home is the perfect lookout post and gun platform for any manner of foot soldier. Old school Iraqi regulars from Saddam's regime would have felt much the same way. Although, they thought that they would repel America from their great tower of shit-bricks. *Right.*

From the intact look of the place it's apparent that no open fighting ever took place here, although it's clear from the layout that Iraqi soldiers have made their residence here at some time before. Scraps of old sandbags dot the floor around windows, and other small loopholes have been smashed into the wall overlooking the market square.

The corners of our new home are populated with old foodstuff garbage and a few off-white canvass Iraqi military cots that have been for whatever reason folded into order, corded up, and stacked neatly. It appears as if whoever left them in the present configuration was planning to return for them sometime soon.

"We can have tons of fun exploring this place! There's probably a ton of old shit to find in here! Isn't there an army post across the street?"

Cole is obviously excited about our new situation, as his Louisiana mind mulls over the possibilities of war-type souvenirs, which we are not allowed to take, as well as the possibility of stumbling upon some long ago buried treasure. A genie's lamp could be buried in the dregs below for fuck's sake; only heaven knows.

Freddy chirps up beside me as he takes a seat to join the rest of us on the dusty concrete floor.

"Yeah, there's a pretty big Iraqi army base just across the street from here. You can see the concertina wire that runs along the top of the fence from the courtyard. Much better than what we've got going on over here, that's for sure."

Cole contributes, "Which explains the old army presence in this building."

I chime in, "You've got it, gumshoe. What does he win, Freddy?"

In his best overly excited 1970s game-show MC voice Freddy declares, "He wins a brand. New. Car!"

"Have to wait a bit for that one, man."

The conversation dies down a little bit, and when it does, I remember that I have to take the piss of the century.

"Holy shit, guys. Anybody have an empty bottle? It just occurred to me that I'm about thirty seconds from pissing my pants."

Duke also points out that his bladder is going into spasms, and that he too will spring a leak if something isn't promptly done about it.

Being the industrious Humvee pisser that I normally am, I procure two empty water bottles from my assault pack and flip one to Duke. With really no place to go we simply stand and turn our backs to the group as we each piss into our respective bottles.

The release of pressure and pain is at once glorious, triumphant, and exquisite.

With nowhere to put my bottle of piss, I simply put it back into my assault pack, planning to dispose of it in an appropriate manner at the first opportunity that presents itself.

"Hey, thanks, D."

Then Duke throws his bottle of piss at me, which I have no choice but to catch.

"Fuck man! Gross! It's warm!"

"Made fresh daily, motherfucker."

Everyone starts to laugh, and at the same time we all share a measure of distaste for the spontaneous game that erupts: warm, wet-potato.

After about thirty seconds of the germy nonsense entailed by passing a bottle of urine back and forth at close distance at ludicrous speed, the play abruptly stops, as Duke, his own piss returned to him at last, puts the bottle of dreck into his pocket.

"Did you see that guy's head explode?"

After a brief pause Freddy responds, "See it? He was staring at me and just about dancing when it fucking happened. What a poor, dumb fuck; I feel bad."

I say, *"Allah hu'l Akbar,"* and continue, "Maybe we should change the way we fight, you know, as it works so well for the Arabs." The short conversation dies.

Our musing ends abruptly as Cloud, with Sergeant Dick dragging behind him, emerge from the top of the stairwell and proceed into the center of the open bay, where they are presumably about to tell us just what the fuck is actually going on.

The next two days unfold much as we expect. Rather than having a dismounted patrol operate at all times around the borders of our JSS, the only combative shift we run, for now, is a four-man surveillance operation from the top floor of the hotel.

Another platoon from the 1st ID has been tasked with securing the JSS from the outside, conducting foot patrols and reconnaissance of their own, in an effort to give us the security we need to set up shop in our new part of town.

Except for our rotating scout detail on the upper floor and a radio guard in the talk, which has been set up inside one of the central offices in the old police station, the entire platoon has been working ceaselessly, day and night, assisting an engineer platoon transport food and water in from the FOB, as well as amenities like cots and port-a-shitters.

For the rest of us not sleeping a four-hour shift or pulling security from the rooftop, it's sandbag duty.

The courtyard in the very center of the compound is made of nothing but old garbage and desert-floor dirt, which I'm currently helping scoop into sandbags and then spirit away inside, to wherever they need to go. This early morning's mission is simply to plug up all the windows on the first, second, third, and top floors, in an effort to minimize incidents of sniper fire, as well as to protect sleeping and guarding soldiers from errant weapons fire, or the occasional malicious RPG.

Special care has been taken to fortify the windows of the top and third floors with wooden framework, on which sandbags are being placed to create observation loopholes and firing positions. I know, it's not nearly as brave as our gloriously mortal Iraqi counterparts would do it, but I personally believe it to be much more sensible, as does everybody else. At some point, I would love to see America again, preferably still in possession of my face.

The occasional laughs about the local police protocols are over and done with, now that the sentiment has set in that these people are going to be a staple factor of life here with us, and are therefore going to prove themselves to be a continuing liability. Their incompetence is no longer a laughing matter.

135

Make no mistake, stupidity kills people.

"How many more of these sons-of-bitches do you think we're going to have to fill?"

"Don't know, Pearce; I honestly couldn't tell you."

I've been working side by side with Moore, bending over the dirt and bags for upwards of four hours, with no end to the miserable, however necessary task in sight.

Yesterday was much the same. As I am not one of the scout squad's designated cool guys, I'm spending more time of late moving, shoveling, and carrying all manner of dirt, food, water, and construction materials than actually being a rifleman.

Mercifully, the shift change comes a quick four hours later, and I get two hours' worth of down time before I get to take another shift up top.

All of our food and water is now inside the building, along with all the sandbags we need to finish fortifying the positions on the lower levels. It's even rumored that we'll have an electric generator hooked to the wiring in the building soon, which brings the faint promise of electricity, a luxury and extravagance that is rarely found in the field. With such a power source, we could feasibly see about how to get our hands on a refrigerator for water, or perhaps a few workable AC units.

The other scouts are still upstairs on shift, and I don't particularly feel like making the long climb up to the thirteenth floor just to say hi, so instead I lie down on one of the new green army cots furthest back in the chamber. Us scouts like to be in the back. It's quieter and somewhat less crowded than it is for those who choose to live closer to the entryway. It's a rare privilege that others allow us to enjoy with little contest, as most of the others know that we routinely get the short end of the stick in regard to duties, as there are still only six of us and we are still frequently fulfilling the duties of a twelve-man squad.

My body is sore and tired. I entertain the idea of forcing myself to eat an MRE, but fatigue gets the best of me. I rarely feel like eating when arriving at new places or traveling for any length of time, so my lack of appetite this morning is totally expected. I'll probably get it back with a vengeance in a couple of days or so.

I do take a moment to fish a wet-wipe out of my assault pack to wash some of the Iraqi dirt-floor grit off my hands.

I briefly think about the dangers of radiation, parasites, and leishmaniases before I drift off into a heavy sleep, but I'm not troubled. I've never been too much of a germophobe myself.

"Hey, D. Time to wake up. Schools in. Your turn to take a jaunt up top."

It's Cole, and through my hazy, blurry afternoon eyes, I'm not at all pleased to see him. He comes bearing bad news.

"Wake the fuck up, man."

"All right Comrade Stalin, I'm up."

It only takes a moment for me to be up and ready for my shift. Knowing that this moment would come quickly, I never even took the time to remove my boots. There will be plenty of time for that later when I get a real downshift.

By the time I don my armor and helmet the leeching feeling of sleep has already left me. This will be my very first over-watch shift up on the top floor. Some of the other prima donnas can enjoy a turn or two at the sandbags out in the open. Everyone's been talking about the stellar view since our arrival, and I must admit to myself that I'm a little excited to see it.

Back at the FOB our freedom to walk up to the upper levels of the barracks is restricted by the rules; there's too much risk from sniper or rocket fire to take afternoon jaunts to the lookout points above. It'll be good to get up off the ground for a while. Fuck it, who knows, I might even get to see the horizon. Been awhile since that.

Freddy joins me at the bottom of the stairs just outside our bay, newly taken to a level of pitch-blackness by the sandbags that now plug every window and loophole of the second floor.

"Time?"

Freddy replies to me, "Roundabout 1400."

"We on for eight hours?"

"Nope. They're switching it up for us. We're going to pull four hours up top, and then four hours in the trucks at the ECPs. That's how it's going to be from now on I guess. Four up top, four down below."

"Sounds good to me; any variation should beat our last tower-prison shifts."

"You got that right."

Stuffing MREs into our pockets, Freddy and I begin our long climb up the stairs to the top. Like our living space, the windows that would otherwise shed light into the narrow, dusty stairwell have been mostly blocked, save for small slivers of relief at the top. Since the stairwell is mostly dark we use our red-lens flashlights to light the way.

"It's hotter than an oven in here."

"Yeah. Concrete's not insulated."

Second floor. Third floor. Fourth floor. Fifth floor. Starting to breathe a little from our quick encumbered climb, I can't help but take note of how similar each floor is to the one below it. The only marked differences between each of the landings comes in the form of different patterns of dust and dirt on the bare concrete floor, as well as the smatterings of old, stale garbage left behind from the hotel's previous occupants.

"Probably been twenty years since anybody has stayed here. As an actual guest, I mean."

Freddy, now in the know, informs me of the latest, "Nope, only five or so. While you were busy filling sandbags the rest of us got a pretty good low-down from the LT."

Freddy continues to elucidate.

"This place didn't really get shut down until about 2002. And, I guess the ol' USA is paying the owner, or at least some guy who claims to be the owner, a pretty decent sum of money in exchange for us turning the whole fucking place into a military compound."

"That's quite a rip-off if you ask me. You know that there was nobody staying here before us. Not even any running water or electric current in the building anymore. I don't think we should be paying a thing; we aren't taking any business from prospective clientele anyway."

"I concur. It doesn't have to make any sense though."

"I don't see why it would. Do you have any idea what we're paying?"

"I haven't a damn clue. Millions probably."

We both have a good laugh at that. Knowing Uncle Sam's particular brand of banking, the shoddy estimate is most likely not too far off.

We take a small break at the tenth floor, mainly just to scope out the landing, which appears different from the others, as it's furnished with four small chairs and a low wooden table, complete with ash-trays.

"Looks like I found my designated nocturnal smoking area. Think they'll allow that?"

"Can't see why not. I wouldn't ask though; I wouldn't tell either."

"Good point; thanks for that. Asking for permission to smoke would be gay."

The thirteenth floor is no different from any of the others, except for the fact that the stairwell ends abruptly, leading to a shoddy ladder and a chintzy-looking hatch to the roof. The ceiling is also quite uneven, suggesting that the construction of an exit to the roof was somewhat of an oversight that was not in the original plan.

"You think this passes fire codes?"

There's not even a response to that one; just a knowing silence from Freddy. I thought it was funny anyhow.

Green doors flank the hallway on both sides of us, reaching down the entire length of the building for about thirty meters on either side. At both ends of the hallway, ninety degree corners suggest that the floor-plan and room layout is the same all the way around the upper floor. All of the hotel's rooms surround the center stairwell in a square.

"At least we'll have an easier time getting around than the folks in *The Shining*. Not really any inventive or artistic flair to the floor-plan, if you get me."

"Yeah, I agree. Pretty much utilitarian all around."

Freddy leads me into the main room which will serve as our primary post, up the eastern hall and all the way to the end, first door on the right.

It's clear that the large room has already been appropriated by other squads as well. Small tables, low chairs, and beds have been put into place to act as seats, as well as knee cushions and supports that line the floor beneath each of the four windows in the room. Two of them face the east, while the other two, closer together than the others, face to the north.

"You guys were busy up here."

I say so because of the rather fantastic fighting positions built around the windows. Wooden weapon rests and reinforced platforms bearing sandbags surround each of the windows, but they are placed far enough back that a viewer from street level would remain totally unaware of the fortifications. Across each one of the window openings hangs camouflaged netting, also a good distance back, so as not to be seen from the outside.

The netting appears closely knit with green, black, and beige leafing, so as to cast the entire position behind the window in shadow. In the afternoon sun, the camouflaged darkness within should be impenetrable from even the most linear view, straight in from across the urban sprawl. Better yet, these are the highest seats in this part of town, leaving us with the best sniper platform self-respecting infantryman could ever ask for.

"Sweet digs, man."

We drop our assault packs near the door, keeping only our weapons and armor on our persons. Like bad kids we take our helmets off to stave away a bit of the mid-April heat.

"Come on, I'll show you the other positions."

Taking a short field-trip down to the twelfth floor, I'm shown the same room, only on this level there is only one firing position on each side. Also, this particular spread lacks the luxury of the furniture that has been accumulated upstairs. This room will primarily be used for an alternate firing position in the event of a longer fight. It would be unwise to stay in one position throughout the duration of a lengthy engagement.

After moving back upstairs Freddy shows me one last fighting position, facing out of the northwestern side of the thirteenth floor, overlooking the market square and the western ECP. This position consists of a long table, meant to be laid upon by the aspiring sniper or machine gunner, so that a prone position can be achieved while still getting a great field of fire out through the window. The position is already complete with netting, sandbags, and an M-240B machine-gun. Personally, she's my very favorite weapon system. I'll call her Vera.

"Groovy?"

"Way groovy. Looks nice, dude."

As we make our way back to our primary hide site, we take a moment to pop open some doors. We're greeted with sights of creepy moldering bedding, and western-looking toilets filled with dried out garbage and age-old human shit.

"This place has everything. Even shit fossils."

"Maybe we can carbon date them later."

"I find that statement funny coming from you, you creationist bastard."

"You know it. Maybe if we look in a few more we can find a pirate skeleton."

I laugh at that comment.

"There's probably some pretty good treasures buried up here."

While most of the doors we pass open easily, a few of them are locked. Two of them give way to our boots during a bit of breaching practice, but some have obviously been reinforced, or perhaps even barricaded from the other side, a fact to which my throbbing ankle can attest.

"We should bring the ram up later and crack the rest open. I think I strained a hammy again."

My hamstrings malfunction on a frequent basis.

As we return once again to our over-watch position Freddy takes the left-most windows, while I gravitate towards the right side. Helmet newly affixed to my dome once again, I take stock of the late afternoon view from my window on the world for the first time.

The view is, as everyone has stated, quite incredible. From my rather uncomfortable wooden seat I can see the impressive domes of a least three mosques, as well as miles and miles of urban landscape that fade into the dusty sky beyond.

All activity in the nearby street market is slowing down by this time of day, and the afternoon is relatively quiet. I can hear, but not see multiple helicopters clipping through the distance, and somewhere far away and below, a pack of wild dogs are barking.

Just below my position, on the outside of the compound wall, a group of Iraqi children are engaged in a heated game of soccer, and the sound of thinning traffic can be heard honking and screeching on nearby streets.

"Three hours and forty to go."

"Getting that exciting, yeah?"

I busy myself right away by scanning for other potential sniper positions in the dense city below. It's not hard to imagine groups of insurgents doing exactly what we're doing right now, especially after our recent sniper episode. Our war is not conducted in war rooms by marking troop movements on maps, strategically divining where enemy lines are, and devising how to surmount them. Instead, our war is here, conducted by playing a very unrefined game of hide-and-seek with an unknown enemy. Fatigue and complacency are evil forces; attention to detail and watchfulness are our primary tools.

After an hour or so I feel well adjusted to the new view. Against my first impression, it's clear that only a few buildings just outside the compound pose an imminent sniper threat. Close fighting positions mean danger; I'm not very concerned with potential enemy positions more than a thousand meters away, so the area which I feel I need to earnestly scan has shrunken considerably since I first gazed out the window. I say window only to describe the square concrete hole through which I'm gazing. It's not clear as to whether or not there was ever glass installed in this room.

One by one, I take my eyes from blackened window to blackened window, pausing every now and then to give special attention to the structure that our most recent sniper attack spawned from. Although it's unlikely Freddy and I could take accurate fire from the position, the workers that remain in the courtyard are still quite exposed to the same angles of fire that posed such a threat the day before yesterday.

"Hey, Freddy, I just had a thought."

"Did it hurt?"

"Almost. What if we're really not in Baghdad?"

"How you mean?"

There's a brief, intentionally goofy pause.

"I mean, what if they really deployed us to New Mexico. What if this is just a very elaborate, very expensive training exercise?"

"I do so wish your stupid alternate reality jokes were the truth."

"Me too, brother, me too. Although we are getting paid significantly more than if we were in Arizona."

"That could just be a very convincing part of the ruse, buddy."

"To chair, my friend. To chair."

The rest of the high-ground shift goes smoothly. Other than some sparse automatic weapons fire off in the distance, the day fades to night with little other noise.

After our four-hour jaunt up top is concluded, Freddy and I relieve the truck crew at the eastern ECP.

The east gate is a boring and simple duty, as Iraqi police and other workers are not allowed admittance through the gate. They simply have to drive a short distance around the small compound and enter from the west side. It's a much busier duty working the other truck, which often involves frequent body searches and identification card checks. For now, our task is simple: if it isn't an American Humvee, it doesn't come in.

From our parked Humvee which serves as our gun platform, guard shack, and radio mount we simply watch the gate, and whatever other visible activity we can see just outside in the market square. We also pay special attention to the rooftops and darkened buildings that overlook the ECP. We haven't yet started to feel comfortable in our new post, as there is really no way to mitigate the danger posed by unseen snipers in the buildings that surround us. Freddy is in the cab of the truck conducting radio duties while I sit as sniper's bait up in the turret behind the fifty, waiting for something interesting to happen.

We switch positions every hour just to make it fair; besides, sitting in

142

the truck can get a bit crampy after a while; standing in the turret, while making one the best bet for incoming sniper fire, presents the welcome opportunity to stretch the legs.

Two hours into our shift an American convoy of four trucks rolls through. We've heard it's the Sergeant Major coming to pay us a visit, but as the convoy does not stop to make small talk, we can't be sure.

The lead truck radios in, gets clearance, and then pulls forward so Freddy can verify the lead vehicle's identification. Then they roll on through. The task at the east gate is rather easy; not nearly as demanding as pulling duty on the west gate.

Working the west ECP of the JSS is a considerably more active job. With the constant flow of civilian vehicles rolling through bringing supplies, visitors, and Iraqi policemen, work on the west gate is spent constantly checking identification, as well as checking every vehicle that comes through the gate for bombs.

Before coming on shift we were given a short, however serious briefing regarding a group of car bombers believed to be working in our area of operations.

Lately it has become a fad of sorts to load up a two-ton truck with high grade explosives and ram it into American entry control points with the accelerator smashed against the floor. It's totally acceptable to get shot and killed by the gate guards, fine, but afterwards, as a man sits dying behind the wheel with his lead foot fully active, the ultimate objective is to have the armed and dangerous truck smash as deep into an installation as possible before detonating.

Our particular ECP has no turns, and no chicanes of any sort in it, which means that if such a truck does suddenly turn the corner and come barreling down on us, we'll have to gun down the operator and destroy the vehicle before it is able to gain decent speed.

A rash of similar attacks have been springing up all around the city this month, so you never know; today could be a very special day.

Thankfully, or not, depending on your perspective, the rest of the shift is quiet and uneventful, save for the departure of the aforementioned American convoy.

When two D Co paratroopers appear mercifully from the deep blackness to relieve us, we bid them a fair and happy adieu.

No rest for the wicked. It's time for our first patrol in our new favorite neighborhood.

"All right, listen up."

SSGT Cloud begins his mini-briefing with his usual serious tone and repetitive catch-phrases.

"I'm not gonna lie, so far Moudan has been pretty quiet, but remember, we're virtually right across the street from the hottest nightclub in town. All the shit you guys have been hearing popping off has been coming from Fahad."

"These are the same groups of insurgents that Charlie was in contact with, and according to the reports coming down from command, they're massing up and becoming as aggressive as ever."

"Some of our friends from the 2nd CAV have reported casualty rates of up to forty percent, because these assholes have been road-bombing the shit out of them. In other words, the battalion casualty rates are getting so high that some of these mounted units are planning on getting out of town early."

A few looks are exchanged in our group, half uncertain, and half enthusiastic. In WWII or Vietnam losing half of a battalion was not unheard of, but in today's present war such losses are totally unacceptable. Casualty rates like the ones we're hearing about are unprecedented in the middle-eastern theatres. Our personal casualty allowance cap rests at somewhere near thirty-five percent, but, after four months of combat operations we're nowhere near our limit, having sustained something like seven percent or so.

"2nd CAV has only been in this part of town for three months. Day in, day out, their Strykers are getting hemmed-up virtually every time they leave Mad, just across the street from us."

"So, what we're going to do is snoop around the best we can and see if we can kill all these guys off, clear? 2nd CAV command is adamant that heavy vehicle support is essential to maintain a presence in this sector. While their adherence to doctrine may be illogically stubborn, it's now become our job to make sure they stop getting owned every fucking day. Hooah?"

Affirmations and nods of ascent go around the entire squad.

"Take three hours to rest up. We'll be rolling out at 0100."

As we move back to our bunks from the center of the bay, we can't help but strike up conversations amongst ourselves.

I break the silence by saying, "We really just made it to the war, didn't we?"

Duke, with his practiced feigned apathy, turns to me and says, "Aren't you glad you're not riding in a Stryker?"

"I sure the fuck am. Airborne."

Dick joins in, "Can you believe fucking forty percent casualties? Holy fuck. Why would they even be driving those things around anymore?"

"EFP magnets, that's for sure. More buck for your bang."

Freddy chimes in, "How do you suppose we're going to find them? See if we just stumble onto them, or pick up a nice camping spot over a route somewhere?"

"I'm all for camping out," I say, as we rustle around, forming our field blankets into little pillows and laying down heavily on our cots. As we click off our red-lens flashlights the bay becomes dark as pitch, and formless once again.

"God bless the twenty hour work day."

"Shut the fuck up, Cole."

Cole and Dick proceed to banter back and forth between themselves, and the conversation abruptly stops when Cole is hit square in the junk by an errant can of Copenhagen.

"Thanks for that, Jackass."

"That's Sergeant Jackass to you."

"I'm sorry. Thanks for the dip, Sergeant Jackass."

"You would. I bet y-"

Boom!

An explosion vibrates sand out of the bags in the windows, takes some of the wind from my chest, and vibrates the cot I'm sitting on. It's by far the biggest blast we've heard so far on our vacation. So big that we can't even estimate how far away it was. Seconds after the blast, reverberations still make the hotel tremble.

"What the *fuck*!"

"What the fuck was that?"

"Hey, Freddy, I think your mom farted."

"Not the time, Duke."

Taking a bit of initiative, I volunteer to be the messenger.

"I'll run to the talk right quick and see if they know what the fuck that was."

Freddy, no longer reclining, profoundly states, "Video killed the radio star, yeah? But a big fucking explosion just killed the ever-loving fuck out of naptime."

145

"Damn straight."

As I grab my boonie and rifle, not bothering with donning body-armor for this particular run, I catch the tail end of the quippy little conversation.

"Hey, Cole, you ever hear anything like that in your trailer park?"

Too far away to catch the undoubtedly witty punch-line, no doubt a propane tank reference, I'm already bounding down the stairs and out the front of the barracks, jogging at a good clip across the ground level of the hotel façade towards the talk. I used to live in a cozy little double-wide myself, in Fayetteville, North Carolina before I was relocated to the present circumstance. I loved the place, so I can make fun of trailer-trash all I want. All of my neighbors were strippers too; just young hard working country girls trying to pay their way through college. This is my smiley face.

It only takes a moment to cross the distance to the police station. As I pass the middle ground, which is a simple, wide stretch of dirt, I notice that we have a few new amenities in the compound.

A fresh, clean looking bank of four brand-new porta-shitters, complete with what looks like Indonesian branding, stand in a welcoming little row at the edge of the dirt path.

"Quaint."

As arbitrary and benign as it sounds, I feel the fleeting buzz of giddy butterflies in my stomach. No more shit-burning details. We have blue water now. Awesome.

Our new talk is simply a small office inside the police station that was requisitioned for two reasons: a functional television complete with electricity, and semi-decent looking third world desks and chairs that even came complete with real padding.

No sergeants or officers are present in the talk, which I find very odd. Maybe they ran off to ask questions themselves. Parker from D Co is stooped over the radio while intently listening to his handset for news that I'm assuming is related to the localized Armageddon of moments passed.

"Hey, Parker, what news, bro?"

"Big fucking blast at the Paper Market. Nobody knows why though. It's not exactly high-noon, and there was no convoy involved. Doesn't make any sense; we're way passed close of business. Just an unexplained blast. You on dismount now?"

"Yeah. We're going out in a minute, looks like. That blast probably cancelled naptime."

Parker continues, "I think this was probably an example of fucking functional Darwinism. If I was going to fix a big old bomb to something, I'd do it in the middle of the night too. Difference is, I'd use a flashlight to do it."

Parker's deep southern drawl makes the comical statement even funnier, and I can't help but laugh out loud as I leave the talk and move back to my mates to relay the news. At least we know we aren't going on a rescue mission. Still thinking about the arms, legs, and guts of a wanna-be vehicle bomber flying headlong into the atmosphere along with the rest of a city block, I decide to delay my return to the squad. Relaying the vague, however pertinent news can wait a spell.

I decide to take a short pause on my return voyage, hopping lightly and happily into one of the new port-o-stalls to take a quick leak. As I piss I inhale deeply, delighting in the fresh, new, chemical anti-septic smell of the plastic surroundings. The toilet has not even been shit in yet, and it comforts me a little bit to be fully inside a modern extravagance that is made of modern materials, with modern bathroom sensibilities in mind. When I'm done jiggling up and buttoning, I switch on my red photon light and examine what kind of toilet paper we're cooking with, only to be sorely disappointed. And, I mean sorely, in rough anticipation of the bloody future. No high grade Charmin for us warrior types here, just John Wayne toilet paper. It's rough, it's tough, and it won't take shit from no Indians. Oh well, you can't win 'em all.

A few more steps and I'm back upstairs, crossing the open bay where Cloud is already waiting with the rest of the guys, crouched around in our standard 'what-the-fuck's-up' formation.

Cloud addresses me, "What's going on, D."

"Apparently, we don't know why the world blew up. We don't think it was an IED, and there were no American forces around. Best that command can tell, someone had a major oops-ident while installing a fresh new stereo system in their car. Battalion thinks it's a failed VBIED maybe."

Freddy has to chip in.

"Motherfucker had some bass, didn't it?"

"Indeed."

Cloud takes the conversation over, "All right. Only one thing to do. Let's go take a look at it."

I huddle around with the others to get a repeat session on the little map that the others were apparently just introduced to a moment before.

It's a piece of laminated paper with exaggerated streets and comically huge Arabic writing, but not a lick of English on it. The map was most likely found at one of the small local businesses in the area, and looks like the printing could date back to the seventies, but that doesn't mean it wasn't printed yesterday. You never can tell in these parts.

"Okay, so our compound is here."

I'm given a brief outline of some local landmarks and our prospective patrol route, cross-referenced alongside a modern American military map of the area. This is done so we can all get multiple perspectives, including both the actual factual, as well as the 'easy-to-understand' theme-park version.

We're given good details of a local school located in what is locally known as the Paper Market, which also happens to be our destination for the evening. Two mosques, one modern and one ancient, as well as a local warehouse serve as the boundaries for tonight's walk. All in all, we're looking at a square patrol route of roughly four miles. Not long at all for respectable infantrymen like ourselves. When we all have a good idea of exactly where we're going and what to expect, we break for gearing up and sensitive items checks.

Everybody checks the batteries in their equipment, also insuring that they have spares handy. After donning my weapon and gear, I send up the radio check, as I'm the designated RTO for tonight's hike, while the rest of the squad equips their racks, body armor, and weapons.

After only a brief moment we're all gussied up and ready to go to the big ball.

Leading the pack in hopes of having a quick nocturnal cigarette break before we take off, I quicken my step a little bit. I can hear the rest of the squad behind me, trundling heavily down the darkened stairwell like a herd of turtles.

Once we're outside, we wait for our LT, who will be walking with us tonight as well as an interpreter, who was dropped off the last time Smag rolled through.

Quite aware of the no-no rule regarding smoking at night, and keeping to my light discipline, I take a seat at the base of a sizable concrete barrier just to the left of our beautiful new toilets and light one up. I'm concealed from the view of the buildings that border the market square, and quite comfortably at rest save for the ASIP radio that slightly digs into my back. Even through my thick armor, I can feel the thick, angular block digging into my shoulders, and I can hear the far away sounding buzzes and beeps of the net in my left ear as they are beamed into my brain by the radio handset wedged into my chin strap. After sending up one more radio check to the talk, I deem myself quite ready to go.

Concrete at my back, facing the hotel, the only vantage point to my glowing cherry comes from our own high-ground positions, so I'm free to enjoy my smoke without the fear of a sniper's bullet.

Word has it that next time we come back to this place, there will be floodlights attached to a high concrete barrier that will illuminate the exterior perimeter of the JSS. Until that time, everyone will have to smoke at a crouch, behind some staunch cover.

"Ready to go, D?"

Freddy takes a seat beside me. He doesn't smoke, but the small curb I've found to rest my ass on, complete with concrete backstop, is as appealing a seat as any. It doesn't matter what you lay your back against in armor; it all feels the same.

"Ready-ready, Freddy. Care to start smoking yet?"

"Nope. Smoked before, growing up."

"Ah. I'm not grown up yet."

"Tell me when you get there."

I smile to myself and take another long drag. "Sure thing, buddy."

After a few moments the entire squad assembles in a loose group, every man standing in a close, very accurate approximation of where he will be marching during the patrol.

Duke and Cole are on point for this one, right and left, while Dick will walk just behind them.

Sergeant Cloud will walk just in front of me, in the very center of the formation for command and control, while I will be just behind. Freddy, as usual, will bring up the rear.

Our Lieutenant doesn't really have a spot. As a non-tactical doofus, he will just sort of float about according to his own whim throughout the course of the patrol, and the interpreter will tag along with our glorious Leftenant.

Five minutes pass as I finish my smoke. Cole helps the interpreter fasten an old army K-pot to his head, and a few members of the squad who've recently departed return from their brief visits to the new port-o-shitters. It looks like everyone is ready to go.

"Radio checks up, Pearce?"

"Roger, Sergeant."

"All right everyone, you know the drill. Infantry, follow me."

With the prescribed melodramatic hand and arm signal, Cloud motions us forward, and we step, not quite in time, out of the east gate.

We say a brief hello and goodbye to our fellow soldiers pulling guard in the truck at the ECP. Moving in our squad column formation, four men on the left of the road, four on the right, we slowly and methodically round the last of the HESCO barriers and take our first steps into the open dirt expanse that stands between us and the rest of town.

I call in to the CP and let them know that we've left the JSS. They acknowledge the fact with a big 'Roger' and beep sharply away from the net.

I like my hands on my weapon at all times, so rather than walk and talk with my handset in palm, I simply tuck the thing under the brim of my helmet, securing it into place with my chin strap. It's not exactly the most technologically advanced hands-free system in the world, but it works in a pinch.

Flanked on all sides by three-story-tall yellow concrete buildings, we make our way into a nearby mulhalla at the right side of the square.

The hot night looks totally green to me; there is not enough lume to see anything more than the faintest of silhouettes through my naked eye, so I crutch on the green view granted by the monocular seated over my left eye. I like to keep my right eye free of the technology in case I ever need to take a shot without night-vision or laser systems.

The PEQ-2 laser systems on our rifles are connected to pressure switches on our weapon grips which, when depressed, send a bore-lighted targeting laser out from the rifle, enabling the night-vision equipped soldier to simply point and click with the beam, rather than deal with traditional sights or aiming apparatuses in the dark. It's a rare privilege which has only recently been granted to modern soldiers. What's more, enemies not equipped with optics that can view IR are unable to view our lasers, as they are invisible to the naked eye.

Along with our targeting systems, each PEQ unit is also equipped with an infrared floodlight which we can switch on much like a flashlight, to illuminate the darkest night for our eyes only.

Most of the squad has their floodlights switched on as we make our way through the dirty, narrow mulhalla. Circular spotlights sent out from our rifles lazily scan around the terrain as we get a feel for our new route. Automatic weapons fire sputters loudly into the night from an unknown and somewhat distant location. The smells of an open sewer and fresh food-garbage fills my nostrils, and I can hear tonight's chorus of wild dogs picking up in time, as if from alleys away they can sense that interlopers have invaded their turf.

As we move deeper into the mulhalla we widen out our spacing and walk a little quieter, and a bit slower.

Every empty soda can and every discarded glass bottle serves as a potential early warning system for the enemy.

Locals in our new neighborhood are smart enough not to come out at night. The only traffic these alleys see at this late hour are either insurgent fighters, homeless people unfortunate enough to find themselves out of doors after nightfall, and soldiers, American or otherwise, who are busily conducting operations. There are no cats. Packs of wild dogs eat the cats.

The long mulhalla is a bazaar corridor lined with open shops lacking any real security measures, and other holes in the wall where people presumably live or small businesses sit locked up for the night. Wooden doors of all kinds, some reinforced and others not, form a long unbroken conga line in the ancient, decrepit stone walls that appear to be as old as Babylon itself. Baghdad is old Babylon. Learn something new every day.

Other homes and businesses built into the residential coral are fortunate enough to bear metal doors or other sorts of wrought-iron grating with padlocks. The barriers are funny though, in their own way. Though the doors may be strong, a simple pry-bar of any make or model would happily pull the old stone away, granting admittance to anyone willing to use the proper tool.

Slowing its pace, our squad comes upon an intersection of sorts that is a lopsided junction between three mulhallas, so we each pull our respective duties. Positions are taken in the front of the formation to provide the rest of us a measure of security while we cross the open space. After looking both ways like any good school children would, our squad finishes its leap-frog maneuver past the linear danger area. Rather than adjusting and taking up our original positions, the squad simply stays inverted. Doubtless, we will have another crossing soon and things will revert back to the way they were.

As suddenly as it started, the mulhalla ends, and we face another open street with what appear to be apartments and multi-level businesses on one side, and the tall fence to the Iraqi army compound, Mad, on the other.

I cross the street quickly with Freddy following closely at my heels.

Twenty meters up the road I can see Duke taking lead of the formation on our side.

The moment I reach the far side of the street, the gunshots reverberating off the near stone walls of the neighborhood sound less muted, and spring into full force. Not yet within a dangerous range, the individual pop-pop-pops and rat-tat-tats of automatic fire become distinguishable, and almost recognizable.

Cloud nods to me and points up ahead to where the approximate origin of the gunfire lies. In a hushed voice he says, "Three hundred meters."

Quietly, I nod my assent, and keeping my right hand on the grip and safety selector of my weapon, I use my left hand to call the data in as the squad presses forward.

"Delta One-Four this is Delta One-Two, over."

"Delta One-Two, go ahead."

"Roger. We're making good time heading up Old Office Road, break; we're approaching gunfire to the north; estimated three hundred meters to the north- northeast, over."

"Copy One-Two, keep me posted, over."

"Will do. Delta One-Two, out."

I speak as as quietly as I can while still being loud enough to be heard through the radio handset. Not being completely satisfied with my transmission, the LT begins his own conversation with the talk, adding his own input in a voice more suited to talking on the phone at the mall rather than sneaking up on a gunfight. I can't fathom what the fuck it's about. After all, the situation is simple. We're walking toward loud noises. End of story. What the fuck ever.

Normally I take moments like this to joke with Freddy about the various and sundry silliness of the day, but being occupied with stealthiness as we are, I decide to keep my choice commentary to myself. Professionalism and all that.

Our sidewalk gives way to an open soccer field fifty meters ahead that is illuminated by a dim yellow lamppost and flanked on all sides by the same brand of dilapidated concrete squares that serve as residences, local businesses, and trash receptacles. Garbage still smolders in nearby metal drums through the pitch darkness of night, sending forth rays of light and heat invisible to the naked eye, but clearly seen as glints of silver lining through my nods. Or green lining, whatever.

Moving through a thin scrim of acrid smoke we make our way into

152

the open space afforded to us by the soccer field.

The weapons fire to our front sounds ever louder, ever more ferocious, but still I cannot discern the origin.

As the thick smell of fried garbage dissipates, we follow Cloud's signal to widen the formation even further, spreading a full five meters from one man to another, and drifting to opposite sides of the large yard in an attempt to stay out of the dim yellow light.

I look around me in a slow but deliberate circle, taking stock of friends and squad-mates, each seeming a great distance away as we cross the rest of the open expanse past broken teeter-totters and abandoned carts that look somewhat like hotdog stands.

As our element nears the far side of the yard, as well as our target mulhalla, we sidle up close to one another yet again without signal or direction, resuming our standard three-meter spread while falling into line with one another; soldiers on the right, and soldiers on the left.

"Call it up; one hundred meters."

The gunfire is close now. Close enough to feel the reverberations from the concrete walls that surround us. The direction of the fire has been lost, at once coming from nowhere and everywhere as it bounces off every concrete surface, and assaults our ears from positions that seem to be originating from north, south, east, and west.

Still unable to see anything dangerous, the squad takes a halt. As we all take a knee in the darkened alley I radio in our close proximity to the gunfire. Once again I'm told to keep the CP posted on the situation, and little else.

I take the time to look behind me at Freddy, who catches my barely-there headshake. *What the fuck are we doing?*

If it were my patrol, I'd have led our squad onto a nearby rooftop by now, in an attempt to get eyes on the gunfire at a position slightly higher than sea-level. Apparently, conservative thought processes are not on the docket for Cloud this fine morning, as it appears that he intends to march us up the street right into the center of a battle between two unknown forces. Maybe he just wants to see if our vests really can stop bullets.

Oh, happy day.

We get the signal to bring it into a quick huddle, and the entire squad disappears into a small alcove just off the main mulhalla: a small fenced yard that apparently harbors no purpose, save for holding three small motor scooters that have been laid down on their sides where they slowly rust in a great puddle of mud and sewage.

The gunfire is close now. I can hear the sound waves bouncing along their erratic paths down the concrete walls and into my head. The volume of the rounds is great, but they lack the dimension of rounds fired in open space. Although loud enough to deafen normal conversation, they do not make my ears ring.

Raising his voice slightly over the growing din, Cloud addresses us once again.

As he begins to speak the group is markedly tense, reduced now to sitting in a small hole, very close to what are obviously dangerous fuckwits. What's more, by the volume of fire there seems to be dozens of combatants; there are only eight of us. One's an LT, and one's a terp. That makes six rifles on target for us. Not exactly reassuring numbers for picking a fight in central Baghdad from street level with no backup in sight.

"All right, listen up."

Cloud continues, "The LT wants to try to get eyes on these guys. We can't enter any of the nearby structures. Apparently they're all suspected to be hostile, and further, there's a lot of women and children living in this neighborhood. We're going to take a look-see from the street.

"Watch your spacing and keep security all around. Pearce, Freddy, and Duke are going up to the intersection. The rest of us will shadow them and pull security. Whoever they are, we know we're dealing with a lot of them. They could be IA or IP, so if you're seen or if you take contact, break the fuck away and we'll roll out, hooah?"

We all nod, and Cloud knows that he still has our rapt attention.

"We're not in a position to fight here. This isn't my first rodeo, and I can tell you this, if one of you kids squirts off without permission this whole neighborhood is going to come alive and eat us, understand?"

Quietly, very quietly, we all give nods of understanding. It's a pretty clear job: waltz up to the intersection and look both ways. The only thing that could put such a simple plan in jeopardy, the way I see it, is if one of us takes an errant bullet in the face. Or having a posse of the happy-go-lucky gunmen quickly round the corner with itchy trigger fingers, forcing us to gun them down and make a run for it. That's it. Simple. No worries.

Breaking away from our relatively safe and sheltered yard, the others fall away farther to the rear and send communications up while providing security for the three of us as best they can while Duke, Freddy, and I

154

move forward.

"Let's go, boyos."

My humor is lost for the time being, and I know that my pulse is not the only one quickening. We're engaging in some highly unrecommended, highly stupid shit, and everybody knows it. Everybody but the LT at least. That's what you get.

Expendable assets us, one and all. Like I said, our unit is nowhere near its maximum casualty count. We've got a little leeway.

As we approach the symphony, Duke and I pull up positions close to one another a good seventy-five meters back from our target intersection, while Freddy does his own thing off to our left.

Every footstep is intentionally placed to insure that a misplaced footfall doesn't make a suspicious noise in the middle of a gunfire lull.

To my front, red and green tracers zip back and forth across the intersection. In between the salvos of gunfire Arabs shout angry words at one another or laugh out loud, as if they were really enjoying tonight's matchup.

I'm pulling double duty with Freddy, checking fields of fire both to the front and to the sides, as well as above and behind. Constantly scanning. There is no way for a full element to look at everything that needs to be looked at in a MOUT environment, so suffice it to say, the three of us try to trudge through the crap as best we can, every one of us wishing we had eight eyeballs apiece; every one of us knows that we're about to step into some seriously deep shit.

Fifty meters away from the intersection we start being very mindful of cover and start to bound as we go. I take cover behind a pile of some unidentifiable, flimsy third-world shit while Duke takes a knee up ahead of me behind a decent-looking concrete pillar, and Freddy starts his bound from the left side of the street.

Moving ahead roughly ten meters, Freddy takes a knee behind what appears to be an ancient industrial-sized garbage dumpster and signals back to me. Getting a nod from Duke, I pop up and continue my quick, quiet advance to a pillar about ten meters in front of him, take a knee, and signal back. We move forward in this fashion, purposefully and carefully.

It only takes a moment for us to arrive at the gunfire.

Uncharacteristically, the Arabs are not using a great deal of tracers tonight. Probably just because they don't have any more; we are a bit late to the party, after all. Even though they offer no real tactical advantage in

155

a fight, save for showing an enemy who to shoot first, and also being terrible for wear and tear on weapons, Arabs love the tracers. They're bright, shiny, and scary. Although at nighttime every fifth round in American machine-gun systems is a tracer, this is done simply to offer a manual perspective on where rounds are impacting. Middle Eastern soldiers never use them for that recommended purpose, but instead, garner a nasty habit of loading up entire belts or magazines full of the things. I suppose they can just blame Allah when their barrels melt.

Upon reaching the intersection the gunfire becomes deafening, finally reaching full force. I use my radio to tell the CP that our squad has reached its target destination, and that we are about to have eyes on the contacts. The noise from the fight is oppressive, and I can't make out the talk's reply.

Freddy lies down on his stomach on the far side of the street, being careful to stay as close to the side of the concrete building as possible without touching the walls. Slowly, he nods and signals at us, so we do the same, lying down on the filthy sidewalks that flank either side of the street.

From my new, low position I can see five feet ahead of me clearly, right to where I want to go. There will be no talking once we take a peek around the corner. Just a quick look and we're out of here.

As I slowly scrape my way up the sidewalk I'm aware of the grime and dirt grating under my pants and gloves, and I feel what I think is moisture in the filth. I don't have the time to worry about getting a hajji sewage disease in my wiener, as I'm nearing the end of my cover.

Pie-ing slowly past the cover afforded to me by the corner of the building at my right shoulder, I begin to see muzzle flashes in the midnight darkness.

My heart was beating loud and proud at a slightly elevated volume before I exposed my body to potential errant bullets and ricochets, but now, hearing the full volume of what could only be a fifty caliber machine gun, my pulse starts to hammer wildly. As I slowly grind myself a few more inches forward I'm aware of my hands and feet starting to shake.

Rifle clutched tightly in my arms, I proceed to finish the rest of my high-crawl on my elbows. Reaching my limit of advance, I decide that I can see quite enough of the street now, and cannot justify crawling out into view any further.

The roars of the bullets are relentless, audibly whizzing passed us one after another as they cut through the still night air, or spark as they strike

156

the ancient cobbled road. They sound like angry mechanical hornets.

I see Freddy to my left on the far side of the street, doing precisely what I'm doing.

Looking around my own corner to the right would be a foolish, quick, and easy way to die, so I look beyond Freddy down the left side of the street, never exposing my head or body to the fire on the near side of the road to my right. Freddy, having the same idea, continues inching a little further into the open space, while looking past me to get more of an angle on the firefight factory to my right.

Through my monocular, assisted momentarily by the showers of light from the guns that illuminate the night like vicious lightning, I can see what appear to be three American Humvees. That can only mean one thing: Iraqi army. We gave them those, because they're so competent.

Slowly, Freddy raises a very tentative hand to where I can see it and it forms the letters IP. Followed by lots of fingers. How many, I can't tell.

I do him the same favor, telling him what I see in the good king's sign language, and as slowly and carefully as we emerged to peek around the corners, we slip back into the safety of the darkness.

I'm immediately relieved to be in the glorious comfort of a middle-eastern street not filled with bullets once again. My ears are also a bit relieved; though the painful brunt of the blasts are gone, I can still hear sirens ringing loudly in my head.

Standing up, Freddy crosses the street to where Duke and I have already begun walking back to the rest of the squad at a good clip.

Amidst the periodic lulls in the gunfire, Arabian shouting still echoes throughout the concrete night. On either side it now sounds as if there are fair amount of wounded. In between the spats of pained wailing and gunfire, insults are now being shouted into the deep Iraqi blackness.

That's the unity of an emerging nation for you.

Nothing is said until we work our way back into our little chain-link hideaway; our safe haven of Football Huddling +3.

Rather than wasting time giving Cloud a formal dissertation, I simply call the talk and everyone hushes in extra-quiet so that they can hear the soft transmission.

I relay the best numbers we have, knowing that they are generally not accurate, as there was no way from our low vantage point to see a clear view down both sides of the entire street. I tell the CP that there is a mounted group of heavily armed Iraqi soldiers to the west of the intersection about fifty meters down, shooting wildly down the street and engaging a large number of dismounted Iraqi policemen about a hundred meters to the east.

I'm immediately questioned on this. Am I sure they were policemen? Freddy nods to me, very definitively with his two sizes too big nocturnal Kevlar head, and I reply that yes, roger, affirmative, copy, I'm fucking sure as hell that Iraq is trying, with great panache and gusto to viciously blow its own dick off.

Newly enlightened as to the true nature of the situation, the D Co platoon sergeant tells us not to do any more stupid shit tonight, move away from the gunfire, and continue the dismounted patrol on a two-mile perimeter, three-hundred-and-sixty-degree sweep around the outside of the JSS, then come back.

Cloud mumbles a word or two in the darkness, prefaced as usual with the telling, "Listen up, guys, I'm not gonna lie."

Everybody hears and understands the rough plan. Which is not much of a plan at all. It's walking. How hard can it be?

Everyone takes up their standard positions with me and Cloud in the center, Duke and Cole taking point, Dick, the terp, and the LT floating around, and Freddy bringing up the rear of the formation once again.

Walking down the wet mulhalla we come once again into earshot of our new favorite group of resident hounds, and I take the time to wonder just exactly where they are. Dog-biting would surely be a nasty surprise on an evening such as this. Thank God for long-knives. They have knives for things like that. I've got four of them on me; wet wipes too, just in case.

Rounding through different mulhallas we see much the same stuff, and smell much the same mush. Eventually we make our way back to the brightly lit soccer field adjacent to Old Office Road.

There's really no way to tell if there is an old office, and I make a mental note to inquire about the general commercial situation in this town at a later time, or to discover if there ever was such a building of its kind in this city. That sort of thing implies infrastructure, after all. Probably way back in the 'Golden Days.' Those are the days just before the 'Golden Shower' days. That's a different town.

Around the periphery of the park, the gunfire, or what little remaining puffs of it ring out every now and then sound friendly, far-off, and quiet. Nigh inconsequential, I'd say.

The night drags on, hour after hour on our first patrol. After running the eight-mile route once at just under three hours, Cloud suggests that we have time to run it again before day-break, so that we can really get a feel for our new neighborhood. Although most of us are dead tired by now, nobody really voices a complaint about the idea of going one more time around the block. We all know that it is quite sensible to take another turn around a new neighborhood. It's likely that we will pull light duty on our next patrol besides, provided some great emergency isn't going down on our shift.

We walk again, and then we walk some more. Endless miles of cracked concrete, dirt, and shit are graced by the presence of my American boots and deft nighttime ninja footwork.

At around five in the morning the smells of cook-fires start emanating from apartments and small street-front restaurants alike.

The welcoming smells, accompanied by the blue, pre-dawn glow of the rising sun remind me of how very hungry I am as we make our way back over the last mile to walk into our new ECP once again.

Chapter Five: Good Times Travel Inc.

If your travel agent smiles at you
While he cleans his gun,
You might do best to reconsider where you'll go.

The world is filled with magic places,
With music, booze, and sun,
But just because you see some palm trees
Doesn't mean it will be fun.

I'd like to shoot my travel agent.
I'd like to hang him out to dry.
I saw pictures in this brochure,
Looking so peaceful I could die.

But what I see keeps me laughing.
I can't seem to hold it in.
Someday I think I'll stab my travel agent,
And I'm never coming here again.

Please be wary of the tickets.
Take this good advice, my friend.
Be wary of your travel agent
Because some road trips never end.

Oh, Hell yeah!
You bought it hook and line!
You've been duped again,
By a grinning travel agent.

Back in the safety of our open bay it's business as usual. In a stroke of good luck, we've ended up with a full two hours on the clock before our slated rest rotation begins, which gives us a full ten hours of down time.

Before the relaxation festivities can begin, however, the daily chores of an infantryman must be completed. Talking amongst ourselves quietly, so as not to wake any of the other squads, we converse about the happenings of the night while we begin to clean our weapons.

"Dishkas are loud as fuck, man."

"What?"

"Come off it, Freddy, you heard me."

We have a good chuckle in our quiet, murmuring weapons cleaning circle. There's a genuine shortage of humor going around today and it shows. Everyone is beat.

My cleaning goes slowly, thoroughly, and methodically as usual. Brush in hand, I scrub residue from oil, ammunition, and dirt from each of my main weapon's components in the same order I always do.

First, I like to give the innards of my trigger-well a good scrubbing, and then lay my entire lower receiver aside. Before I rest it on a small towel I extract my buffer spring and buffer from the butt-stock, also laying them to the side. Next I brush off and wipe the bolt, the main hunk of moving metal in the upper receiver, and lay it out alongside my charging rod where it awaits further disassembly and cleaning.

After I've scrubbed the main haul of grime and debris from all the main weapon groups I set in with my dental picks. Dental picks are always the fastest and most effective way to get grit out of the hard to reach places.

A deeper disassembly is conducted after the exteriors of all my components are mostly clean. Thoroughly I brush, pick, and wipe all of the weapon's smaller disassembled components until I find them to be in a passably clean state. With the brunt of the cleaning done, I quickly assemble the weapon, small parts to big ones, and finish by fastening the upper and lower receivers together.

After an hour or so I deem my weapon to be as impeccably clean as it's ever been, and complete my weapon's maintenance by applying a very light, fine scrim of oil on all of the weapon's moving parts, followed by a rust check on the exterior.

There are many who would assume that weapons don't rust during long deployments in the desert; those stupid words are uttered by idiots who've never spent three days at a time sweating over their weapon in a hide site. Shame on them.

A little oil here, some wire brushing there, and I'm through. I complete my chore while listening in on the waning conversations of the others; everyone is hurriedly focusing on their business in hopeful anticipation of the good rest that is about to come.

Very quietly, I manipulate the selector lever, trigger, and charging handle of my weapon to perform a quick functions check.

The healthy, tight sounding actions of my weapon let me know that it's very clean, lightly lubricated, and functioning perfectly.

Laying the weapon aside, I can't help but look at it a bit. I always do. I love the way it looks when it's pristinely cleaned, with the bluing on the exterior lightly oiled. It truly is a beautiful machine, and I take a special pride in having no carbon in my star-chamber. That's soldier talk. Maybe I just like it because my life depends on it. If I had the choice, I'd take an H & K any day of the week.

Mentally patting myself on the back for a thorough job well done, I recline on my once new army cot, still lightly damp and salt-cured from the sweat of the man that was sleeping on it before me.

With no air conditioning to speak of, the dark hole of a bay we're living in is already developing the token fungal, musty ambiance that generally denotes a place of residence for infantry of all kinds, from time immemorial.

Making my staple to-go pillow with my woobie and placing it under my head, as is my custom, I allow my mind to wander off a bit.

I'm a torn man. On the one hand, I could eat food. Or I could do that later and enjoy myself a little for the time being. Over a week's worth of long days await us during this rotation, so while I would like nothing more than to whip out my PSP for a round of Spectral Souls, I tell myself that I'll feel like batteries are more of a precious commodity later in the week, and I shouldn't squander my game-toy's charge at the beginning of the rotation. Wise words from a wise man.

Most of the others are conducting basic hygiene operations, otherwise known as 'whore baths.' Armpits, feet, balls, and ass cracks are unceremoniously scrubbed in our semi-public space, with little thought given to modesty. Actually, a lot of good conversation pieces come up this way. For example, this morning's quip is brought to us courtesy of Cloud.

"Hey, Cole, is your ass still sore from yesterday?

Dryly, Cole simply gives a questioning gaze to Cloud as he scrubs his nuts with a small rag that is already falling apart, with a little smirk on his face that says, 'I don't know, but I'm eagerly awaiting the punch-line.'

"I don't know what you're talking about Sergeant."

"You know. From you stuffing wet-wipes into it all the time."

"Cleanliness is next to godliness, Sergeant."

I have to pipe up at that one.

"Cleanliness in Louisiana? I don't buy it. You people created gumbo for God's sake."

Pulling his pants back up and discarding his defiled rag, Cole, deciding that he's not yet done having a social experience, proceeds to empty his mind.

"You're goddamned right they did. As well as the flood; invented that too. As a matter of fact, a more perfect shower, I cannot think of."

"Touché, my friend."

I take the time to wipe my own armpits and dick, and then discard the small, once soapy rag into a tiny bagless waste bin that somebody appropriated for this dark purpose, no doubt stolen from somewhere deeper in the hotel. Who knows, we're probably doing the plastic can a favor. It probably used to hold Arab shits.

Deciding fully against recreation of any kind, I decide that a meal is in order before sleep can come. Luckily, I got good dibs on one of the hamburger simulators, complete with totally digestible BBQ fluid and chemical cheese approximation spread. Beggars can't be choosers, and I'm McFuckin' it.

I finish the heavy meal quickly, not bothering to heat it up first. After making quick work of the food, I discard the garbage and thirstily consume a quart of water.

As I lay down on my cot, I don't bother to think much of anything this morning. I don't really want to. Time has already begun to drag, and the newness of the Iraqi adventure has already begun to slip away.

I try to guard my thoughts as best I can against attempting to calculate the rest of the wait in this country, or even to speculate when we can return home. All talk of a late-August return recently flew out the window during a company briefing. We were told not to expect to start packing our shit until at least Christmas.

Christmas at the soonest. From my life, here in mid-April, that seems a considerable distance. The longest distance between two points is time they say; I think they're right.

Realizing that I've failed in my grand plan not to count the days, I sigh and roll over on my side waiting patiently, as I'm used to doing, for sweet sleep to take me away.

Thankfully, I wake up naturally before our guard shift begins. For a moment, I take the time to be a bit giddy; although I'm quite sore, I don't feel foggy headed this morning. Sleep is a truly magical thing.

None of the others are up yet, save for Cole. I think it may have been his turn to pull a radio guard shift, so I expect that he's sitting busily in the talk, monitoring radio transmissions and watching Arabian music videos piped in from Kuwait and the Emirates.

Having to piss like never before, I grab my rifle and a magazine, don my boonie-cap and Oakleys, and head downstairs where I move out into the bright noon sun. It's a short journey to the wonderful blue plastic shitter where I take my morning piss.

Through the thin blue plastic walls I can hear the sound of the market square in full swing. Floating just above the din, a not-so-bad Islamic hymn is being broadcast through loudspeakers for all to hear, announcing that mid-day prayer time has arrived.

Idiots attempting to drive through the madness honk their horns and shout, as if in total surprise that a regular bazaar has blocked their travel plans. Hawkers and food-stand dudes call out into the bustling air, and a bit closer, within the low walls of the compound, I can hear a loud and jocular conversation being held by two IPs, although what the conversation is about I cannot understand. Most likely, it's about the latest 'same-same' porno.

I decide to confirm my guess that Cole is pulling a radio stint, so I lazily walk to the talk, stopping every so often to 'Salam Alikom' somebody.

Just inside the door to our newly appropriated office my suspicions are confirmed. Cole sits wide-awake at his post, lackadaisically doodling on a piece of waxy green 'Write in the Rain' notebook paper and doesn't even look up when I enter.

Just behind him at a long, low plastic table our LT is slumped over, taking a very privileged nap. Hey, who's going to stop him? I myself would be concerned about escaped prisoners or a maniacally demented Iraqi policeman sneaking in through the open doorway and slitting my throat. But hey, that's just me being unnecessarily paranoid, right? It's not like we're in the middle of a hostile neighborhood, actively engaging in armed combat with a religiously murderous and determined insurgency. My mistake. Mayhaps I'll indulge in a radio nap later too.

Our own sleeping quarters are constantly guarded by an infantryman located at the bottom of the main stairs in the lobby, which happens to be the sole entry point to our most recent dwelling. There is no such measure in the talk, which is why it is recommended that all personnel working in the talk remain armed and vigilant at all times. *Right.*

"Hey, buddy. Any news?"

I flop heavily down on one of the sparsely padded chairs as Cole swivels away from his drawing to address the question.

"We might be in for a real day, man."

I'm taken a little aback by the sunken, restless, excited look in his eyes. That could only mean one thing.

"Well, apparently Redwater just found themselves in a shit-storm about a half an hour ago, just about three miles away, and they think that over a hundred fighters are going to storm this place sometime today and kill each and every one of us. They're creepin' on us pretty good, looks like."

"Good thing that we don't let IPs work the gates. Goodness knows they can be paid off easy enough. That fight last night could have involved any of the guys from this post."

"None that I've heard of. Best we can tell there's a small, temporary duty station over that way, overlooking a little bridge over a canal of some sort. I guess it was the guys working that post, whatever they were up to."

"Cool. If there are no IAs that we aren't allowed to shoot back at doing mid-morning .50 caliber drive-bys on our hotel, that's a good thing."

"I concur, doctor."

The news, though a bit far-out, makes me a little concerned. I had better go smoke a cigarette, restore some of my personal calm, and wake the other members of the squad. No doubt Cloud's 'listen-up' will take place sometime very soon, and I'd like to be fully ready when it does.

Bidding Cole adieu, I leave him in the warmth and comfort of some Arabian pop song, the chorus of which seems to be *habibi, habibi, habibi,* over and over again. Good beat I guess, although the vocals are a bit too jumpy for me. Cute singer though.

Cole's shift is over in less than fifteen minutes, so he'll be back to the bay shortly.

Next-door to the entrance of the hotel, within the compound, and sharing a wall with our building, is a small café operated by a private individual that services the police station's every need: Smokes and chai.

As I stroll on by I'm assaulted by the store owner and accompanying group of children, each wanting to know if I want a soda, or a falafel, or some chocolate, or cigarettes.

La, la, shukran. La, la, shukran. I'm well versed in the art-form of politely refusing goods and services by this point, and I feel that the internationally understood 'no thank you' should be acceptable, though I can't verify whether or not the syntax is grammatically correct for this region. I'm not a local language authority. Even so, it seems like an awfully difficult phrase to fuck up. *No gracias. Nein Danke. Nye spasiyba. Bu hao*, or something. I always forget the Chinese.

I do want a cigarette; I want one very badly. I don't want a *Miami* or a *Royale'* though. Good old AAA Marlboros. That's what I'm fixin' to have.

On my way to the twelfth floor to take advantage of the temporary smoking area I found, I'm pleasantly surprised to discover that a similar set of furniture, complete with glass ashtrays, has been set up on the third floor. It's not close enough to the bay to disturb the non-smokers, but it's close enough that frequent trips up here will neither be physically demanding nor take too much time. I'm serious when I say physically demanding, and I'm not a lazy person. Quite fit, I should say. No, you run around for eight days straight in cramped trucks and full body armor, usually running on a lack of sleep while surviving on nothing but packaged food, and tell me you don't feel the effects of three flights of badly formed Arabian stairs. See; I'm right.

Sitting on a low wooden chair on the third floor, I sling my weapon onto my back and lean forward over the little table. I listen as best I can to the sounds outside while I draw a cigarette and light it, but I'm very surprised as I realize I can hear nothing from this floor, save for the lone humming of a gasoline-powered generator that the engineers set up yesterday. Currently, there is still talk going around that the engineers will have flood lights up around the JSS by our next rotation. There's also a rumor that they will eventually be supplying a steady stream of power to our floor of the building, but I highly doubt that's going to be any time soon; that sort of thing takes a lot of wire, and a lot of gasoline. They also told us that we would have an AFEES Post Exchange on the FOB by November. Even though I'm greatly looking forward to buying a Butterfinger any time I want to, I'm not holding my breath yet. Though more than half a year seems like an adequate amount of time to set up a small store, I'll believe it when I see it. Army time is different time. Sometimes it moves at light speed; sometimes it simply moves infinitely slower than average. Mere mortals can't understand these things.

After extinguishing my smoke in the unexpected ashtray and laying it to rest next to a dozen other used up filter corpses, I return downstairs to quickly wake the rest of the squad. As predicted, Cloud is already on scene, simultaneously shaking Dick and Duke into consciousness.

I can hear Cloud speaking as I enter the bay, "Wake up, guys. We're going up top a little early today; grab your shit."

Freddy, wiping the sleep from his eyes, asks, "What's up, Sergeant?"

"We don't know much, but a bunch of Redwater types just got lit up about two miles west of here, in Fahad. One of their birds just reported that there is a force of eighty-something armed revolutionary-looking types heading this way in the mulhallas. We're going up top to see what we see. Make no mistake, all regular positions and shifts are stopping. Everyone, every squad, is going to battle stations, clear?"

Everyone seems a bit nervous. It's not every day that you awake to a sure, impending fight. Dick starts to laugh.

"Did you just say battle stations Sergeant?"

"Yeah, so?"

"Nothing."

The rest of the squad catches the contagious giggle, and Dick shouts loudly as he throws on his armor.

"Man your battle stations! Man your battle stations!"

The whole squad is openly laughing now. As always, with a little bit of nervousness and surprise comes giddy excitement. Each and every one of us wants kills. Every man wants a piece of the enemy. It's not every day that we get the chance, which is the frustrating reality of a ground war like ours. We're lucky if we ever get to see anything other than a muzzle-flash, let alone an advancing enemy force. Who knows? Today just might be our day.

The scouts are not the only soldiers hurriedly making ready in the bay. All around, extra soldiers from the other rotations are checking weapons and gear while getting ready to go to their designated posts to get ready for a thick fight.

Everyone quickly drinks water and inspects their equipment. As we don our armor there is a pronounced sense of hurry. If the report came in an hour ago, these unknown potential combatants could be anywhere. Even more alarming is that the insurgents in our neighborhood traditionally crutch on bombs and sneak attacks. If they move through a neighborhood together, they usually do so without weapons in view, with no kit, casually, looking every bit like unarmed, peaceful non-combatants. This is very strange indeed.

Before five minutes have passed all six of us are quickly and enthusiastically moving up the stairs while checking radio equipment, and checking the chambers of our weapons to make double sure that they're hot and ready to go.

The stairs don't feel tiring to me this afternoon. Instead, my quick legs impel my weightless-feeling body up the stairs without any effort at all.

As we pass the landings to the other levels I can see some, but mostly hear other squads making ready for battle in their assigned locations. Although common sense dictates that a full assault against an entrenched American force is an unlikely circumstance, it has also been made pretty clear to us that such a thing is not totally unheard of. Some terrorist types have a real big death wish and will stop at nothing to try to get to Allah a little bit quicker than everyone else. It's even better if they can try to steamroll some sectarian westerners while they brightly burn into cultic salvation.

Reaching the top floor, I head to the northwest facing room, the one with the M-240 Bravo and the prone-ready table. Freddy is pretty adamant about wanting to spend a little time behind the machine gun. I'd like a turn at it, but I can't argue with his enthusiasm, so I make ready for the day by cleaning off the lenses of the resident binoculars that never leave the station.

From down the hallway I can hear Dick and Duke setting up our two long guns in the northeast room, the M-24, and the Barrett 107. The Barrett is the long gun that I'm personally signed for, so after the events of the day, however they transpire, I'm sure to be the one to clean it.

Ensuring that he's locked and loaded and all set, Freddy asks me if I can see anything. I see a lot of things.

I see thousands of windows, both whole and broken, staring at me for thousands of meters all the way to the horizon. I can see straight down half a dozen of the straighter mulhallas for at least a couple hundred meters. To my right and below, a group of children is playing a heated match of soccer in a muddy field just under the hotel, and to my left masses of passersby and the occasional automobile trundle down the street, doubtless heading home after a busy day of shopping.

"Nothing yet, man."

Freddy is lying down a bit closer to the window than I am; however, his body is completely concealed from sight at street level due to the large amount of camouflaged netting that covers both the front end of the weapon system, and the window itself.

Slightly more exposed, I crouch on a knee on top of an old dresser about halfway back in the room. I'm far enough away from the window that I can see at least within twenty-five meters of the hotel from street level, but far enough back so as to be invisible to an enemy sniper.

Leery of the nearby buildings, some ten stories tall that stand about four hundred meters to the west, I start looking through my binoculars, focusing on windows one-by-one in hopes of seeing any movement at all.

"What do you see, Freddy?"

"Everything looks totally normal to me. Just people going about their daily business. No heavily armed crazies yet."

"They probably won't try to engage us from the street. If it was me out there I'd spend the afternoon making cozy fighting positions in neighboring buildings. They could get right up on us that way before popping off."

"I was just thinking the same thing."

Many soldiers underestimate the cunning and tenacity of the insurgency. Yes, the enemy might be ill-educated and overly fanatical, but that has nothing to do with how well they can fight. These people have the necessary combative street smarts. Some of the insurgents we're up against in these bad neighborhoods have undoubtedly been fighting for years. Some Iraqi youth, much like the warrior children of Africa, have been fighting turf wars in this city for the duration of their entire lives. Many of these people have never done anything but fight.

"No. Probably not from the street."

Taking leave of Freddy for a moment I make my way to the other post. When I get into the small room the other scouts are already set up. Sergeants Cloud and Dick are engaging in a behavior that mirrors mine, scanning with binoculars from positions deep back in the room, checking far into the distance, as well as moving up close to the window to examine different positions directly below us in the street.

"Ya'll ready to shoot something?" I say.

Cole, not taking his eye from the optic of the M-24, gives me a hearty affirmative reply.

"You fucking know it, man. It's about goddamn time."

From behind me I can hear footsteps approaching in the long hallway. When I peek my head out of the room to see who it is I'm greeted with the sight of SSGT Brass moseying his way up the hall in full kit.

"Howdy, Sergeant."

"How you doin', Pearce?"

"Just about fantastic. Come up top to see the view?"

"That's right."

As he enters the room he quietly strikes up a conversation with Cloud. As well as the proper NCO duties of informing each other of exactly where they've put their men, and with what weapons, they take the time to socialize a little bit and talk about the events of the morning so far. Not wanting to keep Freddy by himself for more than a minute, as that would be bad form, I head back to our position for the day.

"Well, no fucking foot patrol today maybe."

"Who knows, D." A brief pause. "If any other assets from the battalion get tasked out here to help, we may get to kick in a few doors today."

Although that's an enthusiastic fantasy, it simply won't be happening. Our platoon of twenty-five people, with really only twenty-two working combative roles, is very limited in how far we can spread our reach over the city.

Out on a mounted patrol, clearing sections of town and going door to door searching can be a pretty standard experience. We've engaged in the practice many times while working in different neighborhoods. That tactic here, based out from the JSS, is not a capability problem. It's a manpower problem. At all times, it takes no less than twenty people to secure the entire JSS. That's putting it mildly, as the more populated companies do the job with over thirty-five soldiers. With soldiers tasked into static guard positions protecting our barracks and our trucks, as well as the high-ground positions and radio shifts, that only leaves six to eight of us that can actively leave the JSS to fight the enemy. Of course, those are situations where the compound is not under the threat of immediate attack.

It's doubtful that the battalion would supply us with additional soldiers as well. Many of the other companies are in the same staffing and security conundrum as we are, with only about three hundred working soldiers between them, counting those left back at the FOB which include our medics, mechanics, and such.

Not even our own lieutenant is foolish enough to send six men out to fight sixty in a gunfight in their own neighborhood. That would be abject madness, especially in the day time. I can wrap my mind around doing a stealthy combat mission at night with only six of us, but never in the day. Logic says that would be a catastrophic failure.

If one man goes down in a fight, one man has to carry him. One armored, screaming, bleeding soldier is heavy to carry, and therefore slows down the entire squad. With only one casualty, a six man squad loses two of its guns and nearly all of its mobility, especially if immediate medical attention needs to be performed.

In a city like Baghdad, six men placed in that situation would rapidly become four. Then two. Then none, just like that. Our scout element is highly specialized, but very fragile. That's the brutal reality of the situation. I, for one, don't want to have a cameo holding a local newspaper on Youtube any time soon.

It would be a different story, and a different feeling, if we enjoyed the luxury of backup or additional infantry support. The idea, on paper, is that we are not alone. We're supposed to be here in the middle of town, quite among friends, what with the Iraqi police and army to help us. As illustrated by the bedlam last night, it's clear that, indeed, we are alone in the world, at least three miles away from any additional American ground support, other than the Strykers across the street from the 2nd CAV, or the occasional Apache CAS coverage courtesy of our avian friends, weather permitting.

The 2nd CAV is no longer actively patrolling; their casualty rates are too high, and last I heard, if we want birds this week we'd have to really need them, and call a good while in advance.

"We are so fucking alone in this part of town, Pearce."

"I know. Exciting, eh, Freddy? We've made it to the war, I believe. Don't sound so disturbed. We're making this place into a fucking fortress."

"You think this wall will stop an RPG?"

"You think an RPG can make it accurately all the way up to this fucking wall?"

Not the slightest bit worried about his life or well-being, Freddy laughs when he thinks about the logistics of the aforementioned situation.

We've had no less than eight RPGs fired at us in the last three months. They're easily recognizable because of the way they flip crazily through the air and impact far, far away from whatever they've been fired at. Dangerous and horrifying up close, the brand of rocket propelled grenade that Baghdadi locals have demonstrated to us are very old, and not well maintained.

Brand new, a modern RPG system is a weapon to behold. Easy to operate and incredibly accurate, they are the choice of militaries all over the world for destroying emplaced positions and vehicles alike.

Baghdad's RPGs are not new, nor the finest in the world. Baghdad's RPGs have problems. Most, if not all that we have seen, have had shot at us, or that we have confiscated are at least twenty, if not thirty years old. Arabs get these weapon systems from ex-Soviet and Eastern-block countries that have more use for selling them than using them. Which means most of the weapons sat mothballing for years before they made it to the desert, where they became used as walking sticks by Arabs who inadvertently filled them with dirt.

The actual grenade projectiles are quite beautiful brand new. I had the privilege of seeing many in New Orleans during the hurricane, along with some classic stielhandgranates. Also confiscated, they are a story for a different time. Long story short, most of the ordinance available in this country is old, discolored, bent, and rusted.

It's not a wise idea to smash a grenade around with a hammer, and even hajji extremists are smart enough to realize that. So, knowing of no other way to adequately repair the bent grenade fins which are meant to stabilize the weapons in flight, they simply fire the bastards off, bent or not. The result is always frightening, as well as comical. Hajji shoots off and says a prayer. I've even heard somewhat accurate stories from our interpreters that locals often place bets on where one will end up before the shot is fired. If one of these old weapons is used to good effect, it usually has to be from very close range.

Muhammad likes to shoot from a distance, so the threat facing us today is most likely going to come in the form of an AK-47 clutched in the dirty hands of a man in a black man-dress, standing slightly back in the shadows that the broken windows of the cityscape provide.

While scanning with my binoculars, I believe I see the shape of one such man, far back in his hide. I see his weapon, placed next to him leaning up against the back wall of the room. He appears to be having an earnest conversation on a cellular phone. It's pure luck that I'm able to see him; the rays of the sun are positioned in just such a way that I can see into the south-facing windows that look towards the JSS. The window that I'm looking into belongs to a structure that is nearly three hundred meters away, standing alone in a large dirt field of sorts, surrounded by piles of garbage.

"Freddy, got one. You see him?"

"If you're looking where I'm looking. Black robe, window, three hundred meters or so northwest, then yeah."

Foregoing radio transmissions, Dick shouts to us from down the hall. "Hey guys, you see all the movement by the market?"

Not only in the building that I'm currently spying on, but also in the mulhallas below and to the north, numerous would-be shoppers, now armed from some unseen cache no doubt planted in the darkness of the early morning, begin to take the shape of an armed horde, calmly walking into neighboring structures, as well as having their own cell phone conversations. It's clear that they're under the impression that nobody is watching them as they prepare for their assault. Here's one for good intel reports.

Other men, some armed and some not, move toward the JSS, making sure to stay out of the middle of the square, instead running along the periphery of neighboring buildings. Some men continue to maintain small groups as they calmly walk in our direction, while more individuals peel off from the main groups, disappearing into building facades and nearby mulhallas.

From behind my binoculars I shout down the hallway, "Yeah, we got 'em, Sergeant. You want me to call it down?"

"We just called them in. Talk says we're weapons free. Go loud!"

"Roger! Roger!"

Well, this is certainly an odd day.

Looking back to the window overlooking the market, I respond to Freddy's previous question, "That's the one. And, that makes two of us. Waste him."

"Never thought I'd see the day."

Freddy squeezes the trigger.

My ears start to ring before my mind registers the sound. The concrete room immediately burns into life with the sound of 7.62 rocking as I peer at the enemy position, trying again to find my focus through my own weapon optic.

The M-240 Bravo is a beast. It's my favorite, and it's angry. Freddy continues to fill the room with its pissed off reverberations in short

173

3-5 round bursts. No need for him to lay down on the trigger and go cyclic on a single target. After the space of about five seconds and three bursts, he silences the gun.

More gunfire erupts at the other end of the hallway as the other scouts open fire on their targets. In a flash, the square below empties itself of the armed men, and the view immediately presents itself as the view from a ghost town postcard.

Looking through my rifle's optic, I find the window where I originally saw the would be hero, and see nothing. No man, and only one or two errant pockmarks that betray Freddy's own automatic fire on the outside of the window. He must have made good shot-groups on the inside.

"You get him?"

"If he was standing in the same place where he was when I opened up."

From down the hallway, amidst the fire from the scouts in the other room firing both the M-24 and their M-4s, Dick calls out to us.

"You motherfuckers getting any?"

"Yeah; some! What have you guys got?"

Radio discipline goes straight the fuck to Hell. They know we're here. We made them absolutely sure of that. Shouting is now the protocol of the day. Automatic weapons are rocking off all throughout the JSS now, and noise discipline has also gone out the window along with the opening discharge of Freddy's weapon.

I have no trouble hearing the conversation, but I have to strain a little through the newfound ringing in my ears. Though not comfortable, it's invigorating in its own right; a staunch reminder of what is happening at present. The smell of spent shell casings and gunpowder fills our small room, and I become aware of the growing, uncomfortable heat of the day.

Below us and outside, as well as echoing up to our position from the depths of the stairwell, a flurry of single-shot weapons fire noise fills the air, signaling that the rest of D Co down below us have targets as well.

More fire comes from the street. Finally, those of the enemy now entrenched in fighting positions or who are unlucky enough to be caught in the street or market square see fit to return fire at us. The gunfire starts to land in random windows, on random floors of the JSS. Camo netting has been hung across nearly every window, so the enemy would have to be very lucky to pick the right one. I can hear a salvo of AK rounds impact the brickwork a few stories below, but there's no sign yet of the scouts

174

being in immediate danger.

Suddenly I see two fighters quickly running across an open mulhalla, toward the building where Freddy just wasted infidel Exhibit A.

Believing I have a good shot, I quickly squeeze off five rounds at the running insurgents as they cross the small path.

"I think my last two were late."

The shots feel good, but a kill is uncertain as the targets, under fire from others of our ilk, are halfway across the street when I engage them.

A 5.56 round doesn't kill a man. It wounds him, so that he can crawl someplace safe and bleed to death. NATO believes it's a more humane round because the wound is smaller. I beg to disagree. Given the choice, I'd take a 7.62 any day. Death would come quicker. Much quicker.

After the scouts and D Co pick off our first easy targets the combat becomes a loud, sinister version of 'Whack-a-Mole.' Minutes pass with no movement or gunfire, with our time spent waiting for an enemy to do something foolish. Every once in a while, hajji becomes bold enough to fire from a window or make a run for different cover, each in kind trying to make it ever closer to the JSS. It's clear that their attack was not supposed to begin yet, and we've interrupted their peaceful morning tea time. What the fuck did they think we were doing here anyhow?

Our first hour goes by with nothing out of the ordinary, save for random gunfire from different fighting positions below, or shots from the other scouts. On three occasions I engage different targets. Although the movement always disappears after I fire, not once do I see the body of a man I killed, lying gloriously in a pool of blood like a bandit in a wild west film. I soon tire of endlessly searching windows in the far buildings, so I round my binoculars on the street, where I scan our field of fire looking for suspicious behavior of any kind, or people trying to hide weapons.

I pay extra attention to the contents of push carts and donkey wagons as they pass, but after surveying the thirty or so that I can see from my vantage point, I glean nothing definitive. It may very well be a long day indeed. As the brunt of the gunfire ebbs, dozens of Arabs emerge once again out into the street to go about their daily business, as if the random bullets whizzing through the air do not bother them in the slightest.

"Hey, Freddy, why don't you just stick your head out the window and politely ask if somebody is hiding anything, where they are, and what they look like?"

"How about I flip my shit to cyclic and waste every man, woman, and mother-fucking child in the street and be done with it. Maybe after that they'll send me home."

"Oh, sure they will. Straight the fuck home on the first, finest red-eye that Uncle Sam can muster up. You'd be in for it then."

Freddy softy laughs to himself. As always, even though lying behind a machine gun, aiming constantly at civilians, checking for anything and everything amiss, Freddy remains one of the sanest, most giving Christians I have ever met. He jokes hard about killing innocent people or about how his mother is a whore, but it stops there. Just jokes after all.

"You have a very healthy, very special sense of humor, Freddy."

"True dat, foo. True dat."

"Man, you really do love being a turtle."

"No other choice but to love man."

He reaches under himself and rights a fold in his blouse, making the wear of his armor more comfortable before moving his hands and eyes back to the gun.

"No other choice. You want to work at Wal-Mart?"

"Nope, brother-man, can't say that I do."

I assume from the lack of new fires across the market square that we're slowly being surrounded. In this urban environment, snaking through mulhallas and back alleys to cover the distance to the JSS in cover and concealment would be a simple matter. From the conversations drifting down the hallway, I can tell I'm not the only soldier thinking such thoughts. Maybe we've killed five men, or twenty, but it doesn't matter number-wise if the reports from this morning are to be believed. From the accuracy of the reporting thus far, I'm inclined to keep listening. I keep scanning my sector with Freddy, every once in a while breaking away to have a look out the windows on the other side of the building, scanning and examining yet another endless city-scape. Everyone is sure that the fight isn't over. We didn't deter them from three hundred meters, no less in a single hour. We're being surrounded.

Four hours pass with little to report. Most of the crowds have now gone, and in the light of the rapidly setting sun Freddy and I continue our vigil. We watch. We wait. We watch some more. It's not yet a regular shift, and it doesn't appear that things will return to normal today.

Being the somewhat sensible man that he is, our LT will hear none of it. An attack is imminent. There are an unknown number of armed hostiles looking at our positions right now, readying themselves for another attack. That has become the gospel truth, and nothing in the world will change it.

Our squad is still well rested, and we pass the time by making periodic visitations to each other's positions to have small, quick conversations about the events of the day, and then return to our posts to look at more of the same: everything, and nothing.

I think about home for a while, and then I think about Emily for a bit. Usually I upbraid myself for thinking such cruel thoughts while the sun is up, for the specific reason that sleep, and any subsequent release is far, far away.

Far away. Far away. She wore it for her soldier boy who's far, far away.

My thoughts drift to the peace and quiet of my brother's backyard, as well as to my parents' homes, and the times I've spent with Emily in those places on leave.

They play softly on, like a silent movie in the back of my brain, as my eyes endlessly grate over the blasted city again, and again, and again.

Conversation between Freddy and I is no longer an entertainment option, as we've played it out already. Instead, we busy ourselves with radio checks to the talk, telling them that we're still looking, and periodically fire off one question radio checks to the other positions to make sure coms are still up, as well as to remind ourselves that we are still awake, and alert.

"There's no place like home."

A brief pause, and Freddy replies, "What, are you fucking Dorothy now? Don't ask, don't tell."

"Since you mention it, I'd say Dorothy and I go way back. Right now, I wouldn't mind having a quick Technicolor fu-"

Automatic weapons fire erupts from a set of low buildings about two hundred meters away, dead center and just to the right of our field of fire.

I can see movement in the street, but no muzzle flash, as it's not quite late in the afternoon yet. Taking a knee, I look through my optic towards the origin of the gunfire.

"Freddy, you see it?"

"Not yet. Lookin' though."

Unable to see anything but running women, children, and unarmed

177

men in the city streets below, I grab the handheld short-wave radio and report the contact.

"Delta One-Four, this is High-Ground Two, we have contact to the north-northwest, how copy, over."

"High-Ground Two, you are cleared to engage. Call in additional information when you can, over."

"Copy, out."

The radio transmission is quick and to the point. It's intentionally brief, so I can get back to doing my job.

More contact opens up to our front, but Freddy still cannot see a target to engage.

Below us, from the belly of the JSS, another M-240B opens fire, and it's very clear that somebody else can see the thing we seek.

Out the window and just below our position, I can hear the tell-tale pops and thuds of automatic weapon's fire striking the building just below our floor. Doubtless, the enemy does not have an exact target for their fires. They simply know that Americans are in the building, and that they want to shoot us. It proves to be an immediately ineffective enterprise.

While continuing to search my sector, I use the handset to call over to the scouts in the next room, to find out what they can see. I get a brief reply back that they can't see shit.

Before the fires lull for more than a few seconds, we hear more shooting that sounds like it's originating far to the east. Which could be anywhere, given the stony nature of the room we're living in.

Without delay, the recognizable report of the scout's M-24 announces its presence throughout the building.

The gunshots echoing through the concrete hallway exhilarate me. We finally made it to fucking contact in a high-ground position, just like we're fucking supposed to do. Hallelujah.

Suddenly from another window, a dark, not quite square recess in a three story building, I see what I know, believe, and understand to be a small arms muzzle flash from a man standing much too close to the window for his own personal safety.

Fully attuned to the third world and my place in it, I can feel the tremors of adrenalin start to rack my body. The world seems to shift somehow, and my body feels lighter.

The acrid-sweet smell of cordite and gunpowder fills the room as Freddy starts rocking on the gun once again. I see another target in a window, closer this time, and ride the adrenal wave anew, putting five well-placed rounds into my target.

Freddy's gun goes quiet. "Ammo!"

"Got it."

I quickly leave my position and hop down to the floor, grabbing another two hundred round can of ammo for Freddy. I quickly draw the rounds out, as the case was already opened to facilitate a fast reload, and hand Freddy the business end of the belt.

As he is no stranger to the weapon, his reload goes smoothly. With great haste, rounds are gently laid into the feed-tray and aligned, one round in, beneath the feeder claw. After the claw is dropped, Freddy slaps the feed-tray cover shut and charges the weapon with a healthy sounding clink.

"Combat test-fire!"

Once again, the room fills with the din of healthy 7.62 bursts. Our exclamation of test fire comes across as mostly a joke, as the weapon was to be fired, test or no, as soon as reloading was complete.

Moving back to my position, I start looking for another target.

A burst of AK fire blasts through our window, invading our cozy little room. It looks like they finally found us. One of the sandbags in front of Freddy shakes and sputters a small plume of dirt, while the wall to the rear of our room takes a pounding. Six smacks in all, the rounds hit flat on the concrete at the back of our position and thankfully do not ricochet. Hell of a good group for an AK too. Praise for decent automatic marksmanship aside, I'm going to kill the bastard.

Outside my window, rejuvenated somehow, the gunfire grows thicker. It's louder, and becoming closer every minute.

There is no need for me to call up enemy numbers on the radio. The net is already frantic with soldiers and NCOs calling out enemy positions, of which there must be twenty, if not forty.

I aim at another suspect window and pull the trigger.

In the building below us an entire platoon is shooting, squawking on the net, and shouting.

Together, the roar of the sniper system in the other room coupled with the reports of my own weapon, and Freddy steadily rocking along form a sort of chorus that is accompanied by the rhythmic thumping of twenty guns below.

Outside, from the direction of our enemies, comes wave after wave of gunfire. In the growing cacophony I can hear a man painfully screaming in Arabic, echoing his misery across the expanse of concrete and open space. The man is obviously seriously wounded, or has just lost his mind. My radio crackles again.

"All positions, all positions, this is Delta One-Four, break."

The break signals a pause, and Freddy and I listen as best we can through the cloud of gunfire.

"The IPs are leaving, break; I say again, the IPs are leaving, over."

A sergeant down below responds to the chatter, "What do you mean they're leaving, over?"

"I say again, we don't know why, but the Iraqi policemen are leaving the police station in droves."

The following silence from the radio signals that there is simply no more to say about the matter.

Freddy blasts his gun again.

"What the *fuck*, dude. Worthless pieces of shit!"

Alone in the world, the twenty-eight of us continue our fight. Our only allies in the compound are leaving, letting us deal with what they perceive is only our problem, and not theirs. It's not difficult for the Iraqis to forget that this fight is not an American war, but rather, it is a chance for the Iraqi people to regain their own country. My family in Nevada could give a shit about Muhammad and his AK. These fucktards will have none of it though. Rather than pursuing freedom and peace in their local neighborhoods, they'd rather get falafels and let us fight in their stead.

"This country will always be a fucking shithole.

"You said it buddy. No end in sight."

The fight drags on, slowly losing its tempo, until after the space of twelve hours and under the cover of total darkness, the desert city becomes blissfully silent once again.

Cloud pays us a visit in our position to make sure we're still good on ammo. Knowing that we need a few dozen more magazines and a half dozen fresh cans for Freddy, I volunteer along with Cole, to make the necessary supply run to the bottom of the building. Can't fight a war without bullets these days. If only I could stand behind a tower-shield and stab a gladius into Hajji... That would really be something.

Deciding, quite against the grain of battalion recommendations, that we don't need body armor to go down the stairs, we make our run with nothing but our weapons and undershirts. Pants and boots too, of course.

180

As we quickly hop down the stairs to make our journey more expedient, we can still hear the sounds of a small fight coming from somewhere outside the stairwell windows. Currently the trucks, two of which have been mobilized, are having a small fight of their own at the east gate.

The Browning .50 caliber machine guns cough their angry lead into the Baghdad night in sporadic bursts; not too frequently though, as targets that dare to show their heads are gradually becoming fewer and farther between.

It's highly likely that most of the attacking force have either been killed or have fled by now, overwhelmed by the gunpowder and lead of the good old US of A.

Not caring to continue the long journey to the bottom of the stairs in total silence, I pose a question to Cole.

"I could really use a stiff drink about now. You?"

"In my fondest fucking wishes and dreams. Got Cope though."

"Hey, it's supposed to satisfy."

"Damn right it does."

"Care if I lift a pinch off you?"

"Go ahead."

Cole flips me the healthily weighted can as we round the last stairwell at the bottom of our decent. With little time to worry about socializing, we don't bother to consult with the rest of the platoon, but instead, we travel directly past the open bay to the area behind the reception desk, one flight down, where our ammunition supply is stored.

One flight down,

There's a song,

And it drifts like smoke.

Dismissing the unwanted intrusion of one of my favorite songs, I banish Norah Jones from my mind.

By the time we reach the cans and pre-filled magazines I already have a new wad of moist, delicious dip in my mouth, and so I flip back the can back to Cole, who deftly catches it.

Before grabbing spare ammo cans for Freddy, I take the time to grab personal ammunition for myself, replacing four of my spent magazines with fresh ones from the cache.

Cole busily starts filling a bandoleer full of fresh magazines, as the rest of the squad up top has fired considerably more 5.56 rounds than Freddy and I.

After stocking up on magazines, I grab four new cans of ammunition for Freddy, two handles clutched in each hand. It may not be enough to totally plus up the position; if it isn't, myself or somebody else will doubtless make this quick trip again to grab what is needed.

After the short vertical trip and another small conversation regarding booze fantasies, we once again reach the top of the stairs.

By the time our ascent is complete the gunfire from the truck-mounted fifties has stopped. Blessedly, the city no longer sounds like it's about to swallow us.

I bid adieu to Cole and make my way back to my position.

Dropping the ammo cans at Freddy's feet, as he is now standing, having himself a little bit of a stretch, I marvel at the fact that nobody was hit this afternoon. Not a single scratch on any one of us.

"It's funny that the IPs would leave. It doesn't really seem like it's turning out to be too hazardous of a day."

Jovial, and in a chipper sounding mood despite the late hour, Freddy replies, "I know, right? You think they would have stayed to develop more of those 'bold Arab soldier' bragging rights. Guess not."

"Guess not."

"There's really something to be said of cowardice, however."

"Or a good old-fashioned buy-out. It's more than likely that somebody simply paid them off."

"You have a good point there, Freddy. Probably paid them in foot-bread."

"Big money that, don't cha know."

"Understood."

Settling into our respective guard positions once again, Freddy and I survey the nearby streets, as well as buildings and potential fighting positions all the way out to the horizon.

Where the market and surrounding apartments and streets were mostly quiet before the world started to disintegrate, now the neighborhood has become a complete and utter ghost town. Tonight, unlike any other usual night, not even the wild dogs are barking, doubtless startled away by the massive amount of gunfire in the afternoon.

"I could really use a nap right about now."

"Yeah. You and the rest of us."

The night outside my window is a post-apocalyptic bas-relief, carved entirely in hues of green and black stone. Inside our hide, the blackness is complete, and through my unassisted eye I can barely make out Freddy's silhouette.

In the total darkness and the safety it provides, I open my newly donned body armor's Velcro a bit at the top and recline against the wall, slightly nearer to the window than before, in an attempt to get a breeze of any kind from the outside world.

Although the heavy smell of gunfire has already started to leave our room, the smell of dirty soldier has not. The heat is stifling within my armor, and the breeze I seek is not anywhere near cold. Instead, it's the lukewarm tease of an early summer's night, that in a fashion most cruel, reminds me in the fondest way of home.

The fight comes and goes throughout the night. Though not yet having reached a state of sleepy delirium, I could really use a rest.

The initial thrill of the engagement has long since passed, and I no longer feel surges of adrenaline or fear. Instead, myself and the rest of the crew have adopted the mindset of construction workers, road crews, or long haul truckers. We just have to perform until the job is done.

Information comes down over the net that the enemy has been reinforced by neighboring Al' Qaida forces, but largely, we are not concerned.

So far in the fight, the enemy have been lucky to advance to within two hundred meters of the JSS, so it is rather unlikely that they will be storming our barracks in force any time soon.

Perhaps if they had the manpower and bravery to wage a full assault against us with a hundred soldiers we would be in real trouble. But they won't, and we're not.

For them, the cruel reality of the situation is that they made a big mistake: a AAA grade fuck-up, and they're paying for it now with dozens and dozens of dead and wounded, and doubtless as many deserters. The waning fire signals to us that we've broken their spirit, at least for the night.

A double plus, the night is our time. The night is when we train. It's where we feel the safest, operate cleanest, and also where we have the definitive edge in technology.

Regardless of our good luck and ample performance through the fight thus far, reinforcements or a shift change are not coming. Battalion command has decided in all of its infinite wisdom that life should carry on, as far as platoon rotations are concerned, by the decree of the already established calendar.

Whether we like it or not, the JSS is under our command for the next four days.

Our only real concern is that D Co and the scouts together possess only twenty-four working soldiers. Currently, there are over thirty-five positions that need to be filled, including the four trucks, high-ground, fighting positions, and duties at the talk and barracks CQ.

Until we're told otherwise, we're going to be awake.

At 0400 gunfire breaks out again. Though not as dense as in the previous afternoon, impacts from bullets continue to pepper our position, and we fire back in turn.

I give ammunition to Freddy when he needs it, and make the occasional trip down the hallway for a generalized situation report from the rest of the scouts. The situation is groovy.

Other than using my laser to point at suspect movement behind the occasional vehicle or an ominously flashing window, primarily to spot for Freddy, there are no huge engagements in the night. There are no Hollywood John Woo dives out the window where I empty my magazine into a mass of advancing terrorists while surrounded by a flock of doves.

A flash appears in the night like a cheap firework, or a flashing headlight. We shoot at it, and it vanishes. Sometimes the position stays quiet, leading us to believe that we have a kill. Other times, the fire simply opens up again from another location nearby. It's not an assault at this point, just mild harassment. However, a bullet shot in jest can kill you as easily as a well-intentioned one.

By the time the morning breaks, the world has grown quiet.

Potential shoppers and other pedestrians trickle from their dwellings to engage in their morning rituals; they set up shanty market stalls, or socialize over cups of chai.

All the while, through sleepy eyes, we watch the scene unfold, constantly on alert, looking for signs that the fighting is not yet over.

Hours and hours drag on without end.

Freddy and I speak to one another in earnest now about anything and everything, in an effort to stay awake. It's simple to do with a partner. Approaching thirty hours without sleep, alone, the task of staying awake would prove itself much more painful.

Sweating once again in my armor, I scan the jagged horizon and

184

streets again, and again, looking for signs of hostiles moving, or civilians appearing to move anything that looks like a weapon.

To stay awake we drink water; more than we really need to stay hydrated. The exercise of blearily moving the wet, heavy bottle gives me a momentary task: it's an effort to stay awake, basic training style.

Periodically, Freddy or me will move to the other room to converse with the others, imprisoned on the top floor as we are. With no enemy contact in the last six hours, our new adversary has become fatigue, and we do anything we can to stave it off.

Though the idea of sleep is blissful, it is an unnecessary risk. If one man were to rest, giving the other man a solo-watch, the lone guard would most certainly fall sleep.

There are still more positions to be filled than can be, so we double down, and buckle ourselves further into our never-ending shift.

Every once in a while Freddy and I take turns taking off our body armor to step out into the hallway for a brief reprieve.

Dip is no longer having a positive effect on me, so I've turned to coffee grounds instead. Dipped, the instant coffee grounds give me a satisfying but temporary pick me up. As an alternative, or simultaneously, I step into the hallway and smoke two cigarettes at a time. This gives me a new, brooding fear that I'm exceeding my self-imposed ration, and will run out of nicotine before we return to the FOB. All is not lost though; after my next four packs of Marlboros are gone I can always defer to local brands. Though not quite the *Ritz Deluxe*, they'll do the trick in a pinch, dog-shit taste and all.

Other than substance abuse, we turn to PT.

It's almost impossible to fall asleep while doing jumping jacks or pushups, so as Freddy and I take our revolving turns in the hallway, we work ourselves almost to death, jumping and jumping, pushing and pushing, all the while remaining awake and alert, in a constant effort to hear transmissions from the radio, as well as to listen for sounds of the firefight renewing itself.

Most assuredly, that would give us something to do.

The fighting has worn thin. With still no casualties to speak of, the 82nd airborne stands triumphant, still staking claim to our own private block in the very center of town.

Though half-assed sporadic gunfire pops up every now and then, there is nothing that compares to the lengthy battles of the day before yesterday.

Below us, the truck gunners and line squads of D Co have started to take rest shifts, with half the force down at all times. The scouts have been told that we will get our much deserved rest after battalion command gives the all clear, which, God willing, should be any moment.

Freddy and I, as well as the rest of the scout squad, decided to break proper protocol as of an hour ago, through force of sheer exhaustion. Going on nearly sixty hours without sleep, we're as combat effective as the living dead; we're submitting to nature, and going one up, one down amongst ourselves.

At 0300 I decide to give Freddy the first naptime shift, one hour long, which I will wake him from to take my turn. I'm hoping against hope that this whole fracas will be over with and done before then, so I can settle into some real sleep. I have the notion that any small nap I take will simply not do the trick.

Out of boredom, the scout squads have shifted rooms. Freddy and I have migrated to control the sniper systems, as well as to survey the northeast corner, while Dick and Cole have taken up positions in our previous location.

This room, the primary hide, is much more spacious and accommodating than the small room where we have spent the last fifty hours, so I am afforded the opportunity to pace back and forth, to and fro whilst waiting for the shift to end, as well as periodically surveying my field of fire and the great nothing beyond.

The last of the contacts died down hours ago, and little of note occurs in Baghdad at three AM if there is no problem to be found.

Though on my feet and diligently pacing about the room, I feel my head begin to nod. Trying to fight my way through the fatigue, I press on through my silent vigil and ignore it.

I'm rudely and suddenly awakened when my bobbing, walking body smashes boldly into the concrete wall of the hide, immediately shooting sparkles of light and pain through my head. I suppose I should have been wearing a helmet.

Roughly awakened by my sleepwalking oops, I decide that a smoke is in order. It's my second to last one that I'm permitting myself until noon the following day, where I will allow myself to open the last pack of my favorite brand.

Stepping out of the room so as not to be a visible smoker from the street, I step into the hallway, slightly aside from the doorjamb. My observation post has now become a listening post. In my opinion, for now, that will do just fine. Better a listening post than a sleeping post, and right now, I'm positively looped. I've read somewhere that a lack of sleep can kill you, but in my humble life, I have yet to die from such nonsense.

I light my cigarette with my hands carefully cupped around my Zippo to kill the light as much as possible. Though difficult to believe, it's not impossible to imagine that some of the hostile forces in the city may have had night vision optics fall into their hands, so one can never be too careful.

I prefer Zippos to regular lighters. I suppose it's the dependability and quality of the thing, provided you conduct regular maintenance. As a soldier, such tasks are not merely doleful chores, but sometimes are sought out simply to pass the time. You cannot spend a good hour taking care of your Bic lighter. With Zippos, cotton filling needs to be changed, fresh lighter fluid needs to be applied, fresh flints need to be loaded into the system, and every once in a while, a full tweezing escapade is in order. Wicks need to be cut, lengthened, or replaced. Quite stately in my opinion, the traditional lighter adds a burst of class to the whole dirty business of smoking, and adds a sheen of quality that is not to be found with a plastic piece of shit. If you stoke it right, it won't spontaneously run out on you, leaving you high, dry, and flameless. Also, there is a pretty wicked pirate skull on mine that I'm rather fond of, and it lives in a position that is easily accessible in a small, button-up leather utility pouch that hangs daily from my belt. Can't beat that. That, and Zippo tricks are most amusing.

Snapping my lighter closed, holstering it without much flair or flash, I take my first drag of the first cigarette I've had in hours, and immediately I feel better.

The cool, dry, flavorful smoke fills my lungs with a minty goodness, and though I know the feeling is fleeting and temporary, it revitalizes me somehow. Immediately, evil sleep is held at bay and I feel more wakeful. I take a furtive glance at my watch. 0315. Forty-five minutes until sainted naptime.

Thinking about Emily while falling into a sort of smoker's reverie, I'm startled half-awake out of my smoky haze by footsteps heavily approaching from the main stairwell.

I feel a fear that only a soldier can. That could be one of my buddies coming up the stairs to chat, or an understanding platoon sergeant. In either of those cases, I'm golden. And, the company will be nice. On the other hand, it could be a Sergeant Major or LT coming up for an impromptu inspection of the diligent fighting positions. If that were the case, I'm doubtful I would be given much slack or credit for having been awake these last sixty hours. Smoking inside? No-no. Letting your buddy take a nap? No-no. Not having a helmet on? Also, you guessed it, it's a big fat no-no. I could be totally fucked, and in for some pushups, or perhaps even a stripe removal. Technically, by stepping into the hallway I have abandoned my post.

Fully awake, resigning to the fact that I can't properly extinguish the smoke, get rid of the smell, dress myself appropriately, and wake Freddy in time, I stand as I am, doing what I'm doing, waiting in mute apprehension to see what manner of dark force impels itself towards me from the gray concrete depths.

A deep, gravelly voice, thankfully one that I know and love, emerges from the top of the stairwell.

"What the fuck do you think you're doing?"

"Doing what I do. How are you this fine evening, Chapps?"

"I decided not to turn in quite yet. Doesn't seem right, seeing as you poor, oh-so-special fuckers are still awake."

"You scared the ever-loving *fuck* out of me. I didn't know who was coming up the fucking stairs at this early hour, and I'm not exactly what you would call army-standard battle ready at the moment."

"I really wouldn't sweat it. We've been in a real deal here. Smag would probably tell you to remain as you are, and commend the whole high-ground for a job well done. Everybody's still up in arms as a matter of formality. It's pretty clear that we made them tuck-tail and run away – those that lived."

"I certainly hope so. I'm due for some good naptime, I think."

"Are the others down?"

"I'm letting Freddy take a rest. Sergeant Cloud is in the talk, I believe, and Duke and Cole are taking the other room. I have no idea where Dick is. Probably jerking off to stay awake or some shit."

"Been a long night."

"How is it below?"

Chapel takes a Camel Wide from a modified chemical decontamination kit that he keeps just for the purpose, as the plastic container keeps cigarettes dry in the rain, and lights one up to join me in the hallway.

"Mind if I bum one of those from you? The rest of mine are way down under."

"Sure thing, greenhorn."

Chapel and I are close. You can tell, because we don't keep track of the cigarette commerce anymore. I know he'll always have one for me, just like I'll always have one for him, and that's just the way it is.

Unceremoniously grinding my dead cigarette under my boot, I happily take the new victim from him, and proceed to immediately light it on fire.

"Two more days here, then back to the FOB for laundry and hot chow."

"And the dad-gummed inter-webz Chapel. Don't forget the inter-webz."

"If we're not on blackout, as usual."

"Yeah. At least we won't be to blame this time."

Chapel and I finish our smokes, mostly enjoying the silence of good company. Just as fast as he appeared, he vanishes down the stairwell, and once again I'm alone with nothing but the darkness, my thoughts, and the short, slowly smoldering cigarette.

Tiring of the act of smoking, I crush the cigarette out like so many others that have gone before it, and enter the room again, resuming my post, protecting the free world from the unholy wrath of the infidel scourge.

0340.

I know a nap won't do my any good. Besides, the small chat with Buddy-Dude One and a nicotine overload has given me a second wind, so I resolve to myself that I will stand watch until the sun rises. What's a few more hours? Anyhow, Freddy was just about to lose his mind, having exhausted himself with pushups, and having already sung every Third Eye Blind song he could think of three times over.

When I sleep, I will sleep the sleep of the dead. Until that time, I will content myself to stare at more empty dirt and bricks.

I tell myself that if I start to wane again I still have one more cigarette.

Barring that, giving up on my pride, I could always wake Freddy and take a swing at this whole naptime concept once and for all.

Settling in behind my gunner's port in the walled-up window of sandbags, I lean forward with my hands on my knees, rifle slung across my back, and helmet still off.   If the fighting stops and we can get away with it, the scouts will take it off, I can assure you of that.

Gazing out at the blackness with both eyes, one biological and one enhanced with the optic, I take in the scene one more time.

Signaling the true end of the fight, the dogs are back.   Their plaintiff wailing carries on the warm pre-dawn air as they tell me stories about hunting for food, or being lost and alone.

Not wearing my helmet, the mount of the day for my night-vision optic is a skull-crusher: a small series of rather uncomfortable nylon and rubber straps that encircle the head, supporting the technology without the need of a helmet and the corresponding mount.

Desiring a more natural, less cybernetic view, I flip up the nods, leaving them on my head in case I need to quickly inspect something at a moment notice.

Mostly, without enhancement, the night is black and blue.

The square silhouettes of plain buildings are accompanied by the round spires of mosques and other decorative structures that appear like phantoms against the bright blue night sky.

Sporadically, around my field of view the occasional streetlight or electric lantern casts yellow and orange glows around the city.

My eyes are drawn to a rooftop just below the JSS that is near enough to see clearly, but not so close to our building that I have to lean out any further to accurately see the entire roof.

In the still of the night,

As I gaze out my window,

At the moon in its flight,

My thoughts all drift to you.

Thanks, Mr. Porter.   I needed that.

In the soft, low light of an electric lamp, an Arabian couple, disclosed to me only by their silhouettes, is sitting on a low bench on their apartment rooftop.

Peaking my interest, as they are the only other living people in view, I focus on them as best I can and simply watch.

A young couple, I decide, from the look of the man, as I can make out no beard in the dim light.

Wondering what they're doing out so early, I return my attention once again to the unmoving skyline, but then bring my gaze back to the couple, for nothing else is yet moving this morning.

Seeing them together puts me in a good mood.   It's wonderful to see that even amidst the worst of all circumstances, two people can still hold each other. Because of the early hour, I can only assume that they are generally happy, just enjoying each other's company, and are most likely in love.

They sit close together, obviously moving back and forth, innocently kissing each other's lips in the pale orange light, as they lean their heads in close together to speak and share secrets that nobody else is allowed to hear.

Being way out of earshot, I don't care to put my nods down to try to snoop and lip-read. I'm a bit too far away for that, and I don't speak conversational Arabic. I wouldn't get too much out of a full-fledged eavesdropping spy session.

I feel the cozy, begging feeling of fatigue and sleepiness all over my body now, and long more than ever for a good night's rest. Rather than giving up and waking Freddy, I'm transfixed by the young couple and privately delight in my secret voyeurism. As this man and this woman, who I don't know, talk and laugh and cuddle while gazing at the stars above, I can't help but feel a kinship with them.

I want those things. I'm looking forward to those things. I'll someday have those things again. It does my heart good to see them, and I imagine me and Emily there, laughing as we secretly talk the night away, lost in each other.

At about five-thirty I sit triumphant, having not succumbed to the evil clutches of illegal, dangerous sleep. I know my time will come soon.

As I look at the horizon I think I can detect it brightening a bit, in anticipation of the full sunrise that is to come. Combing the horizon once again, I'm met with the feeling of satisfaction; the fight is over, and our endless shift will soon be done.

Deciding to finally give in and wake Freddy, I look one last time at my couple, who have been sitting quietly all night now, presumably to watch the sunrise together.

I'm shocked, and awed, and empty, when I find that my lovers are pieces of drying laundry hung across a bench beneath an open window with large, irregular stones about its opening.

I look again, closely now, at once highly disappointed, but also very interested at how my mind forged the lines of their bodies and faces out of the flat, empty, soulless stones of an abandoned rooftop. I *know* they were there. They were there, and alive, and happy, as plain as day.

Still looking in disbelief at inanimate objects that moments ago were

191

happy lovers, still trying to second guess myself or make sense of what I have seen, I become aware of footsteps in the hallway once again.

This time they are not alarming, originating from the other hide site rather than from down the stairwell.

Leaning away from my window on the city, I look over my shoulder, back at the doorway, in anticipation of whoever it is that's about to enter.

"Everybody awake in here?"

"Just me, Sergeant."

It's Dick, hopefully come to bear good news.

Just like me, he looks like a fucking zombie.

I say, "Is it in your head?"

"What's that, D?"

"You know. The Zombie, of Cranberries fame."

"Oh, that. Yes it is."

"What's the word then?"

"The bird is."

Without another bird, Dick takes a seat across from me atop one of the low tables that we've recently re-appropriated as a Bench of Restfulness +4.

Without the handheld short-wave walkie-talkie, my position has been dark on communications for upwards of four hours, as Cloud decided that the radio should stay near the heavy gun. That, and if we have a real emergency, help is only a shout down the hallway.

"We're going to stand down and resume normal rotations again at 0600."

Ecstatic with the news, I hurriedly glance down at my watch.

0545.

"Fuck me, that's fantastic!"

I don't make an attempt to hide my jubilation, and I quickly start to don my gear in anticipation of the short trek downstairs to the bay. The best part is, I have one pre-naptime smoke left.

"Hey, Pearce, when was the last time you ate, man?"

I draw a blank. As I strap on my body armor and rack, clicking my weapon into my quick release, I look thoughtfully at the floor through my tired eyes and give the question some good thought.

"What day is it?"

"Friday, I think."

"Wednesday night then, maybe."

"Yeah. I don't think I've eaten since Tuesday. I'm more

concerned with sleep right now, but we should all definitely eat something."

Sometimes Dick can be a bit endearing. He is a handsome man, though he's a bit short. Through his incessant, nonstop bullshit and pride-mongering, every once in a while I get a glimpse of the NCO that he tries to be. Apparently, not sleeping for three days has dried the bullshit right out of him, and to myself, I think a slight soliloquy of almost positive thoughts about him. Times like these, the NCO in him tries its best to shine through. I concur, and I approve of his message.

"You know, I hadn't really thought about it, but I am hungry as fuck. I wonder if they have an elephant meal in the MRE menu?"

He chuckles a bit at my feeble attempt at exaggerated humor, yawns, and leans back on the bench, stretching his spine as best he can in his constricting armor, palming the centers of his eyes with each hand, trying to wipe the sleep away. From the bleary, bloodshot look in his eyes that I can see through the brightening morning light, his attempt at wakefulness has failed; he remains as glazed-over as me.

Having assembled, donned, and otherwise collected my assortment of battle-rattle, I gently shake Freddy awake, experiencing a brief moment of pride in my charity, as he has been sleeping contentedly and soundly, not stirring over the recent conversation.

"Hey, Freddy, time to wake up man. Time to pack up."

"Is the war over?"

Though grasping at humor, the quickly thought out and sleep-drunk comment makes all of us laugh out loud.

Dick decides to prod him on, "Yeah. Grab your shit; you can go night-night in cot-cot land now."

"Not yet then, maybe. The war I mean."

Freddy stands up and stretches, completely disregarding the imminent sniper threat outside as he yawns deeply and says, "I think I need to make a couple of plop-plops before going night-night again."

Just like that, we've mentally regressed to the old words.

As me and Freddy hurriedly pack the sniper systems back into their cases I can't help but feel a sense of giddy relief.

For today, the fight is over. Soon, I will be asleep. I think we definitely got some kills, and none of us are injured or dead. It's a great morning for any infantryman, past, present, or future. We're tired, but exhilarated enough to enjoy it.

Without another word, packed and ready to go, we sit and close our eyes, waiting the long wait until the sound of our saviors' footsteps begin to echo up the long stairway.

Four D Co soldiers, whom we all know and love, appear magically and enter the doorway to the hide, conveyed as if through a dream, into our reality to relieve us from our wakeful Hell.

"Thank you, brattahs!"

"Don't mention it."

"Thank you, Jesus!"

"No. Thank you."

The tired D Co soldiers, with fresh sleep still in their eyes, quickly assemble their kit, dropping their helmets for the time being as they move themselves into our little home, depositing their assault packs around their respective positions.

We're a quiet bunch as we link up at the top of the stairwell. Even though we've not left the building in a good long time, protocol cannot be deviated from. Dick checks our sensitive items one by one, and together we move down the stairwell toward the promise of blessed sleep at last.

I arrive at my bunk already in a dream. Quickly, and without much grace, I drop my shit under my cot, making sure that my weapon is still on 'safe.' I even take the precious time to take off my boots and change my socks. Though I've not undergone any serious hygiene, or even brushed my teeth for the last three days, small comforts dealing with personal cleanliness are the farthest things from my mind.

Completely stripped down to my undershirt, items accounted for, and kit successfully downloaded, I briefly think about what Dick said about food, and seriously entertain thoughts of eating.

Try as I might, sitting on the edge of my cot while staring at the floor, I can't muster up the feeling of hunger; it's simply gone from me.

Taking a hearty drink of water, I do realize that I need to piss, unable to recall when the last time was that I did such a thing.

Grabbing my rifle once again and putting a magazine into my pocket, I lackadaisically slip my feet into my boots without tying the laces. I highly doubt anybody is going to give me any shit about my appearance this morning. If they did, I would most likely tell them to shove it, nevermind who.

My journey to the pisser goes quickly, and I decide that I much prefer it to our protocol upstairs, which is pissing down an old, unused service elevator shaft in the middle of the building. Watch your step and all that shit.

Although my relief-effort goes quickly, by the time I'm back up to the bay some of my squad, along with another squad from D Co that is also blissfully down, are sound asleep. There are no patrol shifts slated for the day. It's resting up time.

Careful not to wake any of my compatriots from their heavenly slumber, I sit once again on my cot, place my rifle gently underneath, and quietly slip off my boots like the house-slippers they are.

My woobie: my friend, my pillow, and my blanket is still in my assault pack, but after being slumped in the guard positions for days, I feel like laying my neck out flat. Besides, I think I'm just a bit too tired to get into my pack at the moment.

All around me the quiet rustlings of infantry soldiers getting ready for sleep fill the concrete chamber. I decide, since it's assured that sleep will come soon enough, that unconsciousness will have to wait a bit longer while I eat something. Although Cole is already asleep, the majority of the scout squad is still awake, beginning the short journey to the kitchen area for some early-morning foraging.

With my stomach newly reminding me of the necessities of life, I take a moment to leave the group and move to the back of the bay, to what obviously used to be an area appropriated for kitchen duties, where we have common-sensically placed our foodstuffs.

Selecting a lonely victim that is already naked without its box and pallet, I take a Meal no. 2, Pork Rib Meal, back to my cot where I delight in the action of taking my cold morning instant breakfast. It's the first one I've had in days.

After each of us has ventured back from the kitchen area we settle in amongst the cots, where we engage in the routine and expected bout of Mornin' Trade 'em.

Peanut butter is traded for cheese, and flat bread is exchanged for wheat-snack-bread or crackers. All the jam gets passed up and thrown out, or placed quickly into pockets where they will either break, or be remembered at a later time. That crap's dog shit.

Ingesting an MRE is about getting full, rather than being satisfied. The processed peanut butter and cheese sit on the stomach like a lead brick, whereas the jelly is near worthless, having the consistency of purified water. It's common for soldiers to leave it living in their pockets for later to be used as a solo candy-snack, rather than as a bold accessory to a full meal. I can't complain about it though; at least they feed us.

I slam the meal down in about two minutes flat, squeezing the packets of food goop down my gullet as fast as I can, then chasing the slop with canteen water. After disposing of the garbage left over from the meal I just decimated, I lay down on my cot once again. This time, after having just pissed, drunk, and eaten, I feel positively fantastic, as nothing can hold me back from sleep now.

As the other soldiers around me finish their quick meals and hygiene chores, they too grow silent, dropping off one by one into the land of sleep. I don't have a difficult task before me in my bid to join them. I don't think any more thoughts. I don't harbor any dreams.

I submit to the blackness of my mind, and I feel myself simply fall away into oblivion, as if I am sinking through the very cot itself.

I don't softly drift into sleep, and I don't try to make it come. I neither toss, nor turn, but simply wait a moment.

Sleep doesn't gently come to take me; it crashes into me, forcibly abducting me, rapidly pulling me into the void.

Blessed darkness at last.

My sleep is sound, and the deepest it has ever been.

I awake just shy of noon, two full hours before our shift is slated to begin again. Not quite feeling the pull of wakefulness yet, and eager to get a little bit more quality rest in before work begins again in full, I decide to take a little time to brush my teeth and wash my face.

Still tired even though I've plussed-up on over six hours of sleep, I decide to lie down again to relish the time for all it's worth, anxious to not feel as tired as I did the day before at any time in the near future. Lying on my cot, I softly reflect on the events of the previous days. What a fight. Fortunately, we only had one small casualty downstairs: a paratrooper from D Co that will be returning to duty after he recovers from a very small grazing wound in his shoulder.

I'm grateful for our safety for the moment, and I take my lightly wakeful morning time to say a small, but very heartfelt prayer to God above, thanking him for the safety of myself, and also my buddies through the turmoil of the longs days and nights that just passed.

After the short prayer is done I simply lay back on my cot and stare at the ceiling.

Not unlike any elementary or high school in America, the ceiling is covered with pock-marked foam panels that are seated in flimsy aluminum framework, producing a grid of repeating squares.

As I have often done throughout my life, I take a moment to reflect on the random faces that my eyes and brain can construct out of the random dots above me.

It's always the same for me, whether I'm passively observing carpet, stucco, paint, or clouds, my mind slowly builds faces out of the dotted patterns and brings to life skeletons, beautiful women, devils, and other fantastical creatures.

I marvel for a moment about the simplicity of these things before I feel the sweet, heavy sensation of fatigue coming to take me away again.

Before I resume my quiet slumber, before the sleep can fully get me, I take a long draw on my canteen. Camel-Baks are for pussies, and I'll have none of that.

My thirst sated, I give myself over once again to the darkness of our private chamber and calmly drift to sleep as I listen to the sounds of the wide-awake and bustling city on the other side of the thick cinderblock walls.

Cars and taxis, most likely white and orange Brasilias, honk their horns at passersby, briefly drowning out the sound of market stall owners hawking their wares to any and every pedestrian within earshot. A thought of Disney's Aladdin briefly pops into my head, unannounced.

"Sugared dates and figs! Sugared dates and pistachios!"

I briefly ponder the validity of the animated statement, wondering if pistachios, obviously of Italian origin, have ever made it to the reaches of Middle Eastern civilization. Unable to complete the thought, I'm once again taken by the thick blackness of sleep.

I'm not awakened by my buddies roughly shaking me at the shoulder like I'm accustomed to. I'm not awakened by a programmed clock, happily announcing to me that the day is about to begin, and that I might miss it.

Instead, I'm brought roughly into consciousness by an explosion that shakes the building and threatens to hurt my already ringing ears, even through the acoustic shelter of the concrete walls.

As I sit up and rub my eyes I notice the rest of my squad immediately popping to, roused from their deep slumber over an hour early by the sheer violence of the blast.

Though sounding not at all near, the force of the explosion is quite pronounced, and as we wake our uneasy curiosity fills the heavy, sweaty morning air.

"What the fuck was that?"

"It was a fucking Arabian alarm clock, Jackass."

Dick and Freddy hold their small morning interrogatory conversation as I stretch my arms high above my head, taking a private delight in the fact that I've already brushed my teeth this morning.

"Rise and shine, sleepyhead."

Cloud joins in from a bunk just over yonder, "Up and at 'em, Adam-Ants."

Dick looks a bit perplexed, "What was that?"

Waking up to that exact statement from my mother, perhaps every day of my elementary school attendance, year after year, I immediately recognize the phrase.

"You've never heard that one before?"

"No. I haven't. Where's it from?"

I stare at my camouflaged knees for a moment, having never really thought about it before.

"Honestly Dick, I can't say where it's from. Only that I've heard it a time or two before. Revolutionary war, maybe? Up and at 'em? As for the Adam Ant appellation, I have no idea."

With no more talk about Adam or his coterie of ants, the squad begins to make ready for the day ahead.

Unexpectedly, there is no further hubbub about the blast. We only receive a small report from the talk that no American forces were involved in the explosion, so the matter simply gets brushed aside for the time being. Apparently, even though it seemed very close, the origin of the blast was located somewhere on the other side of the Mad compound, far out of our usual patrol area. On our next foot patrol, we will no doubt attempt to visit the blast site, but for this morning it's business as usual as the squad prepares itself for yet another high-ground shift on the top floor.

This rotation, we will be splitting up, with Freddy and I going up top, while the others head to the ECP trucks. After a four-hour block, they will take our place above as we relieve them at the ECPs.

Bidding a fond farewell to the rest of the squad, Freddy and I begin the long trudge up the never-ending stairwell once more, to resume our duties. Freddy packs the sniper system with him, and will deploy it as a matter of 'just-in-case.'

Arriving at the top floor, we immediately head into the primary hide. In the event of another fight, we can always split up if we have to, covering both the sniper system and the machine gun emplacement in the other room.

Freddy, not usually a tobacco abuser, asks, "Got any of that queer Skoal apple shit?"

"Nah man, just vanilla today."

"I'll take one anyway, if you don't mind."

Without a thought to my rapidly dwindling supply I flip him the can. It feels good to be a dispenser for once, rather than the token chew-beggar of the squad, albeit my dip is less masculine than the others.

I developed a taste for the Vanilla stuff in New Orleans during Katrina, as an introduction to the whole filthy affair of dipping. Since that time I've equated the taste of a good, moist, full pinch of vanilla Skoal with army drill movements, rifle maintenance, and now, full-fledged combat operations in a foreign land.

"Thanks, brother."

"Anytime, man, you got it."

After both of us have our fresh morning dip in, the conversation stops. The morning sun has already given way to the intense heat of the midafternoon, and an obnoxiously bright ray is currently striking its way in through my camo-netting from above, in a malicious attempt to bake me alive, even before I can properly begin my shift.

I gear my mind up for the long hours that are to be spent peering out into the endless urban nothing.

Fifteen minutes gives way to a half an hour, followed by a full hour, and beyond.

A few hours into the shift I stop glancing at my watch, as the numbers don't matter anymore.

The conversation held between Freddy and me branches fluidly from topic to topic, jumping between a broad range of subjects such as movies, books, modern dance, and aerospace technology, until the tired talking dies in the increasing heat of the day.

With nothing left in all the world to speak of, I gaze out at the bustling city, settling my newly awakened eyes on the usual sights of traffic, commerce, and the occasional bitch-fight between weak and angry shop-goers.

Drawing Freddy's attention to one such particular bitch-slapping Arabian fight, we each place a small bet of five dollars on our man of choice. However, our sport is disappointingly brought to a premature close as both men involved in the altercation decide that hitting each other in public is no longer the answer to their dispute. They obviously apologize to one another, then walk their separate ways into the deeper market below. Good that nobody got hurt. Bad that the only entertainment to be found abruptly ended with no clear winner.

"That was goddamned disappointing."

"True that, motherfucker. True that."

The hours of the late afternoon drag on without end as I busy myself with drinking water, thinking thoughts, and surveying the dull landscape before me with heightened, though dull and uninterested eyes.

"When does it all end, Freddy?"

"Months and months from now, I'd wager."

"I concur. Comfortable yet?"

"Like a tick in the skin man. Like a tick in the skin."

An hour from the end of our high-ground shift, Cloud joins us up top along with Brass.

"How's it hanging, Brass?"

He drags on in his southern drawl, "Short, bored, and unattended I'm afraid."

A report has recently come in to the CP that another assault, considerably smaller than the first, may come at us today from the east.

As a result of the new intelligence, regular maintenance trucks from the locality have been denied access to the JSS. Further, the ECP rotations have been advised to treat any incoming non-USA forces as hostile.

Heeding the new news, all eyes in the high-ground positions pay special attention to the mulhallas and main streets to the east of the market, where this highly rumored but also fairly unlikely attack is supposedly going to originate from.

As a result of the new alert, D Co soldiers have replaced the rest of the our scouts in the ECP trucks, sending them up top to join us.

Freddy volunteers to hold down the fields of fire in our two primary hide spots, while me and the rest of the squad follow Sergeants Brass and Cloud to alternate locations on the east and southeast sides of the hotel to get some different angles on the eastern roads.

Our new position provides us with a more direct view of the neighborhood bustle, as well as a spot-on central vantage point to the wide open road below.

Puzzling enough, though it's not yet four in the afternoon, the marketplace lies quiet and empty. This could be the result of two different scenarios: one, being that another market in the area just exploded today people probably just got wise and decided they purchased enough dye and turnips to make it through the day and simply went home, or two, that the locals have been tipped off that some highly stupid shit is about to transpire in the neighborhood, and obviously want nothing to do with the undesirable side-effects. Either way, the market is empty and still.

Itching to get himself some action and being a good friend of Dick, Brass has arrived to provide his eager southern expertise on the M-24, in the hope of being able to take a shot for himself.

Though weary of allocating squad resources to an outsider, Cloud has acquiesced to Dick's request, allowing Brass to take up a position as a temporary shooter for the squad. The rest of us are to act in a spotter's capacity, as well as to provide good old infantry support.

We are all quite surprised when our platoon sergeant appears from the hallway and joins us in our new east-facing room.

SFC James, our platoon sergeant, is not a cocky man. Unassuming, and about forty-five years of age, his demeanor suggests that he himself has had a long and industrious career in the US Army.

Not quite a stranger to the 82nd Airborne, he has spent the majority of his career in armored units assigned to various cavalry positions. Any conversation that pours out of SFC James is rife with memories and good, soldier-worthy stories about the action in the Persian Gulf that was.

As a staunch lynchpin of army values and integrity, he is not a favorite of my scout platoon. In him, I see a man biding his time and awaiting the fateful day where his duties as a soldier will come to a close. A good soldier by heart, he's a man set firmly in his ways, and knowing full well how things should be done, he simply provides the best leadership for the platoon that he knows how, knowing that if he does everything right he will forsake none of the soldiers under his command.

Dick's occasional disregard for procedure and discipline clearly put the platoon sergeant on edge, which invariably causes some friction from the rest of the scout squad, who naturally want to side with Dick. I could give a shit about the delicate nuances of internal squad politics.

Alone in the world, I feel that I can see James's view clearly. He is a man that knows exactly what needs to happen, and he knows exactly how he wishes to accomplish his tasks.

Relying on the scouts for manpower alone, he is forced to deal with Cloud and Dick in the best way he knows how, but it's clear that he doesn't enjoy a minute of the experience. Instead, it seems as though he would be much more content in dealing with traditional soldiers under his command, rather than attempting to cater to the needs and wants of want-to-be prima donnas like Dick.

I like the man, and personally, I wish the scout platoon was run in the same way that James runs his platoon. He's both competent and knowledgeable, and any contention with the scouts that occurs on a day-to-day basis, in my opinion, can be traced directly to the immaturity and thrill-seeking impetus that generally issues forth from the rest of my squad.

Traditionally, brash and unthoughtful glory-seeking behavior is frowned upon by Big Army, as reckless behavior is usually a precursor to tragedy. I fear, in my heart of hearts, that my squad is barreling toward such an unfortunate eventuality under the direct tutelage of Cloud and Dick. It gives me comfort in some small measure, to think that my destiny, in some capacity, still lies, at least in part, in the hands of a man like SFC James. I get this sort of wave, because he's never made me rappel down a third-world elevator shaft for fun. Dick has done that before.

I find it very strange that he has allowed Brass to man one of our weapon systems. Usually a platoon sergeant would squash such a request in times like these, rightfully refusing to allow someone to take up a shooting position specifically for the purpose of sating his own curiosity and need. I suppose it flies, in this case, because everybody knows that Brass is a squared-away crack shot anyhow.

With news of a different group of hostiles fresh in our minds, or perhaps remnants of the same group from earlier in the week, we, our normal squad, plus the few NCO extras, resume our surveillance of the city-scape to the east.

Having well-defined and specific orders to keep the streets clear of all through traffic, half of the scout squad, with its new NCO accompaniment, provides over-watch and security coverage to the street below, with each of us hoping that soon we will have a viable target in our sights. All of the locals have been advised today that any unauthorized traffic near the JSS will be fired upon, without question. This information was simply disseminated throughout the local neighborhood over an hour ago, through the majesty of our own loud-speaker system attached to the Iraqi police station, as well as through sending out informed Iraqi policemen who enjoy the simple task of spreading information around, as there is no real effort involved in the exercise.

Neither Brass nor James say much, while the scouts are content to scan the surrounding buildings and roads, as well as keeping our status current on the net.

Breaking the humdrum reverie of the quiet Baghdad afternoon, the engine of a small vehicle betrays its presence, echoing up from a small side street, and apparently heading toward the center of the market from a street to the northeast.

A clear view of the road where the car can be heard is inaccessible from our current location as it's too far to the north, so abandoning our new position that favors the east side, our happy band quickly moves down the hall again, back into the primary over-watch room where we can clearly see for over a mile up the main road.

Hearing the steady thrum of the accelerating engine with deft celerity, Duke calls it up on the radio.

"Delta One-Four, this is High-Ground, over."

After a very brief pause, his transmission is responded to.

"High-Ground, this is Delta One-Four, go ahead."

"Roger. We have a vehicle approaching from the northeast, no visual yet, over."

The response comes with a declaration of understanding, as Brass, unable to contain his good-natured enthusiasm, takes up a solo position behind the M-24.

Brass braces the weapon upon the sandbags stacked beneath the right-most window of the room, where I myself prefer to sit and endure my shifts. Crouching over the now posted weapon, he has the perfect sniper's position overlooking the main road that leads into the eastern ECP of the JSS.

With nothing to obstruct his view, he acclimates himself quickly to the sight of the weapon, looking out at the streets and market below the window, and waiting.

Before ten seconds can fully pass, a traditional taxi cab, a Brasilia model from gross estimation, rounds the corner onto the main drag at a distance of about four hundred meters away, and begins travelling on a straight bee-line toward the JSS at approximately thirty miles an hour.

As the vehicle sounds off and visibly accelerates to cruising speed, I take a moment to call it up on the radio and ask for the talk's advice.

Without the need for further explanation, we get the approval to take the shot, provided that the vehicle shows no signs of stopping and continues on its current approach.

Listening in on the news, Brass takes aim at the lone cabby, suspecting along with the rest of us that some sort of foul play is about.

From behind me, while I gaze at the rapidly approaching unauthorized cabby, Cloud instructs Brass to fire a warning shot into the hood of the vehicle.

As we have been stationed in this neighborhood specifically to thwart violence and provide a stable aura of peace, it would not benefit us to shoot and kill random, lost, or confused civilians just because. That wouldn't generally be good for public relations. So, announcing that he is about to take the shot, Brass begins to apply pressure to the trigger of the long gun, aiming directly at the center of the approaching vehicles hood in an attempt to discourage the driver from maintaining his current course, as well as to try to disable the vehicle entirely.

The sharp crack of the rifle fills the room, and Brass maintains his focus down the optic of the weapon.

Nodding, signaling a good hit, he maintains his aim on the approaching vehicle.

Bearing no signs of being hit at all, the small white and orange taxi-cab continues on its path directly toward the JSS, visibly accelerating as it swerves slightly, a clear sign that the driver is quite aware of, and very alarmed at the event that has just taken place.

"He's not stopping Brass."

"Fuck no he ain't."

Quickly Cloud, obviously wishing for Brass not to kill anyone who doesn't absolutely deserve it, tells him to take another warning shot.

The cab, only a hundred and fifty meters out now, provides an easy target for the request.

From my own ACOG optic, I can now see that the driver of the cab is an elderly gentleman, obviously distressed somehow by his current state of affairs.

However, after the second warning shot rings out, rather than stopping to wait for new news, Muhammadio Andretti smashes down on his accelerator, heading directly for the funnel of concrete that leads directly into the eastern ECP.

James, clearly feeling uncomfortable with the order, which he knows is standard operating procedure, tells Brass to take the kill shot.

"End him, Brass."

"Roger."

Prepared for the third shot, fingers placed tightly in my ears like a boy-scout on his first day at the shooting range, I hear the muffled report of the third round going out. I watch as the windshield of the speeding car spider-webs with the impact of the well-placed bullet.

A small hole, accompanied by spreading cracks of annealed glass mark the spot where the intrusive bullet has newly penetrated the cab, dead center on the mark, just above the steering wheel.

Though I can see no immediate splash of blood, which would be indicative of a head or throat shot, the car violently swings to the left, smashing head on into a support pillar on the façade of one of the neighborhood businesses. The impact is intense, immediately bringing the car to a sudden halt, smashing in the front end in a good two feet, and visibly moving and cracking the heavy concrete pillar. I think briefly and fondly of airbags as I turn to face the squad once again. It takes a moment for the echo of the dull concrete-on-metal impact sound to clear the air, and the day becomes quiet once again.

Duke speaks out, "That was a fucking quick stop, Brass."

And it was. The room is silent as we collectively take stock of the now smoking vehicle, interring the undoubtedly freshly-dead driver, that was brought forcibly to a sudden halt a good fifty meters before the driver could even entertain thoughts about entering our quiet, peaceful JSS.

I immediately have an intrusive thought of Miracle Max, waving his index finger in front of his pointy nose and insanely bushy eyebrows, smiling and saying, *"Not mostly dead; all dead."*

From the back, Dick speaks up.

"You just get a kill, Brass?"

"I believe I just done did."

His southern dialect is unnatural, forced into a form of humor that he utters in an attempt to dispel the serious ambiance in the room. It's not every day you get to melt another human being by personal choice alone.

I take a moment to reflect on what's just transpired, and although it was highly unrecommended, I silently congratulate Brass on a well-placed shot, shutting down a vehicle that could, no doubt, be harboring any number of pounds of high explosives.

There again, it could have just been a very lost, very scared old man. Which is what I saw through my ACOG. I saw no religious maniac or terrorist beast. I saw a cute, frightened 80-something that didn't need to

205

die today. And I know Brass saw him too.

The shooting incident goes over without further remark. Another day, another dollar. Or body, in this case. Thankfully, it fell over to Iraqi army jurisdiction to clean up the mess.

Expecting unexploded ordinance as much as the American forces, an Iraqi Army EOD team, surprisingly professional in their disposition, has been dispatched to conduct a controlled detonation on our target vehicle from earlier in the day.

With our shift up top over and done with, Freddy and I have made our way downstairs. For a change of scenery, I link up with Cole to conduct watch in the truck stationed at the western ECP. Since the eastern ECP is regarded as being the safer post, being as it's less exposed to the ominous windows overlooking the market square, Freddy heads off to man his truck for the next two hours alone. After two hours is done, I will assume the solo shift and he will join Cole at the west gate.

For the most part our shift goes quietly, with very few passersby, as the Arabian workday ended hours ago. At 1730, a good hour and a half into our truck rotation, conversation between Cole and I grows stale, and we simply look ahead to the ECP, lying in wait for anything unauthorized trying to make its way through us and into the compound.

Blissfully, Baghdad is rather calm this evening. With my window and door opened, mostly covered by the nearby HESCO barrier, I take the time to inhale deeply and feel the sweet warm early summer's breeze drifting in from the market. Surprisingly absent of bad smells, the air is clean, fresh, and dry, tinged with the barely-there scent of home cook-fires and ginger spice.

Though it's not yet setting, I'm looking forward to the pseudo-lightshow of the fading sun. No clouds usually grace the Middle Eastern sky at this time of year, and beautifully, though briefly, the sun tinges the sky with a unique brand of fire, before it returns to its dark home just beneath the horizon.

With no IPs or civilians attempting to gain admittance to the JSS, I lose myself in a silent thought while passively scanning the nearby windows for any sign of a remaining threat.

Unplanned, and out of schedule for this area of town, the nearest mosque opens up the evening sky with songs and chants of prayer time.

Normally unintelligible and obnoxious, conducted by underage children and aspiring vocalists, the city around our JSS during morning, noon, and night prayer time becomes a cacophony of echoed gibberish and wailing, with dozens of loud speakers coming to life, each spouting different prayer skits of syncopated chanting and off-key screeching.

The misguided shouting from brain-wiped eight-year-olds, amplified by the best 1970s audio technology dinar can buy, usually echoes through the city, exceeding any reference to fingernails on a chalkboard tenfold. It's normally enough to make one's ears bleed.

This evening, rather than being treated with an onslaught of irritating and unwelcome discordant noise, a man takes the microphone and fills the dimming city air with a peaceful, melodic song.

Allah Hu l'akbar la, Allah, Hu l'akbar.

God is great, God is great.

God is great. And the song is great. Starting at a low pitch, the melody rises into a crescendo, gaining pitch, where it falls back into low tones to finish the phrase.

Uncharacteristically of Arabian music, the song does not rely on the simple fluctuation of slipping constantly into minor tones, and decidedly lacks the token 'Arabian Nights' vibe that so much of the local music normally possesses.

Instead, the song remains in a major key, sounds intensely prayerful, and lends a blanket of audio-peace over the otherwise troubled city.

Though completely major, it's not quite western of course, retaining some of the exotic allure of Arabian music while at the same time avoiding the homogenous tone of a protestant hymn.

It is at once beautiful and arresting.

God is great, God is great.

"You know Cole, God really is great."

"Fuckin' right he is."

After a brief pause, he continues the conversation, "This guy's not that bad either. I rather like this guy."

"Me too," I say, "much better than the standard fare. I think this particular one does what it was intended to do."

Sitting peacefully in the Humvee for an hour, waiting for the song to begin its final descent into silence, Cole and I simply listen, and are for a moment taken away by the beauty of the well-sung chorus echoing off every city wall, filling the barren streets with its hopeful strain.

Basking in the message and the rhythmic, simple, repetitious beauty of the sweet melody, it becomes easy to appreciate the beauty and simplicity of life, as it was intended, that exists within old Babylon.

Only after the song dies and the loudspeakers go quiet do we once again hear the wail of hungry dogs, the occasional siren of an Iraqi police truck, and the eerie quiet of a city that is literally trying to eat itself alive.

Just behind our truck, two IPs newly returned from their spontaneous hiatus smoke cigarettes and joke loudly into the evening air.

As soon as the fire died down yesterday and it was officially declared that the JSS was no longer directly under attack, the police force returned, non-committal like, as if nothing had ever happened. I'm sure that if we ever asked one of them why they left, it would be because they had some pressing errand to attend to, or some weighty family matter.

Rather than broaching the subject, not wanting to sour our welcome and be forced into the mass killing of all the local IPs, our command has also remained hush-hush about the subject.

It's been made abundantly clear that they will not stand together with us in a fight. We can count on that as a hard fact in future engagements. For now, we can cater to them while attempting to stay in their good graces, in the hope that they will not abandon us entirely. It's a clear and well known truth that we are not occupying this part of town as an operation of expanding empire, but rather, we exist here in this place with the permission of the locals, and are continuing to pay them accordingly.

The majority of the battalion thinks that's bull-shit, as do I, but still, sacrificing our lives and well-being to the whim of popular media and local politics, we have no choice but to comply, and continue to be an all-in part of the dog and pony show.

I pose an innocent question to Cole, "Do you think any one of these errant AK rounds or RPGs could make it across the Atlantic to America?"

"Highly doubtful, my pasty Nevadan friend."

"That's what I was just thinking."

Sitting alone in the world, waging our own private war in the middle of a hostile Arabian neighborhood, it's abundantly clear that we are not serving any direct American interest at all. Rather, we are indirectly serving our purpose, vainly attempting to plus-up and educate Iraqi forces in an attempt to enable them to take charge of their own government. This is done in a feeble, never-ending attempt to bolster the Iraqi populace and government with the aim of fortifying Baghdad, and the rest of Iraq beyond against Iran, who would be more than happy to appear on the scene as the next invasion force.

Saddam Hussein's war against Iran brought over a million deaths from both the Iraqi and Iranian sides of the conflict. It's not far-fetched to imagine that if Iraq were left unattended, with no adult supervision, that it would be quickly gobbled up and be assimilated as a new Iranian territory.

"They should be hanging him soon, eh?"

"I don't know exactly when. Sometime around Christmas I've heard, maybe sooner."

The capture of Saddam made news headlines in December, just days before our deployment was confirmed and we were dispatched to the conflict overseas.

It's still a small matter of interest on everyone's tongue as to when exactly Sodum Insane will be hung, and just exactly what the geo-political ramifications will be afterwards.

"A short drop with a jerky stop."

"That's for damn sure. Or the chair. Do they even have those?"

Deciding to enlighten all of Louisiana, I deign to share my knowledge on the subject.

"Yeah. As a matter of fact, Saddam used to like torturing people with a device called the 'black throne.' Apparently, what you have is a normal wooden chair with an iron spike sticking out the middle of it. You just take your allocated undesirable and sit him down heavily on the spike. A quick impalement in the ass, like a pointy iron butt-fucking, and then you flip on the juice. Run an electric current straight up some poor motherfucker's asshole until they bleed to death, or otherwise die from the shock. Mr. Saddam had a thing for sodomy. Quite a humanitarian, if I remember correctly."

"Shit man, that sounds awful."

"Yeah, just about in line with the rest of it. Offer your political competitors free scenic helicopter rides, then after you take them up on the offer, push them out over the middle of town. That will teach the people blind loyalty real fast."

"I heard about that one. His cousin, I think?"

"His nephew, maybe. What does it matter? It's sick shit, either way you slice it. Right up there with Hitler, Stalin, and all the rest. They have a statue of the nephew or cousin or whoever he was, two stories tall, just a few blocks away from here in one of the other main marketplaces."

"There's no place like home."

"You said it man. Now, where's my goddamned ruby slippers?"

"Hajji probably stole them in Kuwait. I wouldn't waste any time looking for them."

"Good point; what the fuck was I thinking anyway?"

In the fading evening light, the traffic coming through the ECP is minimal. Small groups of Iraqi policemen flash us their plastic name badges as they walk by, sometimes stopping to smoke a cigarette with us, or to show us something really neat about their cell phones.

Cellular telephones made it to Baghdad about five years ago, but apparently, they took a little while to catch on. Probably riding the wave just behind the local service providers, following as fast as they could set up the transmission towers.

Most gimmicks with the phones are videos of policemen's families and homes, or little Tetris knock-off games, as well as dirty pornography from some of the goofier, younger policemen.

The second time I've seen her today, a young girl, probably no more the thirteen or fourteen years old, walks by us into the police station.

"What's the deal with her, Cole? I've heard she lives here?"

"Yeah. Works here too from what I understand."

"How you mean? In the café?"

After a brief pause, sounding sad, though with a bit of a satirical smirk in his voice, he tells me, "From what I've heard, the IPs pay her the equivalent of a dollar a pop to fuck her in the mouth. I've also heard that sometimes they pay her with food."

"Man, that's pretty messed up."

"Tell me about it."

The disparaging words, which may or may not be true, put a dampener on my mood, pushing me further into the realm of distaste for this post, these people, and this country.

"She's pretty cute too. Doesn't seem right."

After another long half an hour, an Iraqi policeman appears beside my open Humvee door, with his AK-47 in his hands, eagerly trying to tell me something.

"Mista, Mista. Look."

He holds his unloaded AK out to where I can see it clearly in the fading light and works the charging handle a couple of times. Not being completely inept at international sign language, I can immediately tell what he wants. The rifle sounds like the tin man on a bad day, and I can hear the bolt audibly scraping against large pieces of dirt and debris in the chamber.

I say, "You need to clean it first."

The man looks at me blankly, then says, "Yes, Mista. Clean."

210

From behind me, Cole joins the conversation.

"Lube? You want lube?"

"Yes Mista. Yes. Lude."

"All right, here's your lude man."

Cole passes me the black bottle from his position in the turret, and I pass it on to the needy. Taking the bottle of CLP gun lubricant from me, the man sets in to work doctoring up his rifle a bit. And he does it wrong.

Racking the bolt of his weapon to the rear, he boldly upturns the large bottle of CLP directly into his open ejection port, directly into the chamber of the weapon while giving the bottle a hearty squeeze, so tight that I can visibly see the bottle compressing and growing lighter in his stupid, dirty hand.

"Hey, no no. *La la. La.*"

Stopping the massive deluge of weapon oil at last, he smiles and hands me back the now half-empty bottle, which seconds before had been chock full.

"Thank you, Mista."

As he walks forward, moving past us and the truck, leaving the compound doubtless to join the rest of his post buddies somewhere, I can see a dripping, oily trail following him, even in the low light.

"Cole, I know you're pissed, but don't shoot him please."

I can't help laughing a bit, as that was some of the stupidest shit I have ever seen. Also, it wasn't my bottle.

Cole is not really angry; he's simply amazed, as I am, as well as markedly irritated with the context, stupidity, and generalized retardedness of the display that we were just party to.

Weapon lubricant is precious. It is also expensive. It is an important, indispensable commodity for weapon maintenance, and new, full bottles of the stuff are not easy to come by. The full bottle should have been enough to last Cole a year or more.

Though always applied, every day, it is done so carefully, with measured consideration.

All parts inside the weapon that undergo metal-on-metal contact or friction need to be lubricated regularly. However, one Q-tip head full of CLP is usually enough to cover every surface inside the weapon with a very light scrim of oil. On other occasions, that same q-tip worth of oil can be spread over the barrel of the weapon to prevent rust, as well as over the rest of the weapon's external metal surfaces. A little bit of the stuff goes a very long way.

"He better not be planning on shooting that shit tonight."

"I hope that stupid motherfucker finds himself in just such a situation, and I hope his shit blows up in his face when he pulls the trigger."

"It'll probably happen after a soccer game. *Allah hu' Lackbar!* Bang! Bang! Poof! And lights his God-damned self on fire."

I'm assuming CLP is flammable in large quantities, though I'm not exactly sure. I've never been in the mood to try to light a bottle of it on fire just to see the aftermath. That's what hand sanitizer is for.

In excess, gun oil becomes the enemy of any weapon, breaking down woods, plastics, and any other non-metal component parts, such as those found on the AK.

Further, excessive lubrication does more than assisting with glide; it will actually fill spaces that are not supposed to be filled, resulting in more heat and friction building up within the weapon, which can cause any number of problems that range from innocent and annoying, to catastrophic and deadly.

People have a tendency to forget that a modern rifle is simply an old-fashioned cannon, nothing more, nothing less. Granted, the ergonomics, convenience, and technology have changed, but the underlying principles remain the same. A ball is placed into a tube, and propelled out of it by pressure from an explosion. It's not a good idea to hold a cannon in your hand that's literally been soaked to the screws in petroleum-based industrial lubricant.

"He'll probably just light himself on fire is all. Did you see how sodden and drippy that was? I've never met an Arab who didn't smoke. Watch for the fireball, my friend."

"God, I hope that shit's flammable."

Trying on a slightly Hispanic accent, and holding my face in an expression of extreme dignity, I say, "I don't always oil my weapon, but when I do, I try to commit suicide."

At 2200 hours, the squad assembles to go on our final walkabout for this rotation. Everybody is eager to get relieved and roll back to the FOB early tomorrow morning, provided that our replacements arrive on schedule.

Resuming my usual duties as the squad RTO, in my normal position at the center of the squad, I fire off one last radio check with the talk before

212

our small patrol gets under way.

On tonight's docket is a thorough investigation of the blast site in the Paper Market that woke us so rudely earlier in the day.

With no maps this time, and no briefing, the idea of the patrol is simple. We will quietly make our way into the heart of the market to the shut-down part of the street and assume residence in one of the nearby structures, or on a cozy rooftop for a couple of hours, and see what we see. When it's all said and done, we'll walk back here and be finished. Cute and quick; neat and simple.

The walk goes quietly and smoothly as me and the squad trundle slowly along, careful so as not to make any unnecessary noise.

Blissfully, the air tonight is not filled with gunfire, but instead we're greeted with the usual sounds of people talking from windows and rooftops, as well as our old friends, the resident local dogs.

Our walk takes us past some of the now familiar sights: the schoolyard, the small soccer field, and the Old Office Road, which is perhaps the most unique street in town I've seen.

As we walk, the left-hand side of the street is covered in easily recognizable store front facades, while the entire right side of the street is a three story wall that stretches on for two or three city blocks that belongs to a long, old structure that I think must have been a factory of some sort at one point in time. I have no other conjecture: it's just big.

Making our way further down the dim road, periodically lit here and there by the occasional streetlight, we round a bend, and the shapes on the left-hand side give way to mulhallas and smaller free-standing apartment buildings.

One of the larger structures, standing all alone, has been filled to the brim with garbage and is periodically set on fire, in lieu of having no functioning trash system in place for the neighborhood. The junk repository is a constantly smoking pile of detritus; an unsanitary eyesore that would only be permitted right here, right now. There's no place like the Baghdad.

Rounding a dead-end corner where our only choice is to turn ninety degrees to our left, we enter the main drag that we all call the Paper Market.

Supposedly, back in the day paper, typewriters, pens, pencils, paper, schoolbooks, and other literary supplies were exclusive to this large stretch of road, which was the premier shopping center for such things in the 1970s. Now, it appears to be a random mish-mash of businesses that

213

have absolutely nothing to do with printing, reading, learning, or otherwise.

Looking up from the very end-point of the market street I can clearly see exactly how large the market is. Wider than is customary, the dirt street that runs through the center of the market is wide enough to accommodate four American road lanes. It's huge by Arabian standards, far more permitting than the usual mulhalla. Just behind us, barring the way if we had decided to take a right turn at the end of Old Office Road, is an iron gate leading to a large, open atrium Roman-style children's school.

With no other way to go, our squad spaces itself out to occupy both sides of the street. We scan our environs as we make our way forward, deeper into the darkened market.

The first order of business is to find a nice perch where we will be able to see any and all goings-on.

The market is flanked on either side by tall four and five-story buildings, many of which are currently undergoing repairs or some other cosmetic activity. Over half of the buildings on either side of the street have large, unstable looking sets of scaffolding clinging to the outside facades, making it clear that some sort of manual labor has been underway in the market on a massive scale for quite some time.

As we walk slowly on, using market stalls and concrete pillars as cover, my supposition is further proven correct by piles of bricks and tools, disorderly stacks of metal piping, and the occasional workbenches that have been scattered about seemingly at random, blocking portions of the sidewalks, as well as protruding into the street itself. From the look of the chaotic disarray, it is clear that despite the large roadway, the primary traffic that frequents the market is comprised of people pushing and pulling small handcarts or simply walking.

Cloud holds up his hand, signaling for the squad to stop and take a knee.

Silently, I take cover behind the nearest concrete pillar and observe both the environment, and my fellow scouts.

We've reached the blast site, and I can see it clearly, about thirty meters up the road.

A massive crater marks the epicenter of the blast; the destruction seems to have ripped a hole in the middle of the street at least two feet deep, and as much as six feet across.

Being marked as dangerous and impassable, the outside of the crater is roped off with foreign-looking orange plastic tape of some sort.

It's a wonder that the nearby buildings did not come crashing down as a result of the force of the blast. Though damaged, the nearby storefronts are still standing, and appear to be largely intact.

With no proper cleanup yet having taken place, pieces of carts, clothing, and what debris remains of the stalls, which previously hawked goods and services to random shoppers, now litter the street in their broken, anticlimactic glory.

I take a moment to focus in on some of the finer details and notice that every man in the squad is kneeling in different consistencies of powdered, finely shattered glass.

Looking for the shine, I confirm my thought when I see lakes of the stuff up and down the street on both sides that shines a dim, sparkly, off-color green into my nods.

It looks like every window, as well as every other piece of glass down the street for two hundred meters, was violently shattered all at once from the brute force of the blast.

After taking his time to select a building, Cloud settles on a structure not quite ten meters away from the front of the squad, roughly five meters shy of the edge of the crater.

Having been badly burnt, though clearly not recently, the blackened concrete building provides us with the perfect operational platform from which to overlook the market, provided that it is still structurally sound after having been nearly burnt to the ground ages ago, as well as quite bodily blown up just a few hours before. It's not the building I would have chosen. I would personally prefer to saunter up the street a little ways more, looking for a better building in a concerted effort not die in a heavy structural collapse this evening.

Naturally, I feel a bit uneasy about entering a scorched-out, blown-up, six-story Arabian building that appears to have been constructed completely of limestone-like yellow bricks, assembled in what looks to be very much like the Lego fashion. More joy.

We enter the tall building and find the inside to be absolutely jet black, both from the soot covering every surface, as well as the absence of any light illuminating the inside of the structure.

As we enter, Freddy and I go right, while the rest of the squad takes the left and center of the big open foyer. We will clear the rooms one by one, searching every inch of the building all the way to the top, to ensure that we are alone when we set up shop for the evening.

Going room by room, we flip on our IR flood-lamp illumination toys from both our nods and the laser systems on our rifles. Though still pitch black to the naked eye, the six of us light up the interior of the building brighter than the brightest IR Christmas. So much so that I have to use the adjustment knob on my nods to dim the intensity of the light.

Not being permitted to speak, as we are quite stealthed-out at the moment, I make a mental note to comment to Freddy later that this feels just like one of the black entrances to one of those chintzy theme-park or county fair haunted house rides, though it definitely smells much, much more frightening. Must be the shit.

Whatever may have occupied this structure before us has clearly been gone for quite some time, after having cleanly looted and stolen every item in the building before departing. Aside from the charred stones, nothing remains in the structure save for random piles of feces and the occasional odd piece of garbage.

We reach the top of the structure quickly, after falling into a rhythm with the repetitious layout of the identical floors, quickly ascending yet another open stairwell. One slip in the dark, and it would be a horrifying fall all the way to the bottom.

I don't give too much thought to walking up another largely unsupported stone staircase, on an uneven, rickety, burnt-up path which instead of a railing has a precipice.

I wouldn't want a lurching stomach or dizziness to spell my doom on the stupid climb between floors, so I don't look down into the five-story pit that flanks the stairs.

Making it alive and in one piece to the top, we at last permit ourselves to whisper to one another, checking whether anyone has seen or found anything interesting, as well as taking time for Cloud to designate our fields of observation, two men per post, rounding the edges the building.

Not wanting to silhouette ourselves on the roof, we decide it best to take up a quick residence on the top floor, just beneath the roof, shortly after having checked the roof for terrorists and hobos, of course.

In the quiet of the green night I can see quite a bit from my vantage point; however, the information gleaned from the site proves very little.

I can confirm that there are buildings around, and I can confirm that I am currently standing in one, somewhere in the heart of the Middle East. Those are my only reconnaissance discoveries for the evening thus far. I do not, however, attain or glean any new insight into the methods, force, numbers, positions, or motivations of the Paper Market bombers this night.

216

More deserted than usual at this hour, the neighborhood, and especially our new street, seems dull, lifeless, and empty.

Even the dogs seem to have marked this place as a danger zone, refusing to announce their scavenging presence to us like they usually do.

The night air is still, warm, and heavy. Surprisingly, I think it possesses a little bit of humidity, though it is not bright enough in the sky for me to tell if there is a little bit of a moisture haze.

Clouds are rare here, and although it has rained twice since our arrival, we can never see them. When rain falls, the sky just turns to a monotone empty gray, and nothing more. Not even the bad weather has any character or personality here.

Hours pass while we keep noise and light discipline. I'm dying for a smoke, but I cannot.

Without a word, Cole and I bum different flavored pinches of dip from one another while we silently hold our watchful vigil over the dead city.

Pats on shoulders and exaggerated nods from helmeted heads are the recommended communication methods of the hour.

I break the silence rarely, and very softly, only to call in radio checks to report our situation to the talk. With no new or dire news to report, the conversations are short and to the point.

Deciding that the usefulness of our patrol has been exhausted, Cloud and Dick lead us once again down the zany, dangerous staircase. Hey, it could be worse: at least we're not climbing down the outside of the broken motherfucker for sport.

Once back on the ground, I feel my body becoming tired, and though still alert to the possible dangers of imminent ambush, I'm still getting excited thinking about some time off my feet on the cot. Hell, if I remember correctly, my PSP still has a full charge, as there's not been any time to use it yet this rotation. The time is nigh.

We take our time heading back, sampling some different mulhallas as we go, taking in all of the local flavor our new routes can provide. Mostly what we find are more piles of garbage, hidden in heaps in the back alleys alongside rusted bicycles and the occasional bit of tied up livestock.

Nearly back to the JSS, Dick stops the patrol and clearly breaks a little bit of noise discipline as he punches a donkey in the ass with all of his might. The impact from his gloved fist creates a visible ripple in the ass's ass that can be clearly seen even in the pre-dawn darkness.

Surprised, the animal hitches and kicks, sending its comical scream echoing off the surrounding walls. Thus, we brave soldiers, in line and proud, march on giggling at the distress of the stupid-looking, though sad and defenseless animal. My my my. A real-life donkey-punch. Wonders will never cease.

Calling in that we have returned to the JSS, I walk through the gate with the rest of my squad and participate in our usual brand of hands-on sensitive item checks.

Having verified that I have all of my shit that I'm supposed to, I make my sore and tired way up to my cot, where I flop down heavily on it once again.

Tomorrow I will delight in showering, and maybe talk on a telephone. I will be blessed with the rare privileges of having a decent meal and doing laundry.

As a fantasy, a pure unbridled heaven, I may get a chance to read or play a game after having briefly spoken to my family. As I lay down I think about the FOB, and the good sleep I will get in my bed there. I am excited, quite like a first grader just before recess, or Christmas. It's childish and giddy, but I just can't stop the feeling.

There's no place like home.

A home. A home. A home away from home.

Chapter Six: My Dreams

An azure sky gently kisses my eyes in my dreams.
The moonbeams of your soul could give me everything it seems.
The days roll on and on, lasting so very long,
Until the day abandons everything,
And I'm finally free to dream.

From deep within my darkness I can hear your voice.
My heart beats quickly as you say my name, a reverie.
The night can only go on for so long, gone so quickly.
I'll bravely wake to lose this fantasy,
But for a while it's mine to dream.

We lie beneath the stars just like we always did,
Gazing at the cosmos sharing anything, and everything,
No witnesses to see us but the shadows,
Nothing distant or forbidden.

No one, nothing but each other on the grass.
I feel your beating heart just like I always did,
Transfixed by all your magic held within, hiding,
In your eyes, your smile, your toes, and your glowing soul.
Against your warmth I'll always cry because
When I wake this dream will die.

Your sweet rapture fills my mind with peace in my dreams.
Your vibrant summer kiss could give me everything it seems,
But the day rolls on and on so very long.
After kind night abandons me to everything, and nothing,
I'll wait again to dream.

Deep inside my daydream I can speak to you,
Give to you, show you everything that I've been through,
Now we're both gone; nights awake all seem so long,
The one and only soma that can pull me through,
Is that I can dream of you.

We'll lie beneath the stars just like we always did,
Gazing at the cosmos sharing anything, and everything.
No witnesses to see us but ourselves,
Nothing distant or forbidden but the past,
No one, nothing but each other on the grass.

I'll feel your beating heart just like I always did,
Transfixed by all your magic held within, hiding,
In your eyes, your smile, your toes, and your glowing soul.
Against your warmth I'll always cry because
When I wake this dream will die.

Our last hours at the JSS go smoothly, with nothing out of the ordinary to report.

Wonderfully quiet, our last shifts pass with nothing but the slow passage of time to mark them.

At four a.m. the squad is awake, and by five in the morning we're shaved, whore-bathed, and ready to go. All sensitive items are accounted for, and we're pretty much packed.

A light MRE breakfast passes the time for our squad, as we are luckily on our down shift, all ready to walk out the door.

It's not the same for the other squads, who will have to pack up their stations and run down to the trucks at a moment's notice as soon as our replacements arrive.

Without fail, we will assist them carry all the heavy shit, but for now we simply take our time.

Freddy has already departed to perform a radio check on his truck, as he is the slated driver for today, and needs to be as ready to go as soon as possible when the time comes.

After pissing and throwing away my breakfast garbage I take a moment to visit the smoking area on the third floor, where I enjoy a solitary cigarette by my lonesome, staring at the cheap wooden furniture and the dirt on the floor to pass the time.

An hour later we're running to and fro, grabbing excess ammunition, assault packs, medical equipment, and the long guns, then packing them tightly into the trunks of their designated Humvees.

The back of the vehicles is spacious by civilian standards, but when trying to fit five infantrymen's shit in the trunk, the chore of jamming stuff in can become quite tasking, usually ending with some private jumping up and down on the trunk lid in an attempt to get the bitch to close.

Taking my position in the rear-left seat of the third vehicle, I sit back and relax for a bit as the last of the radio checks go through. With nothing to attend to at last, I simply sit and listen to the route plan as the last quick radio checks are sent up to the talk.

With Charlie Company fully in position, having already taken our place, our small convoy of five trucks makes its way merrily down the curvy barrier-alley that marks the exit of the primary ECP, not to return for four whole days.

Not as simple as returning directly home, our platoon has been tasked with an eight hour mounted patrol before returning to the FOB at long last.

I spend the patrol gazing out of the truck at anything and everything, looking once again for the fated bombs that could end us all at any moment.

Periodically, the LT will deem a random passerby or vehicle suspicious, wherein such a case I get out of the truck with the rest of the dismounts and participate in the frisking of the general populace, as well as the searching of cabs, trunks, and undercarriages of 'suspicious' cars. It seems that suspicion, as it pertains to the day, can be easily defined as any cheap-looking vehicle with an Arab in it.

The morning turns into afternoon with a day filled full of similar tasks. At the end of it all, we have found no bombs, luckily have not been detonated ourselves, and found and killed not a single terrorist or insurgent. I don't feel like we're particularly earning our pay today, but hey, that's just fine by me. Unlike some of the other die-hards, I appreciate having all of my fingers and toes attached to my body at all times.

Still alert at the end of the patrol, I continue to watch from my window while continually marveling at the vast assortment of trash and broken shit that litters every street, paved and dirt alike.

Broken glass bottles, soda pop cans, miles of shredded cloth, broken bicycles and scooters, socks, shoes, underwear, and electronics from the late 70s of all kinds.

Here an old cracked vacuum tube television, there an ancient boom-box, every single one of them busted, broken, and otherwise bashed in, forgotten, lying on their shattered sides in assorted piles of filth, yuck, and human waste. After a while the landscape becomes tiresome to look at, and I can feel the dirty city grinding it's way over my tired eyeballs like pieces of broken glass.

"Almost back to paradise guys," I say.

Freddy hastily replies in a cheery tone, "You know it."

A Few moments later we are rolling through the blessed gate of the FOB that we all know and love.

We pass the Americans at the main ECP along with their dual tower guard accompaniment, waving our ID cards as we go. Snaking our convoy passed the chow hall, we move down the familiar bend in the road as we roll by an improvised helicopter landing zone, finally coming to a stop at the fuel point. One by one we roll the trucks up, TCs sign us in on the ledger, and a crew of dot-type Indian personnel from lands far afield fill our tanks to the brim, 1950s service station style, with smiles to boot. *Terima Kasih!*

After fuelling has been completed, the trucks roll to their second to last destination of the day, coming to a restful halt at the motor pool.

During their short stay, a couple of hours at most, truck crews will work with engineers to look for damage, check tires and air pressure, check the vital fluids of the vehicle, and change oil and filters if necessary.

As the trucks were not directly shot or blown up on this outing, the PMCSs should go rather quickly.

Having no designated vehicle that we are personally responsible for, we scouts dismount and break away from the group along with the majority of D Co, leaving only a few unlucky paratroopers behind to look after the vehicles.

I already feel free as I walk with my crew back to the barracks, with the wonderful feeling that I'm about to be able to drop all of my shit for the next few days, and maybe even get to eat a real cheeseburger, complete with my personal very favorite drink, ice-cold strawberry Fanta.

The barracks feel wonderful. It seems that in our absence, individual air conditioning units were installed in thoughtful anticipation of summertime, where we've heard temperatures in the city can exceed a hundred and forty degrees Fahrenheit on a cool day. At least for four days out of twelve we can enjoy a little chill time.

Having cleaned my weapon only hours before, I simply check the chamber to see if I've acquired any new dirt.

Having satisfactorily passed my thorough inspection, I deem the weapon to be in serviceable condition, and then busy myself with quickly applying a very light scrim of oil to the outside. It never hurts to shine your girl up every once in a while.

Immediately after I link up with Chapel, we hit the town. Chow, laundry drop offs, and phone calls are all in order. Time to kick our 'week-end' off in the right fashion.

"That's fucking bullshit."

"Damn right it is."

Walking quickly back to the barracks from the chow hall, to-go plates bearing tuna-fish sandwiches in hand, Chapel and I have already received the news, via word of mouth, that the internet and phones have been shut down once again.

"Every fucking time. Probably 1st ID again."

Chapel doesn't hesitate to reply. "Not combat either I don't think;

some of the guys were talking about a suicide."

"Some pussy kills his stupid self and we get the internet ganked away for a week. What the fuck. Proper notification can kiss my ass. His platoon should just post that he was a weak fuck, and tell his whole world over his fucking Facebook page.

We are both irritated about the unwelcome news, but we're not really angry. We simply take it in stride. It's one of those things that we've come to expect. Hey, I've said it before: at least they feed us.

As far as soldiers in the field go, and especially compared to other soldiers throughout history, even here at war, we're about as spoiled as they come. We know it, and we're thankful for it. Come November time, we may even be able to shop for ourselves at the newly rumored PX, rather than relying solely on mail from home for tobacco drops.

"It would be nice to have a PX," I say.

"Tell me about it. But, you can look at it this way: there's one less errand you have to run on your re-fit day."

An officer from a non-infantry unit looks at us in a slightly disparaging way as we pass. Stopping his stroll, he barks at us.

"Hey Airborne, they don't teach you to salute a damned officer?"

Not dissuaded or concerned one bit by the leg butter-bar, Chapel quickly rounds on him with a reply.

"You forget where you fucking are sir? You're in a combat zone, you smurfing smurf."

Taken aback by the sudden and disrespectful onslaught of silly language, the man's face grows bright red with anger, in good keeping with the strange patch that he's sporting on his arm – his wrong arm; he's clearly never been to combat before.

"You should respect your officers."

"You sir, are not our officer, and furthermore, respectfully stated sir, we've had two officers on this FOB clapped up by snipers in the past four months. Knowing that, if you want me to, I will happily salute you right now. I will do it in an exaggerated fashion, and with great bravado. Further, I will enjoy every second of the experience."

Reminding himself that thoughtless saluting can mark himself as a target, he seems to notice for the first time the many windows, some within three hundred meters, that have an easy line of sight to his position, just over the protective walls of the FOB.

Keeping a cocky air of false, idiotic superiority, he continues, "Who's your Sergeant Major?" Chapel and I start walking away,

225

thinking similar thoughts, as he poses the question one more time, slightly louder than the first. "Who's your Sergeant Major?"

Stopping in his tracks, Chapel quickly rounds on his heels to carrying out a picture perfect and snappy about face.

"All the way, Sir!"

Flashing the steady, smart gesture, Chapel stands at attention with his hand formed into the perfect parade day salute while staring directly into the eyes of Sir Assimus.

Visibly shaken, the now skittish officer performs a very awkward side-stepping crouch maneuver and gazes, this time a bit frantically, at the many possible sniper hides that have a clear view of his head, neck, and nether-regions.

"What are your names? Names and ranks!"

This officer was apparently taught nothing of attention to detail, as he did not already take note of our name tapes. It's his personal conundrum now, as Chapel and I, both with good reason, quickly walk away from the scene of our silly transgression as quick as our airborne boots can carry us.

Rather than following us all the way back to our den, the marked man quickly turns and goes his own way, with all the leisure sucked right out of his gait.

"Think we'll hear back about that one Chapps?"

"I doubt it. Some stupid fobbit sends out a complaint towards a couple of paratroopers, without a good reason? I think not. Serves him right."

"Nicely played, by the way; I wasn't aware that we've had any sniper incidents."

"We haven't."

At that, we both burst into hearty laughter and continue unopposed along our merry way back to the barracks, to enjoy the somewhat more realistic than usual food in our hands.

"I have a couple of years on you yet noob; you'll get the hang of it soon enough."

Much like the rest of the conversation, the comment is meant in good spirit and jest, and it gives us something that we can both smile about for a while.

"What a fuck he was."

"Yep." Chapel enunciates slowly, with exaggerated breaks, "What. A. Fuck."

With still a good walk through the layout of familiar buildings ahead

226

of us, there's still plenty of time to carry on a good conversation.

"Hey, Chapps, has your stomach been funny lately?" I pose the question as a result of the very unhealthy, very sudden feeling of urgent pain that springs up in my guts for the third time this week.

"Yeah, I get you. I haven't had a solid shit in over three weeks now."

"Me neither. It's getting old real fast."

Chapel speaks from experience, "They probably slipped us a batch of old MREs. That happens from time to time."

My stomach lurches from within again, and it forces me to slow my pace slightly.

"How old you think? Desert Storm? Vietnam era? Revolutionary War, mayhaps?"

"Something like that. I wouldn't trouble yourself about it too much. It'll do enough of that by itself."

"Gee, I really can't wait to eat all this fish and mayonnaise."

"It'll do you just as much good, I guarantee it."

When I reach the upstairs bay of the barracks I only take the time to remove my blouse and deposit my fresh fish sandwich on my bunk.

Dressed down to my undershirt, I leave my glasses and boonie on my bunk, taking only my rifle and a magazine with me.

Rough biology forces me into a steep run as I tilt my body forward and unceremoniously fling myself down the stairs three at a time, then out the door. I don't take the time to sign out with the CQ.

Moments later I'm safe, in the fourth and rear-most, somewhat freshly cleaned bathroom stall of our KBR shitter-trailer. Although not the best digs one could hope for while doing one's paperwork, it's far better than shitting into half an oil drum, or an open slit-trench. Gotta love porcelain. That, and you don't have to burn your own shit in diesel fuel afterwards.

As usual lately my guts are quite wrapped up, in the worst way. I sit patiently waiting for nature to take its course, feeling the awful pressure of bad food-stuffs preparing to clear themselves from my system. That's when the sirens start.

Springing to life, I can hear the sound of WWII style warning sirens echoing cleanly through the plastic sides of the trailer, followed by the unfeeling, pre-recorded announcement voice. *Incoming. Incoming. Incoming.*

Horrified about the present situation, I start manually trying to push

227

the shit out of my body, hoping desperately not to die on a KBR shitter with my pants down around my ankles. At least I'm not whacking-off.

Refusing to abandon my dignity and lie down as I'm supposed to, with a shitty ass, face down on the bathroom floor, I simply try to make myself small.

I feel the hair raise all over my body as my heart quickens its pace, and I reflect briefly about the medical terms for such an immediate sense of dread: the feeling of impending doom. Piloerection and such.

Having no reason to really start panicking, other than being trapped taking a shit in a plastic box in the middle of an impact area, I defer to the rules of 'psychic says' to explain to myself that there must be a very good reason why I'm shaking and freaking out far worse than normal.

God in heaven, please bless me and watch over me this day. I really don't want to die with shit on me.

The sirens continue to escalate. Having finished my crap, I don't want to risk standing up to wipe only to get mortar shrapnel in my poopy ass, or have my dick blown off by a rocket.

Instead, I simply lean forward on the shitter in the most self-deprecating pose possible, and in the very cliché fashion I grab my ankles.

Having fully assumed the position, I'm horrified both by the sensation that bombs are about to fall, as well as the cold sensation that my naked cock is touching the bare inside of the front of the very public porcelain bowl. No time for that now though.

Tremendous thunder hits all at once. The report of a nearby impact is close enough to make the entire trailer lurch and brings the ringing in my ears back anew.

Another close explosion forces me to open my mouth and squeeze my eyes shut, the horror of the situation being too great for any other action.

Shaking violently, I re-evaluate my decision not to lie down on the floor, but still, even in my terrified panic, I have too much pride to lie down on the floor with shit on me.

Another explosion sounds further away than the last, and I feel suddenly brave. All of a sudden, I come to my senses and shout,

"Fuck it!"

In a second I'm on my feet, reaching for the John Wayne paper with shaking hands.

Crinkling the toilet paper, as is my custom to get deeper cleaning traction, I quickly scrape my ass once, hard enough to get a glob of the shit off me.

One more time.

Two more times.

Boom!

Another impact sounds off close enough to nearly scare the shit out of me again, and I decide to wipe just one more time for good measure. I refuse to die with shit on me.

Taking the time to flush like a good soldier, I hike my pants back up and secure my belt with one quick motion just as another impact strikes, seeming to be somewhat farther away than the last.

Slinging my rifle onto my back, I fling the shitter door open and make a run for it.

It only takes the space of six strides to clear the courtyard before I go barreling into the concrete safety of our building.

"Jesus Christ, Pearce, you were in the shitter for that?"

"Yes, I was."

I try to regain some sense of personal pride and composure as best I can while at the same time I make a mental note to return to the shitter during a quieter time to finish my thorough clean-up.

"I had better go check in. Catch ya later, dude."

Quickly ascending to the top of the stairs, I'm happy to find that I was the only one missing during the attack. The rest of my squad is well-accounted for.

"No cause for alarm, guys. I was just takin' a very loud dookie."

Cole looks up from his bunk and says, "You were poopsterbating."

"Nope. Not this time Cole."

Freddy speaks up from his bunk, "I just poopsterbated."

"Good for you. Now, you stay away from me, Fredward Penis-Hands."

Andrews, the out of place young paratrooper that I've taken under my wing, Chapel, and myself decide not to go to sleep this evening, but instead we decide to weather the storm of waiting and agree that we should all stay awake to see when, and if, the media blackout will dissipate today.

"Three fours."

Andrews slams his cup down with uncharacteristic gusto, and Chapel calls his bluff.

The casual game drags on for a few hours, until each of us tire of the sport.

Not solely focused on the game, we take our time and play slowly, simultaneously watching episodes of Drawn Together, which Chapel has had his wife send him from home, along with a very handy portable DVD player, which is now our collective savior from the clutches of mass boredom.

With several episodes of the nonsensical Comedy Central cartoon over, and as we've grown far too tired of the dice, we decide to go our separate ways for the time being, saying that we'll link up again at around midnight to take a nocturnal jaunt to the phones and computer center, in the hopes that we'll find them in good working order.

I decide that the time is ripe for a smoke, and Andrews accompanies me though he's not a smoker himself. He's too smart for that sort of thing.

Lighting up just outside the barracks, being careful to maintain the minimum distance that is allowed away from the building, I light up and take a very satisfying drag, as I've been returned at last to my stash of American cigarettes. Nothing like good American Marlboros. Camels too, for their smoothness; anything is better than *Royale's* and *Miamis*.

"How's your week been, Andrews?"

He looks dejectedly at the ground for the space of half a minute before he answers me. I genuinely feel sorry for him. Although he knows that the land outside the wire is no place for him, it's clear that his never-ending duty to guard the entrance to the barracks provides him with absolutely no excitement, entertainment, self-worth, or job satisfaction.

"Just the war on boredom I guess. My fam might be sending me a laptop soon. That would be fantastic. You play RPGs, Pearce?"

"I do, shamefully and obsessively. It's my dirty closet secret. I can't wait to get back to the states and check out Oblivion. Of course, I'll have to buy a Playstation 3 first."

"That the new Elder Scrolls?"

"Yes indeed. Sequel to Morrowind. I've got a magazine article about it if you'd like to have a look."

"That would be great."

We talk about familiar things from home every day: games, movies, books, or anything else just to pass the time. From our daily routine of weapons maintenance, guard shifts, patrolling, and fighting, it's easy to be lead to believe that the droll hum of disciplined life will roll on forever.

It's a good hope for the future, as well as a good boredom alleviating conversation piece, talking about fun things from the world that we were all originally born into. Talking about the prospects of sitting down to a nice glass of booze and a nerdy game does wonders to brighten my own outlook on the future. It's a damned mouth-watering prospect.

"What are you going to do, Andrews, first thing when you get back?"

"I'm getting drunk."

"You're eighteen. Why would you want to go and do a silly thing like that?"

My question is jocular, and rhetorical. Most underage paratroopers drink in the barracks. In most companies it is not only allowed, but actually encouraged. Paratroopers in the barracks aren't tearing around Fayetteville getting into real trouble. The idea is that as long as you're in the barracks, you're hopefully not going to do anything illegal, and further, you're hidden away in an environment where state and federal authorities would never find out about the transgression, provided that you don't try to start practicing parachute landing falls out of a fourth-floor window. The third floor is acceptable as long as nobody breaks anything. I've never tried it myself though. Heights and booze never seemed like an intelligent combo.

"Well, more power to ya. I'll be doing much the same thing, in between packing all my shit to ACAP."

"You're a lucky man, D."

"As you too shall be, my friend. You too shall be."

Flicking my cigarette butt aloofly into the designated can, I pat Andrews on the shoulder in a gesture of genuine reassurance as I make my way back up the short staircase to the scout bay, where I aim to get me a little bit of nerdy alone time.

Fully aware of the health risks, I throw a fresh wad of Skoal into my lip as I lay down on my bunk.

I decide to spend a little bit of quality time with my PSP, as it is still fully charged. I haven't had any time to use it over the past week, so the opportunity to have some downtime with the device makes me almost giddy.

Settling into a turn based strategy role playing game, my favorite leisure time of the whole war, I notice, most irritably, that mosquitoes are trying to eat me alive.

"Anybody else getting the holy fuck bitten out of them?"

Freddy, from the bunk just across from mine, replies, "Yeah, we think that they're all coming up from the old plumbing."

"We'll have to send out requests for mosquito nets and bug-zappers if it keeps up like this."

Sitting on the edge of my bunk, really looking at the environs for the first time since returning, I become immediately aware of the contagion that has overtaken our home. Looking closely, I count no less than a dozen of the malicious creatures; some fly around merrily, while others lie in wait on the top of the sleeping bag that serves as my comforter.

Without pause I start smacking at the creatures, killing them one by one, trying as best I can to murder as many of the little bastards as possible before I start to get bit again.

Satisfied that my murderous rampage has thinned the ranks of the intruders in and around my bunk, I nestle myself back into the corner, reaching into my assault pack to withdraw my PSP, which will at long last afford me some real entertainment.

I play intently for an hour or so, doing my very best to shut the world out for a while. I have a few intrusive flashbacks of my most recent experience in the shitter, but then quickly dismiss them before I brood on them too much.

The expedition to the phones and computers that I had planned is cancelled once again, this time by Duke and Cole returning to give us the fresh bad news.

"Well, apparently the phones were on for a few minutes, but we missed it. One of the KBR handymen was killed by shrapnel during the last attack while crouching safely in one of the shelters."

Few and far between, some very sturdy sandbag and concrete bunkers have been built at strategic locations around the FOB in an attempt to give soldiers and private contractors a place of safety during the frequent mortar and rocket attacks, in the event that they are caught in the middle of an expanse of open terrain when the bombs begin to fall.

"Any idea which one?"

"One of the bunkers by the fuel point. Probably the target of the attack. Lucky that one of those things didn't go off."

He pauses briefly before continuing, "They think it was a rocket that got him. Came in horizontally along the ground, and went right through the door of the bunker."

"Man, that's unlucky as hell."

The room is briefly filled with improper, hesitant laughter. Though tragic, the situation reported to us is comical enough. However, nobody can help but to feel sorry for the unlucky man, whatever his name may have been. It's also easy to understand that any one of us could be visited by a similar fate in the days ahead. Maybe even tonight. It's not really a laughing matter, although the premise of the 'lucky shot' is quite comical.

"Just when he thought he was safe."

Freddy speaks up from his bunk, "Nope. No safety in this shit-hole."

Letting the conversation take its course, I settle back in and turn my mind's attention once more to moving my characters on their grid, much like a digital board-game, and strategizing as how best to defeat my own digital enemies while taking little or no casualties among my vicious, magical sprites.

Before retiring for the evening I round the corner at the back of the small hallway leading to Chapel's chamber, wondering if he is still awake.

I find him much as I was, playing his PSP. Unlike my more refined tastes, his small library consists primarily of action and adventure titles.

"How's the Ratcheting and Clanking going?"

"Good. I'm stuck again though. I can't seem to find where to go next."

Unlike myself, Chapel doesn't really get lost in games as a source of a good time. Rather, he uses them as a time passing tool, in an effort to prevent the lonely boredom from driving him crazy. Chapel doesn't play games to simply enjoy the experience; he plays them to win.

Characteristically, the small barracks room smells delicious, filled with the fresh, warm aroma of newly brewed Folgers coffee.

"Mind if I raid your pot, Chapps?"

"Knock yourself out. Or rather, stay awake all night. That's what it's there for, smurf."

Chapel takes a moment to slap his face and neck. Apparently the scout chamber is not the only one currently being overrun by the winged menace.

"Are you current on your malaria shots?" I say as I pour myself a fresh cup of coffee from the very state-side looking pot that is plugged into an adapter, sitting neatly on a plastic shelf that Chapel has appropriated from some distant quarter.

He doesn't answer, and he doesn't need to. It's a facetious question, as all of us have had our malaria shot recently. That, and no less than twelve others.

I don't have a coffee cup. Instead, I've simply cut a plastic water bottle in half with my knife, keeping the bottom portion as a vessel for barracks delicacies such as tea or coffee from the states. Although not insulated, and with very sharp, thin edges, the makeshift cup does the trick in a pinch.

Hot sugared coffee in hand, I decide to grab my own PSP once more and hang out with Chapel in his barracks room for a while, as my own has grown dark and quiet, with all of my fellow scouts already having fallen fast asleep. There's no real sense in going to bed yet anyway; my CQ shift begins in just under two hours. I'll have plenty of time to get a good rest tomorrow morning, and provided that no emergencies are announced or new chores crop up, I'll be able to sleep in as long as I please. I finished all of my chores and running around already, so other than picking up my laundry drop and getting a quick haircut, I have a free day ahead. We all do. Sleep is just about the most precious commodity that can be awarded to us, as it is always in short supply, especially after our last jaunt out on the town. However, being tired as I am, I simply can't pass up the opportunity to have a little more down-time tonight.

Two hours later, with play-time over, I store my device in my bunk and grab my rifle, leaving my blouse behind. Full uniform is not required, no matter what duties fall to paratroopers in the barracks, be that mopping, CQ, sweeping, or other types of chores.

Relieving another D Co paratrooper at the bottom of the stairs, I take my position in front of a shoddy desk in a flimsy, uncomfortable chair, and glance at my wristwatch to see that it's 0150.

I'm on until three, so by being early I have extended my shift a bit, while at the same time I've done another paratrooper a favor.

Not being allowed to busy myself in any way while on shift, I prepare for the very short hour by enjoying the slightly warm breeze from the outside world, as the flimsy wooden door leading to the courtyard has been left ajar.

Getting prepared to stare at the doorway, the ceiling, and the surrounding beige walls for the next hour, I quickly make a robotic sounding radio check with the talk. The talk constantly monitors the battery life of radios, and also ensures that the CQ posts have them switched on at all times to enable a quick battalion-wide response if a medical emergency or an attack of any kind happens at the front doors to any of the company barracks.

Emily is probably pissed off at me now, as I've not had the opportunity to touch base with her for the better part of three weeks. As I sit and pass the time in my chair I think about what I'll try to talk about when I get the opportunity to speak with her again, but no topic immediately comes to mind.

Going to college in New York, I'm sure she's having a good, though busy time. I briefly wonder if she's safe, and what kind of company she is keeping before I allow my mind to move onto other thoughts. Against my will, my mind keeps returning to her. I can't wait to see her again.

By 0230, all foot traffic by my temporary night-time post has petered out completely, so I busy myself with listening to the sounds of the city, just short meters out the door and over the walls.

I can hear Humvees rolling towards and away from the FOB, followed by some sort of siren, no doubt issuing from an Iraqi police truck. After that, I hear distant AK-47 fire. Maybe it's directed at American soldiers, or maybe the locals are just trying to shoot the moon out. Either way, it's over the fence and too far away to be of any concern to me. That's what tower guards are for, two of which have their post above the perimeter barrier in a sturdy tower that stands guard over the area along the wall just above where we park our vehicles. If any trouble is afoot outside, they'll be the first to report it in.

The fact that our building's paratroopers don't take rotating tower positions is a blessing. Instead, tower duties are permanent posts on this FOB, allocated to untrustworthy soldiers that have dropped the ball in some major way. Punch one of your buddies, and you get to spend a few months on tower guard. Try to kill yourself and you get to spend a year, or the rest of your deployment on tower guard. Get caught using steroids? Permanent tower guard. Lose a piece of sensitive equipment or a weapon? You guessed it: tower guard.

I, for one, disagree with the practice. Though a droll and thankless duty, I am of the opinion that good soldiers, alert soldiers, should have the security of our living space in their hands, as opposed to a gaggle of hand-picked fuck-ups. This practice most likely explains why we have IED occurrences on the roads that lie just outside of the FOB that are clearly visible from the tower positions. The surrounding area should always be secure, however, the lackadaisical tower guards can't seem to keep the nearby roads from exploding. Surely, if they were not busy sleeping or jerking off, we would have fewer incidents immediately outside the walls.

On two occasions within the last month trucks entering or leaving the FOB have been struck by IEDs that were placed conspicuously close to the walls and towers. If people are sleeping up there, shame on them, and what's more, if they are sleeping up there, hajji knows it.

There are plenty of Arabs that have gotten passes of some sort which permit them to engage in a set of very lucrative business dealings on the FOB that are not directly related to the activities of the KBR. Duties of industrious Arabs of the entrepreneurial sort include providing us with cigarettes, lighters, cheap local souvenirs, or inexpensive electronics like the televisions and coffee pots that now dot our barracks floors. Other Arabian merchants provide services such as shoe shining or haircuts. I'm pretty sure that we're paving the way for the haircut guys to have rather opulent futures, as they charge five American dollars a pop, and we are required to have a fresh haircut every week. Although five dollars does not sound like a lot of money, it's important to realize that the amount is equivalent to thousands of Iraqi dinars. And these barbers have dozens, if not hundreds of appointments every day.

It's extortion, but we do it anyway. To the barbers' credit, they do a neat, quick, and clean job of it.

Thankfully, my shift ends as quickly as it began as Freddy, for reasons unknown is already awake, and magically appears from the mouth of the stairway to start his shift.

"I was just about to come get you."

"Yeah. I woke up to piss and noticed that it was just about my time to head down anyway. I'll be right back."

I hold down the fort for another couple of minutes as I wait for Freddy to return from his late-night jiggle, deciding that I could use a piss and a smoke myself.

Upon his return, I make quick work of the pissing business, once again finding myself in the rest-room trailer, this time comfortably mobile in front of a urinal rather than being held captive by one of the merciless stalls.

Stepping away from the urinal, I take a quick look at myself in the mirror, reflecting on the fact that I desperately need a good shave if I want to avoid getting into some kind of trouble tomorrow. It's been two days at least since I last shaved. Being that I'm not endowed with the most masculine of facial hair growing abilities, I've been successfully getting away with murder. Not shaving every day is a big, big no-no. But I'll take care of it in the morning.

I gaze at my reflection for a bit longer, thinking about a moment I had while in-processing into the army about a week before basic training began over four years ago.

I remember how my newly bald head both shocked and amused me, as I have always loved wearing a ponytail or simply going about with my hair all the way down to my shoulders.

Looking at my closely cropped hair and the twenty-one year old face underneath it, I can't help but take a moment to think about the whole of my life and chuckle a little bit.

My face looks tired, and I'm getting a bit older. Though wearing the same brown shirt as on many mirrored occasions similar to this one, my face always slightly changes.

Now, I notice that I have slightly purple, sunken eyes, complete with bags that have never showed themselves before.

I think about the mortars one more time and I feel suddenly selfish, and a bit sad. I want to grow old. The mirror easily reminds me of the slow passage of the long years, brought to life before my eyes as a sort of cameo, or a window into my own mental state of affairs.

I wonder what I will look like when I'm old, and I desperately want to see the day. I don't want to die in a war-zone at 22, as my birthday is right around the corner, but I will if I have to.

I want to see myself age.

Clearing the depressed thoughts of never seeing my twenty-third birthday from my head, I once again feel elated with the day, and am genuinely happy as I step out of the trailer, with the light tin door slamming merrily behind me.

I flip out my zippo and fire up a smoke. Looking up at the night sky, I can see my favorite, and most easily recognizable constellation, Orion.

I smile as I think to myself that I've always thought that he is an archer. I'm quite surprised to have just very recently learned that he is actually a warrior with a club, facing off against a fearsome lion, with no bow to be found.

I stubbornly remain set in my ways as I look up into the night sky, not allowing myself to see the lion and club, but instead being satisfied with seeing the constellation as I have always seen it. An archer, boldly drawing back a well-aimed arrow, dagger or long-knife hanging from his belt with his spectral feet planted firmly on his own astral turf. I've always seen him that way, and I will continue to do so.

Unconcerned about the possibility of incoming rockets or mortars at this late hour, I continue to stare at the quiet night sky for the duration of my smoke break while privately delighting in the fact that I'm genuinely stress-free at the moment.

The blessed silence is rare; the spats of gunfire from the day ceased long ago, and no helicopters are taking flight over the hostile city this morning. Even war can provide a good peaceful ambiance every once in a while, I suppose.

Nearly burning my fingers, smoking the cigarette to its filter in my daze, I quickly flick the butt into the provided can, freeing myself of evil nicotine's grasp once again, at least for now.

A short walk later, I bid Freddy a good night, returning up the stairs once again to my own little corner, in my own little room.

Although I feel that another digital battle, or maybe a spot of reading is in order, I decide to fall victim to sleep at long last, letting further recreational activities wait until later tomorrow, after the rest of my chores are done.

We only get one re-fit day. During the remainder of our stay in relative paradise, we will conduct two eight-hour mounted patrols far away from here, in our own designated sector .

One real day off and two nights in a bed, with a twenty-four hour chow-hall nearby. Can't beat all that.

I think about how lucky I am as a modern soldier to enjoy the privilege of such creature comforts, even in the heart of a warzone.

I continue to think similar cozy thoughts as I drift away to sleep.

The following day is wonderfully uneventful. Early in the morning we set about doing the rest of our FOB errands before settling into a long bout of relaxation, where Chapel and I pass the time with Andrews by playing our handheld games or engaging in vigorous matches of pirate's dice.

Cheese sticks and hamburgers are on the menu in the dining facility, along with copious amounts of Rip-It energy drinks and Fanta, which we scuttle away into our deep pockets, to be consumed as a quick pick me up at later times, during the long night-shifts ahead.

Blissfully, the phones are up and running again and I'm able to touch base with my immediate family, as well as Emily.

My brief talk with Emily is awkward, which is normal lately. Our conversation is filled with empty spaces, and our search for fresh topics is labored and rough around the edges. We're constantly grasping for new things to say, even in the absence of nothing new to report from either of us.

Though not the most uplifting conversation of my life, the simple verbal contact is very satisfying for me.

After phone calls and a brief but effective stint at the improvised gymnasium on post, me and my coterie of friends, with fresh haircuts and bags of clean laundry, return once again to our barracks to spend another peaceful night in our home away from home.

Everyone remains jocular and overly optimistic, their time being spent trying to enjoy the day as much as possible before work begins in earnest again tomorrow.

While the rest of the scouts, joined by others from D Co, sit down in the warm glow of the television to bask in a friendly multiplayer session of Call of Duty, I return once again to my bunk, this time settling into a spot of philosophical and calming reading by Paulo Coelho, a newly acquired favorite of mine.

One after another, my mother sends me copies of his literature, and while some of it doesn't exactly strike me right given my geographic location, some of it resonates very well with me.

After a bit of easy reading, it's night-time once again.

I'm taking an earlier shift on the desk downstairs, so Chapel offers to grab me a to-go plate from the D-Fac and I gleefully accept.

At around midnight, ready to go to work the following day, I settle in for a good sleep after having a little bit of fun with my PSP. For a soldier in a warzone, life is not all that bad sometimes. I delight in the events of the day, and retire completely satisfied.

Nobody tried to blow us up today, which is the first event of the like in some time. Always a plus.

0600 is upon me before I know it. Only taking the time to shower and brush my teeth, I don my gear and ready myself for the quick briefing that will be held just outside our living quarters. Freshly assembled outside, we gather around the trucks for the formal briefing that will inform us of the recent battalion news, as well as the latest enemy activity in our sector. We will also receive a specific briefing on the route plan of the day, complete with alternate routes that are to be taken in the event of emergencies or contingencies. After the usual formal briefing is over and done with, we will take the time to say a prayer, as the chaplain has come out to visit with us this morning.

Before taking a quick leak followed by a morning cigarette, I place my rack, weapon, and armor inside my truck, with the aim of being slightly more comfortable for the morning briefing.

"All right everybody, listen up."

SFC James and the LT begin their briefing, using larger-than-average laminated road maps to chart, primarily for the drivers, but also for the rest of us, the primary and alternate routes that we will be taking throughout the course of our day's adventure.

We will also be stopping during our travels to conduct random checks of vehicles suspected of carrying bombs, weapons, or terrorists, as well as paying a visit to another local police station and an open bazaar style market that is held daily among the wrecks of a squadron of old busses, presumably at the center of what was once a bustling transit station.

After we are briefed as to the preferred routes of travel for the day, all named, of course, after Hollywood women, tobacco brands, and hard liquor, the chaplain takes a step forward to grant us all a morning prayer. Most of the paratroopers present take off their boonie-caps and bow their heads as he begins to speak.

"Our dear lord and savior Jesus Christ, our almighty God, please watch over us this day and keep us safe in our travels, as we travel along these roads to which you have led us far, far away from home."

"We ask that you would be with us, sheltering us from harm and evil, as we attempt as best we can to bring some of your grace and comfort to this chaotic land. We ask that you will bless us by helping us to remain alert, and that all of us will return safely today, and eventually home, into the waiting arms of our loved ones."

"Dear Lord, you are truly our rock and our salvation, our armor, and our sword and shield. Bless us and protect us this day as we venture out into harm's way for the sake of others, and see us all back here tonight safe and sound. Glory be to God. Amen."

"Amen," the new congregation replies in unison. Come to think of it, it is in fact Sunday morning.

It's a good prayer. Although sometimes open religion feels somewhat out of place to me, especially in military settings, the rare morning prayer lifts my spirits somewhat, and allows me to feel, if only for a few short minutes, the presence of a protecting and guiding force.

I know that I'm not alone in my reflection this morning, as the rest of the patrol's preparation duties such as mounting weapons, issuing grenades, and inspecting equipment go on with not much talking at all, and even less coarse humor.

Except for the rustling of tactical nylon, heavy metal thumping on the same, and boots shuffling to and fro across the gravel, our morning duties, with the exception of the radio checks going up in the trucks are conducted in a sort of thoughtful, reverent silence.

Many of us have not been to church in a long while. I haven't been in months and months. Years maybe.

With the majority of us already seated and ready in our trucks, it's nearly time to go.

"You dudes ready for another one of these?"

All of the replies are in the affirmative, although they freely foreshadow portents of the boredom and discomfort that lies in store for us today. Eight hours mostly spent inside a hot army Humvee leaves plenty of respect and appreciation for the spacious comfort of other means of modern transportation. I'm prepared, mentally and otherwise, to spend yet another cramped up day in the back seat. Lucky for me, as a dismount there will be plenty of opportunities for me to leave the vehicle and stretch my legs today.

Once final radio checks go out and every man's weapon is locked and loaded, the convoy rolls slowly out of the ECP. We trundle down our little dirt road, the window on our war, and into the dirty city beyond.

I'm in the lead truck for today's outing, with Brass as my acting TC. As usual, Cole is in the gunner's position on the .50 and Freddy is driving. Moore is across from me in the driver's side passenger seat.

With the rest of the scouts in the fifth vehicle with the platoon sergeant and LT, my truck is much quieter than normal. Though I know Brass, he is unfamiliar to me as a truck commander, and the general mood in the vehicle has taken on a serious nature. There will probably be considerably less jocular behavior on this patrol than is normally customary to pass the time.

"How are you this fine morning, Brass?"

Brass takes the time to hawk a huge wad of Copenhagen-laden spit out the window, which he promptly closes, and replies, "I'm fucking fantastic. How are you today?"

His voice is optimistic and chipper, though forced a bit for the sake of a little comedy, as he poses the question in his thick, North Carolina drawl.

"Same shit, different planet."

"I hear ya."

241

Our convoy turns to the left at the end of the long dirt driveway of sorts, pulling onto the main drag that will lead us into the heart of the eastern side of the city and deep into our sector.

Fully paved, the four lane highway is one of the best roads in Baghdad.

Frequented heavily by crews of general supply vehicles, engineers, and route clearance EOD teams, one would expect this stretch of road to be totally safe, though it frequently isn't.

In an effort to minimize the risk of IED placement garbage, wooden debris, rocks, and signage have all been cleared as best as possible from both sides of the road, however, and without fail, explosive devices invariably slip through the cracks of observation almost every day. As we move down the innocent seeming blacktop road, every man in every truck starts the never ending search for anything out of place or anything that looks like it could go boom.

Driving under an overpass, individual trucks break free from the line formation and randomly swerve left and right in an effort to emerge from the overpass in different positions. Insurgents frequently throw anything from urine or gasoline, to hand grenades and heavy rocks down onto passing trucks from the far side of overpasses like this one. The gunners in our turrets are exposed when viewed from above, protected only by thin sheets of camo-netting that stretch over the top of the turrets; the netting itself serves mainly as protection from the sun, as well as providing a small bit of insurance against grenades falling directly into the cab of a Humvee. By coming out from under the bridges at different intervals, and rarely on the same line of entry, the likelihood of being timed-out by a would-be assassin playing a rhythm game is strongly reduced.

Safely on the far side of the overpass, our convoy once again forms into a straight line, in an effort to better follow one another through a tight pattern of suspected bombs -- cardboard boxes and the like -- as well as the slow moving motorists and pedestrians that already threaten to choke the flow of morning traffic as we enter a marketplace of some sort, despite the early hour of the morning. Hajji, being the genius that he is, prefers to do the main body of his shopping before the midday sun graces greater Baghdad with its presence.

Without signal or reason, a few hundred meters beyond the overpass the crowds grow markedly thinner, and the through traffic that one would normally expect to be on the way to the nearby market this morning is suddenly suspiciously absent.

Grabbing the radio handset, Brass notifies our platoon sergeant immediately, while at the same time telling Freddy to slow the vehicle, and then stop.

"Delta One-Three, this is Delta One-One, over."

"Send it."

"Roger. Anybody else notice that somethin' fuck'n weird is goin' on with the vacancy around here? It's normally bustlin' here in the morning. Over."

"No profanity over the net. Brass, keep a lookout, but proceed forward. Hit counter-flow when you can get over the median."

My pulse quickens a bit. Something *is* definitely amiss in the neighborhood. To the left of the truck and up ahead about fifty meters, stands a small concrete cube that serves as an Iraqi army guard post that usually regulates the flow of traffic, as well as presumably protecting the road from IED emplacement. Uncharacteristically, the post is empty today.

Beyond the guard post a line of traffic has been halted for no known reason, creating a wall of trapped motorists that are currently sitting in precisely the lanes that James has told us to move into at the first opportunity. The wall of cars almost chokes the entire road, save for a small lane to the right. Buildings line the left side of the road, and the sidewalk is far too narrow to accommodate our vehicles. Our only option, if we wish to continue into town this morning, is to hug the right side of the road with our tires rolling up on the sidewalk, with nothing but a barren field on our right hand side.

To nobody in particular I say, "That looks like a bit of funneling if I ever saw."

Brass from the front, "You're damn right it is, and I don't like it. Everyone keep an eye out."

Rogers and affirmatives fill the truck as we start our journey anew, this time at a slightly slower pace, examining anything and everything that we can lay our eyes on.

Though limited, from my small angle of vision to the front-right side of the vehicle I see a maze of debris and junk that has obviously escaped the attention of EOD route clearance crews for the better part of a decade.

With no buildings to the right side of the road visibility is good, stretching far beyond the sidewalk into hundreds of meters of open wasteland filled with broken fences, piles of garbage, and the old rusted husks of burnt-out automobiles.

Close to our vehicle for dozens of meters ahead, piles of wooden garbage, suspicious heaps of metal tubing, and broken vegetable and falafel stands give no hope of ever seeing anything suspicious at all. It's all suspicious, and a monkey could hide a bomb quite easily in any nook or cranny of its choosing, and we would never be the wiser.

"Pick it up a little."

Without saying anything, Freddy applies more pressure to the accelerator and we start approaching normal cruising speed once again, making good time as we move deeper along the wall of still, halted traffic.

I feel the blast more than I can hear it.

The explosion is deafening; the weight of it slams into the right side of our Humvee with enough force to make the tires squeal as the vehicle lurches violently to the left, smashing mightily into the sides of abandoned civilian cars while still grinding forward. The world folds in on itself with the raw violence of the blast.

Accompanying the deep, ringing near-silence of my ears, I can hear the shouting start.

Brass orders Freddy to stop the vehicle and shouts something unintelligibly to James across the radio net.

Freddy brings the vehicle to a stop. I see him working the controls through bright rays of the sun coming in through the windshield, hanging beautifully in the cloud of dirt and dust that instantly filled the cab.

Through the dust I can see the others start to move in their seats, checking themselves to see if they've been hit. Slowly, my hearing tries to return, and all the world sounds as if I were underwater, the sea blanketed by a ferocious ringing.

From across the radio net, we are told to check in.

Brass wheels around as best he can in his seat to get a good look at all of us through the haze.

"Anybody hit? Anybody hit?"

I look at my hands and feet, patting myself down slowly to feel the integrity of my body armor and limbs. To my left I see Cole's legs, still attached and supporting him in the turret, and Moore, apparently unharmed and in one piece.

"I'm up."

"I'm up."

"We're all up Sergeant."

We shout through the deafening fog of war, still prisoners in our stopped metal shell, awaiting the status of the others.

"Truck One, Up."

"Truck Two, we're ringing, but we're good. The truck is dead, over."

James, seeming undisturbed by the news, keeps the roll call going. "Roger that. Truck three, sound off."

"Truck Three, up."

"Four up."

"Truck Five," It's Chapel's voice, "We have a man down. Duke is down, over."

Over the net again, from the platoon sergeant, "Is he alive?"

"Roger that."

"All trucks, security, move to Lazy W. Dismount."

There's my call to arms.

I jerk my door handle downwards and push open the heavy door. Clumsily, my equilibrium still seriously affected, I step out into the bright rising sun.

Not lingering, I quickly shut my door to protect the gunner, driver, and TC while examining the street and curbing immediately around the vehicle and beyond as I drop to a knee. A secondary device could still be waiting to explode somewhere nearby.

Seeing nothing in my immediate vicinity that looks like it could be a secondary explosive, I take cover at the rear of the vehicle and pick up a sector of fire to the right side of the halted convoy.

Cole has swiveled his fifty towards the quiet market, busily surveying the open shop doors, window, and facades of the neighboring businesses. It seems we made it to the other side of the roadblock, and the market, empty of people only moments before, begins to come alive again as people return from their hidey-holes to start buying and selling their wilted produce once more.

As security is already pulled to the left side of our direction of travel, I turn my attention behind me to the naked field. I see nothing in the empty wasteland save for a group of old men and their women who stare dumbfounded at our halted convoy from their huddle around a pile of flaming garbage.

Taking the time to look back at the rest of the convoy, I crane my neck to examine the damage.

The second truck was hit directly, though how bad the damage is I can only guess.

Around the truck red transmission fluid and diesel fuel visibly spew into the beige dirt of the road where they pool together and glint in the bright morning sun. It's a wonder that all of the paratroopers who were riding in the vehicle are up, moving, and accounted for.

There will be plenty of time to survey the damage later. A proper BDA can wait. For now, I simply pick up security and look for any evidence that would give me a hint as to where the bomb was activated from. With the technology present on our trucks the blast was most likely not activated by a cell-phone, though stranger things have happened. The blast hit the rear of the second vehicle, so thermal triggers are also out of the question. This blast was either generated by command-wire detonation, a timer, or a fuse.

"EFP!"

The other truck crew communicates to us the kind of explosive that was used, and then continues in their duties.

Back in the third truck James is still communicating over the radio, doubtless informing the command post at the FOB about the events of our morning thus far and dialing in a wrecker, as the second truck is going no further today.

Adrenalin starts to leave my body after a few minutes have passed. The blast was shocking, but as I survey my surroundings I can feel my pulse slowing down, recovering from the marathon sprint that surprise explosions frequently cause.

Dick, forming the scouts up for a small walkabout, motions me over with the rest of the squad leaving Cole, Brass, and Moore to continue upholding security to the front of the convoy from in and around the lead truck.

Everyone's voices are elevated to speak over the ringing in our heads.

"What have we got, Sergeant?"

"We're just going to walk around for a bit along the front of the market and see if anyone speaks any fucking English, and then see if they know anything or saw anything!"

His hearing seems to be a bit more shot up than the rest of ours.

"What happened to Duke?"

"We don't know!"

"The fifth truck, right?"

Dick appears annoyed and disinterested in the question; he knows what I'm getting at, but there will be plenty of time to solve the mystery later. The fifth truck was farthest away from the blast. With no casualties anywhere else in the convoy, even in the truck that was directly hit. Something is a bit off about Duke's collapse.

Now standing much closer to the second truck and crew, I can see that Forrester, the gunner on the second truck, is bleeding mildly from his neck.

The turret, though high above the ground, has been destroyed, leaving a very alive, but very stunned Forrester still manning his MK-19 in the mangled truck. Steel armor and ballistic glass, nearly three inches thick and meant to withstand just about any force, are melted and cracked, bulging in toward the gunner's position. It looks as if the turret was a victim of Hercules as he passed the fastest basketball in known history. All along the passenger side of the truck, pockmarks and indentations betray where smaller molten projectiles were thankfully stopped by the Holy Armor of Might +6 that did its job. Steel has served us well today.

The trunk of the vehicle, having taken the brunt of the explosive force, has been transformed into still smoking, curiously crafted meshwork. The frame is completely perforated, and from my viewpoint I can see directly through the rear of the vehicle through dozens of baseball sized holes; anything other than an EFP is clearly out of the question. The little bastards melted clean through the steel as if it were nothing. The bottom of the truck, still bleeding massive amounts of vehicular life-blood into the street, shows signs of being mightily raked across the bottom, and both rear tires of the vehicle lie shredded and flat.

The morning air is already filling with the shouts of local Arabs as they congregate in force to rubberneck, trying to understand what is going on. That is, if they didn't help orchestrate the whole ordeal in the first place. Most likely some were in the know, and some were not.

As our squad moves forward the stench of recently detonated high explosives, dry and chemical, hangs in the air as we press into the crowd to begin asking our standard line of stupid questions.

Dick, despite his newly attained and very impressive functional knowledge of the Arabic language, cannot seem to illicit a good response from anyone. His deafened state isn't doing him any favors either.

I busy myself by looking at the faces and hands of a hundred spectators, looking for nothing, and anything.

I'm searching for a weapon, a detonation device, a cellular telephone, or anything else that could signal that somebody had something to do with the blast, from the actual detonation itself, to surveillance or reconnaissance. It's not that simple. I don't see any Arab waving a cell phone in the air or standing before me with binoculars hanging about his neck.

"What do you think, Sergeant Cloud?" I have to shout for him to hear me over the ringing in my ears and the garbled decibels produced by a hundred shouting people, "Snow day?"

"Snow day, Pearce!"

While Cloud shouts at the top of his lungs into my damaged ears I notice that his accent has vanished. It's probably just me.

Dick gets a call over his radio, "Bring it in."

The message is given to us short and sweet. Apparently battalion command, just a short mile up the road, still stationed in the comfort of the FOB, did not deem that it was safe enough to send us out a tow vehicle, what with there being dangerous bombs about and all. Instead, it falls to us to get ourselves home.

James is busy overseeing the reclamation effort, which has already begun in earnest.

The convoy carries tow bars with it at all times, and we are continually prepared to deal with a situation such as this. While they are not the preferred method for dragging a destroyed up-armored vehicle with flat tires, they will do the trick in a short pinch, provided that the wear and tear on the towing Humvee, already straining under its own weight, does not give out with the effort.

Already, the driver of the fourth truck, under the ground-guiding tutelage of Chapel, is backing its way in front of the number two truck while a small crew of D Co soldiers manipulate the one hundred and twenty pound tow bar into place, securing it to tow rings located conveniently on the front of the damaged vehicle.

Before five minutes have passed everyone is seated in their respective trucks except Duke, who has been placed long-wise in the cab of his vehicle between the new gunner's legs where he remains unconscious for reasons not readily apparent to the rest of us. At least he's breathing.

Our convoy rolls out again with damaged truck protected at the center of the convoy and performs a very wide, slow U-turn, taking us back from whence we came.

Brass turns to us, "What did ya'll think of that?"

"Fuckin' scary shit, Sarge. We're lucky bastards, we are."

"Amen to that, Pearce."

We just bonded.

The rest of the drive is silent, and the awkward thought process of the day is somewhat suspended in limbo as everyone thinks about what a close call we just had. Every man has taken a noticeable, quiet pause during the short drive, obviously taking a moment to think on his own mortality.

We troll along on heightened alert at about half the speed of our normal cruising pace. Despite the clip of around ten miles per hour, the towing Humvee seems to be keeping its paces well. Shortly behind the rescue vehicle the damaged truck is pulled along while Forrester still pulls security in the broken turret, and the driver still steers the front wheels, helping out with navigation the best that he can.

James announces over the net that we are RTB, and less than a minute later we're rolling, though somewhat pre-maturely, through the southern ECP of the FOB.

All of our trucks will forgo the fueling process today. Instead, they will be taken immediately to the motor pool where, along with the obviously destroyed vehicle, they will all undergo a thorough inspection, insuring that no unseen damage rears its head to bite us in the ass later.

Before the trucks are dropped off at the motor-pool, James directs the formation to drive along the front entrance of the aid station so that we scouts can unload Duke and see that he gets the immediate attention he needs. Freddy, now freed from his driving duties, and Cole, also newly liberated from his turret accompany the rest of the squad as we carry Duke on a stretcher into the medical facility.

James leans out of his Humvee window before we are all the way inside the medical building.

"Be advised, guys: it's coming over the net that the towers are in contact to the northwest, just about by the barracks."

"Roger, Sergeant."

I hadn't guessed that the proximity of the gunfire I have been hearing for the better part of a minute was so close; I don't think any of us did. Every one of us became just about useless for the purpose of listening shortly after the fireworks display.

Walking with my squad with one hand on one of the stretcher's carrying handles, I try to dissipate some of the grim and serious ambiance.

"Does anybody have their hearing back yet?"

"What?"

Dick says the word loudly, and in an exaggerated way that gets small smiles out of the bunch, although no laughter at this time is permitted for the sake of propriety.

As we reach the end of the short hallway we round a corner through a doorway on the left and emerge into a large open bay that is complete with dozens of bunks, IV bags on hangars, and rushing medics who whizz to and fro as they take care of freshly wounded soldiers and mop up, as well as prepare equipment for the next batch of casualties.

Our lead medic, SFC Brickman, is on station today, and he recognizes us immediately.

We quickly deposit Duke onto a mobile gurney, from the looks of it fresh from the states, and give a brief synopsis of the events of the day to SFC Brickman while a junior medic busily stoops over our friend and begins performing a cursory pre-examination.

After the short hand-written report is filled out, we are unsure as to what we should do next.

Though we're slightly out of place in the medical center in full combat gear, we decide to stay a while to see if Duke snaps out of his temporary coma. Knowing that we will be around for a bit, without saying a word, I put down my armor, helmet, and other gear on the floor out of the way, in the hall just outside the main medical bay doors. The rest of the squad follows my example and does the same.

None of us feel like sitting, so we content ourselves with leaning against the walls like a bunch of cowboys in a saloon while we wait to hear any news.

I hear a sudden commotion from the front of the hallway. Knowing that another wounded soldier is most likely inbound, the rest of the squad and I move further away from the main entrance of the med station and scoot deeper into the old brick hallway.

The door to the med-station bursts open.

1st ID soldiers, of whom there must be at least six, rustle through the doorway as best they can while carrying one of their wounded comrades. They've got a lot of speed on, obviously much more distressed than our group. Immediately, I can see the blood spatters and I know why.

Not a single one of them in battle gear, they look at once both shocked and surprised to be summoned to a place of trauma and death.

Parking their buddy just inside the doorway to the medical bay, they immediately start talking amongst themselves, taking turns to stoop down to their buddy on the floor, issuing one-by-one sentiments of reassurance to the fallen man.

"It's going to be okay, Zimmer. Everything's going to be fine."

One accompanying soldier, a sergeant, seems to think that he is in full control of the situation, and as a master of life and death, it is clear that he will not allow his fellow soldier to expire this afternoon.

Brickman, who has on other occasions educated me in the proper application of a tourniquet, as well as offered insight about the proper way to oil and give a surgical edge to a field knife, steps toward the new visitors.

"Why don't you all step outside."

Clearly bearing a burden of hope for their fellow man, an E-4 speaks up.

"What can you do for him doc? Come on, he's still breathing."

"He ain't breathing. He's been dead for a while. You all get along now. We'll send word when he ships out."

Everyone takes a moment of silence as the grim truth begins to marinate a little. The scouts and I are at a loss for words, so we simply stare at each other and the floor, waiting for the awkward moment to pass.

The soldier on the gurney looks as alive as can be. He stares through me with pleading eyes, and quietly asks for help. He looks as though he is trying to draw breath.

Brickman is correct, however.

The soldier, no older than myself, handsome and fit, has suffered multiple gunshot wounds.

One clearly enters the front of his neck, while already hardened blood forms a morbid pancake under the stretcher beneath his skull. Entry wounds, three in total, can be seen in his chest. It's clear that the wounds are massive and mortal, though the soldier stares at me with moist, open eyes, and an expression that could be easily misinterpreted as surprise, or excitement.

"When was he shot?" SFC Brickman attempts to complete his report, discovering that the incident happened in the tower flanking our own barracks less than three minutes prior. They ran him over here mighty fast.

The living soldiers attempting to save the life of the wounded man made an incredible run to get here. An admirable and concerted effort, though it was not enough. The soldier was most likely dead before he hit the floor of his tower.

I speak out, "Sniper?"

"Roger, Sergeant. We came as fast as we could."

I want to offer words of encouragement and condolence. I want to

251

tell these soldiers that they did all that they could. I cannot. A sort of stage fright grips me. Who am I to tell them about life and otherwise? Who am I to give credence to their effort? Who am I to understand, as I wasn't even there in the first place.

Rather than offering my paltry condolences for a man I didn't even know, I simply shut my trap and watch helplessly as the rest of the drama unfolds before me.

Military orderlies promptly wheel the body a short distance away, to the far left and rearmost corner of the bay. From my vantage point along with the rest of my squad and the dead soldier's buddies, I watch as a final synopsis of the unnamed soldier's condition is taken into account. I watch as his pulse is taken, reading zero, and his breaths per minute are counted, also reading zero.

Uncommon for a combat zone, but time permitted and safe here in the med station, the medics continue to perform three full rounds of CPR, to see if they can elicit any kind of vital response from the fallen man.

The aids pump and the body shakes, but no breath is heard.

Again the chest is crushed, and the heart is pounded with even more force on the second go-round. Still, no life is seen in the broken body.

Our eyes glide, as if ordered, to the floor in contemplation as two medics grab a clean white sheet and hurriedly drape it from foot to skull over the top of the lifeless body.

Determined to stay and hear about the status of our own squad-mate, my group of dudes is undaunted, standing idly by as the scene unfolds, waiting patiently to hear any news of our buddy's status. Duke is out of our field of vision, already undergoing treatment of some sort in the rear of the bay. Although I can't see him, I can see two medics doting to-and-fro around his gurney, and a fresh IV bag gently swinging on a chrome hook above him.

"God bless his only-child bratty fucked-up-ed-ness. I hope to goodness gracious that he's okay."

The squad says nothing, but nod their heads in silence in acknowledgement of my words. It's a terrible thing that's happened to us today sure, but nothing compared to the gravity of a sudden, bullet riddled death on the FOB.

Freddy speaks up knowing full well the impropriety of his statement, caring to add a little brightness to the general mood anyhow.

"Blackouts again, huh? We can't seem to win this week."

"No, Freddy, most assuredly we cannot."

I take leave of my squad with the aim of stepping outside into the fresh desert air to indulge in a cigarette.

Just outside the aid station Baghdad is in full swing.

Two convoys pass each other, one route clearance EOD team leaves the FOB while another platoon of infantrymen like ourselves comes trundling in. The city seems quiet today, with no sirens, no gunfire, and no screeching tires or screaming.

As I light my cigarette, it seems like a most peaceful day.

I think about Duke and what may have befallen him.

Nobody else in the convoy lost consciousness. Nobody even in the second truck, the truck that was directly hit by the IED. Duke was the gunner in the fifth truck, about twenty to thirty meters away from the epicenter of the blast. With no visible wound on him, there is no reason why he should have gone down and out.

Crushing out my smoke, I walk inside to rejoin what remains of my squad once again.

We wait together in silence as the dead soldier is packed into his stretcher and prepared for final dust-off, then wheeled away.

Another half an hour passes as Brickman, accompanied by his coterie of helpers, administers aid as well as his diagnostic expertise to Duke and a few other new arrivals, who are already busily recovering on gurneys deeper within the bay.

"All right. Ya'll can clear out now. Stay, and you'll just be in the way even more than you already are."

Dick fulfills his leadership role as he asks the important question.

"When will we get more news?"

"I can't tell you that. Today, we'll arrange a flight to the Green-Zone. One of you will accompany him and then come back here. Other than that, there's not much I can tell you. Your CQ will keep you posted."

With that, our squad, now reduced to only five members, takes a slow, silent walk back to our barracks.

"Snow day, ya'll?"

"Snow day for certain."

When I'm safely back in the barracks I drop my kit, feeling thankful for being back so early in the day, but also experiencing a private, heavy burden of guilt for allowing myself to feel good in light of the somber

253

events of the day.

I also feel a deep hatred for Duke, and cannot help but think that some sort of dastardly malingering or cowardice is afoot. There is no reason that he should have lost consciousness. There is no reason that he should not be here with us in the barracks, and there is no visible damage on his body. He wasn't even near the shockwave for fuck's sake.

I do not say so in front of my squad, but it appears from the standpoint of a slightly medical perspective that Duke has been the victim of a well-timed panic attack.

I ask, to no none in particular, "Did he hit his head, you think?"

"Shut the fuck up, Pearce."

Dick is uncharacteristically defensive, and Cloud, still busily organizing his gear, doesn't utter a word in my defense. Understanding that Dick knows what I'm getting at, I don't say anything else for the sake of harmony in the barracks today.

There is no debriefing. Everyone knows what has transpired in the last hour, and there doesn't seem to be any proper motivation to explain or critique today's performance. It was a normal patrol, everyone did his part, yet still it ended badly.

As per a small statement made by the LT, it's apparent that we are to take the rest of the day off as well as another re-fit day, as our scenic tour slated for tomorrow has already been cancelled. The platoon will not roll with fewer than five vehicles.

In two days' time we will venture out to the JSS once again on schedule, to resume our normal rotations. In the meantime another D Co soldier, not a scout, has been selected to catch a Blackhawk ride with Duke's sleeping body to the medical center in the Green-Zone. He will stay at the facility until Duke has a definitive prognosis and then return to give us the full report. Maybe he'll even come back with Duke, provided that the sleepy bastard wakes up in the next little while. We'll just have to wait and see.

I settle in, without an idea of what else to do, to play a bout of digital war scenes on my PSP, although I can glean no joy or satisfaction from it today. Rather than being an exciting pastime, it simply serves to fill the bored, uncomfortable space.

Taking leave of my own chamber I return once again to Chapel. As I round the corner I announce my presence with a question, "Good to be back, Chapps?"

"Good to get fucked and go home with your tail between your legs?

Sure; good as I've ever been."

The exchange is less than light-hearted, bearing less frivolity than we are used to in our exchanges, given the gravity of the day.

"Do you know when we'll have word on the truck?"

"We already got it while you scout types were dealing with your resident epileptic. The truck is down for good. We're slated to receive a replacement day after tomorrow. Until then, it's ours just to kick back and wait on the supply chain."

It's clear that Chapel is upset with the events of the day. It's clear that he's also filled with disdain, and a general lack of sympathy as am I, for the downed scout. He sounds even more contemptuous about it than I do, and I'm pretty cynical.

Being the disciplined career soldier that he is, Chapel instead seems disheartened that we are not out patrolling today, or for that matter will be doing nothing of the sort tomorrow.

Chapel has a soldierly work ethic the likes of which I have never seen before, and it's not difficult to see what his real thoughts are through the jocular, nonchalant character he presents to the world around him. He wants to get out there. He wants to take the fight to the enemy, and he doesn't want any problems, logistic or otherwise, to take him away from that pursuit.

"Two weeks," he says to me.

I sit heavily on the bottom bunk beside him. "Two weeks? How you mean?"

Chuckling to himself, he proceeds to answer my question.

"Two weeks. You know. That's how long we have left in country. Always remember that. We just have two weeks left. Any fucking body can do any God-damned thing for two fucking weeks. Two weeks is nothing, and that's all there is to it. Two weeks."

"Two weeks. I dig it."

"You had fucking better. Tuna fish run?"

"Tuna fish run."

Both being afflicted by the damnable dysentery, Chapel and I have found comfort in the resident fish sandwiches here on the fob. For whatever reason they seem to contain considerably less of the toxin that seems to be adversely affecting everybody else, as well as providing us with some balanced nutrition without the unseemly side-effect of shitting water three times a day. We also take care to load the sandwiches, packed neatly onto hamburger buns, as chock full of lettuce, tomatoes, and onions as possible to ensure that we are also getting a good intake of vegetables with our salted, mercury-laced fish meat.

Our walk to the D-Fac is brisk, and we gather the meal quickly.

The walk back to the barracks seems to be shortened, as we are both engaged in our own private thoughts as we reflect on the events of the day.

After the meal is finished I take my leave of Chapel and make my way back to my bunk, with the aim of going to bed early, as all of my chores are still done and nothing remains but to wait.

As I lie down in my bunk I think of Emily for a moment. She's been a bit demanding, if not temperamental lately, about not hearing from me often enough. As much as I would love to run to the phones and give her a call, surely they must be down again after the death on the FOB today.

Though I know that the next time we speak I might face a little animosity, I'm not too concerned about it. She knows I can't speak to her whenever I wish, and even in my absence, I know she loves me anyway.

Though still in the early afternoon, I close my eyes and sleep once again.

The next two days pass with little event.

Our truck that was struck by the EFP has already been replaced, and D Co soldiers have already returned from the motor-pool after inspecting the new truck, making sure that it is up to par.

The squad is already packed and ready for our next adventure in town. In a few minutes we will trudge downstairs to the trucks once again to set out on our next rotation, as we should have done two days ago. Hopefully we can make it there in one piece this time.

Our rotation has been extended. Rather than spending an eight day jaunt at the JSS, we will spend the prescribed eight days at the hotel, followed by a five day jaunt at the neighboring Iraqi army base. Our rotations are to remain that way until our deployment is concluded. From the very cusp of summer, that day seems to be a great way off; a veritable eternity in the dusty, blood-laden heat.

Down at the trucks, responsibilities have been changed. My duties for the new cycle, at least as it pertains to basic transit to and from the JSS, have been changed to gunner's work. I lug the Browning .50 caliber machine gun up into the turret and secure it firmly on the pindle.

Having worked in a gunner's position before, I'm no stranger to it. I'm actually looking forward to a little bit of breeze and sunshine.

Another added perk is that I get to stand up for the entire patrol if I so wish. Barring standing, I could affix the gunner's sling just below the turret, which serves as a quasi-tropical ass-hammock, and sit for a while. Having a few options at my disposal makes me happy indeed.

Not loading the weapon yet, as that will be done shortly before exiting the FOB, I take the time to seat a two hundred round ammunition can into the bracket on the left side of the gun, and then insert a cotter pin into the pindle, locking the gun into a horizontal position so that the cannon doesn't wobble and flop around unsupervised; our platoon always enforces a rather 'hands-free' policy until we leave the wire. What's more, leaving the pin in ensures that the weapon system stays locked into place making loading a much simpler, quicker, and more stable process.

Running one last inspection over the gun, I feel that everything is kosher and as it should be.

Before I leave the turret to run back upstairs and grab the rest of my gear, already neatly laid out on my bunk, I strip a .50 caliber round out of the ammunition belt and wedge it underneath the butterfly trigger, which is a heart shaped mechanism that sits horizontally between the weapon's grips, allowing it to be pressed equally with both thumbs. Wedging a round underneath the trigger is the only sort of safety available to me, as there is no mechanical safety present on the weapon. With bumpy roads and quick vehicular movements around piles of trash, as well as the surprise explosions that happen from time to time coupled with my own Caucasian clumsiness, a safety is absolutely necessary.

Conveniently, the round will stay tucked tightly into place, protruding a good inch on either side. In the event of contact a gunner simply has to smack the round sideways, bumping it out of the trigger well, thus freeing the weapon for immediate bang bangs.

Up in the barracks, as is still customary these days, Zombie plays out while the rest of the scouts make ready for our jaunt. Freddy is already seated and waiting, no doubt conducting radio checks in the truck, and Duke is still absent, apparently hell-bent on malingering like a bitch for the rest of the week.

"They say that it should get to be over a fucking hundred and ten degrees today," Dick proclaims as he hook-and-pile-tapes his body armor tightly onto his torso.

Cole joins in the conversation, "How hot does it get here, you think?" So I decide to add my two cents.

"About a hundred and thirty is fair all summer long over the rest of

257

the country, but here I've heard it can get to an excess of one fifty-five. The damned concrete city is like a ceramic oven in late July."

"Fuck, man, who told you that?"

"I looked it up in the computer lab."

"You would.   I hope to God you're wrong."

"I know I'm right."

"You would."

"Make me."

Make me continually solves every goofy conversation, and I would recommend the flagrant use of the phrase to anyone.

"Any word when Duke will be up again?"

Cloud tells us, after a pause, "None yet."

"Well, at least he gets a bit of a vacation for a week or so."

Cole pipes up, "And a purple heart from what I hear.   LT was talking about it earlier."

I desperately want to say rude, uncaring, facetious things, but knowing how my squad has previously responded to such drivel I decide to keep my trap shut in an effort to further maintain a deeper measure of tranquility throughout the coming rotation.

Freddy enters the room just as I get all kitted up and ready to leave.

"We need to make sock water!"

Sock water, justly named though it sounds decidedly unappetizing, is the way to go, especially in lieu of the newly present and ever brutal summer heat.   Though still early in the season, the Iraqi summer is upon us.   Rather than sitting idly by and blaming El Nino for our temperature-based misfortunes, we are always on the lookout to devise new methods for keeping water cool.   Even though the chow hall functions and has a refrigerated drink cooler, there is still no ice on the FOB; at least there is no ice that is accessible to us.

Sock water is a distant, but well-attempted second option.

All of our water comes from bottles, Oasis brand, apparently cheaply bottled by Mormons somewhere in northern Utah.   As the bottles are only a liter apiece and quite slim, they fit neatly into any of our issue socks, which nobody really wears anyway.   Hanes makes a much better black tube-sock, and everybody gets away with wearing civilian socks from home.   So, being the industrious infantrymen that we are, thanks to a little bit of creative thought from Forrester, our military-grade socks have become refrigeration tools.

Placing the bottle of water in a sock, preferably clean, and then soaking the whole thing with water creates a sort of heat diffusion mechanism. Thanks to good old conduction, or convection, whichever the fuck it is, the wet bottle-socks are then hung out of the windows of our moving Humvees, cooling the water slightly as we drive. Although never anywhere near cool or refreshing, the new system takes the bite out of the water, resulting in a refreshing, lukewarm plastic flavored beverage.

Moving generally together in our gear laden turtle conga line, we trudge downstairs and into the waiting trucks below.

There is no briefing today, and no prayer. The drivers know the routes that we are taking and the mission is simple: get to the God-damned JSS this time.

We'll do our best.

I'm somewhat relieved, as my walking load for this rotation is going to be much lighter than normal, as RTO duties have been reassigned to Freddy for a bit, though he's still our truck's active driver.

Before ten minutes have passed our convoy is rolling; the scouts are in the first vehicle once again with Cloud working as our acting TC.

As our convoy halts at the lock-and-clear barrels, I use the crank on the turret to orient myself towards the large dirt berm and proceed to load the .50.

I take pleasure in it, as it's something new to do. I'm also already enjoying the natural air conditioning that comes standard with hanging the better part of my body out of the top of a moving truck.

Taking the belt of ammunition in my left hand, I open the feed tray cover with my right. Carefully, I insert the rounds by laying them down in their designated place beneath the feeder claw, which is the initial mechanism responsible for feeding and holding the rounds in place.

Locking the claw down, I firmly but gently slap the feed-tray cover closed and aim the weapon system square at the berm.

Holding onto the grip with my left hand, I take the charging handle in my right fist in an underhand position and rack the weapon's bolt to the rear.

Letting the charging handle go, I'm met with a satisfying thunk. My weapon is hot.

Done with the chore, I quickly load my rifle insuring that my selector lever is switched to the 'safe' position, then wedge it into a secure bracket in the turret beside me.

Having gone about the necessity with great speed, I simply hang out for a bit in the turret, waiting for ups from all the trucks, and for our eventual, unavoidable drive to begin, which will take us eight long hours to accomplish.

Though the drive to the JSS could take as little as a half an hour, we have a slated eight-hour mounted patrol block today, so as we begin to creep forward out of the gate I try to get myself as comfortable as possible for the long day ahead.

As lead gunner, it is my responsibility to scare traffic out of the path of our convoy. I will do this by firing warning shots if need be, and generally aiming at anyone who doesn't quickly respond to my polite suggestions regarding how they should quickly move the fuck out of way.

Beyond that, in this position I have the first, and highest vantage point in the convoy. If there are to be enemies or bomb-type troubles about, it is my job to see the problems first.

As we move along our main route to the west, I feel refreshed in my new position. Rather than being restricted to a meager ninety-degree view from my armored window, I can see all of Baghdad splayed out before me, and the miles of road up ahead which we are going to traverse today.

We're all on high alert as we approach the bridges, and the area just a few hundred meters short of where we got hit just days before.

As our convoy makes its way under the overpass, we conduct our random lane switches.

I have an affinity for the neighborhood on my left, as we've been told that it is a predominantly Christian neighborhood, right here in the heart of heathen Baghdad.

Not visible from my current position on the road, there is a decent-sized church in the middle of a residential city block that is complete with bright, twenty-four hour lighting and topped with a steeple and cross. It's amazing to me that the local rag-brains allow it to exist at all. As much as it seems terribly out of place to me, I find it equally beautiful. Sometimes we take a detour through the residential area nearby and drive past it, but today is not such a day. Eager to get away from the area surrounding the FOB and into our main area of operations, we are determined to make good time travelling to our sector today, sticking primarily to the main drags until we reach Moudan.

As we come upon the crowded market district the convoy slows further, with all eyes peeled for any signs of devices that may or may not go boom. Though impossible to see even if they were present, we are somewhat assured of our safety today, in spite of the blast earlier this week. Apparently route clearance traversed the road using imaging toys, scanners, and whatever the hell else they use to find bombs just hours before. Granted, a device can be placed in a matter of minutes. Regardless of the cold reality, there is a bit of assurance to be had knowing that they were recently here. At least I can take comfort in the fact that if we do get nuked today, at least EOD made the effort to try and make sure we didn't. Neat thoughts to live by.

We pass through our previous expedition's explosive kill-zone with little event and no detonations. Everybody breaths a little easier. I enthusiastically call down from the turret, "Well, guys, we didn't explode and die and all that shit!"

Freddy from the driver's seat replies, "Amen to that brotha."

The rest of the drive breaks into neat mini-missions to pass the time throughout the rest of the patrol. Sometimes we halt and dismounts are called to get out and talk to locals. Sometimes we just halt, wait, and watch. More and more throughout the day, with dwindling options for new routes to take through the same square city blocks to look at the same scenes, we find ourselves traversing the same routes, in the same lanes, over and over again. Come and get us. Lap two. Come and get us. Lap three.

Being early in the day, traffic is heavy, but most vehicles are smart enough to move over and get out of the way of the passing military convoy. Some people, for whatever reason, are reluctant to do so. In such an event, I scream at them at the top of my lungs, leveling my weapon at their startled, apathetic, or horrified 'But why Mista?' faces, and I make them move.

A common ambush tactic in any theatre, in any part of the world, is to park a vehicle in front of a convoy before an attack is initiated, hopefully barring the way of advance. This is what we're constantly on the lookout for, and also the very same situation which prompts my rage-aiming and lack of cordial mannerisms towards the general public.

Provided that the traffic is flowing, we move with everyone else along the right side of the road. When that is not a feasible option, we take some liberties with the local traffic laws (Who gives a shit anyway?) and drive on the left side of the road, counter-flow. Who's going to stop us?

If both lanes of travel are sufficiently packed, but there is room in the median, we move to the center of the road and continue, sometimes forcibly grinding our Humvees along the sides of any traffic that cannot manage to get over far enough or fast enough to accommodate us.

Sometimes in turning lanes, sometimes half up on strips of concrete that serve as lane dividers in the center of the road, we continue down the middle of the street. Our tires are big, and we have great suspension systems. Common sidewalks are an easy enough obstacle to surmount, provided that one of our drivers doesn't fail to see an open man-hole, having us end up as prisoners in an up-armored truck, high-centered at the hip in a sewer main.

We've been pretty good about that lately, as we've not created that awkward and unsightly situation for a few months; we've learned our lessons.

As the day begins to drag on I can feel the heat of the new summer roaring to life.

My hands and neck are covered in sweat that already saturates my gloves and armor. I can feel more perspiration constantly dripping from the back of my neck and helmet, and yet more running down the insides of my clothing, all the way down my ass and legs, where the wet yuck has begun noticeably pooling into my boots.

I drink water constantly, as we all must.

I don't care much for the extra chore of sock-water creating, and drinking warm water doesn't bother me much. I've also read somewhere that the body is able to process warm water faster than cold, so the temperature of the fluid, while not delicious, is just fine by me.

Halfway through the patrol I feel myself starting to bore a bit, so I have Cole pass me up a pinch of Copenhagen Black and it helps me to regain my focus, as well as giving me something to do with my tongue.

As the sun starts its descent into evening-ish-ness, our patrol comes to its end with our convoy rolling happily through the ECP of the JSS, and I think to myself, BOHICA.

Doubtless the crew stationed here will be quite glad to see us, as their rotation was scheduled to end over two days ago. We're late, and as a consequence so are they. The rotation will continue as usual as if the two lost days never took place at all, and that's the end of the story. Calendar days mean very little to us.

My truck is slated to be parked at the west ECP, which is good for me. I get to leave the weapon system as is, and simply have to take myself inside, sit down upon a cot, and wait with the rest of the squad to hear what our rotation is going to be, when our patrols are, and what positions, up or down, that the scouts will be manning first.

Scouts are blocked in to be on high-ground first, followed by an early morning patrol. Our rest shift this cycle will begin as the sun comes up.

We perform our shifts. High-ground and gate shifts go as planned, and our foot-patrol is largely uneventful, with locals constantly assuring us through our interpreter that life in the neighborhood has never been better, that there are no problems with violence, and that things are really just whiz. Fucking right. I believe them. There is also a common request to get the public water up and running again in Moudan, and we tell the local people that we will look into that matter and solve the problem, if at all possible. I'm sure that Cloud will take it up with command. Maybe.

Of course there are problems with violence in the neighborhood. The nearest morgue is five miles away across town, so the locals bring their dead to the JSS. There are bodies every day.

The days drag on, each one much like the one before it. We drink water, eat sparse MRE meals, stare at the jagged city, endlessly walk, and do our best to stay alert for the next attack, looking, watching, and biding our time.

Our JSS shift will come to a close in a half an hour, at 0600. My squad should be waking up shortly, but I beat them to it by having one of the last scheduled radio guard shifts.

Sitting in the command post in front of the radio, I listen to transmissions as they fly across the net, trying to glean any information that I can from the actions and happenings of others that may pertain to us. Every half hour I perform a radio check with battalion command insuring that there is a good, constant communications link between this outpost and the rest of the battalion at the FOB, as well as across the theatre.

Alone in the post save for the LT, who is currently slumped over upon himself, sound asleep in a shitty, sparsely padded chair, I enjoy the one perk of having a running television, three channels included.

Two of them are too fuzzy to make out, but the Iraqi version of VH1 is up and running splendidly, and coming in loud and clear.

While I listen to the radio, make radio checks, and take notes, I rest my tired eyes on the comforting and familiar early morning glow of the tube.

The channel coming in is obviously piped out from either Kuwait or the Emirates. Also, it could be coming from another developed, secular Arabian nation that I don't know the name of. Either way, the music videos are filled with beautiful exotic women, handsome men, and catching, modern sounding pop-music, although the songs carry strong undertones of Arabian and Indian influence.

I enjoy the quiet music. It's exotic, and it reminds me that I'm very far away. It reminds me that the world is a wide open, fun, and energetic place; at least it is everywhere else but here.

In great contrast to the bloody, dusty, dying city in which I find myself, the images on the screen are filled with dancing people basking in afternoon sunshine, complete with ocean views and palm trees. Partying, dancing, clubbing, and romancing. I even saw one a moment ago that appeared, although set against the backdrop of almost tribal sounding music, that all the Arabs had gone to New Orleans for MardiGras.

The jovial beats, happy flutes, rapid drums, and optimistic tones of love songs lift my spirits a bit. It's good to see a little bit of proper Arabian culture every once in a while, even if these sort of broadcasts are somewhat outlawed by states which adhere to Sharia government.

I make a mental note and decide to take a vacation in a 'good' Arabian land sometime in my life, be it Kuwait City or Dubai. It would be nice to see the good part. Soothing for me, I think, to see a modern Arabian civilization as it should be. The experience of an exotic vacation locale would surely stand in stark contrast to the twisted, violent, and bombed-to-Hell cultural climate that I've become so accustomed to these past months.

My radio shift comes to a close as a member from the newly arrived platoon, who I do not know relieves me from my chair, and subsequently, my music-video fueled cultural experience. Also, I've found that most of the women in these parts are hotter than Hell, unveiled faces and all. I would love to get me one of those.

Back up in the bay, my squad as well as the rest of D co, is hurriedly and jubilantly throwing on the rest of their gear, happier than larks knowing that we are soon to be free of the dreaded JSS once again.

Unlike usual we will not be returning home today, but rather, we are simply gathering up the trucks and virtually moving just across the street, taking up residence with soldiers from the Iraqi army and the Second Cavalry Division, camping out in the new location for four or five more days. How long the rotation will be has not yet been decided by command. We are going first. The length of the trips that follow will be dependent upon how effective our time spent in our new home proves to be.

The checks on the trucks are half-assed at best, with everyone knowing that we are to park them once again in five minutes' time. Radio checks go up regardless of the short stint, and our five truck convoy departs the JSS with all soldiers and equipment accounted for.

Taking a right, rather than the customary left after leaving the JSS, the drivers must pay grave attention and be exceedingly careful as they maneuver the trucks through a narrow alleyway that cuts between crumbling brick buildings and bad masonry work, and is also flanked by bollards and trees.

The alley proves surmountable, though at considerably slow, careful speeds. I'm rattled back and forth a bit in the turret, feeling the cratered, uneven waves of the broken alley as we creep through, in some cases coming to almost a complete stop as fine movements are made with the steering wheel; our side-view mirrors narrowly miss some of the bollards by a matter of inches, and a brick wall by even less.

Emerging from the narrow alleyway we arrive in a wide open round-about, overgrown by an open bazaar market that seems to have fallen out of the sky, splattering dirty Arabs and vegetable carts haphazardly about the crowded space. The chaos of the market does little to facilitate smooth traffic, but the locals move out of the way and allow us to pass easily enough.

I feel jubilant today in my turret, out in the early summer air. I can hear everything from my new position: the conversations of those who pass by, dogs barking, vendors hawking their wares, distant gunfire, and the rhythmic sound of incoming helicopters.

Though it's miserably hot, I feel brisk today, with the promise of some new scenery, a new chow-hall situation, and the curiosity of whether we will be receiving bunk-beds, cots, or neither.

Working at Mad should also be a refreshing turn of events for us, as I've heard it told that they have no Americans on tower duties; the only real shit job seems to be working the ECP, which is currently being handled exclusively by an American MP unit as their sole occupation.

This means more directed patrols and operations, as well as less time spent trying to defend ourselves. A guard-free rotation means that there will be more time for planning and orchestrating important and complex operations, rather than simply filling the space with endless high-ground shifts and the monotonous work of continually checking vehicles and IP identification cards.

The ECP that leads into the Mad compound is well guarded, and the entire post is completely surrounded by towers and heavy, tall brick walls. Much, much better than the shit we've got going on less than two blocks away.

Rather than a simple open entryway, we pull into the compound and are greeted by lines of shifting toll-booth like barriers, as well as privates and specialists from the MP unit moving long strings of concertina wire out of our way.

I can't speak of concertina wire's stopping power against a floored truck laden with explosives, but it's comforting to see that the MPs are trying to do active things with the ECP regardless. It's a good sign. Maybe we won't be blown up in our barracks here after all.

"Looks like a new home, eh boys?"

"Pearce, it looks like more of the same brown crap. Watch your mouth with all of that optimistic 'This is Vegas!' horse-shit."

"Roger, Sergeant. Although, flapping my gums as I am wont to do, I've heard it told that they have a functioning dining facility."

Nobody bitches at me for that particular comment. Instead of griping, there is a pleasant silence as we roll unopposed through the ECP, as the rest of the minds in the truck wonder off to prospects of chocolate muffins and breakfast bacon.

Freddy says, "Point taken. Wonder if it's any good?"

"We'll find out soon enough."

Mad is a much smaller post than our home FOB, and we make our way towards our designated parking area quickly. It's a small dirt field, maybe half an acre at most, that lies in the shade of some old yellow cinderblock buildings that were obviously destroyed by missiles or bombs in years passed, and have since suffered no repair. I'd put my money on the good old 'shock and awe' campaign.

Bushes of a kind I do not know flank the small dirt square, at once giving the place a sort of park-like feel which I find to be very much to my tastes, however out of place the thought seems.

Since Mad is a base that is not under direct American control, we cannot simply leave our trucks open and the weapon systems hot, so we lock and clear our heavy weapons and take them with us, taking care to lock our trucks with heavy padlocks, as well as sealing off the top hatches of the turrets from the inside.

Carrying all of my personal shit including my rifle, assault pack, and the .50, I fall in with the others, clumsily stepping along with the rest of my squad as we follow our LT like a bunch of ducklings, each of us uncertain as to exactly where we are going. Everyone except the LT and the D Co platoon sergeant that is, who have already received an advanced tour of our new digs.

"We doing eight hour mounted patrols this shift here, like the FOB?"

I ask the question to nobody in particular, but I'm a bit eager to divert my attention from the load I'm carrying, as the Browning is digging into my right shoulder something fierce, and I'm having to work double to keep up with the brisk pace of the rest of the squad.

Freddy speaks up, "I heard we're going to be on for a four-hour patrol every day. Beyond that, I think we're going to act as a QRF for the surrounding forces. Seems like kind of a wonderful sham gig to me."

"Amen to that. That sounds all right."

Standing just up ahead about thirty meters or so, I see our new home. I'm immediately impressed, as it doesn't look the slightest bit destroyed. It even looks a bit peaceful, surrounded by more strange exotic greenery, as well as other buildings that seem to have also survived the war thus far. There's even a bit of shade, and that's just swell.

In the hopes of new bunks and a bit of much deserved relaxation, we form a line as a platoon, and the twenty-five of us march slowly up a lopsided concrete staircase and past what looks to be the building's designated smoking area, then into the ground floor doorway.

The building is much different from the others that we have become somewhat accustomed to during our time in-country. Rather than a dilapidated looking structure made out of faded yellow cinderblocks or simply of structured, poured concrete, our new home is made of brown bricks, looking from the exterior much like any American elementary school, or a local library that could be found in any town in the states.

Though I'm not the best critic of architecture, I like the building. The familiarity of it does me some good. Three stories tall, the interior has entirely finished dry walling and paint, which is a huge surprise in this town. As me and the squad march toward the stairwell that will take us up to our new home, I'm also pleased to find that the floor is covered with some rather nice panels of brushed concrete or slate, rather than the usual barren concrete and dirt floors that we have become accustomed to.

Down the hallway just beyond the rest of my advancing brethren, 2nd CAV soldiers are busily mopping the far hallway, preserving the dull shine of the floor in true army style.

I say, "Who remembers how to run a buffer?" as we start walking up the staircase to our new home on the third floor.

Cole addresses the group, "I will buff anything. Any floor, any tile, any slate, granite even. Shit, I'd happily buff linoleum if they fucking give us chow and we don't have to rot in a fucking concrete room for eight hours a day."

"Would you buff a cock?"

"Shut the fuck up, Pearce."

I see the comment for what it really is: not a quippy snipe, but comedic, jovial assent. We're all quite happy to have arrived, if not exactly at the Taj Mahal, at least to some new crap to look at.

Our path leads us up an even, modern feeling staircase before it empties us out into another clean, newly polished hallway. LT calls out from the front, "All the way to the back boys; bay's on the right."

With that, our gaggle makes its way to the end of the long hallway and takes a right turn into a sizable open bay, which is in fact much larger than even our permanent living quarters back at the FOB; this room makes our usual accommodations look very tiny in comparison.

Rather than joining us for the initial moving-in process, our LT and the rest of the squad leaders gather across the hallway in a small room that has already been established as a functioning CP by the 2nd CAV soldiers that previously used it.

In patent scout style, my squad moves unopposed to the back of the bay as we claim our bunks as far back in the right-hand corner of the room as we can go.

"Well, beds fuckin' win out. No cots to be found."

There is a subdued, bubbly excitement present as me and the rest of the guys place our gear down on our newly claimed bunk-beds, complete with mattresses both above and below. The mattresses are horrifying, as they are adorned with cute little teddy bears and other multi-colored cartoon characters. They also present a repeating, calligraphic script that says *'Love you, Love you,'* over and over again.

Though I can't vouch for the aesthetic value of the décor, I can't hate the mattress. It's a real mattress for fuck's sake, thin and naked though it may be.

Cole turns to the group as he deposits his gear, "You think these were donated by Disneyland or some shit?"

"Naw, dude, the Mickey on there is a clear copyright rip."

I say so, because the assortment of Disney-esque characters and Mickey look-alikes, although surprisingly well rendered, are all colors of the rainbow. A tan mickey in particular catches my attention. *Love you, love you.*

"Hey, Cole, your mattress loves you."

"And, Pearce, you should know, I love my mattress. Love it, love it."

All gear having been downloaded, we lie down on our backs for lack of anything else to do. If we were free to explore our new home or to seek out food or coffee, we would have been told to do so. Instead, while we wait for the word to come back from the CP pertaining to which squad is going to do what and when, those of us on top stare at new shapes on the ceiling, while those of us below, heads peacefully resting in the shade of our new bunks, hidden away from the glare of bright fluorescent lights, reflect on the words etched in front of our faces: *Love you, Love you.*

Sure you do, teddy man. Sure. You and all your friends.

Rapidly losing the battle to remain conscious, I resign myself to a quick afternoon nap. Doubtless, in the event of any excitement, I will be among the first to know.

One time, just this sweet blessed once, the scouts are not called onto station only fifteen minutes after arrival at a new post. Even more remarkable, is that nobody is. D Co is given a straight eight-hour nap, all squads included, save for a few unlucky privates whose destinies are entwined with that of the radio in the CP.

I awake from my heavy slumber at about six in the evening, along with a few others.

Chapel is among them, and over a quick drink of canteen water and light speculation about what the rest of our rotation will entail, we think, each of us in his own way, about the future, and just how long we will be staying at our new post. Which at this point, from the view of my lower-level, comfortable, and shaded mattress, staying for an extended period of time doesn't seem like such a bad deal at all.

Word has it from the LT that aside from a few mounted patrols that will be conducted later in the week, we will be assuming QRF duty for the rest of our rotation at Mad, which basically means that we're on call to respond to any and all local emergencies, not unlike any local fire department in the states. Only our job won't be to fight fires; our job is fighting firefights.   Those are two totally different things.

To break the monotony of our rotation and to add some variety to our scheduled mounted patrols, there will be a joint operation to clear and sweep local neighborhoods with the Iraqi army in about five days from now.   Until then, it looks like we all have some much needed quality time with our reading back-logs and our PSPs.

Fully rested, with nothing new yet on the docket, Chapel and I decide to venture forth into our new post in an attempt to find something to eat, a place to shit, and generally just get a feel for the new environs.

I grab my rack and weapon to prepare for the adventure.   Not being on a totally secured American FOB, it can't hurt to take all of my ammunition with me, even though body armor is not required, thank the gods.

"Two whole hours to kick it, Chapps; whatever shall we do?"

"How the fuck should I know, cupcake?   Let's go have a look-see."

There is a platoon briefing scheduled at eight o' clock, where we will undoubtedly be informed of the recent neighborhood goings on, as well as officially beginning our QRF rotation.   Far from symmetrical, our seemingly endless week of responsive down time is going to be punctuated with eight-hour drives, as well as the aforementioned neighborhood clearance operation, the details of which will be disclosed to us at a later time.

It doesn't take Chapel and me long to find the chow hall, although the amenities leave much to be desired.

Rather than a full-service joint like we are used to back at the fob, chow is conducted by a series of deliveries over ground and air from surrounding American posts.   Foodstuffs that are only a little bit removed from the standard MRE fare are moved in bulk to Mad, where they are served by privates from all battalions present out of thick green thermal serving tubs, much the same way that field chow is served back in the states.

The menu is roughly the same as any training exercise in the woods of Fort Bragg: instant mashed potatoes, flattened pork rib patties, and American-imitation Japanese-style yakisoba, which is a personal army favorite of mine.

Tonight we get the pork rib patty, some rolls that could have been made by somebody's crazy aunt, well-meaning though not as skilled as we would like, and some sort of cream-corn gruel.   As a big accompanying hooah, our staple 'Rip-It' energy drinks are here as well.   As an added perk, located just outside the chow area on the first floor in the hallway are a series of shelves that stock chocolate muffins, immortal type, quantity: many, at all hours of the day or night. I plan on being good friends with the chocolate muffins, as they are much better than the bricks found in random MREs, and apparently they are quite free, and available in bulk. No, seriously; we are actively encouraged by the chow-hall personnel to fill our pockets with them. It's just that fucking awesome.

After Chapel and I finish our meal, clean-up is a relatively simple process; rather than setting trays in their appropriate bins, chow here is conducted solely upon paper plates, which we promptly throw away in real plastic American style trashcans.

"Downright satisfying. Where's the can, you think?"

"Fuck the can, D. Where's the smoking area?"

The mention of fresh, sweet tobacco fills my stomach with a sort of happy tingling as I realize that I've not smoked for upward of ten hours now.

"Right. Pissing can wait. First thing's first."

"Little brother, you have to get your priorities straight."

Across the hall from the small bay filled with plastic tables that serve as the impromptu chow hall, a number of certifiably legit Arab merchants have set up shop in small rooms adjacent to the central hallway, three of note. Not the butcher, the baker, and the candlestick maker as in days of old, but rather, the shmog guy, the pirated DVD guy, and the aspiring barber guy. All of which we plan on frequenting in the near future, political affiliations be damned. Like John Lennon said, religion too.

Chapel says to me, "I think there's a line of shitters just outside the building to the east. You got your Charmin, pipsqueak?"

"I most assuredly do. Care for a loaner?"

"Please."

"Pashalooista."

I take some of the ready roll from my pocket, wrap about two poops' worth about the flat of my hand, and rip it free as we walk down the long hallway.

"No Russian please, danke, you know I don't understand a lick of that shit."

"Konyechna droog moi; neither do I."

Pleased and a bit self-assured by a bit of my own linguistic foolery, I hand the ripped-off wad of nice, mailed straight from home American-grade toilet paper to Chapps as we step out into the fading

271

summer light of central Baghdad, together as brothers in arms. Or in this case, brothers in porta-shitting.

The smoking area is just to the left of the building's primary exit, elevated on a slab of concrete that serves as a sort of mini-porch, and sequestered away from the main entry by a group of unknown trees that are different, although not too far removed from the normal, run-of-the-mill swamp trees that can be found in Georgia or North Carolina.

"Can I bum a Camel Wide?"

I'm sporting a full brick of Marlboro Menthol Lights, my brand of choice, but I like to mix it up every once in a while.

"Only out of the kindness of my heart. I'm already running low. I bought a stash of *Miamis* though, just in case."

"Cool, Chapps. I still have half a carton of minty-Americans if you're inclined. I got ya."

We don't really keep track anyway. Talking about cigarette commerce is drummed down to mere formality. If I'm ever out of smokes, God forbid, I know Chapps has one for me. I know it's the same way with him. Besides, I like a break from menthols every once in a while.

As we light up, with the scent of the Tigris river on the light summer breeze, I smirk to Chapel, "You know, I hear from some of the Mexican types that menthols make you impotent."

"Bullshit. But it couldn't hurt to stay away from additives. If it doesn't make your dick fall off, surely it does something else nasty to ya."

"Like crystals in your lungs?"

"Bingo, Small-fry."

"I haven't discovered any yet, but next time I cough up a geode you'll be the first to know."

"You just wait, brother; you're not my age yet. You'll be coughing up all kinds of civilizations by then."

The smoke feels good on my lungs and fulfilling to my soul. A little taste and feel of the American way of life, right here in the middle of Hell's septic tank. Thanks to Allah for the fresh air. The Tigris River is not sanitary; tonight's relaxing river-breeze smells like a thousand-year-old open slit-trench.

We smoke the rest of our cigarettes in silence, puffing in and blowing out our smoke in a sort of mock-synchronization, with nothing much more to say.

As the sun sinks low in the Baghdadi sky, the fading light of the evening threatens to tell my mind that I'm somewhere just off the Vegas strip. The meditative, mechanical exercise of smoking gives us something to do, as well as sating our addictions. There's nothing like it. Reveling in the last tendrils of the fresh smoke, staring at the bleak early summer horizon that's visible between the jutting concrete buildings that can be seen over the walls of the Mad compound, I know Chapel is thinking the same things I am. I'm thankful to be alive. I'm happy I got to eat. I'm glad to be smoking. And, I'm going to be happy as fuck when I get the Hell away from here.

"Shit?" Chapps says.

"Shit-poop."

"Shit-poop?"

"Yeah. Shit-poop. And I think I'll nickname a dog that someday."

"What the fuck, D. Troubled youth nothing. That sounds like bad parenting."

"Yeah. Like Killer's any better."

"Killer can, and will eat your face."

"True that. Ditto and stuff."

We put out our cigarette butts in a staple Folgers coffee can, no doubt set in place by some Sergeant Major as the tip of the spear in a feeble attempt to curb the rash of Middle Eastern cigarette butts that litter every square inch of the city.

Dare to keep Baghdad beautiful.

We make our way down the short concrete staircase and onto the dirt road that separates our living quarters and chow hall from the rest of Mad, as well as the beautiful, clearly visible line of porta-shitters that eagerly await our presence just a few short meters away.

"Catch you on the flip side, yo."

"Whatever, Boondock."

Chapel laughs at my humor, but it's not altogether undesirable. We got a copy of The Boondock Saints by mail the other day, and since then it's been the platoon DVD whore. We all pass it around, and everyone loves it.

Although it's not at all dark yet outside, the inside of the porta-can is almost completely dark. Lucky for me, I'm normally quite the prepared soldier. Extricating my red lens head-lamp from my right cargo pocket as I take a seat, I affix it to my head and switch it on.

I stare at the surprisingly clean floor of the little plastic shit-house as

I let nature take its course, and for once, simply delight in my situation and where fate has seen fit to find me. Much better than the JSS this is. No getting shot at yet either. Yet, anyway.

A few minutes pass before I tidy up, suddenly feeling much better about the world and my station in it.

As I link up with Chapel just outside my own little plastic door, we begin the short journey back to our bay to await the briefing that will outline formally our responsibilities for the rest of our stay.

It's a quick walk back up to the barracks: simply across the little dirt road, up four exterior concrete steps, into the building, up a small staircase, down the hall, then through a doorway to the right. It is a journey that we will hopefully take many, many times in the near future.

Still having a bit of time to spare, Chapel and I each go our separate ways, back to our bunks in our own designated squad areas. Being fully awake, I decide to succumb to the call of my PSP and silly tactical war game, in light of the fact that I've been a man about town for going on eight days now, and have not yet turned the machine on.

Happily, I reach into my right pocket and pull out one of the clear cellophane wrapped brownies, no doubt imported from a happy place made entirely of sugary glaze and chocolate clouds. I bet they even have a castle there. Beer too.

Bit by bit as I play, I pop pieces of the delightful pastry into my mouth, and it reminds me ever so slightly of the wonders of the outside world, far from war and fear; far from death and despair.

I move my little sprites through digital battle after battle, as there is still at least an hour to relax before our briefing is scheduled to begin. Between each instance of pixelated combat I take the time to outfit my troopers with healing items and tactical diversions, as well as to outfit myself and the rest of my group with newly researched and manufactured weapons and armor. I give my soldiers as much as I can spare, me being the tactically proficient and benevolent general that I am.

After only a half an hour of triumph, I resign from my quest by placing the machine back into its designated living space in the black darkness of my assault pack, not so much out of boredom and satiation, but instead with concern for the longevity of my own battery supply.

I neglected to bring my charger on this particular outing, being completely unaware back at the FOB that our newly appointed duty station would be complete with electrical outlets and a reliable supply of juice, undoubtedly supplied by a real power plant somewhere nearby,

274

rather than an improvised network of gasoline-fueled generators.

I make a mental note to remind myself that from now on, electronic extravagances and luxuries will be fully available at the semi-modern Mad, and I should prepare myself accordingly. Time to start packing some adapters.

Happily thinking that the remaining six hours or so of charge in my childish toy will get me fancily through the next week of drudgery, I let my eyes close, shortly after one more furtive glance at the script just above my eyes, mechanically scrawled onto the lowest-bidder's mattress above me.

Love you, Love you.

I think sarcastically to myself, 'I love you too,' as I slip away for a quick nap in the half an hour that remains until our formal briefing.

The time passes quickly, and before long I'm awake with the rest of the crew.

As directed by our platoon sergeant, we gather up our kit and prepare to assemble out at the trucks, ready to go, where we will receive the formal briefing that will hopefully detail the coming escapades of the long night ahead.

Chapel is most likely already down at the trucks with his own squad, doubtless making sure that his troopers are squared away. Since he's not present to accompany me on my walk to the trucks, I simply make the journey in silence with my own scout squad.

Duke has still not returned since becoming a casualty, although we hear small updates over the radio channels day by day. Apparently he is on the road to recovery and his diagnostics completed; soon he will be deemed worthy to come back to active duty, RTD style.

My squad and I walk in silence through the late evening, our feet treading upon the dusty concrete sidewalks and dirt roads of the Iraqi military installation.

There is nothing much to talk about this evening. Not, at least, until we are duly informed of the duties we will be pulling tonight. After our briefing maybe there will be something interesting to say.

I will be a dismount this evening, and Dick, excited about the possibilities of manning the gun, will be taking Cole's usual position in the turret.

Cloud will be filling in as a TC for one of the other trucks, while

Brass will be the TC for my truck.

Freddy is driving as usual, and Cole will serve as the left side dismount in my truck once again.

When we arrive at our vehicles the majority of D Co is already assembled.

Relieved of my position as fifty gunner, I simply drop my kit and armor in the rear right passenger seat of my designated truck and seek out the rest of the smokers to do my duty before the formal briefing begins.

There is one cigarette, mostly partaken of in silence, and then another. Then another.

More than an hour passes as groups of soldiers mill about their trucks, with their sensitive items accounted for, and their radio checks completed.

Some soldiers set their gear up as temporary backstops or pillows on the ground, leaning against them and simply nodding off, or waiting in semi-comfortable positions while staring at the ground or sky.

More than likely, the orders we were no doubt set to receive over an hour ago have since changed, having already been replaced by a new condition, situation, or route.

Smoked out, and not desiring to stare and listen to the night sky anymore, I sit rumpled up into an almost comfortable ball amidst my gear in the back right passenger seat of my vehicle, eagerly waiting, half-awake, for the news that will shed light on exactly what the Hell we are supposed to be doing tonight.

Before I can fall fully asleep our LT and platoon sergeant finally muster the group into a twenty-five man huddle.

The smokes are put out, though the dip spitting continues. Idle chatter stops and body armor is donned as we all press in close to hear what needs to be said.

The LT begins, "All right, listen up."

Though not assisted by night vision I can see everyone clearly, illuminated by the familiar white-orange glow of a street-lamp much like I would find in any city in the states. The long shadows of my fellow soldiers are cast across the dirty concrete and road as recently kicked up dirt and dust from stomping boots form a strange sort of fog in the blue glow of our Humvee headlights.

Unanimously, the drivers have all turned the engines over in their trucks, ensuring that the radios are fully charged, and that the trucks themselves are ready to pull out when needed.

"Drivers, go ahead and turn your vehicles off."

During the brief pause five paratroopers leave the group, and five diesel engines cut off one by one with their echoes dying in the night, giving way to sounds of far off prayer chants in the city, as well as the braying of a lost-sounding donkey. There's a newly relaxed feel to the briefing, as pairs of headlights blink out one after the other.

"Tonight we had a scheduled patrol in and around the neighborhoods of Fad and Moudan, but that's changed."

"Elements from the second CAV, First ID, and Redwater are all working ops in those areas tonight, so to stay out of the way we're pulling QRF for the next twelve hours. Relax. Shoot the shit. Chill out. Take your cute little naps, but we're on call all night. Run the trucks for the AC if you like, but stay by 'em. Make sure to run them enough to keep the radios at full charge. If we get the call we'll be pulling out at a moment's notice. Hooah?"

"Hooah," we all reply. It's not a loud and boisterous basic-training huzzah, but rather a muted, simple, unanimous acknowledgment. Amen.

With that, we all break back to our trucks to resume our small time conversations about the worlds we've all left behind. We resume our tobacco breaks and our tiny, however effective naps, ever grateful to be freed from the wretchedness of eight-hour tower and high-ground shifts, at least for the time being.

I find Chapps amongst the dark faces milling about the trucks and proceed to smoke one more cigarette with him while generally talking about nothing, and everything, as the night wears on.

We wait. And wait. And wait. 0145. 0210. 0247. Not a damn thing changes.

Foregoing my hot, small space in the back of the Humvee, I've laid myself bodily out across the back of the truck, lazily reclined while looking at the stars with my hands folded behind my head in the quiet night, with my legs hanging freely off the back of the vehicle a good three feet off the dirty ground.

Somewhere not too far away, small pops and rat-tat-tats can be heard echoing away from distant concrete surfaces. Although not close enough to cause immediate alarm, the sudden fracas makes my stomach tighten ever so slightly. That could be tonight's siren call.

I do my best not to focus on the distant gunfire, and I try to divert my attention to other things.

Knowing full well that it would be quite against the rules, I wish that

277

I had brought my Zune with me tonight. Some tunes would do me just right about now, looking up at the sky, dreaming about Emily, and awaiting the bright rays of the morning sun so that we can get on with our duties and pass one more day. I just love leaving the days behind.

Nodding just slightly, I'm roused by a rally call from the LT.

Knowing full well what that means, me and the rest of the squad catapult ourselves off of, out of, and up from the Humvees and the ground, quickly grabbing our gear and armor as we gather hours later as we did in the beginning, huddling around our LT for the latest news.

It begins in the same monotonous fashion that it always does.

"Listen up, men."

As if we could figure out how to listen down for fuck's sake.

"Redwater elements in Tiger square, smack dab in the center of Fad, are getting hemmed up by an unknown-sized force of insurgents fighting from emplaced positions in a three-story building that flanks the main traffic circle; mount up and get your game on. We're going to bust 'em out."

The distant gunfire can still be heard in the city, now having picked up frequency and intensity. The angry cloud of noise now makes perfect sense, as does our new mission. We're going to drive right into the middle of it.

Just like that, we're in the trucks, this time acting as a fantastic quick reaction force, firing up the engines and performing our last radio checks.

Rather than waiting until we arrive at the berm or clearing barrels as is the usual standard, we are given the order to lock and load in place, right in the middle of Mad.

With knives and my M-4 being my only weapons, loading goes quickly. Insertion, charging, bolt release, and safety. Dust cover closed, and I'm already ready already.

"Truck One, up."

"Two up."

"Three up."

"Four good to go."

"Five's good."

Even through the thick ballistic glass of my window, now tightly shut against the night, I can still hear the not too distant reports of automatic weapons fire, no doubt originating from tonight's scenic destination.

I'm concerned. I'm happy. I'm nervous. I want to kill one.

"How we doin', guys?"

"Ready to drive into some shit, Pearce?"

I give my enthusiastic reply to Cole, "You God-damned know it. Let's get us a couple."

Freddy from the front, "A couple? Fuck you, D." He's good natured in his speech, "Why not a dozen? Why not the whole goddamn town?"

"You ready for some Carmageddon then?"

"Fuck the steering wheel, dude. I'll hit one if I can, but I'd rather just shoot out the fucking window."

"Fucking Carmageddon nothing then. You're goin' GTA."

"Fucking right."

"Your mom."

"Fucking right."

The rest of the truck laughs at our excited interchange, including Dick up on the gun, laughing loudly and intentionally through the intercom system on his headset, though we can hear him in the flesh just fine anyway.

Cole sits in the passenger seat beside me, ecstatic as the rest of us, not saying a word while busily packing a fresh can of Copenhagen, looking to get a fix before what is certainly going to be a bit of a fight.

"Hey, Cole, pinch man?"

No banter. No harassment. None of the usual condescending bullshit, Cole just smiles at me and flips over the can.

Gratefully, I fill my lip full of the fresh stinging chaw and flip the can back to him. Though not southern by origin, I can give a pretty good yee-haw noise now and then, and I promptly do so, temporarily filling the quiet truck with more welcome chatter.

Our estimated time of arrival at our place of business is only three minutes away, leaving precious little time for speculation and small talk.

In near silence our small, but heavily armed convoy rolls out the gate, waved off by cheerful seeming MPs, ever vigilant in defiance of the late, or early hour.

Bon Voyage.

Our trucks take a right hand turn onto the main road that serves as the primary entry port to Mad. We drive around the large traffic circle which normally serves as the central market for this locale in the early mornings. Now the space is bare and quiet, save for a few Iraqi army trucks scattered about the square while the soldiers that belong to them talk, smoke, and sleep the hot summer night away.

279

Taking another right hand turn, the trucks are given the order to pick up the pace. Rare enough due to the normal amounts of traffic on the road, the acceleration feels good and excites me. We're on the way to a fight.

"Ho, my leg's shakin'. It's gonna be a good night, motherfuckers!"

Dick reports his physiological condition from the gun, but he doesn't sound scared one bit. On the converse, it's clear that he has a case of the excitement quakes. There's probably a bit of fear in there somewhere, but no more than mine, no more than Cole's, and no more than Freddy's.

I crack my window a small hair, less than an inch so I'm still protected by the bullet-proof glass, and take a deep breath of semi-fresh night air in an attempt to slow the beating of my heart. Another left turn.

Here we go again.

The city looks a bit macabre and totally abandoned tonight, just on the other side of my small tourist's window. I can smell garbage and the token smell of tan, dry dirt. As we near our mission area and the site of gunfire to which we are running, I can hear the noise escalate.

Our platoon sergeant croaks across the radio, "Four hundred meters. Keep your eyes peeled. Dismounts standby. Oh, and gunners: watch your lanes."

No reply comes over the net.

Brass, directly to my front, calls out over his shoulder, "Okay, you guys. Be cool. Heads in the game."

Just outside the mock huddle in our moving bullet sump, I can hear the gunfire picking in volume and intensity.

"Watch the rooftops!"

The call comes over the radio, but I'm uncertain of which truck it issued from. From my window I do just that, scanning the rapidly moving concrete pillars, windows, and bits of shadow that glide across both my naked eye and my night-vision monocular.

Somehow the deep, electronic green looks more freakish than average tonight. The lights are brighter with heavier blooms, and the shadows are more pronounced, and somehow darker.

One more left turn and the gunfire becomes deafening, surrounding us all as we pull into the center of Tiger's square.

Brass from the front, "Call them when you see them."

His order, though completely sound advice, is rather unnecessary as the combative scene unfolds before us.

From across the massive traffic circle to our one o' clock, at about two hundred meters away, dozens of muzzle flashes and fully automatic reports fill the still night air, directed already at us, and still upon the small three truck element of Redwater troopers that for whatever reason are still parked in the center of the square.

As our trucks slow to a halt I can see the shadows and silhouettes of the contractors crouched behind the trucks, pie-ing out as best they can to stay covered behind their lightly armored pickup trucks and return fire.

Fighting against a large force in a fortified position, it is clear that they are desperately in need of assistance as none of their trucks are sporting any heavy weapon systems. With the volume of fire hailing down on them from the target building, it's a wonder that they are still alive, though the combat has only been on for four or five minutes at most.

After eagerly anticipating the order from our platoon sergeant, our gunners begin to have their field day.

Over the net, "Gunners, check fire on Redwater in the square. White trucks are friendly. Heavy enemy elements are present in the building to the one o' clock. You are clear to engage."

There is no verbal acknowledgement. No reply. Instead of common verbiage the night suddenly grows much louder.

Dick starts rocking off with the .50 in proper, violent six round bursts.

The sound of the massive weapon's angry shouting immediately dampens all other noise, and my ears begin to ring.

Thump-thump-thump. Thump-thump-thump.

Brass from the front seat yells at the top of his Southern lungs, *"Git you some, Goddamnit!"*

Our convoy rolls to an easy stop as we round the bend in the traffic circle and parks in its Lazy-W formation seemingly of its own accord as we arrive at the battle. The position forms our convoy into a jagged crescent, with the front of the formation nearly perpendicular to the target building, which is now only a hundred meters away.

I call across to Cole, *"Get a can ready!"*

The bright trails of tracers and sharp whizzes of naked rounds fly past my window; the wild sounds of ricochets and our own gunfire reverberate into the night as the smell of hot gunpowder and burning brass fills the musty air inside the truck.

Nothing further needing to be said, Cole and I work frantically to unstrap the pile of ammo that sits tightly secured between us in the back seat.

After freeing some of the boxes from their ratchet straps with my shaking hands, I proceed to crack each 200-round can open one by one, checking that everything is in order, and that the rounds have not become entangled in a way that would interrupt a smooth load.

Another radio call comes through the din, "Dismounts, prepare to step off."

As I place my hand on the door handle and look out the window I can only see the blinding flashes of tracers, American and insurgent alike, as all of our trucks and dozens of the enemy sling everything they have at each other. At least we've taken some of the pressure off our friends.

I jump in my seat as a round impacts the truck somewhere near my door, and dozen more whizz by, giving my armored seat the over-under treatment.

Looking out the window at the green hailstorm, my testicles try to climb their way into my ass.

From my angled position, looking on from the safety of my now tightly shut window, I can see four or five muzzle flashes from enemy positions in the windows. Dust and debris fly free of the target building in small chunks, as the façade and windows of the structure are being continually filled with our own two cents.

Thump-thump-thump. Thump-thump-thump.

"Feeling a slight pucker, Cole! You ready to hit this shit?"

The noise in our truck, the lead truck, has become slightly more deafening since the Mk-19 behind us started to open up, blowing away not only our ear-drums, but also any living thing, be it man or beast on the first floor of the enemy structure.

"Ready as I'll ever be, motherfucker!"

"Can, I need a can!"

Dick's gun has gone quiet, all out of baby-batter, so I hoist him up another can. His reload is shaky and filled with colorful language, but it's quick. Before much time passes the gun is up and running again, deafening us all with its reports and showering the inside of the vehicle with hot brass. Hopefully it's showering somebody with hot caffeinated death at the other end too.

There are no real signs of enemy casualties yet, as the gunfire refuses to cease.

James comes across the net once again, "Lead truck, we have Apache CAS on the net; shine the motherfucking one o'clock. Dismount."

This is, having finally arrived, the nightmare call for dismounts. It is also the savior call of the evening, as we have some avian help close at hand this morning, ready to lay some leaden Hell in the name of Jesus and 'Merica. And me, for fuck's sake.

"Get it!"

Thinking of nothing, lest my spirit abandon me, I quickly throw open my door and step out into the maelstrom erupting in the very center of the square. We're pretty good targets now.

Lucky for me, heavy concrete supports stand just a few meters away from my truck door to our three o' clock. I quickly shut the door behind me, exposing my body to the enemy fire while taking the time to politely close the door behind me to protect those still inside the truck. With my metal cover closed up and gone, I start to run for concrete as Cole rounds the back of the truck behind me. There is no orderliness to our dismount. Ten of us have now exited the vehicles, with six paratroopers in my group, and four in the other; we begin our fervent run in a chaotic gaggle, moving to the far side of the road as fast as we can. Angry sounding bullets impact the ground in front of my feet, and especially eerie projectiles miss us by flying only a few inches above. I find this extremely motivating, so I sprint even faster.

Sliding into home, I take up a position of cover amongst the sturdy concrete pillars as Cole takes a professional and hurried dive, landing just behind me and to my rear, finding safety behind his very own cylinder of concrete.

Brass has also dismounted into the crossfire with us to do the honors of aiming a heavy infrared laser at the target building.

Our job is not to engage targets in the building; that's already being attended to by the heavy weapon systems in the trucks; our M-4s could not do a better job than two .50s and three Mk-19s. Firing our own weapons would only serve to give away our new position and complicate the very important task at hand.

Instead of firing, Cole and I cover our trucks by pulling security on an alleyway to our right-hand side, scanning rooftops across the square, and generally protecting Brass from any unseen enemy activity as he aims his laser at the target building, now a mere eighty meters from where we crouch behind cover.

On the other side of the square to my nine o' clock I can see our other squad of dismounts, four in all, doing much the same thing we are, securing the areas on the outer periphery of the traffic circle while doing their very best not to expose themselves any further to the enemy fires.

The night drowns in the din of men screaming and the thick, acrid smell of gun-smoke. Reports from dozens of weapons echo from every wall, and the traffic circle has become an orchestra pit for the dark symphony of murderous instruments.

The enemy fires continue on, refusing to die. The mass of fighters that greeted us are most likely heavily wounded or dead, but the fight still drags on. There's no telling how many enemy fighters still remain in the structure.

Nothing detrimental has come across the net yet, which means that somehow in all the fray, our Redwater friends are still alive, and apparently, they are quite excited to be fighting from the open now that they have some heavy hitting friends in their corner. There are no casualties that I know of on our side, though through the fervent gunfire I can hear the dying screams of enemy combatants bellowing out against the night, trying as best they can to let their pain be heard.

Through the sharp explosions from the 40mms and the thump-thump-thumping of the fifties, some of the screams that can be heard emanating from the target building sound as if they are angry, in a rage, while others are clearly fading laments. The pained screams are windows into dying minds and bodies; souls that are being ripped bodily away from their sundered hosts.

It chills me to the bone with fear; it excites me and tempers my own sense of righteous indignation. I hate, hate, *hate* them. I can feel the hot fear starting to leave my body; I love that I can hear them die.

I scan my sector and see nothing, save for a bit of movement in a few lighted windows across the street from our position, but I do not fire.

If I was a terrorist genius, I would not have left the light on.

It's more likely that the movement belongs to frightened children or housewives, trying as best they can to understand exactly what is happing to their neighborhood, just outside the windows of their homes. Shouting at Cole I ask, *"You got anything?"*

"Nothing, man. Looks clear."

The three other D Co soldiers that dismounted with us also give small negatives and head shakes. Nobody can see shit, other than the maelstrom still erupting from the target building directly to our front.

Brass holds his laser, visible only through our night-vision optics, steadily at a third story window of the building that is the sole target of our selective rage. Amazingly, AK-47s still fire at us into the night. Though most of the enemies appear to be somewhat smarter than they were a short

284

minute ago, now mostly firing from relocated positions on different floors, their side of the fight is sounding decidedly less motivated than ours. I can now see no more than six different flashes from enemy weapons, which is less than half the volume of fire that we were subjected to when we arrived.

I can hear the report come over Brass's M-bitter radio. "Tally, one mic out."

One minute until the big noise. One minute to salvation, elation, and the total silence of death from the fuck-sticks who decided to make a big row out of all this tonight.

Apparently in the know, the Swiss-cheesed Redwater trucks, somehow still operational, break from their small formation in the center of the square and proceed to pull out behind us with personnel firing at the target building from driver's seats with pistols, passenger seats with rifles, and truck beds with as many cuss-words as would make a seasoned seaman blush.

"Dismounts! Mount up!"

Though somewhat diminished from the severity of the fight, enemy fire continues to rain down all around us. Though it was necessary for us to have left the vehicles in an attempt to get a more thorough grip on security around the square, I feel uneasy and naked at the prospect of crossing the Tracer-Styx once again.

Aware of the call to mount up, the gunners on our trucks double their rates of fire, going cyclic in order to make sure that our enemies put their heads down, thus making sure that we survive our return journey. Here's one for suppression.

No time. No choice.

Together, the six of us take a sprint back to the trucks.

As I run I can hear a new, hot salvo of 7.62 rounds whiz crazily above my head; I hear another pop and see a round impact the dirt just inches in front of my running boots.

Should have learned to lead better, motherfucker.

Arriving first, I open my door for Cole, who barrels directly through the middle of the truck, eliminating the risk that would arise from running all the way around the truck again. I'm sure he's more than happy to bump Dick in the legs as he passes as a worthy trade for making a markedly shorter journey.

Taking cover behind the door, I slip inside the vehicle, relieved and feeling safe once again, tightly behind Cole; Brass is already safely inside, seated once again in his position of command, now leaning slightly out of his open window while still aiming his green laser at the target building.

"Tally Ho!"

Immediately, immensely, the night is filled with noise louder than the fervent gunfire.

The roars of engines and rotor blades scream from only thirty feet high, as two AH-64 Apaches burn through the night above us, flying overhead at what seems like a hundred miles per hour, emptying everything they've got into the target building. They've got quite a bit.

Chain guns belch and make the night shake. Through my green eye, from corner to corner, two floors of the building erupt in sparks, concrete chips, and fire, as the structure and whoever still reside within are mightily ripped apart by thunder and steel.

Dick shouts down, *"Holy Fuck!"*

The display is quick, but it is unequivocally the most intense and amazing sight I have ever beheld in my mortal life.

Quickly, a second chopper passes overhead, firing a barrage of hellfire rockets into the structure, one per floor, blotting out the world with its fury and causing a pounding in my head like I've never felt before.

I don't need to say anything. We saved the day. Our work is done. And the birds have saved our day. Though admittedly, we were doing a pretty good job by ourselves.

I listen in mute shock as another report comes over the radio telling us all to sit tight, as the birds are coming around another time for a slower, more thorough pass. The square is bathed in a quiet, deep ringing stillness, filled only with the close sound of helicopter blades and the nervous excitement that foretells of their return.

"Ten Seconds. Tally!"

The birds clip in again, this time at much slower speeds, hovering just above our heads as they make their pass. Not shooting rockets this time, each bird, one of which is clearly visible through the gunner's turret just above me, unloads another volley of chain-gun fire, methodically sweeping the floors of the target building.

It's beautiful. The sparks and the pure noise of the brutal display is somewhat spiritual. I take a moment, helpless now from my voyeuristic passenger seat as the might of a superpower rips the small dirt-people fortress apart. I feel prideful, as a veteran might on the fourth of July. I feel jubilant and safe. I was just out there. I feel… I feel like a fan of the winning Super Bowl team. *See, I told you so!*

In a moment the display is over, and the report comes over the net that the birds are on their way home, after being given a prompt and audibly heartfelt thank-you over the net from our LT.

"Man, those guys are fucking cool." I say to nobody in particular, and nobody refutes the fact.

I crack my window a bit, just slightly, and press my face near to the hot summer morning breeze and inhale the sweet smell of life, of danger surmounted.

Danger surmounted smells like melted concrete, cordite, and Fear-Spice body odor.

On the still darkness of the morning air I can also smell the exhaust from our trucks and the gunpowder of recently fired rounds. I can hear the ringing in my ears telling the story of the small, but somehow meaningful fight that just took place, and I can clearly perceive in small measure, the scent of blood, shit, and burnt hair on the light early morning wind.

"Radio checks. Trucks sound off."

"One up."

"Two fuckin' up."

"God-damn three up."

"Four, Hella up."

"Five, break." There's a pause. "Five up. Shit."

Our platoon sergeant strikes back, "No swearing on the God-damned, mother-fucking radio."

Nobody gives a shit about the sudden, illegal, and unanimous bout of senseless vulgarity. Nobody is going to bitch at us about it tonight. Nobody gives a flying fiddler's fuck. We can say whatever in the Hell we want to say tonight. I guess there really is a time and a place for everything.

In the new quiet of the morning, in the total stillness, save for the lonely sound of rubber on dirt and the steady rumbling of diesel engines, we turn slowly around the circle as we head back from whence we came with our gunners still scanning their zones. Us dismounts stare out of our windows once again, every man in overt, quiet reflection and deafened disbelief, each himself considering the boisterous events of the hour in his own way as we pull back through our small slice of town, back toward Mad, and indelibly, indisputably, a bout of good, sound sleep. That is, unless we get called out again. Hey, when I was little, I thought I'd like to be a firefighter. I had no idea, mind, what manner of fire that would be.

The drive back to Mad goes quickly; the radios stay hushed, and no conversations are started. We listen to the radio reports as we drive, snooping in on the aftermath play-by-play as a trite, quick synopsis of our sector's events are relayed to neighboring units and friendly elements around the zone.

As our truck pulls lazily into the ECP I can feel my whole body relax; the tremors are gone and a sudden, peaceful exhaustion courses through my entire body.

Rather than the usual hurried breakdown, as we are still on call, we simply park the trucks, shut the engines off, download our gear, and wait in smoky, red-lit huddles for the next word from our LT or platoon sergeant.

"How'd that feel, Dick?" I omit the customary 'sergeant,' and am excused, as everyone could really care less about now.

"Like a fucking game, dude. Like a surreal, loud, high definition fucking game. Just wild, man."

"You think you got you one?"

Freddy, coming around the truck, lends a hasty reply, "I think you took out the entire third floor by yourself. Just sparks, man, saw the whole thing out the windshield. When I wasn't trying to plug my ears, that is. Jesus, that was loud."

With nothing to do but wait, I seek Chapel out among the rabble from the other trucks.

"Hey Chapps. What's up?"

"Fucking Armageddon, same as every other day." He smiles at me, a large stream of Camel smoke issuing from his mouth as he laughs a bit.

"How your ears doin', D? Dick got his rocks off, yeah?"

"What?"

"I said – you're a jackass."

Knowing full well that my ears aren't that far gone, he quickly tunes in on my cliché joke, and the comment is forgotten.

I light up a cigarette of my own, while silently excusing myself from the rest of the group to stare up at the dark and cloudless sky, thinking about just how quiet the night can be, and how quiet it has always been throughout the majority of my life. I also wonder if I'll ever be able to hear the sound of silence ever again. My ears have always had a slight ring in them. From music first, and the army second. Now, with the healthy ringing blasting through the amplifier in my head once more, I wonder, as I drag on my sweet smoke, if it will ever truly go away.

Our smoke breaks and excited conversations about the evening don't carry on for very long, as soon we are summoned forth by James once again.

It's casual and not intense like the first briefing iteration.

We are told first and foremost to stay close by the trucks, letting our respective squad leaders know if we break away to piss or shit. We're told to keeps coms checks up and running every hour on the radios, and blessedly, we are also commanded to drink some water and take a nap.

As we break away from the circle, I'm giddy with the elation that I'll soon be unconscious once again. 0400. Just a few more hours of QRF standby and we'll be clear to go back to the barracks, take care of our gear, and then grab some real shut eye before the slated mounted patrols and joint Iraqi operations begin.

I'm not long in the back of the truck before I nod off, tucked tightly into the cozy, safe space amongst my helmet, nods, armor, and weapon.

My weapons cleaning episode is quick and easy; none of the dismounts fired during the engagement. The same cannot be said of the gunners, however, and they are all busily cleaning their heavy weapons, fully dirtied in the intense fight just hours ago. Sensitive items checks are carried out as usual, and once again I lie on my bunk and stare at *love you, love you*.

It must be roughly eight o' clock in the morning, but my head still says that it's just past midnight. I forego the opportunity to grab some simulated breakfast foods, but instead take the time to lie down and catch a few winks after changing my socks and undershirt. For not having engaged in a particularly large amount of physical activity, I sweated like a horse at full sprint last night. Running through a hail of bullets will do that to a man I guess. It's all well though; my blouse has been sweat starched for upwards of a week now, and I don't feel that it could get any crunchier anyway.

I awake at around ten, my nap having naturally concluded itself. I take the time to brush my teeth, bath my underarms and crotch with baby wipes, and apply a fresh coat of deodorant under my armpits. Morning, sunshine. I'm ready for the day.

We're not pulling out on our operation until noon, so I figure I have time for a sit in the privy, as well as the obligation to myself to grab some chow before we head out into our new neighborhoods and proceed to do some knock and talks accompanied by the local Iraqi army.

It should be a pretty chill detail, except for the fact that our dismounted foot patrol is slated to last a full eight hours. There are running bets that suggest the day of knocking will be over after only four hours or so, which is the usual breaking point of the Iraqi army work ethic. That is, they can feasibly hold out that long if they are given a steady IV drip of chai tea, cigarettes, and falafels.

Finishing my personal maintenance activities, I make the long walk to the Humvees quite by myself, beating the rest of my squad there by a good fifteen minutes. No reason in particular; I just have no other place to be.

When I arrive at my designated truck, the lead truck as usual, the doors and roof are still chained and padlocked, so I drop my kit and light up a smoke for lack of anything better to do.

Before long, the rest of the gunners and drivers trickle in. I offer a hand, helping to hoist the heavy weapon systems onto their pindles, and I help with coms, firing radio checks back and forth with the drivers.

Another half hour passes, and we find ourselves pressed into the early afternoon huddle once again.

Although not yet dressed in my armor, I can already feel the sweat starting to bead down my back. We've been told that it should be over 125 degrees today in the summer Iraqi sun. It's early July, and I'm told the brunt of the summer heat has yet to hit. Over the next month or so we can all expect temperatures in slight excess of 150 degrees; we're not very excited about the news.

"All right people, listen up."

"Today should be a simple affair. Stay close to your interpreters and Iraqi pals. Also, command wants us to directly report any instances of Iraqi soldiers stealing from the houses of locals. There have been a lot of complaints of that nature recently, so we're going to step on that shit if possible."

"That being said, written reports. Don't attempt to apprehend, beat to death, or shoot any of the IA who are doing this, understood? Killing all of our joint-patrol buddies would certainly be bad PR, hooah?"

We give a unanimous acknowledgment, but it's not all seriousness. Chuckles and guffaws radiate throughout the platoon. It's a wonder this country is still even here, with the manner of stupidity that issues forth from its so-called protectors.

Our sectors and routes are promptly briefed to us, and then, as is usual, we're back in the trucks and on our way to another nearby traffic circle where we will link up with a detachment of nearly one hundred IA soldiers, and then move east to west, door to door through our entire sector.

I laugh quietly to myself in my passenger seat, just thinking thoughts. Back in the states we jump out of airplanes at least once a month. Sometimes as many as three or four times depending on jump schedules. The 82nd Airborne remains the largest and finest parachute infantry group in the world, but still, we drive everywhere we go.

We'll be using interpreters to talk to locals, assessing their living conditions to see if we can help at all with basic considerations such as humanitarian food relief, electric power, and culinary water supplies.

Linking up with the IA goes smoothly, except for an incident that startled the crap out of us. An accidental discharge from an Iraqi soldier's AK ripped the sky open in three places just after we arrived. Nobody was killed. Nobody, at least for the next two city blocks. Beyond that, who knows?

As prescribed, our patrol goes clumsily and slowly, with Americans on one side of the road and Iraqis on the other. Our gray formations keep their proper spacing, and we're all business as we roll through city block after city block pulling security, remaining focused on the task at hand. The American side of the street looks like a military patrol.

It's different, there on the other side. The Iraqi soldiers cluster together, look for nothing in particular, and talk and smoke cigarettes as they be-bop along with their rifles hanging forgotten at their sides, or sling-less, swung clumsily about in their hands. Those that carry their rifles in the low-ready position put us constantly on edge, as they sweep their careless muzzles across us time and time again, without a single thought for 'don't flag your buddy' protocols.

Also as predicted, many chai tea breaks and falafel stops are needed. For minutes on end we stand idly by and wait for the IPs to stand around and smoke, eat multiple lunches, and sip away at chai cups before having our interpreters goad them into continuing on.

Three hours into the joint patrol, Freddy and I cue onto a curious phenomenon.

"Hey, Freddy, is it just me, or are there like, only forty or so IAs left?"

"You are astute my friend.   Either there's a bit of attrition going on, or we're under a well- planned, deftly executed ninja assault."

"Hashishins."

"Ah.   Right.   A Hashishin assault."

"Good Lordy."

Breaking away from the central group, ten soldiers from D co, us scouts included, proceed down a narrow mulhalla with the small remainder of half an Iraqi element, maybe fifteen soldiers in all.

We walk quickly, with the early afternoon sun-dot reminding us that we won't be pulling this detail for much longer.   One more hour is the word coming across through the ASIP radio slung onto my back.   The larger operation has apparently been cancelled, as command can no longer deny that our friendly elements have been slowly but surely abandoning us, and will soon leave us alone, in the very center of Moudan on foot.

"One more hour roundabouts, Freddy."

"Yeah.   This particular mission didn't last very long, did it?"

"Nope nope nope, as predicted."

I do my best to keep pulling security and stay alert as we traverse the small mulhalla, making random, thorough, and quick stops to peek inside dwellings while talking to locals about any pressing matters of the day. Primarily, we try to find out whether they have concerns about, or have witnessed any recent suspicious, violent, or dangerous behavior in the 'hood.

The answers are always the same.   *Nope Mista, everything is great. Everything is fine.   We're just living here, safe in paradise, without a care in the mortal world.*   More likely, closer to the truth, their smiling faces and calm assurances about the groovy present state of life is probably a simple mechanism to get the IA soldiers out of their homes, lest any of their personal property be illegally requisitioned for the greater good of Iraq's finest.

I walk two meters in front of Freddy, and about three behind Cloud. The rest of the scouts and D Co march on ahead, trying as best they can to communicate with the IA, as well as putting forth effort to remain vigilant about scanning windows and rooftops for any present threats.

Just to my right, about three feet off, I walk side by side a tired looking IA.   We tried to speak moments ago, but he speaks no English, and I stopped giving a flying fuck about the Arabic language a few months ago.   So, rather than communicate like a bunch of modern folks, we just smile at each other while pointing to windows, pieces of strange garbage, neighborhood children, and anything of interest to make the walk seem to go a little faster, and a bit more sociable.

Weapon at this side, with no sling, just his fist, he walks beside me with an MP3 player earphone plugged into the right side of his head, and a piece of foot-bread clutched tightly in his left fist.

Apparently, one of his tactical pouches is filled with some sort of cream cheese in a plastic bag. He does his best to avoid stepping into the large rivulet of sewage that snakes down the center of the mulhalla, all the while busily stuffing his face.

Across the street to the right, about fifty feet away, I can see a mural depicting canoes on a stretch of swamp land, sailing their fishing rigs across an impressively painted stretch of cinderblock wall.

Nodding to my new friend, I point with my index finger and motion towards the mural, for no other reason than to receive a nod of assent back, in an effort to keep the primitive conversation going.

He looks in the direction of the mural and suddenly trips, causing the cheese laden chunk of bread to launch crazily out of his grasp.

With the reflexes of a small cat, he lunges toward the errant missile and promptly trips again, this time with horrifying results.

As his body lunges forward one of his loosely hanging frag grenades slips its spoon, and in a terrible, butt-fuck-on-ice pirouette, he clutches at thin air and misses again as the armed explosive plunks dramatically to a splashing halt in the dirty water at my feet.

Less than a half second goes by, and I'm diving toward the brick wall and dirt floor to my left, screaming at the top of my lungs,

"Frag out!"

"Fuck."

I hear Freddy exhale the fuck-word before I feel him slide into home beside me. Some members of our squad dive for cover, while the rest dumbly turn to stare slack-jawed at us in an attempt to understand what has happened.

Akhmed. I'll call him Akhmed, stands by for another whole second as he stupidly gazes at the fallen frag.

Some of the IAs begin to backpedal in mute horror, while others simply stand, stare, and attempt to process the last moments of their lives.

I look away from the frag, craning my neck to the left; I feel the grinding of my helmet biting into the old yellow bricks a half-inch from my face. My buttocks tightens and I open my mouth; I brace for the blast, and the pain.

Three seconds.   Four seconds.

A heavy, anticipatory stillness hangs about the crowded alleyway, as everyone has no alternative but to wait and see how the grim event will transpire.

Five seconds.   A bit more.   Seven.   Ten.

Freddy and I let out a long sigh of relief as we come to grips with the fact that we may indeed not be mutilated by an errant explosive device, dropped in a river of sewage just three feet away.

"Okay, Mista.   Okay."

Akhmed laughs and smiles at me, then promptly reaches into the sewage to extricate the soggy grenade from the swampy fluid.

Brown and gray tendrils of moss and shit hang from the glinting wet metal of the device.   Looking closely, it becomes clear that Akhmed, in his infinite wisdom, simply had the grenade hanging from his chest by the spoon, for God knows how long.   Rather than the spoon having been triggered, and the explosive armed by the absence of the pin, the whole spoon and release mechanism had become unscrewed from the grenade; it was never armed, and the blasting cap still hangs peacefully and friendly-like from Akhmed's chest.

"No problem Mista; no problem."

Suddenly speaking decent conversational English, and with a cheesy smile, Akhmed proceeds to screw the blasting cap back into the explosive device, restoring it to its former position once again, where it hangs sodden and inert from his chest.

"Right."

"Right."

Without another word, Freddy and I climb onto our shaky legs to catch up with the rest of the dudes for the next half hour or so of the doomed patrol.

Dick can't help himself.

"A little jumpy there, huh D?"

"No.   Not jumpy one bit.   Before, at least.   Nope, just following standard procedures."

The joke is only a small prod; a miniscule sarcastic gripe.   I saw the look of mute horror on Dick's face, the mirror twin of mine, while the shit-bag drama was unfolding itself.   Gotta love the Baghdad this week. At least I didn't pass out, hit my head, and get a purple heart.

"Maybe I'll get a purple heart for that."

Dick's gaze immediately transforms from amused to disappointed, angry, and sullen.   He has taken Duke's side in the matter, and obviously takes offense to my ill-witted statement.

With marked spacing between each word, he flatly, angrily says to me, "Shut-the-fuck-up, Pearce.   I'm serious about this."

I smile.   "Rod-Ger Sah-Gent!"

I could really give a shit.   I'm still pumped from almost being blown into Kibbles.

Chapter Seven: Far Away

If you lie beside me I'll show you my mind,
About all my anguish as I left you behind.
I'll hold your hand tightly and try to explain,
The inexorable torture of war's lonely pain.

The days unforgiving that stretch on without end,
The soul thus unfettered with these words that I bend,
In effort to show you how my life has changed,
I'll tell you my story, though roughly arranged.

In the violence and turmoil of hands from the sky,
Of the fear and the waiting, so slow to pass by,
It's of these that I'll tell you, those remembered best,
As you hold me tightly, my head on your chest.

I'll tell you I love you; how it's always that way,
In lands far off distant and filled with the fray,
How I longed then to hold you, but always I feared
That a letter would reach you and bring you to tears.

So I thought not of the bad things; of the killing and death,
But I thought of your body, of your light and your breath.
I'd think of the good times that have all passed me by,
And the heaven that's waiting right here by your side.

So tonight it's hard for me to tell you
Just exactly how I feel,
For words are always hollow
When one has lived for real.

The rest of the patrols go smoothly and without significant events. Mad is kind to us with its steady supply of chocolate brownies and readily available porta-johns. Love it. Love it.

Another eight-hour patrol, and then it's back to the FOB. Home sweet home, yet again.

Having been gone in the city for fourteen days, after cleaning weapons and fueling the trucks, all of D Co shotgun scatters throughout the FOB, eager to fill our bellies full of real food, and maybe make a phone call home.

Talking to my family on the phone is wonderful, although there is not much new to say. Regrettably, I cannot get ahold of Emily. Knowing full well that it's the dead of night in New York, it's no surprise that she's not picking up her phone. Resigned to the fact that I will not be hearing her voice today, I trundle along, Chapel in tow, to the computer lab to fire off a barrage of e-mails, updating my family on what little news that there is to tell, that I'm allowed to tell, and also to write a mushy letter to Emily. Doubtless, it's time for her to be a little angry with me, feeling as she does from time to time that I'm not talking to her out of some sort of neglect, rather than what is realistically permitted.

Just inside the computer lab door, a fairly modern place aside from the building it finds itself in, the main room looks much like any computer lab that can be found in any high school or public library across America. From each console the clickety-clacketyness of hammered keys sound off through the air, as those fortunate enough to know how to type communicate with their families as efficiently as possible, from a virtual world away.

Some of the computers are even equipped with cameras that enable a bit of choppy, lagging, low-resolution video chat, although I've never tried it myself.

As usual, my father's Yahoo messenger is running, so it's a quick and simple process to start typing directly to him, although we don't talk about much. We love each other. He can't wait until I get home. The dog says hi. Everyone misses me. The usual, boiler-plate 'soldier away from home' stuff. It's comforting, if not a bit cliché.

Having just found out that I will be getting leave against my will in November, I decide to write my brother and tell him the good news, in the event that he wants to do a couple of liquor store runs and get pre-emptively stocked up before my arrival. When I think about going home to spend a bit of time with him a smile lights on my face, quite without manual control. Even back stateside, it's been over two years since I've been able to go home.

Next comes e-mail from Emily delivered through Facebook; the first half-dozen or so she fired at me soon after my last disappearance, while the last e-mail in the bunch was written over a week ago. Doubtless, she grew tired of me not responding and simply decided to wait. Which is just great; I'm a bit pinched for time today as it is.

> *Hey Dal,*
>   *How is your week going? I'm being driven up the wall right now. It's almost finals, so I'm busily cramming away to get ready for them. I got another job! The men's store just across the way from Target was hiring, so I just went in and got the job. I'm very excited to be so busy! I'm going to enjoy the break from school as best I can, and hopefully start living it up a little bit more with the girls ☺ I can't wait until you can come see me! I'll be a senior next year, and you know what that means ;) A room all to myself! No roommates equals more privacy for you and me! There are so many places I want to show you when you get back. Namely, a cute little Japanese bistro me and my cousin discovered a few nights ago. I really miss you! I think about you every day, and I hope you're staying safe! Tell me what you can when you get the chance; I know I'll hear from you as soon as you're able to get back to me. Any word on when your leave bracket is yet? I love you, Teddy Bear!*
>   *Love,*   *Your Choochie-Face.*

Reading Emily's words makes me smile. I love hearing about the pressing issues of her day back in reality. I can't wait to be able to share with her some of the day-to-day events from my life over here, many of which I'm not fully allowed to speak about over the internet, for the obvious electronic security reasons. Hajji's listening maybe, but Big Brother is for sure.

I don't take the time to reply to each small e-mail snippet about Emily's emotions or daily to-do lists. Instead, I read through them one by one, savoring every word until it's time for me to write one cohesive, and conclusive reply.

The last e-mail in the bunch, written as she doubtless gave up hope of ever hearing from me again, sounds like it has a different tone, by far measure, from the first.

Hey D. I hope you're all right. We keep watching the news every day to hear if we can learn anything new, and I'm constantly looking at the soldiers to ever see if I can find you in a crowd. I know how silly that sounds though; I know they don't allow reporters to go where you are. Give me a call whenever you get the chance! I'm really worried about you. I hope you're not dodging me for whatever reason. Just send me a quick mail when you get the chance. I'm dying to know that you're all right. I'm thinking about you a lot tonight. Hear from you soon.
                                                                    Love you, Emily.

After we've recently corresponded or spoken over the phone, Emily's letters are always upbeat and filled with excited punctuation. As the weeks of silence drag on, the tone of the letters gradually becomes more serious, as all the exclamation points and smiley faces see themselves out. The last letter is very robotic and dry, with not one flare-up of happy to be found.

I set my jaw, and sit up straight for the smoothing-over task at hand that is about to take place.

Knowing that I have a few good pages of response in me, as well as plenty of 'hang in theres' and 'I love yous,' I get to work as quickly as possible, typing away as fast as I can in an effort to say as much as possible in the remaining fifteen minutes I have allotted to me in the lab. If I were to go over time, I would need to log out, and go wait in line once more for my turn to show up again. Which means I have one shot to get it all out before I can hit the send button and vamano.

I begin by responding to her life and times, her week, her new spots, and her crazy work schedule.

Then I tell her about the places I want to take her when this is all over with, and what we'll do when we get there. Wink.

Three minutes left. "Computer 13, three minutes."

"Roger," I say to the fat, insufferable 10th Mountain sergeant that somehow got tasked with the duty of overseeing the computer lab. Maybe he hurt himself in the shitter somehow. Who knows.

I finish up the letter by saying that I love her more than anyone or anything, and that I'm doing my best to stay safe. There is still no real danger, and everything is going good. But I don't finish. I never press send.

Horror of horrors, in an instant there is a massive power outage that treks its way through the lab, plunging all of the dying computers and angry soldiers into pitch darkness.

"Fuck!"

It's not just me that says it. It's a syncopated chorus that rises, builds, and echoes around the small stone walls of our cozy lab. In an instant the power is back on, but my time is up, and my chance has flown. I'll have to come back later this evening for a re-write. If I don't communicate with her soon there will most likely be emotional hell to pay. Not so much for her, but for the guilt trip she will doubtless send me on. I know what's coming; my bags are already packed.

Back in the barracks it's life as usual. Platoon chores have been accomplished, and scouts, as well as the other paratroopers from D Co, unwind by playing games on handheld devices and modern game systems hooked up to third-world television sets. The bravest soldiers watch movies and play real-time strategy games on their laptops sent from home, or on new, high-speed machines that they recently purchased online and had mailed in. I myself would worry too much about having such high value electronics in this place. My computer is safe back in North Carolina where it belongs.

Lying in my bunk, rifle and other sensitive items accounted for, I take a moment to make sure the mosquito netting on my bunk is tightly sealed against the new contagion plaguing the barracks.

Dozens, if not hundreds of mosquitoes zip around the inside of our small home; we've been told that they have probably all issued forth from the sewer system found beneath the building. Thank god for inoculation and immunization; the mosquito infestation is becoming a seasonal occurrence.

Luckily, I have only been bit a couple of times in the hour since our return, and now, satisfied that the little bests cannot reach me in my nylon-webbing shelter, I take my PSP out of its case for a spin, as well as a necessary charge up at its preferred power source: a regular enough seeming outlet that sits just above my mattress to my right side, seated in a modern, mostly intact plastic mount on the wall.

Not feeling hungry tonight, I forgo a chow hall trip; maybe if I get the inkling later I can link up with Chapel or Andrews for a midnight tuna run.

The scouts, all except Freddy, who is sound asleep in his bunk though it's only seven in the evening, watch an HBO series that reminds them somewhat of America.

I'm only able to play for a half hour or so before I get both frustrated at the situation with talking to Emily, as well as sleepy after the long day's drive.

Switching off my device, I hook it into the bottom rungs of the bunk above me, this one a pale baby blue that is blessedly bereft of the 'love you, love you' script I've become so accustomed to in the last few days.

I roll to my right side and grab my boonie cap, securing it snugly over my face in an attempt to blot out the bright lights of the barracks and the late afternoon sun streaming in high above the sandbags which plug the window above my bunk.

I never get the chance to drift to sleep. In the sweetly dark, relaxed haze that foretells of the coming sleep, I hear a faraway alarm.

Incoming. Incoming. Incoming.

My eyes snap open and I wait pensively, listening for what happens next.

The rest of the barracks falls quiet as volume on televisions is turned down, and everyone consciously waits in a hush to hear how close the wretched ordinance will land.

An explosion, probably a hundred meters off, sounds like a bass drum on parade; it shakes our building, but otherwise has no negative effect.

Another blast. And then another.

Sitting up on the edge of my bunk, I flip back the mosquito netting, bastards be damned, and wait to hear if my squad is up. They're not.

"Hey, Cole, where are Dick and Duke?"

"Chow-hall man."

He talks sleepily to me across the bay, pulling on his undershirt as he does so. We're unaccounted for. We know what comes next.

Throughout the barracks, squad leaders flock across our small hallway to a small room where the platoon sergeant and LT sleep, relaying that their squads are accounted for, compiling the report that is momentarily to be sent down to the CQ, and then by radio across the FOB to the CP.

Freddy, now fully awake and alert, says, "You guys going? I'll go too."

I reply, "It's okay Freddy. We know they went to the chow hall. Stay here in case they come back. We won't be gone more than ten."

Hurriedly pulling on my boonie and grabbing my rifle, I wait just a moment longer for Cole to pull on his blouse.

As I wait for my buddy, Chapel rounds the corner.

"You guys accounted for?"

"Nopeskiy; we've got two at the chow hall."

"We're missing one too. I'll tag with you."

With that, the three of us fly down the stairwell, busting out of the bottom of the barracks to hit the ground running as soon as the loose gravel of the FOB is beneath our boots.

"You think they finally hit it?"

Chapel gives me a sarcastic look over his shoulder as we run. Through quickening breath, he finds the time to speak.

"You know, they say that if you put a thousand monkeys with typewriters in a room for eternity, eventually they would write the works of William Shakespeare."

"Shakespeare was a hack."

"No matter, point is, it's about fucking time that they figured it out, firing from different locations every time or not."

I don't see any smoke, and the sirens and explosions have ceased. Regardless of the disarming stillness that hangs about the FOB, we quicken our pace even further, dodging through narrow alleyways and zigzagging though the parked Humvees in the motor pool as we run as fast as we can, pell-mell toward the D-Fac.

As we Round the familiar corner of the J-DAM building it's clear that something is amiss.

Though no hole can be seen in the outside of our eatery, it's clear that the blasts were close, if not directly inside the flimsy structure.

Chapel slows down in the front, and half jogs in place as he turns about to speak.

"Bastards probably hit square on the roof; can't see it from here."

All fear gone from me, as the bombs have already finished falling, a new anxiety forms in my guts. My squad mates were here.

Just outside the front entrance and exit, a dozen wounded soldiers lie spread out on the third-world sidewalk and the dirt road, freshly moistened to keep the dust down.

Two soldiers farther up the line appear to be dead, as their faces have been covered with their own bloody uniform tops.

I scan the wounded with my eyes the best I can. Thankfully, I do not see Dick or Duke among them.

Shouting out, dumbly walking in the chaos, I see Dick after a few moments, crouched by a soldier from another unit while beginning to apply a tourniquet to the young man's leg.

"Need a hand Dick?"

"Nah. I got it. Maybe. Yeah man, pressure here."

Without taking the time to don a protective glove, I apply pressure to the bleeding thigh of a man I don't know as Dick uses a tourniquet to apply a pressure dressing, although the wound is superficial and shows no sign of arterial spew. Due to the abnormal, shocked-out color of the wounded soldier's face, I can see why Dick has chosen to err on the side of caution. There is no harm in tourniquet application on the FOB anyhow; in a moment he'll be in the med-station, where he will be seen to by professionals.

"How you feelin', man?"

"Been better."

The soldier, Martinez by nametag and Mexican by my best estimate, looks a little gray, but otherwise no worse for wear.

"I got a hole in my leg, homie."

"I see that. You surely do. Impressive."

After a short, awkward pause I say, "You get a purple heart for that, you know?"

"Yeah, homie, I guess you're right."

Dick smiles at me with only a small bit of contempt on his face, finally buckling under my continuous flow of purple heart commentary. I have spoken the truth. We both agree, this soldier deserves it. I win this round.

With the pressure dressing in place and the blood flow stopped, Dick looks around, presumably for somebody else to assist; however, it looks as though the ambulatory casualties have already started walking or are being helped to the med station. The two bodies lay untouched, morbid, and for the time being, forgotten.

Quickly, two orderlies from the med-station appear to take our new friend away, thus concluding our medical duties for the evening. Hopefully.

"Seen Duke?"

"Yeah D. He's on his way back. I thought he would have passed you on his way there."

"Must've missed 'im. We hauled balls the whole way over here."

Most of the first responders' jobs having been done even before me and the others arrived, there looks to be precious little to be done now, save for the repair crews and those who will come to take the dead.

303

Dick turns to me, "Hey, Pearce; go check the patches, man," as he motions toward the bodies on the sidewalk. The dead soldiers lay still and bloodied in the shade of tall concrete T-barriers that were set in place to protect the soldiers within the D-Fac.

Lifting the uniform edges that cover the top of the torsos, I see two patches. One 1st ID, and one from a non-infantry unit that I do not recognize. I do not look at the names, ranks, or faces of the dead soldiers, and having quickly finished the grim inspection, I head back to my crew.

"None of ours. Better book it back and get the report in."

Nobody says a word, but there is a satisfied enough feeling throughout the bunch. None of our guys were hurt, and it's just tits that Dick was there to help out. I can see from the bounce in his step and the light glow on his face that he feels shaken, but good about the events of the day. I'm glad I wasn't in the chow hall for the blast, but I'm also glad some scout representation was there early for the assist.

I interrupt the silent jog, *"Fuck."*

"What, Pearce?"

"The fucking bodies, man. God bless 'em, but the media blackout for fuck's sake. My girl is going to kill me."

"No fuck-stick, she's not gonna kill you. She's just gonna leave you for some bisexual bartender somewhere."

Knowing the danger of the statement, I try not to think about the conundrum that has been created in my love life on account of almost an entire month's worth of silence.

Electronic media is our only outlet to our families and lovers. Snail mail is not allowed for us, as our command has deemed that it would be too dangerous to have our family members' names and addresses floating around the FOB or being driven through greater Baghdad. Media blackout kills the only line home. There is nothing we can send out.

"I'm sure she just enjoys the peace and quiet. Real stressful right now, studying for finals and all."

The group gets a good laugh out of that. They've heard similar things from their lovers lately. The monstrously monstrous stressful workload of school or civilian working life. The nerve racking despair of being a prisoner to a desk for one hour increments and being asked to study every once in a while before hitting the town to go clubbing. Boo fucking hoo.

Our coterie slows its pace as we enter our own little gravel courtyard again, and I run on ahead to relay to the leadership upstairs that all of the scouts are present and accounted for.

Giving the good news that the scouts are up, I also receive news to the contrary. A soldier from Bravo company, thankfully one whose name I do not know, was killed in the attack. Doubtless he was clipped by another mortar, somewhat farther away from the D-Fac. Bad news.

Getting approval from the LT, I take a short hop down the dirty stairs once again to the CQ desk where Forrester sits this fine evening, and tell him to send up to the CP that the scouts in D Co are accounted for and good to go.

Back in my bunk, firmly behind mosquito netting as I listen to the little bastards buzz their endless angry song, I want nothing more than to write to Emily. I know I can't; not for some time, so I simply roll over once again and wait for sleep that won't seem to come.

Our slated re-fit day morning is much quieter than usual. In a half an hour the funeral for our man is set to begin, in an old theatre at the center of the FOB where battalion-sized command briefings are conducted.

Out of a sort of deference for the day music still plays in the barracks, but it's mostly tasteful country at a soft volume.

The funeral is largely optional, though some squad leaders are probably making it mandatory for their troopers to attend.

My squad is not one of them, but Chapps knew the guy. Mason, I think his name was, and I will be accompanying him for this morning's ceremony.

Ducking around the corner and under a hanging wet-weather poncho, strung across the doorjamb as a sort of drape, I catch a glimpse of Chapel as he finishes the chore of pulling on his boots.

"Smoke break time?"

"Morning smoke break time."

We don't say much of anything as we file out of the barracks together with a few handfuls of the other soldiers who will be accompanying us on this morning's short walk.

The sky is a clear blue today, and the city is singing its usual song. Far off gunshots sound away into the early morning light, a police siren can be heard over the bray of a donkey, and a man is trying to hawk some sort of ware just over the fence.

The smoke tastes good; they always do now. I've been good and hooked for some time, and the repetitive activity never seems to get old. Sadly, I can admit to myself freely that I don't just like the smokes anymore: I need them.

Throwing our butts into the appropriate receptacle, then adjusting our rifles and head gear, we set out on the morning's journey, which is a short distance of just over four hundred meters.

"You ever been to one of these, D?"

"Nope. You?"

"A few. Never really uplifting, but I find they help to remind us what we're doing here."

Not having a decent reply, I maintain my silence during the brisk walk, with my ears vigilantly peeled for any signs that would foretell the coming of whistling ordinance, or the cycling up of the incoming sirens.

Attacks are coming more frequently now, with the usual prescribed attacks at dawn and dusk, but also with new iterations happening through the course of the afternoon and throughout the night with no discernible pattern. Just random indirect fire.

As we walk past the chow hall again I can see no discernible damage on the outside. Being the only functional dining facility on the FOB, it opened immediately after the attack, operating in spite of what I understand to be a pretty gnarly hole in the center of the roof. I suppose I'll get the chance to see the damage later today during one of my prescribed re-fit tuna runs. Perhaps Chapps will feel the call of hunger after the ceremony. I'm already pinging for food.

Arriving at the theatre, we can see clusters of soldiers gathered around on the steps leading up to the front doors, smoking cigarettes and holding quiet, respectful enough sounding conversations. Nobody is talking about video games or laying pipe; everyone speaks of military matters. The conversations of the hour focus on the mission here, as well as memories of the deceased from those that knew him.

Moving quietly inside, we're suddenly in a bare stone foyer, the right side being divided into a few different Hajji shops and booths for hawkers to sell their goods to Americans, while on the left-hand side of the entryway there are two doors, the likes of which can be found at any American theatre.

Further increasing the dissociative illusion, the inside of the theatre is very modern, and western, with pseudo-stadium seating, chairs that are upholstered with modern fabric, and red velvety curtains hung at intervals along the high walls, leading down the front of the chamber to where they stop before a standard-sized silver screen, and a small stage with a podium on the left.

This theatre doesn't smell like popcorn and spilled Pepsi. Instead, the light aroma of boot leather, tactical nylon, and gun lubricant hangs in the air. The staple 'Eu der American' armed forces.

Keeping quiet like the rest of those in attendance, Chapel and I sidle down the far left aisle, easing into the center and taking our seats about halfway to the empty white screen.

A projector at the back of the movie house is casting images of Mason's life onto the big screen, while speakers around the auditorium play fitting country songs by Tim McGraw and Trace Adkins.

Quietly while taking my seat, I ask Chapel "How did they get the footage so fast?"

"They go through the FRG, and get anything they can quickly send over the web. I agree; impressive response time. Only a day."

Settling into the warm room, soft music playing, I feel a bit sleepy. I can also feel the heaviness in the air and it makes me feel a sadness I wish I could ignore.

The images that flash across the screen in a telling slideshow for the revered dead continue to put a dampener on my morning mood.

Mason looked to be a real stand-up guy. Wedding pictures, fun pictures of the garage-front family on the Fourth of July, and a pool party, family dog included, play out on the white Middle Eastern screen.

For about fifteen minutes we watch as the footage loops a few times. I give it only half of my attention the second time around. It's a battle to keep myself from feeling a bit misty eyed, even though I didn't know the man, so I don't stare at the slide show anymore. I don't ignore it either. I politely acknowledge it, listen to the music, and attempt to think of happier things, lest I be a blubbering combat soldier losing his marbles for a man I didn't even know, before the ceremony has even begun.

Mercifully, the battalion commander and chaplain appear on the short stage just under the large screen to begin the ceremony.

First off, they relay the short account of how this soldier died. A prayer follows, both for our safety and for a peaceful journey for the soul of the fallen. The lord's prayer comes next. Everything is in good keeping with how a stateside funeral runs, except for what follows.

The commanding officer bellows in a loud, authoritative voice at the congregation.

"Battalion! Atten-Tion!"

In a flash we're on our feet, smartly clicking our heels and standing with stomachs in and chests out, eyes straight ahead.

"Sergeant Major."

"Yes, Sir."

"Commence roll call."

"Yes, Sir."

The Sergeant Major begins reading names from a list, followed by individual soldiers shouting back acknowledgment. It is a traditional role call, the same as which can be heard every morning on Fort Bragg, or at any field-day battalion level function.

"Adams."

"Here, Sergeant Major."

"Alex."

"Here, Sergeant Major."

"Amsdale."

"Here, Sergeant Major."

The list does not drag on through the entire battalion however. Yesterday, a roster was passed around to take the names of those who would be present at the funeral. Even then, this list has been considerably shortened, and it reads on at a brisk pace.

"Curtis."

"Here, Sergeant Major."

"Daniels."

"Here, Sergeant Major."

"Goddard."

"Here, Sergeant Major."

I stare straight ahead, my eyes unfocused as the roll call continues minute after minute, until we arrive at the guest of honor.

"Mason."

The thick silence blanketing the theatre grows denser, and I can feel the weight of the true sadness, wrapped up in the dressing of this simple ceremony.

"Mason, report."

The silence continues, but from the front, from who I'm assuming were his squad-mates, his brothers that knew him best in the world, I can hear muffled sobs. The noise is now too much for me, and I feel a bead of moisture filling my left lower eyelid.

"Mason, report!"

Forceful. Angry. It's the sound of a Sergeant Major that's missing a trooper. Mason's in deep shit now, because later, after PT, he's probably going to get written up for an article fifteen for being AWOL. It's the same voice, and the same sentiment.

"Colonel, where is this soldier?"

The battalion commander replies, "Sound Taps."

With that, a bugler produces a horn, stands front and center on the stage, and begins to play.

The notes are long and empty. The tune, decidedly the most oft repeated and recognizable military blast, usually heard in jest, sounds entirely different to me today.

The beautiful and solemn strain carries its weight above us, echoing lightly from the velvet walls of the theatre, dying out in beautiful diminuendos until silence prevails once again.

"Paratroopers, you may proceed to the front in groups of four if you wish. Thank you for attending today. Dismissed."

We're dismissed, but nobody leaves. Instead, starting at the forward and leftmost part of the audience, paratroopers rise in the prescribed groups of four, do a facing movement together, and walk in a smart file before stopping directly in front of the stage, where they do another facing movement in front of Mason's monument.

The soldiers stand at attention while saluting the equipment of the fallen soldier that has been left behind. Though not a rehearsed or particularly orderly part of the ceremony, every soldier does his best to stay in time with the others. Ordering arms, then about-facing, they march up the center of the aisle in step with one another as four more soldiers rise to take their place, also paying their respects.

It's not all ceremonial business. Some men leave a patch, an insignia, something personal, or a dog tag on the altar.

Walking to the podium in time with Chapel and two other soldiers, I feel a bit silly that I don't have anything readily available to give. It would be a little improper to leave my tags; I didn't know the soldier, and I only have two sets, which I am required to have in my possession at all times.

After saluting, one of the soldiers to my left takes off his name tape and leaves it on the altar. Struck by the sensibility of the idea, I do the same while taking a good look at the monument before we turn to go. I have a bunch of name tapes.

In army tradition, Mason's boots sit at attention where they hold up his rifle, barrel facing down, which serves as the spinal column of the display. On top, his helmet is perfectly straight and balanced, with his dog tags hanging from the chinstrap to dangle down in front of the display.

It's cold and skeletal, sad and empty. The gear should have a man in it.

Making an about face, leading the file, I turn and march up the center of the auditorium, breaking step only when we reach the lobby and are out of sight of the procession continuing still inside.

As I put on my boonie, I step outside with Chapel, this time into a much brighter sun. Slowing our pace at the bottom of the stairs, it's clear that we've both decided that it's smoking time.

"What'd you think, D?"

"Kind of heavy. A bit earthy, I think. Sad, but a good leveling. Brought me back a bit."

My voice croaks a bit as I attempt to speak.

"Sorry, Chapps, I still have a little frog in my throat."

He lights his smoke and flips his Zippo closed with a light click. With his first deep drag oozing out of his mouth and a telling glint in his eye, he says to me, "You're not the only one, brother. You're not the only one."

On our walk back to the barracks a heavy amount of gunfire rips through the air all around the FOB.

"What do you think that's about?"

"It's everywhere, man. Probably a soccer game. Or it could be a wedding. Arabs shoot that much at weddings sometimes."

The sound is raucous. As I walk along the dusty ground I can feel my shoulders hunch a bit. Soldiers in our unit have been hit by errant bullets falling out of the sky before. It wouldn't be the first time.

"The sheer volume of it, for fuck's sake; it sounds like everybody in the fucking city with a rifle is cooking off."

"Chow hall run, D?"

"I was going to ask you the same thing. I could really go for some healthy tuna surprise right about now. I need it."

"You and me both."

"Wish I could have a whiskey with it."

Chapel smiles. "Stop the cruel thoughts."

As if nothing at all happened yesterday, a long line forms just outside the chow hall, the same SPCs check IDs for admittance, and before long we're in the center of the D-Fac, weaving through the crowd hither and yon to collect our prized sandwiches and raid the drink fridge, collecting two drinks per man.

The only difference in the D-Fac today, apart from any other day, are the couple of large, gaping holes in the very center of the chow hall ceiling. Some of the usual fluorescent lights that used to hang neatly in the middle of the tin ceiling are absent, taken down after being mightily put out by yesterday's blast. In their stead, rather than the cold, staple artificial glow of electric light, bright rays of the natural sun now streak down into the middle of the dining floor. Tarps have been laid underneath the tables to cover up the small impact crater, where they will remain until a KBR crew is dispatched to fix the hole in the foundation concrete that was left by the mortar's impact. Randomly across every wall of the facility, with the highest concentrations clustered closely around the entrance wound, black, sooty burn marks left behind from smaller bits of whizzing shrapnel paint the entire interior of the main dining hall like a freakish, large scale game of connect the dots.

The anxious mood of the day is readily apparent, made so by the worried faces of fobbits who eat a little bit faster than usual, each in their own time taking furtive glances at the perfect ceiling that was as they reflect upon what would happen if another mortar were to fall through that same hole again, right now. I suppose it's healthy for the desk-types to be reminded every once in a while that they are in a war zone, after all.

Having always been totally aware of the tactical repercussions of staying for a leisurely meal in the forward operating base's primary impact target, I leave the hall abruptly with Chapps, our Styrofoam plates in hand, and blue skies above us as we work our way back to the relative safety of our concrete building, ever mindful of cover as we go.

"I'm starving."

"I hear you."

Back in the bay I break away from Chapps to sit alone in my bunk, safely behind my prized mosquito netting where I dig into my plate of fish and veggies. Hamburger buns too.

Freddy calls over to me, "Hey, D, you got five bucks?"

I reply through a mouthful of fish and mayonnaise.

"Yeah, why?"

"We're all throwing in for a bug zapper. One of the Hajjis down by the barber shop is selling them."

"Fuck yeah, man, count me in."

I toss Freddy the crumpled bill, focusing once again on my plate of goodies. Besides my tuna staple I was also able to steal a fair amount of French-fries and cheese sticks. It's not the most heart-smart meal, but after twelve days of MREs, I find the experience to be both exciting and delectable.

As I eat my lunch I can't help but think of leave. I initially refused leave, after hearing that I would be slated for a November bracket back in March. It seems ridiculous to leave Baghdad, fly all the way around the world, and fly all the way back, only to pack up, and fly all the way around the world again. The concept pisses me off.

November surely has to lie within one to five months from the end of the deployment. Either way, that's not much time, figuratively speaking, since I will already have been in country for over eleven months by November. Superfluous and stupid, I know exactly what's going to happen.

The days have started to fly by at a quicker clip. With everything falling into a rhythm, the time is moving along at a brisk pace just like it should. After a break, and a return to civilized normalcy, I'm sure that the last few months of the deployment will be a slow drag from Hell. I knew this back in March, and now my worst fears have been realized. Oh well, at least I can be shitfaced for a couple of weeks, a few months from now. Guaranteed, the break is sure to smash up my own personal ops rhythm.

Needing to dispose of my trash, I decide to make the journey to the dumpster downstairs. Once outside, I feel the bright, urgent call of tobacco addiction.

As I light up the smoke, I can swear that today the smell, and the feeling on the air, reminds me of summertime back home in the Nevada desert.

The air has the same dryness, if it's not just a bit hotter. The sand has the same tan hue, and the ambiance of the day feels just the same.

In many atmospheric ways, I feel much more acclimated, and much more at home here in the Middle East than I've ever felt in the alien woods of North Carolina or Georgia.

Smoking my cigarette much closer to the building than is technically allowed, so as to be farther into the shade, I allow myself to engage in a little daydream as I puff away.

I can see myself in the middle of the gravel courtyard stripped down to the waist, with a cartoonish, oversized shovel in my hands, just digging,

digging, digging as fast as I can go. I'm sure that if I dug down just a few more feet I'd be in Nevada. Hell, if my math's off a little bit maybe I'd still pop out someplace peaceful in Utah or California.

I laugh at myself as I relish the silliness and simplicity of the thought.

If only I could tunnel a hole through the shallow earth today, I might make it home in time for dinner.

Softening the frustration somewhat of not being able to phone out or write, on this, our most glorious day off, I've received a package from home.

No paltry, insignificant thing, this box is pretty huge by normal mail standards, being at least two square feet in volume, and I know what that means.

Eagerly cutting away the packing tape with a folding knife, I hurriedly throw back the flaps while seated comfortably on the edge of my bunk, and see what I've been desperately hoping and waiting for: Charmin. *Yes!*

The bleeding and friction-induced hemorrhoids can stop!

Further into the box I discover peanut butter and chocolate no-bake cookies from mum, my personal favorite, as well as an assortment of cards and letters sent from other members of my family. My brother also sent me a game in the package, one of the World Series of Poker games for my PSP. I love poker, and the surprise gift makes me ecstatic.

Taking inventory of the rest of the haul, which is an assortment of much needed AA batteries, snack-foods, and a few more Paulo Coelho books, I take stock of the rest of the squad doing much the same thing.

I even get a few letters from Emily, sprayed with her perfume just the way I like them. As they were all post marked weeks ago, she'll not yet be scathing mad at me for the duration of the pleasant reads.

Near the bottom of the box I find my true lifesavers: two cartons of Marlboros. Thank God for family and all that they do.

"Uh oh." I say to nobody in particular.

"Contraband alert. Got to fess up to this one."

Made safe by declaring their presence in advance to my squad before touching them, all eyes turn towards me as I pull two bottles of liquor from the box.

"Let it be known to all that my father is a fucking idiot sometimes."

"It's known. You are too, fuck-stick. Get out back and smash

313

them right now.   And I'm checking your breath when you get back in."

"Roger."

Dick speaks the truth, but he's not too serious about the reprimand. We have a strict no alcohol, 'god-help-you-if-you-break-it' policy that applies to all individuals division wide, and we all know what is expected of us.

Without further ado I take the precious bottles in hand, wrap them in scraps of packing tape for some minimal concealment, and then proceed to quickly hop-step down the stairs.

Rounding the front of the building, I continue around the side and beyond, into the small alleyway out back that runs behind the naked rear concrete wall of our building, and the tall brick fence that separates our FOB from the rest of the Middle Eastern world.

I'm mad at my father.

The temptation is huge.

The two bottles of Jameson feel alive and warm in my hands.   They look beautiful; their contents gleam with caramel brilliance in the early afternoon sun.

"Someday, motherfuckers.   Someday."

With that final verbal sendoff, I christen the old Arabian wall with its first taste of Irish whiskey.   The heavy bottle gives off a tragic liquid crack as it shatters into a million pieces, scattering its precious booze in a fine mist across the dry desert sand.

"Contestant number two."

I give the second bottle a fling and witness the same effect as the first, this time feeling like an eight-year-old vandal, terror to cheap glass objects everywhere.

Standing for a moment and thinking about what a foolish mail move this was, I toy with the idea of walking over to the wall just to smell the Irish whiskey.

I decide against such behavior, on account of it being wholly and totally cruel, and against myself.   It's bad enough that I got to hold them anyway.

Back in the barracks I'm met with a measure of healthy skepticism.

After breathing into the faces of my disgusted squad mates, fish lunch for the win, everyone is satisfied that our strict protocols have been adhered to.

"I held them in my hands.   My preciouses.   I had to kill them, guys. It was awful."

314

"I'm sure it was, Pearce. I don't think I could have done it."

"It was tough. Prohibition is in again. Yucky times, man. Yucky times."

The next three days go quickly. The squad is fueled up on fob food and well-rested, and our last two mounted patrols went off without a hitch or incident.

Zombie blares in the barracks as we go through the motions like have done a dozen times before, prepping our gear and packing for our two-week jaunt out on the town.

The media blackout never lifted, so as far as Emily and majority of my family are concerned, I've simply disappeared into the great unknown, as have we all.

The drive is the same but different set of chores that it always is. Random traffic stops, questioning locals, searching for bombs, and plowing down the wrong side of narrow inner-city roads while terrorizing locals and donkeys alike.

The conversation is the same humdrum it always is. Poker. Videogames. Fighting, women, and booze. Anything to pass the time.

I can hear all of the chatter through my headset, but I'm busy, and a little removed from it today, as I get to be the fifty gunner this time out.

Our wet-ball thermometer capped out at the high 140s in the shade, so I'm assuming that I have the best seat in the house on this fine August afternoon. At least I get a breeze.

The air conditioning in the trucks, though having already performed admirably during the first part of the summertime, is currently being a bit overwhelmed by the sheer heat of the city.

Rather than a beautiful wind tunnel to a land of reindeer and snow men, the AC vents pump out air that would be considered 'room-temperature' in the states if the AC was on the fritz.

I enjoy my time on the gun. It's free. I'm no longer confined to staring out the same window, at the same slice of passing terrain. I can use my crank to swivel to the left or to the right, at my heart's content.

Standing, I'm no longer forced to slump and cramp in my gear, and the occasional bottle piss on the move is made all the easier for it.

Manning the gun I have a field of fire that is to be monitored at all times, and I have the freedom of choice to point it wherever I like.

As gunner on the lead truck I frequently have to do my duty by aiming the demonic weapon at civilians while screaming gibberish at the top of my lungs, in an attempt to make the local populace less stubborn when it comes to holding their desired traffic pattern.

The constant rotation, screaming, traffic management, security, and scanning make it a much livelier, much more enjoyable drive than usual, the summer heat be damned.

We pull into the JSS, back to where we belong as the sun is setting low in the western sky. As usual, the trucks are parked, but left armed and running to serve as semi-mobile ECP fortifications.

I move with the scout squad to our usual places at the rear of the bay to our preferred cots, this time soaked through with weeks of hot summer sweat, having been abandoned for only five minutes time after the departure of the last down-shift squad. Crusty, they are.

As usual, other squads from D Co are down first, while us scouts will be pulling ECP and high ground shifts followed by our eight-hour dismounted patrol block. At least my cot will be dry by the time I get back.

Before we can quickly move to our first station, a short briefing seems to be in order, as it appears that our local situation has changed a little.

Cloud returns from the platoon briefing to give us our daily heads up.

"All right. Listen close, guys."

"Hajji is up to some different stuff this week. Last rotation had a couple of close calls with bombing incidents. No, pay attention, not the usual stuff."

"To the northwest of here, as you know, is a school. I say school, but it's really like an *oubliette* for mentally challenged women."

Cole looks puzzled.

"A what, Sergeant?"

"An *oubliette*. I don't know. A French fucking word. You ever see First Knight?"

"The King Arthur one?"

"Yeah that one. *Oubliette*, or what the fuck ever. Put shit in there and forget about it. Dungeons and other crap."

"Got it."

"Anyway, Hajj has been abducting these women and strapping bombs to them. They point them in our direction, so then they walk up to us begging for things or acting all retarded, and boom."

"Command wire det?"

"No, bigger than that, open spaces. None of the people pulling the triggers want to be anywhere near the blast. That's why the pussies are using retarded chicks. Has to be radio or timers, so keep a lookout. Time delay systems."

There's a brief pause.

"There's really nothing we can do about time delay systems. We can't go about shooting every woman in a burka we see either. Actually, let me re-phrase that. We can never, never, ever, under any circumstances, shoot a woman in a burka."

"So what do we do?"

"Pay attention. If you need to, grab a terp and try to make these women go away. If not, grab some IPs and try to get them to escort them away. They've been briefed already, so hopefully they won't be letting any lonely retarded girls in through their outer checkpoints."

It's not a happy briefing, nor a very comforting one. But at least we're informed.

After the short brief we break to our posts. Me, Freddy, and Cole are taking the trucks first while Duke, newly returned to our rotation in the field after having sustained absolutely no physical injury, will be posted in the high-ground position with Dick. Cloud is going to babysit us from the CP, as is his usual habit.

It's a short trip down the single flight of stairs to the courtyard below, where Cole and I start our shift at the western ECP once more, checking IDs and screening any vehicle that wants to gain access to the JSS. Freddy opts to take the solo stint at the east gate.

"Duke looks all right."

"Shut the fuck up, D. Nobody knows what really happened. Cut him a little slack."

"What's the problem? I think it's pretty clear what happened. There was a decent-sized explosion, which he was twenty meters away from, and he passed out."

"Just keep it to yourself, man."

"Myself. Sure. The whole platoon would never talk shit about something like that."

It's not an angry conversation, and Cole doesn't really defend Duke. The news spread on its own course like wildfire, while leaving Duke's warrior reputation in a pile of smoking shit.

Better yet, the flak keeps coming down from James. It's always, "How you feelin', Duke?" or, "Having any explosion induced narcolepsy lately?"

I'm a bad person. I honestly can't get enough of it.

The humor is neither clever, nor particularly funny, but the shit still flies anyway. Who's going to stop it? I sure the fuck won't.

"Getting the purple heart, right?"

"That's what I heard. As soon as we get back I think. The battalion will pass it out."

I can't help myself, "Pass it out? *Pass it out!* Now, that's funny shit. That has to feel shitty."

"I don't think Duke gives a fuck, honestly D. I was talking to him about it and he feels genuinely that he was wounded; he feels entitled to the little purple thing."

"Entitled to a panic attack award?"

"Okay, Braveheart, fucking cool it, yeah?"

"Oh, Cole, I'll cool it. I'll cool it right away if maybe, uh, you give me some Copenhagen to encourage me to shut my dishonorably slanderous face."

"That, buddy, I will do. You owe me two cigarettes later though."

"Done."

I'm thankful for the change of texture. I normally prefer Skoal over anything else, but the occasional bitter-sweet Cope is good for the soul too. Mixes it up a little bit, adds some variety.

Cole flips the can at me from his position up in the gun, but I don't have time to put a pinch in yet, so I set the can aside on the dashboard and attend to my errand.

I fully open my already cracked door and stand up to greet a group of three Iraqi policemen who are entering the JSS.

They don't alarm me at all; I recognize their faces. But still, protocol must be followed. We are teaching these incompetent fucks security procedures, after all. They've never had anything like them before.

"ID. Show your ID."

"Mista yes, Mista, ID."

The three men hold up their cheap plastic badges and I give them a satisfactory wave telling them to proceed, but they linger a bit.

"Mista. Michael Jackson? Michael Jackson?"

"Yeah. Child molester, I know; great dancer too. What about him?"

Not fully understanding what I'm saying, the IP ringleader pulls a

318

different sort of small, black mp3 player from his pocket and offers me a wax-encrusted earphone.

"Yep, that's Michael."

Not wanting to insert the contagion into my ear, I simply place my head close to the eighties pop and listen to a bit of Thriller before I nod enthusiastically and smile at the man.

"Yes. It's Michael all right. Very good."

I hand the earpiece back to the IP and give him a thumbs up.

As he walks away, I feel a happy glow -- the glow that indicates that I, Dallas Fucking Pearce, have just fostered warm, heartfelt, wound-healing relations with the 'other people.' What the fuck ever.

"Thriller, huh D?"

"Yep. Now, where was I?"

"You were giving me my can of Copenhagen back."

"Right. Gotta do something first."

I take a sizable pinch, the same sort of favor Cole does for me whenever he ingests some of my Apple Skoal.

I flip the can back.

"Thanks, dude."

"You're welcome. Gotta fucking love mail day."

"Ditto to that."

I don't get to sit and do nothing while enjoying the savory goodness of the fresh pinch for long. The shit truck is here.

The shit tuck is just that: a truck full of shit. Locally contracted, the same blue and green truck arrives once a week to suck the shit out of our portable units, before trundling out of the JSS along its merry, shit filled way.

"I got it."

"You're full of shit, D."

"Eyes ain't brown for nothing."

The truck driver, an old veteran to our processes at this point, causes no problems or tension in the ECP. He stops his truck a good ten meters from our location and simply waits for me to sidle over to him and check his papers.

That chore being done, he simply waits in place as I conduct a simple check of the vehicle, making sure that nobody has stuck a cube of Semtex to the bottom.

I'm sure SWAT would balk at our shitty screening. So would the fucking CIA. So would the fucking Air Force for that matter. There's precious little I can do about that though, as I wasn't issued a fancy mirror or a handheld ex-ray device.

Instead of a standard invasive-type check like the TSA would do, I simply look at the truck in an attempt to deem it safe or otherwise.

I start at the back. Yep. It looks like a truck that is full of shit. I smell. Yep. It smells like a truck that is full of shit.

Stooping in my full armor kit in the 150 degree heat, I do my best to beat the system and crane my neck down to see the undercarriage of the truck. I fail.

Giving in, defeated, in stark contrast to my personal preference to never touch the local beshitted and radioactive streets with my hands, I'm forced to do a half push-up to get a good view of the truck's baby maker. Yep. Still looks like a truck full of shit. The very dregs, the very bottom in fact, of a truck full of shit. Both Semtex cubes, and the red, blinking lights of Hollywood explosives fame are absent. Score. The guy is clear to pass, and I'm clear to get the Hell up off the Hajji dirt.

I wave the shit-man through, returning once again to my station where I eagerly await the next round of excitement.

"Hotter than fucking dog-shit, man."

"Ain't you Vegas people s'posed to be used to that sort of thing?"

"A little. 135 max in the sun, and oh, I forget, you can chill out at the roulette table and have a rum and coke, twenty-four hours a day. That expedites the 'I'm hot outside and that makes me feel okay' process."

"That does sound much better than the current situation. What do you say you show me around Vegas, D?"

"Sounds good to me, in the event of our survival. As long as I can be shitfaced the whole time. You do realize we're rich now, motherfucker. That is, rich by twenty-one year old single guy standards."

"I do indeed realize that. I haven't spent a dime in like seven, no, eight months."

"Same here. No way to do it. Gotta think: Combat pay, hazard pay, overseas pay, plus your regular. Plus, if we're here for over a year, we get the thousand dollars a month kicker."

"Kinda Roman, no?"

"Roman is exactly fucking right. Hail Caesar."

Our conversation is interrupted by a woman. A woman in a burka. I remember the briefing. A woman in black, pushing a wooden cart toward the ECP. I radio.

"Eh, uh, CP, this is ECP one. Eh, I need a terp. Now."

"Roger. We'll, uh, eh, jackass, send him out, uh, um, now, over."

"Righty. Out."

Stepping free once again from the confines of the Humvee, I marvel at how bright, and how God-damned hot it is here today.

In Nevada during the summertime, at distances of more than thirty meters or so away, I can see the heat shimmer in the air like a live-action, first-person skillet view.

Here in Baghdad, it's like a ten meter fade. It's unreal. It's trippy. It's like being fried alive.

I think quickly upon level five plus of Jordan Mechner's Prince of Persia for the Super Nintendo, a private joy of mine that's now many years long past. The world was a badly digitized waving world of red, and the thought makes me smile.

I'm the prince.

I give the internationally accepted hand signal for 'stop right the fuck now,' hand held palm out, straight forward.

The woman immediately reveals herself to be a person of sound mind, and not the slightest bit retarded. She stops immediately, but I'm going to need the interpreter anyway. The load she's pushing on a rickety set-up of rusted metal, wheels, and splintered wood is caked in flies.

I let her know why we're waiting by saying "*Multhaljim,*" a locally accepted word that I believe means 'interpreter.'

It's an awkward pause. Cole stands in the turret behind me, casually behaved yet ready for anything, while I wait the few lengthy minutes for the interpreter to arrive. He's dressed in American army ACUs, sans patches and a name tape, with a black handkerchief wrapped tightly about his face like a cowboy, concealing his identity.

"Hey, Hell-Boy, see what she wants."

Yeah. We call our interpreter Hell-Boy. Apparently, just last year he was shot in the head. Twice. He's proud of showing the scars, and he still walks and talks, ambulatory as ever, as a true Lazarus in the flesh.

I try to listen in as best I can, but the conversation is taking place at a distance of more than three meters away and is hushed and garbled. I don't speak Arabic anyway.

After some time, Hell-Boy turns to me and gives me the complete synopsis.

"It's a body."

"I gather that. She is the sole owner, operator, and proprietor of a rotting dead guy. I get it. Tell me why."

The interpreter turns back to the woman, moving closer this time, although it's clear that he's having trouble thinking over the smell. I'm getting plenty of the back-blast from over here, and I already feel myself turning green.

Gibberish. Gibberish.

After the conversation is concluded Hell-Boy addresses me again.

"Mista, her husband. In an alley. Three days. She doesn't know what to do. She brings him here."

"Good Hell-Boy. Thanks. Wait a sec."

I saunter back to the truck and grab the radio handset.

"CP, this is the west gate, over."

"Yeah, send it."

"Roger. We got a woman bringing in a dead body. Says it's her husband. Three days old, over."

There's a pause and a silence over the net. Doubtless there's a conversation between the IPs and our LT taking place right now.

The situation is not out of the ordinary. There are no funeral homes in Baghdad. The only functioning morgue that we know of operates in a sector of the city located not too far away that we refer to as Medical Town. This body has obviously not been there.

They come back on the horn.

"Yeah ECP, tell her to bring it in."

"Roger, out."

Time for protocols. Can't have just any woman bring in any old dead body to the JSS. Nope, could be a threat. Could be bombs in them there fly infesterdly hills.

I thank Hell-Boy, "*Shuk-ran*," and send him on his way back to the CP; back into the loving arms of scantily clad women dancing the Habibi on Kuwaiti television feeds.

I motion for the woman to uncover the body.

I motion again for the woman to uncover the rotting corpse. This time, she gets it.

As I approach, she flips back a heavy woolen blanket, and I'm sure the rotten body before me would leave CSI Las Vegas completely mystified.

The body is green. It's a freakish, rotten zombie of a man, complete with flies, maggots, and bloating. The whole set.

Trying as best I can to maintain a professional degree of candor, I motion the woman away so I can accomplish my grim search.

Although the skin, multiple shades of green-gray and black is well on its way to full decomposition, I can still see the cause of death.

This man wasn't felled by dehydration, taking a good fall, or shot. He had his head stoved in by something rather heavy. A run of the mill masonry brick, from the look of it.

Around the misshapen jaw of the rotting corpse purple, alien, crystalline structures present themselves to the hot afternoon sun. At one temple the skull gives way and a strange matter, no longer pink, oozes in perpetual stillness from a fetid ear.

Rotten black blood spills down the center of the torso from the mouth, while the rictus of the dead man remains twisted in a look of eternal pain.

Snapping out of my awkward 'hey, look at the rotten dead guy' stupor, I get to work.

I check the bottom of the conveyance and find it clear of explosives. I check the pushing handle, wheels, and the body itself for any signs of tampering, other than the fatal bludgeoning of course, and find no bombs or other command-wire operating indicators.

After bending over, looking at the green and gray and black and purple body closely for the duration of the quick search, I feel nauseous. Hurriedly, before I lose my breakfast MRE all over the ECP, I wave the woman forward.

She pushes the body along, all business, with no tears streaming down her face.

Obviously, she's had a whole week or more to contemplate and ponder the situation, and subsequently has gotten over it. That, or she bashed his dome in herself. Women can do that, you know.

My world slightly spins, like after eight shots of Jagermeister as I make my way shakily back to the Humvee.

"You get a good whiff o' that?"

"Did I ever?" What the fuck, man? Three days, my fucking ass. That guy has been dead for a year."

Though not in the same unit, Cole was also with me in New Orleans during Katrina, at the end of the world. A large part of the operation down south was simply sniffing through buildings and rubble in an attempt to smell out, and ultimately find the dead.

The smell of death is weird. A strange, rusty, sickly-sweet haze of rotten filth, tinged with something that smacks of ginger spice.

Many in America live under the false guise that they have smelt death

323

before, but they have been lied to. They have smelt formaldehyde. They have smelt the tapered, manicured death of the modern, western world. That's a far cry from a rotten, putrid death in the Middle Eastern sun. The medieval death. The 'bring out your dead' death.

"I really need a fucking cocktail."

"Four more months and you'll get one."

"Har, har, har. Hardy fucking har, har, har."

As I sit back down in the driver's seat of the truck to await the next contestant in today's shit twisted game show, I can see the scene unfold behind me in the rear view mirror.

The wife, already conveniently shrouded in mourner's black leaves the scene of the deposit, walking by me and Cole without so much as a word or a second glance.

No identification. No social security number. No insurance policy. Just the dead body of some guy, the original way that God intended it to be.

Behind us, the IPs are apparently engaged in multiple games of some exotic form of rock-paper-scissors, supposedly to determine who is on body disposal detail.

We don't know where the corpse will be taken, but I bet Cole twenty hard-earned bucks that they're just going to dump it in the river when they have the time. After all, it looks like nobody is paying for a proper burial. I've also heard it told that the preferred burial for a Muslim is a burial at sea. Hell, they'd be doing the poor guy a favor.

With no immediate action being taken, the IPs simply lay the body out in the middle of the courtyard, covering the face and torso with an unfolded cardboard box. After hiding the body somewhat ineffectively, they all depart, scurrying back into whatever cracks they came out of, leaving the poor, defiled body to rot further in the afternoon sun. Hands and feet protrude from the half-assed sun shelter of the flattened cardboard box; it's clearly not quite large enough for the purpose. The center fold of the flattened box forms into a triangle, making a silly sort of zombie teepee.

The flies are intense. Although the little demons were present in full force before the body arrived, now they are a division strong, at once harassing and assaulting us. We are not defenseless, however, just sitting idly by in our metal trucks. We're ferocious, fast, and vengeful. We kill the interlopers wholesale with anything we can find. MRE wrappers, plastic bottles, naked fists, name it, the death toll mounts. We are truly

324

the lords of the flies, or rather, the executioners.

After four hours of ID checks, rabid fly assaults, and dead man's perfume testing, we're summoned to switch our posts, and I look forward to the good view and much needed almost fresh air that awaits us in the high-ground position.

Our relief shortly arrives, so Cole, Freddy, and I start making our long climb up the twenty-six flights of steps that lead up to the thirteenth floor, stopping only to visit the bay to stock up on fresh, warm plastic bottles of water. I make a mental note to myself that it's rather funny that the logo for water bottled in Utah would bear a palm tree as a marketing insignia. Wonders will never cease. A snowball would probably be more appropriate.

The climb goes quickly, but I still find it tiring. Logic would state that the long climb to the top would become easier and easier over long months of repetition. This is not the case. Rather than blasting up the steps in full gear and feeling ship-shape at the top, me and the other two are visibly, audibly more winded than the norm. I could attribute the slight physical distress to the hundred and fifty degree weather, but I know better. Our continuous rotations, staple malnutrition, extended periods of dehydration, continual diarrhea, long hours crammed into trucks as well as other static fighting positions, and the lack of a normal PT cycle have all contributed to us wasting away a bit.

I was one hundred and eighty-five pounds of physically fit man when I arrived in Baghdad. Now I'm weighing in at one seventy and falling. Although some of the fat kids are reaping the benefits of being in a sauna for twenty-four hours a day, I'm not quite so enthusiastic about the side effects.

Turning at the top of the landing, we head down the hall into the primary scout hide, and curiously, we find it empty. God, I feel weak.

"Where the fuck are they?"

I make the statement to the room unopposed and receive no immediate answer. Curiously, Dick and Duke's body armor and helmets are still present in the room. Surely they intend to come back to their post today then.

"You think they took the service stairwell, D?"

"Nah. Even Dick knows better than that. We have to swap in person; everybody knows that."

Freddy and Cole look somewhat irritated at me for taking the time to state the stupid and painfully obvious fact. Wasting no time, we spread out and start searching room to room on the upper floors in our quick attempt to find the others. After five minutes of thoroughly searching every nook and cranny of the thirteenth floor, we find nothing. Cole presents a game plan.

"D, go check the roof. Freddy, check twelve. I'll go to eleven."

Although Freddy and I both pull seniority over Cole it doesn't really matter anymore, as far as squad conduct is concerned. The three of us answer to Duke and Cloud, and that's the end of it. Together, the three of us in private are just buddies. There's never any need to pull rank among us, and Freddy and I don't have a problem with taking the light order. It's a sensible thing to do.

Freddy speaks, "And guys, don't call it in yet. Cloud would be pissed, yeah?"

I concur. "Yeah, on the down low. Unless they're dead; we have to report them if they're dead."

Everybody laughs at that one. Of course they're not dead. Gay? Maybe they're gay. But certainly not dead. Maybe.

Breaking from the group, I find my way to a small access ladder at the end of the long hallway stretching away from the primary hide. Without wasting any time, I hurriedly climb the rickety bars to the wooden plug in the ceiling. It's not the kind of roof access that can be found in hotels back in the civilized world. Instead, it's more like the creepy passage to the attic of an old, cheap house.

Pushing the wood aside, I hoist myself up onto the massive roof of the structure, and keeping low to further mitigate the threat of snipers, I take in the view of the surrounding rooftop and what I can see of the city beyond.

I feel like I can see forever up here, but it's drab; there really is nothing good to look at. Although it's the best seat in the house for over-watch, a permanent post on the roof of the building would be unnecessarily dangerous. The constant sniper threat or even the chance of typical small arms fire is too great to remain up here for any decent amount of time.

After looking around for a bit longer, I can say with full faith and certainty that our buddy dudes are not on the roof. Slipping down into the ladder-hole ass first, I find my footing on the cheap rungs and lower myself down into the shaded, secure hallway, pausing only to put the square roof-plug back where it belongs.

As I make my way quickly back to the primary hide I almost crash into Freddy as he bursts forth from the mouth of the stairwell after his search of the floor below.

"Find them?"

"Nothing down there. What about up top?"

"Barren and empty."

"Shit, man. We're like ten minutes behind shift change. They want to see Dick in the talk. This is bad. I know I normally take Duke's side on dumb shit, but this is really, really stupid."

"I know. We could all be fried. Maybe he went for a climb? Let's go check the courtyard."

'The courtyard' is not really a courtyard, but it is a rectangular space between this building and those that surround it on the south side. Instead of grass below, nestled in between our hotel and the neighboring buildings, there is a massive pile of waste and refuse.

The back rooms of the hotel all sport balconies, which we use as platforms to piss off of onto the garbage below, but only after nightfall due to the aforementioned sniper threat.

Emerging onto a balcony on our buildings south side, Freddy and I are relieved. We see them.

Our two buddies, about four stories below us, are making their way back to our position, hopping from balcony to balcony of the adjacent building nearest to us. Some of their journey has been assisted by planking laid between balconies, which appears to be the favorite way to get around by some of the neighborhood's more daring children.

Without armor and racks, they're completely defenseless as they climb about. Worse, the enemy doesn't even need to be involved to kill them. Their pursuit of feeling cool has led them onto balconies that I'm sure would not even pass code in this country, if they have them, and across supportive junk that was not meant to hold heavy American adults.

It only takes them about two minutes to reach the far corner of our building where they climb in through a window almost directly below our position. Thankful to get out of the sniper lane from hundreds of nearby windows myself, I'm more than happy to move back into the hallway to greet our deserter friends. About two minutes pass before we hear their shuffling footsteps coming up from the stairwell below.

"Where have you guys been? It's passed shift change already. We were looking for you, and fucking nobody has been on high-ground."

Dick looks unconcerned about my statement, and Duke just stupidly smiles at me with an air of superiority.

327

"Relax, D. What's the worst that could happen?"

"You could fall to your death or you could be shot. You're nothing but stupid-as-shit sniper bait out there. You're late for shift change, and you abandoned your post. That's the worst that could happen."

Dick's happy mood leaves him and he immediately becomes angry, growing red in the face and flexing his fists.

"Not a fucking word out of you to anyone. We didn't fall, and we weren't shot. What's the big fucking deal? You need to take that stick out of your ass, Pearce."

"You need to remember where you are from time to time."

My gut sinks a bit. You don't talk to your superiors this way. Isolating this particular incident, I could justifiably receive an article fifteen, have rank and money pulled away, and be in otherwise very, very deep shit for the rest of the deployment. Add in however, that my statement was made in reference to Dick leaving his post, and then becoming angry with the common sense reprisal and the situation suddenly becomes very different. I have two witnesses. Dick's current absence in the talk is a huge no no. Abandoning your post. Dereliction of duty. There's about fifteen other things wrong with this particular situation. I reserve the right to say whatever the fuck I want today. Dick and Duke are both in a wringer, and they're going to keep their positions as scouts as a result of my good graces. Cole and Freddy's as well. And they know it.

I say, "Well, derelict fiddle-fuckery and threats of article fifteens aside, they want to see you in the talk. You better get moving there, *Sarge*."

"Fuck you, D. You wouldn't dare."

"No, you'd probably try to shoot me in the back, you pussy fuck-wit."

"Pussy? A pussy?"

Dick moves towards me in a very hostile fashion, so I plant my feet and brace myself for some fisticuffs, which would be a very stupid move for Dick. I'm wearing sappy gloves and I have my helmet on, I'm in full body armor, and naturally, I have the little fuck by twenty pounds. He's an angry little bitch in a T-shirt, mad that he finally got caught abandoning his post. My kung fu is also strong.

"Yeah. For not being man enough to stay *in your post!*"

"Just shut the fuck up about it."

"I will. Unlike some people, I still give a shit about the integrity of

328

the squad. Chill out, fruitcake. Nobody in the squad is going to fucking tell. Now get the Hell downstairs."

Trumped out by the rest of the squad and being fully aware of the sticky situation, Dick once again becomes calm and laughs the situation off. We're a team. No matter how much we hate each other sometimes, you just don't rat your own boys out. That's how the airborne do it, and especially, that's how it's done in a combat zone. Besides, I've always known Dick is a stupid asshole. It wouldn't do to have him shoot me in the back on a patrol and then have the squad take his side. I'm sure they would. I'm not the most popular trooper in the scout outfit. I don't like to be a prima donna fuck-wad, and I like to play by the rules. 82nd Airborne's rules.

After the others are gone, safely accounted for in their positions down at the trucks, the rest of us sit in our observation post for the next four hours. I'm not angry anymore. As a squad, me and the others have decided to forget about the incident. All's well that ends well. However, I smile to myself a bit, as I know that I have one more bargaining chip up my sleeve. I don't see blackmail in my future; I'm not like that, but it's good to know that I have some silly ammunition to wield against an out of control, dip-shit NCO if it comes to that. Hooah.

Our high-ground shift clips by at a decent pace. Nobody needs to be killed, and none of us get shot at. It's another peaceful day in paradise.

Our JSS week passes relatively smoothly, save for an incident in which a hand-grenade was thrown over the barriers that flank the truck posted at the east ECP. With the exception of a D Co paratrooper with a ruptured eardrum and a Humvee with two flat tires, which were promptly changed out, we're no worse for wear.

Following our stint at the JSS we conduct mounted patrols out of Mad, which are largely uneventful, and our greatest, most present enemy for the duration of the rotation is the blasted summer heat.

Blessedly, after just one more eight-hour drive we will return to the FOB, our sainted pseudo-civilization, for a bit of rest.

As the hour of our relief finally approaches, us scouts and the rest of D Co prepare ourselves for the drive ahead. Inventory of the food and ammunition on-site is taken, the barracks is swept and mopped, body armor is donned, and sensitive item checks are carried out.

There's been a change of plans for our platoon, as we will be breaking from our normal operations schedule to pull six weeks of QRF when we return to the FOB. This is joyous news; it's almost like the promise of a guaranteed vacation in the very heart of Baghdad. Doubtless we will be called up from time to time, if not once a day, but at least QRF has the potential to be restful. No slated eight-hour patrols. If we get called up we'll go help with whatever it is and then come straight back. It sounds like the way a war should be.

Knowing this, Freddy has decided that he'd like to take a spin in the gun today on the way back to the FOB. I agree to swap him out as driver, though I don't usually drive in theatre. Freddy always, always drives, and he's getting very tired of it. It's fun for me to know that I'm giving him a little bit of a break. He gets to stretch his legs, and who knows, maybe he'll have a chance to get the gun off.

"Hey, Freddy, remember to put your DAPs on, man."

"Whatever. It'll be fine."

Not yet mad at Freddy, I simply repeat myself.

"You need them. Put them on."

"Roger, Sergeant."

Freddy doesn't put them on. I'll check him once we're down at the trucks.

DAP stands for some silly acronym for Deltoid and Arm Protectors, or Deflector Around yer Pits. Whatever the hell DAP stands for, they are the modern equivalent of the medieval pauldron, which is the segment of an armored suit that covers the upper arm and shoulder. It's a simple enough task to hook them onto the IBA, and they're not too cumbersome to wear. What's more, they are part of the battalion SOP for any gunner. They simply have to be worn.

The DAPs are said to be able to stop up to a 9mm round, so while they are not the best defense for snipers or AK fire, it can't hurt anything to wear them. I always feel a bit better protected wearing them anyhow, as gunners get hit with IED flak every once in a while. It's just one of those things. It doesn't hurt to wear them, so just put 'em on. Simple.

One last time I say, "Freddy, you'll wish you'd have listened to me when one of your arms gets blown off at the shoulder. Put on the fucking DAPs. I'm doing you a favor by driving for fuck's sake."

"Fuck off about it, D."

That makes me mad. Real mad.

"Wear them, don't wear them, now I don't give a fuck. We'll talk about this when we get back to the FOB."

Freddy then gives me a sarcastic, "Roger, Sergeant." It's not said respectfully.

Loading the trucks goes quickly. Radio checks in and weapons ready to go, we roll out; we go forth to boldly accomplish nothing, for an extended period of time.

The trucks are fueled. Real chow has been had. It's almost night-night time. What's even better is that we have a re-fit day tomorrow before our long QRF shift begins in earnest. Before lying down for some serious relaxation in my bunk, I address SSGT Cloud quietly, so the rest of the squad cannot hear.

I tell him about the DAPs incident with Freddy, and ask for his advice. He then tells me to take Freddy out back and smoke him. As much as I'm uncomfortable with the idea, something has to be done, and a bit of corporal punishment is much more preferable than an article fifteen or a counseling statement. We're going to keep this one in the squad.

Knowing what I have to do, I approach Freddy's bunk.

"Freddy, get up."

"What do you need?"

"You didn't wear your DAPs."

"This shit again? Fuck off."

I shout, *This shit again is right. Get the fuck up. We're going outside Specialist, now!"*

Although I generally have a mild, friendly, quiet personality, my screaming voice is huge. Getting up from his bunk, Freddy looks over to Cloud and sees that this is his squad leader's machination, and not all of my own doing. Knowing that he just dug himself in a bit deeper, and that he's finally, really, no-bullshit in trouble, he leads me, cussing at the floor all the way to the door of the bay.

Dick speaks up, "You really gonna do it? Fuck me, he's really gonna do it! Go be a big NCO! Shit man, this is weird."

Dick generally enjoys fucking up the rest of the squad in good humor or corrective sentiment whenever he gets the chance. However, although it has been done, he rarely smokes us just because he's angry. I never, ever abuse the privilege. I've been an NCO for almost a year, and I've never had to take staunch, uncomfortable, corrective action with any one of my squad mates.

Outside, I lead Freddy around the building to the alley in back, where

331

I can still see the broken glass from my booze breaking party, frozen in time for all eternity.

"So what now, buddy? Big Sarge, huh? Gonna smoke me? What should I do first? Push-ups? Flutter kicks or monkey fuckers? What'll it be?"

Debating a bit on which would be the best course of action, I let Freddy stand and wait a moment. I know I have the power to make him hurt. He knows he screwed up, and by that, he's already learned his lesson. All paratroopers know what comes next. It's well within my ability and right to stand here while I make the next four hours of Freddy's life a sweaty, shaking, coughing, exhausted Hell.

Taking my time, I pull a cigarette out of my deck and fire it up with my Zippo. Freddy doesn't smoke, but I pull out another one anyway.

"Yeah. I'm smoking you right now Freddy. You like menthols?"

"You joking?"

"I'm pissed. I'm angry. But I'm not joking."

"Sure, I'll take one I guess."

Lighting the second smoke myself and taking a drag, I pass it to Freddy, who just stands dumbly in place and stares at it before taking a drag of his own.

"You know I'd really like to fuck you up now, right?"

"Roger, Sergeant, I do."

"You know that this was Cloud's idea, and I have full permission to do so for as long as I see fit?"

"Yeah, I get that too."

"You know me, Freddy. You know I'm not a pussy; I just like to play by the rules. Everything is better here if you play by the rules. You're my best buddy in the squad. I feel like you're my only real brother in the squad. Now, why in Hell would I come back here and break you off. For fun?"

"I disrespected you. For that. I was stupid. I actually felt kind of naked in the turret without them. I do apologize."

"I think we're pretty clear now then. Just don't do it again, yeah? I don't tell people to do much; I know that you know how to do your job. Just listen to me in the rare event that I give an order. I don't do that a whole lot."

"Roger, won't happen again."

We smoke our cigarettes in silence as the setting sun starts to sink behind the wall of the FOB, and I almost think I can really catch a small whiff of Jameson essence on the light breeze. The shattered glass is starting to catch the slanting rays of the sun, and sharply glints in the fading light.

I say, "Between you and me, Dick's an idiot. He puts himself, and us, in unnecessary danger all the time. I'll never see eye to eye with him, and I'll always think he's a worthless fuck because he wants to be special, and because he thinks he has a license to swing his stripes around whenever he feels like it. I've just about had it. The JSS was bad man. You know what would happen if he was caught?"

"Yeah. Court martial, bigger than shit. Dereliction."

"And all that jazz."

"You won't tell on him?"

Freddy stomps his spent smoke out in the gravel.

"Fuck no. Idiot would probably shoot me. He has the maturity of a small child. You do realize that me and you are already in deep shit for not taking this up with command. We had a duty to spill the beans about this stuff, technically speaking, and we've already missed the window."

"Yeah. We'd all be cooked."

I continue, "Yeah. We'd all be, and even if we didn't take action for it Dick sure would, and they'd break the squad apart and scatter us around the battalion again. I know that; that's why I won't tell. Like little kids, yeah? Telling?"

Freddy laughs. Without saying another word, with both of us mutually understanding that our business is done here, we begin the short journey inside.

When we return to the scout bay, Dick is the first to speak up, "Back so soon? You smoke him?"

I don't have a reply, and Freddy just sits on the edge of his bunk, having clearly not broken a sweat.

Dick continues, "What, you give him a blowjob or something? That's not what smoking means here."

Cloud, despite being generally inactive lately in the affairs of the squad, has finally reached his own breaking point with the disrespectful and childish manner in which Dick has been conducting himself of late. The squad leader speaks, and Dick listens.

"Sergeant Dick, the push-up, ready position, go."

"You serious?"

Funny, how this situation is getting rather common in here lately.

"Ready position, move."

333

Dick is pissed, but he's smart enough to keep his trap shut at this point, so he promptly gets ready to receive his dose of military discipline. Cloud, I believe, is doing his best to show the rest of the squad how it's done.

Generally, one superior does not discipline another superior in the presence of, or even within ear-shot of the squad. The same goes for direct compliments, criticisms, recommendations, or scolding. Cloud is making an exception to those rules in this case; he's making a point.

Chapps and I go to chow, and when we get back a sweating, shaking Dick is still in the middle of the bay floor, still working his little heart out.

I leave the barracks again with Andrews to do a laundry drop-off and check the phones. They're on blackout again. When we return Dick is doing flutter kicks. And jumping jacks. And mule kicks.

About three hours after it began, the punishment stops. Dick grabs his boonie and leaves the room, and nobody says a word about it.

But I'm going to smile about this for a while. At least a week, I reckon.

QRF is a slow drag, but the pace is welcome. In the first three weeks of the task, we have been called out only ten times, with each and every call focused on providing help with security and towing after IEDs have exploded in sectors nearby, or sometimes even directly outside the FOB.

The media blackout eventually ends, so I make two attempts to reach Emily over the phone, but both times all I can do is simply leave a message on her voicemail. She never picks up. It does me good though to make a few phone calls to catch up with my family at home, and they do pick up.

Making the relative down-time of QRF duties that much more savory, we've been told that we will be participating in a battalion-sized crackdown on high value Al' Qaida targets in Fahad after we return to our normal rotation.

Apparently our higher-ups have come into some credible intelligence which has pinpointed a local center of operations. The details are not yet known to us, but it seems that battalion command has become privy to a series of big ring-leader meetings, or some other such activity that we can feasibly measure, see, and squash.

Knowing that the days ahead are sure to be a big deal, we all take extra pleasure in typing home when we can, eating good food at the D-Fac, and playing our handheld games. As long as everyone and everything is accounted for, and all of the infantry chores are taken care of, they even let us sleep in. It's a wonderful time.

I don't think much about anything. Every once in a while intrusive thoughts about my impending leave bracket rear their heads, but I'm quick to put them away. I don't want to lose my rhythm, lose focus, or get jumpy on account of knowing that I'm about to get the chance to go home, if only just for a little while.

Chapter Eight: Baghdad at Night

There's a tattoo on my memory
Of a burning fire lit plight
And the feeling still that haunts me,
Taken from Baghdad in the night.

A horrid postcard it would make,
This desolate groaning hell,
A land bereft of wonder,
Of singing, or of bells.

My mind it floats and dances
Above these desert sands
Where years of fear and bloody tears
Have shared their lonely romance.

When I watched it from above,
I did but once to think of love,
About the face of ivory white
That I've kissed on better nights.

But this is one I say again,
That stretches on without an end,
And peering outward at the din,
I turn inside, and weep within.

What a dole postcard indeed,
This city view at night.
A more morose and somber scene
Will never take its flight.

Even here from story eight,
I can hear the wild dogs barking,
The radio cackles its dim hiss,
And the night is only starting.

Not beauty here that I have found,
Only waste and blowing grit.
The garbage and the empty streets,
Lie alone beneath the stars.

I'm glad I'll never see in print
A postcard Baghdad night,
As it would bring too many things,
Without any need to write.

Another barracks afternoon. Another chow run. Another mail call, and this time it's a good one.

Chapps has always been a fan of sappy gloves. For those not in the know, sappys are usually leather gloves stuffed to the seams with steel shot. So, while serving as basic hand protection, the added steel-shot within gives you a guaranteed 20 oz. right hook.

Chapps ordered in a new pair of Blackhawk brand sappys for me, and I think that's just swell; now we can be twinners. Besides, my current pair was starting to come apart at the seams.

As a fun added aesthetic plus, the palms of the gloves are reinforced leather, providing a measure of slash protection for the occasional, though highly unlikely knife fight. Whereas most police issue sappy gloves, which are used mainly for riot control have full fingers, these gloves end at the second knuckle. That means full trigger control in medieval-grade armored gear. In a word, they're just tits.

Sitting on the edge of my bunk, I giddily try them both on at the same time, and am in the process of flexing my hands into fists again and again, to break them in and make the leather in the palms a bit more flexible.

Dick also got a new toy today: a high-speed hands free headset that seems to be compatible with our own M-bitter radio handsets.

Dick, while fucking around with the fit of his new Ricky-Recon ridiculousness that's currently wrapped halfway around his head, addresses me, "Hey, D. You know you're not allowed to wear those, right?"

"Seriously? Why not? They're leather, just like our black issue gloves. You wear Oakleys; nobody gives you shit about them."

"Because you could hurt somebody."

My world stops for a moment. I don't know whether to laugh or be angry. This is perhaps the stupidest thing I have ever heard come out of an NCOs face in infantry land.

"Beg your pardon, airborne infantry NCO, could you say that one more time?"

Dick is quickly becoming frustrated with the conversation.

"I said, it's because they're a liability. You could seriously injure somebody with those."

Somebody like you, y'mean.

"Respect intended Sarge, but I carry no less than three knives on me at all times, as well as two hundred and ten rounds of ammunition for my assault rifle. Sometimes I carry the Barrett 107. The fifty fucking caliber rifle. That's perfectly legal. What makes these any different?"

"You're not wearing them."

"Technically, you're not allowed to wear your fancy new headset either."

Getting even more steamed, Dick continues, "My headset isn't going to hurt anyone."

Chapps has apparently been listening in on the whole conversation from just outside the bay on the stairwell landing, and promptly steps into the room to give his own two cents.

"You know Dick, you could get your whole squad killed if coms go down because you can't get through on that thing. It's not issue, and that pressure switch on your chest? What if you need to go prone. You're going to trip the button on accident every minute, blocking, cutting off, and generally fucking up radio traffic on whatever net you're on."

It's sound. It's common sense, and Dick looks ever more foolish sitting on his bunk with five hundred dollars' worth of wanna-be SWAT bullshit wrapped around his head, with the connectors still hanging limply in their protective plastic wrapping.

"Nobody asked you, Sergeant Chapel."

"I know. Nobody asked me; I'm telling. Those are two very different things Dick. Further, Pearce can wear the goddamned gloves if he wants. You carry an automatic rifle everywhere you go for fuck sakes. Think before you invent stupid rules for your squad."

Dick makes no reply.

In a technical sense, the conversation doesn't matter in an official capacity, as our chains of command only come together with the D Co platoon sergeant. I wish Chapel could pull his rightful seniority and put little Dick in his place, but sadly the structure of our beautiful organization has made it impossible for him to do so.

After Chapps leaves the scout bay, returning to the small room at the end of the hallway that he calls home, Dick turns to me one more time.

"You're not wearing them."

"Fine, Sergeant. I'm not wearing them, just like you're not wearing that headset."

"Keep pushing. See where it gets you."

I don't perpetuate the argument. Of course he's going to wear the stupid plastic headset, and of course, I will wear my gloves. I remove myself from the conversation by heading into Chapel's chamber while doing my best not to be angry. I'm going to let this one go. Technically, I have to.

QRF will remain as our primary duty for at least the next two weeks, until we pick up our usual rotation once again: FOB, JSS, Mad, FOB, JSS, Mad, interminably, on and on again.

The primary quest of the day is simply to remain ready to go at all times. Uniform tops, armor, weapons, and sensitive items are laid out on bunks ready to be deployed at a moment's notice. Shits, showers, and chow-hall runs are conducted on a simple, extreme necessity basis. Whenever one of these activities needs to be attended to, individual soldiers sign out on a roster set aside by the CQ that lays out where they're going and exactly when they are going to get back. We have to be ready to assemble, throw our shit on, do coms checks, and roll to our briefing point at the CP in less than five minutes time. If somebody was ever lost on the FOB somewhere, there would be hell to pay at the platoon level. Not to mention the proverbial ceiling falling in on whichever individual soldier fucked up. Simply stated, no foolery. We're prisoners of the barracks for the next two weeks, as we have been for the last four.

The close proximity to one another, the lack of activities to engage in, the lack of a definitive operations schedule, and the continuing media blackouts all contribute to our willingness to gripe at one another. There is a generalized animosity at the squad level right now, but it's not too much of a big deal; everybody knows why.

At 1700 hours I lie down to play my PSP a bit and continue my World Series of Poker campaign. At 1800 Dick, Duke, and Cole start putting their shit on, making it no wonder that they are going to leave the barracks as a group.

"Where are you guys headed?"

"We're meeting with the Platoon Sergeant."

Not the D Co platoon sergeant; the scout one.

"About what? Want me to come?"

"No, D. Just stay here and chill. It's not important."

This is odd. Secret meetings? Cloud is busy at the moment in the battalion CP, and Freddy is fast asleep, enjoying a quiet evening nap.

"Why shouldn't the whole squad go then, if it's a meeting?"

Dick says, "Shut the fuck up, D, and lie back down. We'll be back in a little while. We're signing out, but just in case something cooks off, you know where to find us."

"Roger that. I'll come get you right away if anything pops."

With nothing else, half my squad leaves the bay, dressed up as if they were going on their own QRF outing. Which is normal; they need to be ready if we get a call during their secret soiree with the scout platoon sergeant.

Feeling the same influences that Freddy is, I switch off my PSP and shut my eyes for a bit, hoping to catch a little bit of a nap before whatever random event the evening holds for us.

As I drift away to sleep I listen to our new bug zapper as it kills the mosquito invaders in force, never ceasing its zap, zap, zapping. While the electric killing machine can't totally rid us of the massive infestation, it has served to thin the ranks of the enemy considerably.

A pleasant, dreamless sleep takes me away.

I awake at 2100 hours to Freddy shaking me into consciousness.

"We get a call?"

"No man, squad meeting."

"Ah, I see. Now we're all invited."

Wiping the sleep from my eyes, I can see that the rest of the squad is already seated on their bunks and camp stools that have been folded out in the middle of the bay.

Dick and Duke seem to be presiding over the meeting, while Freddy is still waking up, just as I am. Cole is already seated, looking bleary-eyed himself while staring at the floor, shirtless as usual and taking deep gulps from a bottle of water.

Once we're all seated and mostly awake Dick starts to speak.

"All right guys. Casual meeting. I spoke to our platoon sergeant about some of the stuff that's been going down in the squad lately. We also spoke about some operational differences I personally have with Cloud. Long story short, Rams has decided to transfer Cloud to Charlie company. I'll be serving as your squad leader from now on."

I speak up, "Why? What operational differences? How did you pull this off?"

"None of your business, D. It was mutual between myself, Duke, and Cole."

"And you didn't involve Freddy and me because we're not part of the squad."

Dick with the temper again, "Listen, everyone is part of the squad. We didn't want to involve you two is all."

"You didn't want to involve us because we think it's a stupid liability when you take the rest of the squad repelling down elevator shafts for fun. I see how it is. You want a little bit more freedom, to do whatever it is that you think scout work entails, and you wanted to be out from under Cloud's thumb. And Rams just canned him for you. That's fantastic."

"That's enough, D. Isn't he always in your shit for smelling like cigarettes all the time?"

"Bullshit. That doesn't matter. That wasn't oppressive. I do smell like cigarettes all the time. Cloud has a hell of a nose too. What bullshit story did you tell Rams to get rid of him?"

"We just said some stuff."

"What kind of *stuff*? What kind of shit can you say to an experienced special operations NCO that makes him shit-can one of his experienced squad leaders, only to move a subordinate many years his junior into his former position? I'm not tracking on this."

"I said some basic stuff. Like, we haven't been doing regimented PT here on the FOB. We're going to start doing that. We sit around a lot when we're in town. From now on, we're going to go out further and be more mobile. Just stuff like that. Rams thought it was a good idea, so here we are. Cloud is just going over to C Co. Don't worry about that; he'll like it over there."

Our meeting concludes itself, with slightly guilty looks on the faces of those that pushed the button, while Freddy and I are genuinely concerned and confused.

Surely it's not that simple to pull one over on the platoon sergeant, and conduct your own personal change of command ceremony. It can't be. This is by far the stupidest shit I've ever seen in my life.

PT on the FOB, sure. We're already losing mad weight, so let's run some more, and never get rested. We're all getting weak enough and beat down in the heat as it is. Goodness fuck, even Duke has dropped a little weight, panic induced bed-rest and all.

No, the real crux of the matter is that Dick needs to be in control. Dick has a personal need to make sure he doesn't get caught big time for doing stupid shit like abandoning his post.

Just sitting around huh? We're pulling high-ground security for the JSS, and providing necessary over-watch duties for engineers and EOD on the ground as they search buildings for explosives and dismantle bombs in the streets. More mobile? In the field we do eight-hour foot patrols almost every day, and we cover nearly every inch of our sector when we do.

We cannot modify what we are doing and become more effective at our job. This is Dick's stupid excuse to be able to go rock-climbing about the city, defenseless before the threat of armed assault and snipers, so that he can pretend to be special. So he can get his stupid rush and have a good time at the expense of his squad's safety.

As I lie back down in my bunk I begin to worry. We're now in a lot more danger than we were under Cloud's care. More and more of late, Dick is forgetting where he is, and what he is supposed to be doing here. He has already forgotten that there's a war on. He's forgotten his place. He's taken command, and we're all in big trouble.

The next couple of days are the same, but different. I feel a hole in our squad where Cloud used to be. No more 'I'm not gonna lie,' and select commentary about 'you white boys.' I can tell from simple observation that Freddy feels the same, but there's fuck-all we can do about it. Just have to roll with the changes I guess.

QRF rotations are cycling down earlier than planned, as the battalion is gearing up to put us all back out on the streets again very soon. I'm hoping that we have no more call outs on this cycle; with rarely much excitement at all, I feel that most of our time spent on QRF has been as a necessary precaution at best. We haven't actively done much, save for viewing the aftermath of Arabian bombing runs.

Too much time spent in the barracks is making my whole 'fight the war' experience very dull. I want to get outside and walk around on my own two legs again; be an infantryman, that sort of thing. Yet one more reason why a mood of grumpiness pervades the barracks lately: we are infantrymen. We're not tankers. We didn't sign our lives away to ride around in trucks.

I went to bed much too early yesterday, and as a result, I'm currently enjoying the benefits, or disadvantages of being awake at 0300. Our strange operations schedule has made it so I'm not the only vampire in the company however, and a handful of other D Co soldiers mill about in the dark playing handheld games, listening to music, going for late-night chow-hall runs, or simply taking advantage of the early hour by heading to the phone center to enjoy a wait-free communications experience. That, and calling home at such a late hour gives us a better chance of speaking to our loved ones, as it's currently the middle of the day for them.

I stopped trying to call Emily a week ago. If she wanted to talk to me, she would have picked up one of my phone calls. I have written her e-mails instead, but I'm not too eager for the reply so I only visit the lab to check my own mail every three or four days. I still haven't heard back from her, and now I'm the one who's starting to worry. No matter; she's probably just playing a game with me on purpose.

Eager to do a spot of pre-dawn reading, I reach for my headlamp, secure it to my head, and turn the switch. Nothing happens. I'm out of juice. No matter; I have a ready supply of AA batteries on hand. Time to head for the big stash.

Between the scouts' chamber and Chapel's back room there is a slight recess in the hallway wall that we believe used to be a shower of some sorts. Now, with the plumbing absent, the small concrete chamber has become a storage closet so to speak, holding all of the duffel bags belonging to the scouts and D Co. The duffels are used primarily for the long travel jaunt to and from the states; they contain all the items from our mandatory packing lists that aren't needed on a day to day basis, such as PT uniforms, wet weather gear, extra canteens, and so on. They also serve as a kind of locked bank, sitting out of sight and mind, in the event that a soldier needs to deposit or withdraw anything that he doesn't want hanging around in his assault pack for an extended period of time.

I have batteries in my assault pack, but those are for emergencies at the JSS and on patrol. While FOB-side, I simply raid the huge brick of AAs in my secret stash, therefore never having to worry about sacrificing batteries for mission essential equipment, such as nods or weapon optics for the sake of something silly, like my red lens headlamp for example.

The closet area is totally dark, so in order to quickly and quietly locate my own bag I whip out my Zippo and hit the striker. It doesn't take more than a minute for me to locate my own bag and start to manipulate the combination lock holding the flaps together. 17-13-21. Click, and it's open.

The batteries are the primary article that I routinely access in my duffel, and as such they are placed conveniently on top, so I don't have any reason to embark on a crazy dig.

Snapping my zippo closed and pocketing it safely away, I unscrew the plastic cap on my headlamp as I have done countless times before, slip in the two AAs, and screw the thing closed. Let there be light, ta-da. Red light.

Turning back into the chamber, I almost jump out of my skin, startled by standing face to face with a very fat, very freakishly red Duke.

"Hey, Duke, what's up, man?"

"We need to talk."

In the glow of the crazed red light I'm shining into his face, I can't tell whether he's serious or joking.

"Shh... It's early. What about?"

"Cole."

"What about him?"

So much squad intrigue lately. I can't say that I'm not interested in the subject matter, but I certainly want to go lie down and read, and really, I'm already done with gossip for the day. I could really give a shit.

"Look at this."

Duke holds his right hand out toward me, palm facing up, and presents to me a very strange object.

I lower my voice to barely above a whisper. Even I don't want to hear what I'm about to say.

"A syringe? Where did you find it?"

"In his top. Don't ask."

"You went snooping?"

"Look, that's not important."

We stand in the silence of the red-lit darkness a moment, staring at the needle and not saying a word. It seems we're both thinking.

Drugs are out of the question. No paratrooper in his right mind would do that. No no no. Hell, in a combat zone you could even get life in prison or worse. It's not Vietnam anymore. I say, "What do you think?"

"He's been working out a lot. Steroids, probably; he hasn't been losing any weight. He's been gaining. It's steroids, for sure."

In terms of being in deep-shit with the army, steroids are not nearly as bad as hard-core drugs, which is a relief. However, the implications are still really, really bad.

"We're keeping this quiet, as a squad, yeah?"

Duke looks genuinely concerned and particularly honest, "Yeah, as a squad. I'll wake the others."

"Now? Isn't that a bit suspicious? It's 0300."

"You want us all to talk about this at 1200 when the whole platoon can hear?"

"Good point. Now's just fine."

I make my way, now under the power of fresh red light, back to my bunk where I sit and wait while Duke rouses the others.

Cole has been getting very fit, very fast lately. But why was Duke rifling through his blouse pockets at 3am? And why tell everybody? It gets stupider and stupider every minute here. We are the elite reconnaissance troopers of the 82nd Airborne Division for fuck's sake.

I wish I was in any other of the scout squads. All of my closest friends and the most reliable NCOs, the ones I like best, are all off with Alpha, Bravo, and Charlie. Maybe I could burn Dick's career down and then transfer to one of the other squads. Not honorable in any way, but such a move would surely get me out of this fucking mess.

Once everyone is awake we convene again, just like two days before, only this time we sit in a red-lit huddle, keeping our voices down so as not to wake anybody else from D Co. Of special concern, is our close proximity to the room which houses both the LT, and SFC James.

Duke starts in, "Do you have something you want to tell us, Cole?"

Cole looks confused. "No. 'Bout what?"

"We know you work-out a lot, Cole. More than any of us. Anything you want to tell us? You been juicing, Cole?"

Even though at a hushed whisper, Duke's voice takes on a character of 'holier than thou' pontification. I can't stand the patronizing tone, and I can't decide who I want to choke-slam more. It's a very close three-way tie between Cole, Dick, or Duke.

"What about this?"

Duke carefully hands the empty syringe to Cole, who's eyes immediately lock onto the floor. He slumps his shoulders.

"So what; you caught me. I promise I'll cut it out. You win, all right."

"You had better."

There's not much else to say, but I have to interject.

"Don't worry Cole; we're going to keep this in the squad. We're going to smash it down ourselves. Nobody has to know. I don't even know why Duke brought it to everyone's attention in the first place. Duke, you should have taken it up with him, just between to two of you, and ended it there. Freddy, you sayin' anything?"

"No, man. I got no reason to. As a matter of fact, I'm just going to stay the fuck out of this one."

Good. I continue, "Dick, you talkin'?"

"No. Not at all; Cole's my boy."

"Well, I'm sure as fuck not talking to anyone about this. Cole, get

346

rid of all your shit. Tonight. It stops here, inside the squad. We're looking out for you, you know? You don't have to get busted down for this shit. You're just lucky that they haven't pissed us in a while."

Cole is not himself. He's a few shades paler than average, and he almost looks as if he's about to tear up. Losing rank and going to jail is a big fucking deal.

"I know. I know you guys could burn me for this. Thanks, guys."

It's not a heartfelt thank you. It more like a formal 'thank you for not burning me at the stake' type thank you.

I'm worried for Cole though. From the very depths of me, I don't believe for one minute that either Duke or Dick can keep their mouths shut.

Everybody moves back to their bunks except Cole, who we can barely hear rummaging frantically in his own personal duffel bag, no doubt embarking on his own field expedient version of bomb disposal detail.

After not even a minute, Cole disappears downstairs, no doubt to walk across the FOB somewhere to scuttle his illegal shit into a dumpster far, far away from our barracks. I was serious when I said I wasn't talking. I'm not a talker. His destiny is in Dick's hands now.

Pretending to read with my read head lamp, I decide to stand a private vigil for the rest of the morning to monitor the rest of my squad's movements.

Sure enough, like clockwork, at 0500, Duke and Dick leave the bay. I read a little. At 0600 they return, waking Freddy and Cole once again.

"Hey y'all, squad meeting with Rams, let's go."

That makes me furious. We agreed to keep it quiet. We handled it ourselves.

Everyone knows what's going on, and we all hold our tongues until we're outside the barracks and walking into the darkness of the blue, somewhat cooler than normal dawn.

I speak first.

"What the fuck did you guys do? I thought we were going to keep this down?"

Duke replies, "Pearce, you know I had to take this to Rams."

"No, you didn't. When was the last time they pissed us, huh? Like four months ago? Are they installing a urinalysis station at the JSS that I don't know about? You didn't have to take it to anyone."

Cole speaks up, "Why did you have to? I told you that I was going to stop. I was going to. It's only been weeks, you know. It wasn't affecting anything. I threw all the shit away."

"We had to."

Getting madder and madder as we approach our platoon sergeant's barracks, I can't help myself.

"Do I have to report Dick and you abandoning your posts? Do I? I think this means I do, yeah?"

Our whole group stops, and Dick rounds on me, nearly shouting in the still dark quiet of the morning. "You wouldn't, motherfucker. You wouldn't dare!"

"Of course I would; we're on the way to cook one of your friends right now."

"It's not like that."

"It's just like that."

Cole is silent. He's now on the way to his own personal crucifixion. His career is over, at the hands of the people he called his closest friends.

I turn to Cole as I walk, "Cole, I have to live with these idiots for at least five more months, but they're burning you, man; you should out them, right now."

"Can't do that man."

"Why not?"

"They're my friends."

"What the fuck is wrong with you? Look what the hell kind of friends they are!"

"Shut up, D, please."

I do. I'm mad. I shut right the fuck up.

When we reach Ram's barracks I don't go inside. Maybe I'll saunter in to catch the last part of the ass ripping. The matter doesn't really concern me, so I'm going to stand out in the gravel, away from the shit-storm, where I belong, and smoke my morning cigarette.

They burned him. Their own man: their buddy. My buddy. They hung him out to dry.

Specialist Cole is no more. Only Private, E-1 nothing Cole remains. And he's not a scout; he's a tower guard, and he will remain so for the rest of the deployment.

There is a silver lining to the situation however: one of my best buddies in all the world, Curtis, is being transferred to our squad from the scouts over at Bravo company. So, lose an acquaintance, gain a friend. What a neat way to look at the world.

Curtis, otherwise known as 'Caveman,' for some pretty obvious reasons, will join the squad later, after Bravo Company returns from their own rotation at another JSS, this one miles and miles to the northeast on the very outskirts of the city. Their drive is a little bit longer than ours.

Back in the barracks, for every other squad it's simply a bright new day. No backstabbing, outing of buddies, or vengeful political intrigue. Rather than the newly popular scout rendition of mystery dinner theatre, the rest of the paratroopers in D Co are already joyfully about what soldiers do when they have absolutely nothing to do for months and months while stationed thousands of miles away from home.

Forrester is currently running around the barracks assaulting those who are too slow to wake up and defend themselves with his flopping, naked penis. In a dastardly aerial assault that we have named 'the involuntary dong-copter' by popular vote, he runs about, swinging his dangly-junk in a circle above the unsuspecting heads of the not fully awake. This of course only continues until somebody punches him in the cock, which is, rightly so, every bit as funny as the prank in action. This also stands as a prime example of why queers will never, ever, ever survive in the infantry. It's football team type stuff here. There's no room for weirdos.

One of the other D Co paratroopers, Moore I believe, though it's difficult to tell, is repeating lines from scripture while holding an old broken Hajji cane like Moses would, while wearing an Optimus Prime voice modulation mask. Shipped from America, the new-fangled children's toy makes him look like everybody's favorite transformer, complete with red, white, and blue coloration and a digitally amplified robot voice. The batteries were included, it seems.

Why Optimus Prime would be in the Middle East holding a staff, standing on a broken office chair and shouting "Let my people go!" is quite beyond me, but it must be working, because it's hilarious and it makes me laugh, even more so than the involuntary dong-copter.

Let the kids stomp around a third world country with automatic weapons and minimal adult supervision, and this is just what you get.

Once again I retreat from society back to my bunk, this time out of the necessity of self-preservation. A number of D Co paratroopers from across the hall have dismantled Kodak disposable cameras, leaving the wires exposed so as to generate a painful electric shock whenever the flash button is depressed. Donning fake mustaches, they are currently running hither and yon, shocking the asses of any unfortunate enough to be caught in their terrible path of electric destruction.

Once safely behind my mosquito netting I fire up my PSP, and do my best to pass another lonely day, running and hiding from reality in my digital world, hoping that this QRF business is quickly concluded so we can get back to patrolling. Although this is a safer, somewhat more preferable lifestyle, the QRF cycle has made life's speed nearly grind to a halt. At least, in the danger and discomfort of looking for contact in the summer sun the days seem to fly by a little faster.

1200. Being some time since I've checked for mail, over a week or so, I decide to sign out and take a quick jog over to the battalion CP. This provides me with some fresh air and leg stretching, as well as a chance to see if I've received any more packages.

I say packages, because I never receive individual letters. Over concern of losing them overseas, anybody who writes me anything sends the individual pieces of mail to my father, who lumps them in with the rest of the goodies in larger care packages where they are all mailed at once in a great giant cube.

While this makes it so I only get mail once every month or two, it's always fantastic mail, stuffed to the brim with a month full of letters and goodies. They won't hear any complaints from me.

Upon arriving at the CP mailroom I'm greeted with great news, and I am jubilant. I've got mail.

Though not a monster, the shoe-box sized package surely holds the promise of fresh tobacco and letters from home. Happily, I sign for what now belongs to me, and then make the quick jog back to the barracks, which is much more satisfying to me upon returning than leaving.

Dodging the others, I snake my way back into the shady protection of my bunk and cut the package open.

Yes! Grade A American cigarettes. Hallelujah.

This package is surprisingly light on readables, although there is a wonderful looking pink envelope from Emily inside. Aside from cigarettes and the letter, there is an assortment of Jolly Ranchers, chewing gum, gummy worms, and a small plastic roulette wheel, complete with extremely tiny moving pieces. I think I'll call the currency 'Micro-Chips.' I love the sound of my own voice sometimes.

Without hesitation, I lean back and carefully cut the letter from Emily open with my pocket knife. Carefully unfolding the plain piece of college-ruled paper, I start to read. And then stop reading.

It doesn't take much time; the letter is only three sentences long.

Dallas,

I don't know why you stopped responding to me over a month ago. I don't know what to think; I can only assume that for whatever reason, this is the end of us. I'm dating Glen, my new boss. I'm not looking back.
                                                            Stay safe, Emily

Just like that, my world shifts. She just took my life from me. Everything I hold dear, everything I'm looking forward to is gone in an instant. Five years are suddenly gone.

I'm not sad, not yet. I'm a bit angry. I'll give this some time. I'll try to call her later. I want to kill this Glen fellow. I'm so in love with her. What a bitch.

I'm going to be mature about this. I'm not going to think about it today. Hell, my leave bracket is just over a month and a half away. The weather is already starting to cool down. I'll be home soon, and I'll fix it.

I decide. No more today. I pick up a book, and put it down. I pick up my PSP and switch it on. Then I switch it off. Then I turn it on again. I have the sinking feeling that concentrating on much of anything is going to be quite a chore in the coming days. No matter; there's nothing I can do about it right now. I'll attend to this later.

And she'll be fucking this guy the whole time.

I don't think about it. Bound and determined to let it go, I plunge myself as deep into my digital battles as my mind can go, and feebly attempt to blot out the world.

Every once in a while my mind drifts back to my life, and my eyes start to cloud, my breathing loses rhythm, and my lip begins to quiver. But I won't tolerate that. No, if anything, I'm not allowed to cry about life things right now. There are bigger matters to attend to. Like making a new set of silver swords at the blacksmith, or recruiting more sprites. Attributes, yes, attributes, the numbers, they're the most important of all. The God-damned numbers.

Later in the evening Chapel stops by, sensing that something is a bit out of the ordinary today. "Everything alright, D?"

"Yeah, just fine."

He doesn't buy it.

"I'm doing a chow run; want me to bring you anything?"

"No thanks, Chapps; I'm good. I might go later."

He knows what's going on. He's seen it coming, and he knows me better than anyone in the entire world. We never go to chow alone if we don't have to, and it's not a difficult chore for him to sense that something is amiss.

"Well, I'll bring you back something anyway."

"Thanks."

With nothing more, my buddy is gone, out to brave the evening impact area alone while I sulk, unwilling to move.

Five years we've been together. Engaged, almost. Five whole years, gone. I'll be home in a few months. Probably out of the service in six. It's been five years and she couldn't wait one more month? *Bitch!*

I can't handle the thoughts anymore. Maybe a bit of sleep will grant me a bit of clarity. Not bothering to save my stupid game, I rage-quit the device, stuff it under my pillow, and face the wall.

Having fought the good fight for the entire afternoon, I'm losing control of my flood-gates and I know it. I'm 22 years old. I'm a Sergeant in the airborne infantry. I've been at war for over nine months, and I'm about to cry like a baby.

I manage, with all of my will, to hold back the feeling. I don't hitch; I don't squeak; I don't sob. Water simply pours from my eyes and makes a small lake in the water resistant material of the woobie underneath my head.

Some time later, Chapel returns.

"Hey, man, it's here if you want it."

I don't reply; I don't know if I have a voice. I'll thank him later. For now, I'm content to just stare at the wall.

Eventually the wave of sadness passes. I haven't cried for upwards of an hour, so I'm assuming that my eyes are no longer red. I haven't cried in years. At least nine years, I'd say.

She's fucking him.

I don't feel like eating, but my body is hungry, so I give in and have a go at the Middle Eeastern hamburger and French-fry combination.

After a few bites I feel a bit better, but after half the meal I need to hurl.

Running as quickly as I can, I barely make it to the shitter where I throw up my entire haul of potato meat-water into what used to be a relatively clean KBR shitter.

Cleaning myself up at the faucet so as to conceal the incident, I quickly walk back upstairs, discard the rest of the meal, poke my head into Chapel's room to thank him for it, and lay down on my bunk once again, waiting for sleep that will never come.

2300 hours. I'm still awake, and my efforts to sooth myself into slumber with music of any kind are being foibled by the device itself. It's charged, but it won't turn on. Pressing every button on the face-plate does nothing to bring it back. God-damn it, I need it right now.

Taking the time to dig the owner's manual out from one of my 'Write in the Rain' notebooks, I discover a combination of buttons that can be pressed to back-up restart the system. Conveniently, this entails holding the 'back' and 'up' buttons on the face of the device simultaneously. Why didn't I think of that?

I try to restart the device this way twelve times, and each attempt yields the same fruit: nothing. It pushes me too far over the cliff of the insanely sad and angry. If I can't listen to music anymore, neither can I.

Furthering my motivation to destroy the device, it's filled to the brim with soft-core porno pictures of Emily as she happily poses in a variety of scandalous positions. I want to see them. I never want to see them again.

Without thinking on the matter anymore, I rise from my bunk stopping only to lace my boots, and proceed downstairs with nothing but the dead Zune, my rifle, a pack of smokes, my headlamp, and my lighter.

Only three steps outside the front of the barracks stand a cluster of concrete T-barriers that serve as protection for our gasoline-powered electric generators.

Rage filling my body, I take the best professional pitching windup I know how, and loose the stupid device squarely at the barrier.

It strikes the concrete with a very dissatisfying, very unbroken clunk, and falls to the soft gravel below with no damage to speak of, save for new cracks slowly spreading across the screen.

This is my music. This is my source of peace and joy. This device levels me and connects me with who I used to be, and also with who I love through the technologic mastery of music and pictures. I hate it. I want it to die.

Winding up again, I send the device sailing at the wall once more.

This time, the impact is great.

The plastic frame of the device shatters into no less than a dozen pieces, while streamers of cracked and bent circuitry rip away from the wall at speed, trailed by the jagged edges of what used to be the LED screen behind them.

That settles it.

Immediately feeling better, for now, about the loss of the distraction, I use my headlamp to pick up every piece that I can find.

Satisfied that the evidence of my vandalism has been concealed, save for some small impact scratches on the barrier, I drop the pieces of my Zune, all of my busted music, into the plastic trashcan that lives just outside the barracks door, where they will reside never to be seen again.

I slow my breathing and try not to think about home.

I relish the air tonight; though not nearly cold, it's threatening to show the first signs of chilliness. I hate the summertime, especially here, and nobody is more enthusiastic about the coming winter than I. Bring on the cold.

As I light up a smoke I stare at the stars, and think of the sudden, but somewhat justifiable betrayal of my yellow ribbon girl, and immediately feel empty, furious, and miserable once again.

She's fucking him.

It's a bright new day. Our patrol rotations to the JSS and Mad will resume in four days, so the time of waiting for information is over. Also, we've handed off our QRF duties, so essentially the next four days will be the most care free days of the war for us. That is, until we are told to pack up and go home. That will be the day.

In better spirits today after having survived yesterday's emotional purging of five years' worth of emotional baggage, I decide to take a run with Chapps to the computer lab to type at other people, Emily be damned. I don't feel like talking to her yet.

I fire off one e-mail to my father, one to my mother, and one to my brother. Surprisingly, I have adequate time to do so in one sitting because for whatever reason, there is no line in the computer center today. I decide to stay and type as long as I'm allowed. I'm signed out with the CQ besides, and I have nothing better to do. I'm all ready to go patrolling again.

While perusing my Facebook page, I get the inkling to write Zoe, an old high school fling of mine. While not able to contact her on the chat window, I do fire off a quick message with the basic stuff in it, like, 'How are you lately?' And, 'What are you doing for school and work?' Just boiler-plate stuff. Also, I send her a friend request. Who knows, I might get a chance to see her again when I'm home on leave.

We never broke up, she and I. Instead, she simply moved away; she had to, after our junior year of high-school was finished. Who knows, maybe we could rekindle something a bit. In my defense, I'm angry, lonely, and sad, and have not been laid in over ten months. I still feel betrayed; it's only been a day. This is what betrayed men do. We sulk. We collect ourselves, and then we head out on the hunt again. It's just simply what must be done.

Two days later, Zoe does respond to me. She does so enthusiastically, and fires me back a barrage of questions. More boiler-plate stuff. I take pleasure in catching up over the last four years or so with her, and she knows it. She's also a newly single lady, and it seems very much like she enjoys talking to me. Although, as of yet, we aren't talking about anything serious that pertains to us. I have not mentioned the breakup with Emily, and I have not yet dared to bring up details of Zoe's relationship with me in high school.

There were plenty of make-out sessions in the high-school stage curtains, whenever we knew that we were alone in the auditorium. We used to climb the desert hills around my hometown to fool around at the summits, until we had to scale our way down to the bottom to beat the coming darkness. I remember driving out into the desert in my old Honda Accord to watch the sunset, eat cheap Chinese food, and get each other off. Those were, quite possibly, the best days of my life.

And she's still a fox.

Still skinny as a rail, with a beautiful face and perky tits, most of her pictures capture her doing different modern dance moves or ballet in wilderness settings, always in the sunshine, and always barefoot around different assortments of flowers or trees. Although most of the pictures in my favorite digital album of hers are mostly professional quality, there are plenty of cute, cell-phone-made self-portraits that capture her beautiful face and personality better than the others.

Looking at her through a shitty computer monitor in the armpit of the Middle East, I feel a funny buzzing in my soul that I haven't felt in years.

355

I'm still in love with her. I still want her. I haven't thought about her in years; I haven't allowed myself to.

Tearing myself away from little 'tag you're it' e-mails and photographs is a chore, but I manage to do so with the appropriate level of discipline, and head once again back to the barracks. Surely, I hope I don't die here so I can see that woman again. She was just a girl the last time I saw her.

The immediate and voluntary move against Emily makes me feel dirty and cheap, but then I think 'She's fucking him!' and suddenly I feel quite a bit better. I'm still sad, mad, and jealous of course, but the depressing thought also makes my current communication with Zoe both defensible and justifiable. I'm still mad, but I'm functioning again. That is, I'm functioning as well as any infantryman can while being held prisoner on a FOB, away from any active job or duty, at least for the next two days.

I'm just doing my best to enjoy the empty space. Soon enough, it will be over and I'll be back to the grind. Sore, burnt out, and exhausted, I'll long for a break like this once again, at a time when such a thing is far, far away; I should really enjoy the break while it lasts.

As predicted, the QRF cycle does end. Our normal patrol rhythm cycles up, and we leave the FOB and come back, leave the FOB and come back. Before long, early October is upon us, and blessedly, the weather is starting to cool.

My weapon is clean; my nods are good to go, but I probably won't be needing them: it's the middle of the afternoon. Sticking to pattern and tradition, I fulfill my role as RTO by sending up the radio checks as we scouts, minus one Cole and plus one Curtis, our new addition, prepare to step off into the great unknown. We will also be joined today by two troopers from D Co, simply to have more rifles moving with us.

We have an easy mission today: it has been reported that there is an entire building that has been flooded, and filled to the brim with rotting dead bodies of unknown origin near the Paper Market; we get to verify if such a place does indeed exist, and then find out why if we can. Why is this intolerable? Because it's creepy and unsanitary. That's why.

I'm skeptical about us being able to gain any new intelligence, regardless of whether we find the house of the bloated dead or not, specifically because we have no interpreter with us today. We'll be relying on Dick's not-quite-good-enough Arabic language skills, as well as the gamble that somebody in the locality of our soupy destination speaks a lick of Engrish.

And we're off. The same familiar streets pass by with different faces floating about them. Children play soccer, hawkers bustle at their produce carts, and wild dogs can be heard tearing this way and that through the broken city.

As we pass the long brick warehouses that flank Old Office Road, the afternoon prayer chants can be heard cycling up as they are blasted down on us from a multitude of randomly placed loudspeakers. No longer a cultural experience, the discordant ranting gibberish has turned from slightly exotic and interesting to downright painful and annoying. A couple more weeks of this, and at least I can go back to the states and get a decent break from what is usually an outright slaughter of sanctity specifically, and music in general. Being drunk for two weeks straight will no doubt do me some good before I inevitably return to the warzone.

Having information that the building we seek is not accessible from the ground level, we're on the way to higher ground, gained about four buildings over from our target destination via the roof of an abandoned children's school to the east of the Paper Market.

The school is closed off to us by means of a large wall, complete with Hajji glass on top, that stands no less than fourteen feet high. The pathetic wrought iron gate, however, is only ten feet high, and the somewhat intricate metal work that decorates the gate serves us with the perfect hand and foot holds with which to surmount the obstacle. Go, Hajji, go.

Soldiers pull security in every direction, high and low, while the others climb one at a time, until they land safely on the other side where they begin to pick up security as well. The process continues until we are all on the other side of the gate.

I call it in, "CP, this is Delta One-Two, we're inside the school now, how copy, over."

"Read you One-Two, I have you inside the school. That's a good copy, over."

"Roger, One Papa, out."

Satisfied that our telephonic affairs are in order, our squad +2 makes its way through the empty school, clearing dead space as we go and ascending lopsided concrete stairwells until we reach the third floor, which is primarily a large, open balcony that overlooks the Roman style gap, or park, or atrium space dirt patch that composes the real estate in the center of the courtyard.

Coming together from either side of the third floor, our squad stops at the bottom of a singular stairwell that leads up to the roof.

Freddy, for once walking on point, holds up his left fist, "Stop."

After a pause, he points to a suspicious looking can on the stairs, "What the fuck is that?"

The squad presses closer, and I can clearly see the item of interest.

It's a bomb. Or at least, something that looks very much like a bomb.

"Good call, Freddy."

"Thanks, D."

A bit smaller than a standard-sized coffee can, a green spray-painted, cylindrical metal object sits all the way to the side of the stairs, with an easily seen tripwire that extends from it across the stairwell to a rivet driven into the wall.

Dick states, "We're going up one at a time. Everybody watch that thing and be careful. And remember that it's here if we have to come back this way. Pearce, remind me to bring this up at the CP. We'll get Iraqi EOD out here on it."

"Roger, Sergeant."

One by one, we survive the perilous task of surmounting Captain Obvious's sole attempt to kill us all today, and emerge on the sunny roof, four stories up, in one piece.

The roof of the building has lots of igloo-like structures that are roughly the size of a car, made of poured concrete. No doubt we are looking at arches of some sort for the structure below, but why they are here, I will never know.

As a plus, they do give us some cover as we move across the roof, provided that nobody breaks an ankle on the wonky angles at which the concrete comes together beneath out feet.

A little trickery with broken glass fencing, a few radio checks, and three rooftops later we find ourselves a quarter of the way into the market, on the roof of the building we were meant to find.

It doesn't take long until we locate a hatch into the third floor of the building, made from the same idea, material, Hell, even possibly by the same person who hack-sawed the roof access into the top of our hotel.

One by one we descend quickly into the structure, and right away we know we're in the right place. The smell is horrifying.

We don't need to go deeper into the structure to understand the horror and truth of the reports.

The building is an open hollow shell, with only a few rooms visible coming off the main flight of stairs that circles the main chamber, one flight of stairs per wall, all the way down. It's a design we've seen many times. This building is a great hollow space, complete with two rooms hanging off the sides, and one crazy staircase to bring you all the way up from the bottom.

We can see by light that streams in through the front façade of the building. From our position in the back rear, the sunlight is almost blinding, coming in from six locations at the front of the structure, from two windows per floor.

We don't use the stairs; we can see plenty from here, and we're not going down.

It's clear that the ground level of the building has its own stairway going down to the basement, with a gap in the floor that must be over ten feet wide. The entrance to the lower chamber is filled with water, and other things.

The bloated faces of dead bodies and the backs of rotting skulls, pruney limbs, and randomly assorted floating people bits can be seen hanging motionless in the brown water. There's no telling how many bodies there are; there must be dozens, at least.

"Who do you think they are?"

"People who disagree with the policies of local leadership, I guess."

Our voices echo a bit in the empty concrete space.

Looking closer with my Sherlock eyes, it becomes a bit clearer as to what this building really is.

All along the first floor wall to the east, the wall down below us on our left, bullet holes and dry, splattered brown blood tell the story of the routine, planned, and frequent mass executions that have been going on in this building for some time.

I have an iron stomach, but I'm turning green from the smell. Moore's already losing his biscuits, leaning bodily over a rusty railing and adding his own vomit to the hot mess of rotten body stew below. The squad waits until his retching is over.

Dick talks some fucking sense when he says, "I think we've seen enough here. Everybody else good to go?"

Yes. Rodger. Affirmative. All words can be heard echoing about the room of swampy death. Just like that, we're out of there faster than you can say bubblin' people-goo.

I can't help it. I pull security on the roof, and I speak.

"I can't believe it. That is the most disturbing, and most morbid thing I have ever seen in my entire life."

Dick agrees with me, for once. "You're right. God, the smell of it."

Freddy has a different take, "It's really sad too, guys. Really. Think about it. We need to stop all this bullshit."

I smile, and with a bit of forced sarcasm I say, "We're trying, Freddy. We're really trying."

Freddy to Dick, "Hey man, how we getting down?"

Dick thinks about it for a moment before looking down the backside of the building, which is overlooked by six taller structures, each and every one of them staring at us with dozens and dozens of eyes.

"Let's just climb down this way. We can go around the back of the school then, and come back the way we came in."

Looking at the drop, and being fully aware of the sniper threat, I have to disagree.

The climb is insane for people to attempt in full gear. With a five-story drop to a street considerably lower than the market on the other side below, the only purchase or handholds the whole way down are a series of metal window fixtures, cracked stones, and jutting rebar that protrude from the wall of an adjacent building.

"Sergeant, if I can make a suggestion, that's crazy. We can't make that in gear. Besides, there's a perfectly good exterior stairwell that leads down the front of the building to the market. We can just walk down. Nobody has to get hurt doing this stupid shit today, besides, look at the windows."

I wave my hands toward the structures that surround us on every side, hoping that Dick will listen to reason and understand the danger that he's putting the entire squad in.

"I know we can't do it in gear. I brought cord. We can lower our equipment to the bottom first, then climb down."

"Looking at that, you're seriously going to take your armor off and have your squad do the same?"

"You're doing it, Pearce. Why do you always have to be such a fucking stick in the mud? We have to get down somehow. We're not going to take contact, so just chill the fuck out."

"And when one of those handholds give out, and somebody doesn't

360

make it home because they broke their neck on your silly fun climb, what are you going to do then? You want to carry him back?"

He's angry with me now.

"Nothing is going to happen. There is nothing there. Stop being such a faggot, and climb with us."

"What, you want me to lower the radio down there first, so some fucking Hajji kid can run off with it?"

Dick is over the edge now.

"You're on thin ice, Fuck-O. I'm giving you an order. A direct fucking order. Disobey it and so help me god I will fucking end you, you hear me?"

Freddy finally speaks up, "It is unnecessarily dangerous, Sergeant. That's a pretty scary climb. And I'm a climber; I boulder all the time. I'm with Pearce on this one. It's a stupid fucking idea. We should just walk down the front."

We're at an impasse. Freddy and I have both just displayed blatant insubordination in a warzone, specifically denying a movement order from our NCO in a tactical environment. It no longer concerns me. Wait until the Sergeant Major hears about this one. I wonder who he'll side with on the issue.

I say, sternly now, "You have a whole squad depending on you for leadership right now. You're going to have them take their armor off to fuck around rock climbing for your enjoyment, in the middle of a hostile neighborhood, in fucking Baghdad, over a precipice, for no reason, just so I have it really clear."

"Pearce, you are so fucked when we get back. I'm going to ruin your life for insubordination, you hear me? Everyone else, IBAs off."

The idiots from D Co look nervous as hell about the stupid idea, but that's good. They'll be witnesses in my corner if it comes to that. Curtis doesn't say anything. He also doesn't think much, bless his heart.

I do my part, as does Freddy. We pull over-watch as the idiots remove their gear, lower it five stories with karabiners and five-fifty chord, and then cut it away.

Dick starts his climb first to set the example, to lead the way. Hooah. I want to shoot him. ✱ may actually be justified in shooting and killing him. I hate him. I hate him for being a glory-seeking idiot, and I hate him for the way the other D Co paratroopers obey him because they think he's cool. He's a sniper. He's squared away. He's a scout, and they're too afraid to say no. You have to draw the line somewhere.

Dick is two stories down, and the others, trembling, follow his stupid way, each of them hanging defenseless like meat bullet-piñatas in front of a thousand firing positions in a warzone. My radio crackles.

"Delta One-Two this is CP, what's your status, over."

"CP, wait one, over."

Looking over the wall, I can see that Dick just went gray.

Who's in control now?

"What should I tell them, Penis? What's our status?"

"Tell them we're reconing the objective."

"Reconing the objective, fair enough. That sounds professional. How about, 'We've dropped our armor, ammunition, and radios, and we're hanging off a building in the Paper Market, five stories up, for no reason. I like the sound of that a little better."

"I swear to God I-"

"You do remember that you're hanging off a building that's full of rotten dead people?"

Dick starts to retort, "That doesn't matter, it-"

I shout. Attention from the locals would be just preferable right now, silence be damned.

"Or you'll what? You'll fucking what? Don't lose your grip there, Sarge. Hey, you D Co fucks, you know what happened just now, yeah? What are you gonna say? What are you gonna say about it? Dick, you're lucky I don't fucking shoot you dead right now. We'll see you at the bottom, fucking ass clown. You know that you're derelict right now, risking others. Ordering me to lie to the CP. Dereliction of duty, stupid fucktard. Go ahead and fall. I'll see you at the bottom."

That was probably a little much, I might pay for that later, or I might not. Dick doesn't know it yet, but he really, really owes me. That is, if he doesn't die now. Because I'm dropping security and heading down the stairs.

"CP this is One-Two."

"One-Two, go ahead."

"Roger, we have recon'd the correct building, break, we are looking for an alternate way down to street level, time now, how copy, over."

"Roger, that's a solid copy One-Two, CP out."

"I just covered your fucking ass, Dick. But I'm never pulling over-watch for your stupid ass again. We'll link up by the school gate."

"You have to keep pulling security! You can't leave us out here! Fuck you!"

362

"Oh yes I can. Go ahead and report me, Dick. Report me all you'd like. I can't wait to tell my version of this story. Good credibility you've established in the past too, getting kicked out of Ranger Bat for being DUI. Good call. See you at the bottom."

"You piece of shit."

"You're a good friend, Freddy. Thanks for sticking with me on this one."

"You too, D. That's a bold fucking move, by the way. Not something I would have done. Bad, bad idea in my opinion. I'm just tagging with you so you don't go into the market solo. That's a no no."

"Only two is still a no no, remember that?"

We start audibly laughing. What's the point anymore? The whole market can see us. They've been listening to the Americans angrily shouting at one another for upwards of five minutes now. If we're going to get ambushed, now's the time.

Our convenient metal staircase, if a bit rickety, leads us safely down to the second floor, where we must stoop to get through a low window and into another interior, which serves as a series of wonky platforms linked together with crazily built steps.

Shoppers, tea drinkers, and could-be terrorists all look up at Freddy and I in befuddled puzzlement as we walk, just the two of us, through the throng as we head down the stairs and out the front door.

"We just need the cantina band, Freddy."

"True that, my friend."

It's a quick walk back to the school gates. The whole journey has taken Freddy and I less than a minute; a fair amount of time to get to our link-up point by any stretch of tactical imagination. And I didn't even have to take my armor off.

I feel naked, standing in the market with only Freddy to keep me company. With only the two of us, there is precious little we can do to mitigate the dangers posed by sharpshooters, so we simply take a knee while we watch, scan, and wait.

Nearly fifteen minutes later, Dick and the others appear on the opposite side of the gate, and Freddy and I continue to pull security for them as they climb over, newly encumbered once again in their gear.

Dick opens his mouth to say something to me as soon as his feet hit the ground on my side of the fence, but I cut him off.

"I made a good radio check. Nobody knows anything about this little stunt, and it's going to stay that way unless you want to make a fucking fuss about it. If so, we'll play ball. You do remember that we stepped over a trip-mine to get to the roof?"

Apparently, the bad idea, and the unnecessarily frightening situation as a whole has been like some sort of sobering up therapy for Dick. He doesn't threaten, and he doesn't argue. Like me, he seems relatively calm.

"Deal."

Freddy chips in, "Deal."

Dick pretends to be a squad leader again.

"All right, everybody fall in. We're breaking back to the JSS quickly. We need to put a hustle on. We've been out here too long, and they know we're here. And you two motherfuckers better keep this quiet."

Nods of assent and approval from our D Co friends.

That's not the Dick I'm accustomed to. I think I've done the boy some good today. I scan my sector, but I relax a bit as we make our way back the JSS. I smile. I take a private joy in the day.

Mad is a welcome sight. Even better, I truly need the fresh, clean, blue-smelling shitter this evening, something fierce.

I don't know what it was; I just know the aftermath.

Grabbing a roll of precious Charmin, I head to the shitter bank, quite in the middle of the night. My wristwatch reads 0230.

I can't quite see my breath yet, though it's late October. Stepping out into the black chill, probably only fifty degrees or so, my body begins to shake.

After the extreme temperature of the Iraqi summertime, it will probably take my metabolism some time to adjust to the cold. Normally I'm a winter-loving type guy. 45 outside? No problem. Sleeveless shirt time. I have Germanic and Russian heritage. Bring on the cold flakes.

Now it's different. Though I revel in the fresh, brisk chill of the perceived October cold, my body rejects it entirely. Now, while I move my shivering way to the shitters, guided solely by the red lamp hanging just above my pained face, I take great pleasure in donning my black neck-gaiter once again.

Safely de-pants'd and sitting in the shitter, I can't wait for it to get colder, and also for my body to adjust. It's supposed to get down to thirty degrees or so here in the winter time, and December is rumored to be this city's rainy season. I need to buck up, sure, but I can't wait. The cold and I are happy together. Especially when armor is added to the equation. Anything is better than the 155 degree situation, and I'll take a few chills any day over frying in a wheeled metal skillet.

There's nothing to do while I wait for nature to take its course. I stare at the blue and beige door in front of me, the 'occupied' handle being locked, smashed bodily to the left. The light yellow smell of urine coupled with the presence of blue purifying liquid hangs in the air, emanating from the piss-funnel by my right knee.

I let one loose, and my ass cheeks involuntarily flex together to shelter my asshole from the uncomfortable and no doubt disease-ridden assault from the splashing shit-water below.

To further protect myself from the medieval contagion, I sit with my right hand wrapped around my cock and balls. It simply wouldn't do for blue fluid to splash up into my pee-hole, thus profaning my balls and dizzak.

This is not an infantryman's situation. Infantryman are generally accustomed to leaning back over a community slit-trench in the woods and letting loose in the company of flies, wasps, and chiggers. This is a rare luxury, the same caliber of which is enjoyed by private contractors, framers, farmers, electricians, and all of the manual blue-collar working class across America. I am one of their rank, and while I'm not currently on a well-paid detail erecting drywall in a house somewhere, I know that some motherfucker in Oklahoma is doing the same as me. At this very moment. Right now. That's patriotic thought for you. We're connected, and he doesn't even know it.

Oklahoma where the wind comes sweepin' cross the plains, and the waving wheat, can sure smell sweet, when the wind comes right behind the rain.

When I was young, in the long days before my soul died, I attended an arts high school. Oklahoma was a staple, and I do my best to avert my mind from it but fail, feeling empty about my life and sad for days gone by. I think about romance in high school, a world away, before I ever killed anyone.

Zoe.

Oh, the wheels are yell-a the upholstery's brown, the dashboard's genuine leather.

"Shut up!"

I say the words in a cutting tone to myself, and the snake-like verbiage cuts a small echo across the plastic that surrounds me.

She's fucking him. I'll kill him, I swear to God.

Staring at the floor, I take a deep breath of the blue air, hand still protectively wrapped around my cock, and take stock of my life.

My porta-john is vibrating, pulsing back and forth with the plastic reverberations of the masturbation of a soldier next door. I think of whacking-off myself, but I decide against it.

Emily left me.

I exhale once, directly through my mouth. Though my body shivers, I cannot yet see my breath.

Two weeks.

You can do anything for two weeks.

She's fucking him.

And I'm shitting. I'm shitting in Baghdad. I'm shitting in a little plastic house in old Babylon, and my shit house is vibrating.

I stare at my boots through the freakish red light, and then switch my headlamp off. I want to go away.

She's fucking him.

I wait in the darkness and try not to think.

I wait.

When I feel that my solitary confinement has concluded, I switch my red light back on, take my Charmin in hand, and finish doing the necessary.

Chapter Nine: Blind Man's Theatre

Dim the lights, raise the curtain,
Now it's time, though we're not certain,
To watch the show, in the evening glow,
With their silly jokes and microphones.

The actors take their places on the set,
With what kind of picture are we met?
What's this picture when they die?
If they fade away, this program lies.

Clapping, laughing, smiling, singing;
In the darkest harmony and dissonance:
This is the theatre of the blind.

Lives kick and scream here lost in pain,
Sing the verse in time and turn the page,
In brighter light it looks the same,
Wrong or right, we're not to blame,
Welcome to the theatre of the blind.

They crawl alone, gasping, grinning at you,
But you can't see what's funny in their smile;
It's all lost, the screen is fuzzy;
I hear the screams and I can't laugh anymore.

All the paying patrons drop their jaws,
Not a voice or murmur, no applause.
Just distaste: disgusted horror fills the place,
Thank God that everyone is blind.

Nodding nearly napping in their chairs,
They're wounded and bleeding, but nobody cares,
They try to stab and kill each other,
And no one here is laughing anymore.

The children cry, there's women screaming,
This must be where Dante takes his meaning,
They all start running towards the door,
Nobody wants to watch this anymore.

The grim macabre, bloody hands,
What will it take to understand,
There's nothing to be found here,
Save the dying and the blind.

It's time to go again. Turning away from my bunk in the bay at Mad, I take a moment to stuff my neck-gaiter and full-fingered gloves into my left cargo pocket. It's now late October, and some nights are starting to be significantly colder than what I have become accustomed to.

Armor on and weapon slung, I walk casually out of the barracks with the others into the fading evening light, with my helmet loosely hanging from my left hand.

I'll be in the gunner's position this evening, and being the proactive bastard that I am, I set the weapon up on the truck fifteen minutes ago.

The walk to the waiting trucks goes quickly, and as soon as I arrive, I drop my gear by the lead truck and find Chapel in the smoking crowd.

"Big one, huh Chapps?"

"Same as any other. Just watch your lane; you'll do fine."

Huddling up with the group, I fire up a smoke of my own. I look for the sun, but fail, as the globe has already fallen lower than the walls surrounding Mad, and the only trace left of it is a pink-orange hue that casts a surreal light across the quickly darkening sky.

"I wouldn't worry yourself too much, D. The idea is to be in and out real quick. With the whole battalion here, it shouldn't be too much of a fight, if any."

Chapps is just trying to reassure me now. He knows as well as I do tonight is going to be a hot one.

As far as we know, rather, all we know, is that a number of high value targets from the local insurgent leadership are said, via informants, to be conducting a rather large meeting tonight in a three story structure on the outskirts of Fahad.

The main problem with the operation, according to the thinkers among us, is attributed directly to the involvement of the Iraqi Army. They've been gearing up to hit this operation with us for the last two days, which means there has been plenty of time for them to play double-agent games among themselves, informing the enemy of what we're planning to do, when, and how.

Loose lips are the frequent and continuing problem with operational security that we face whenever we involve local police or military forces in our operations. They simply cannot, or will not keep their mouths shut. After all, each and every Iraqi soldier's loyalty can be purchased for weeks at a time with ten bucks or so. It's good to have such reliable allies.

We will not be having a formal briefing at the trucks. With twenty Humvees, and just under a hundred soldiers present, the briefings for this particular outing were handled at the platoon level. Each element, composed of the standard five trucks, is aware of tonight's operational plan, as well as the specific tasks that have been set out for them.

Delta company will primarily be providing over-watch with the heavy weapon systems on the trucks, while Alpha and Charlie companies will move around either side of the target building, assaulting past the objective as they move, as well as taking up dismounted high-ground positions to pull a mobile sort of perimeter security.

While the rest of the operation's perimeter is taken care of, paratroopers from Bravo company are simply going to kick the door in and kill or capture every Hajji they find inside the target building.

Delta is going to hang to the rear, cutting the target building off from the rest of Fahad, as well as standing ready as a mobile flanking force.

Aside from the dismounted crews that will be handling business at the ground level, all truck crews are to remain in the fight at all times, with the aim of totally encircling the target building. Our trucks will pull security and actively engage the enemy throughout the duration of the mission.

Iraqi army elements, believed to be about one hundred strong, are simply going to charge the building. They don't know how to do anything else, and Iraqi command has assured my own superiors that their veterans have done this dozens of times and know exactly what to do. Our primary concern is that they will become scared, disoriented, or confused, and subsequently attack our own troops. Hell, maybe they've all been paid-off to go turn-coat on us. If that's the case, then we certainly are in for a Hell of a fight.

No small meeting, the social get-together that we're crashing this evening should have more than two hundred guests in attendance.

"I know I've said this before Chapps, but I think I really mean it this time: we really just made it to the war, didn't we?"

"I think you're correct, little brother; I think we're arriving tonight."

In lieu of waiting around for a formal briefing, the battalion simply mills about by the mass of running trucks spilling out of the overcrowded parking area, standing by as soldiers check night-vision batteries and perform radio checks, simply chilling out until it's dark enough to move.

We should be on site tonight no later than 2100 hours. Our target for RTB is no later than 2300 hours. So, if in the event that tonight turns into

371

an awful grinder, at least it shouldn't last very long. Two hours at most. I'm bringing extra water just in case; I've seen this movie.

Five cigarettes later and about a half an hour after full dark, it's time to get moving. I bid Chapps farewell as I don my gear, then make the short, awkward climb through the cab of my truck into the turret. Standing in place, I feel the token vibrations and compressions in the shocks of the vehicle, the frame slightly wobbling, as four other soldiers climb in and take their positions for the evening.

As is our custom of late, we do not wait until we get to the clearing barrels to load our weapons, but instead do so immediately, in the very center of Mad. It looks like we're already pressed for time as it is, and word from the LT is that the operation needs to start. Now.

Supposedly, the Iraqi Army is already on the move, the majority of which are waiting for us less than five hundred meters away from the target building.

Brass is my acting TC for the evening, and addresses us all.

"Heads on a swivel, guys. You ready to get you some?"

"Roger, Sergeant."

"Don't pass out on me now, Pearce; I know how you scouts are on the gun."

Way to go Duke; pave the way.

"Negative, Sergeant. I don't feel at all sleepy tonight."

"Good. Keep it that way."

Brass isn't being his usual, stoic, serious self. He's having a hard time keeping himself from laughing, obviously delighted with his own sense of humor. He has nothing against me; he's my buddy. The same can't be said of Duke.

Our Sergeant Major comes over the net, "All trucks, proceed to phase line Alpha. Repeat, mission is a go."

Rather than being safely tucked back at the FOB for tonight's operation, the Sergeant Major has joined us in spirit over the coms net from our command post at Mad. High ranking heavy hitters are managing battalion communications for this run. A good comfort, Apaches from a nearby post will be on standby to support us with CAS tonight. The Sergeant Major, as well as our own battalion commander, will be in direct communication with them throughout the evening to direct the aerial assets as they see fit, should the need arise.

Delta Company is last in line in the caravan this evening. I sit and wait in the turret, feeling the vibrations of the truck in my feet as Bravo and Charlie pull out first.

Brass spits a wad of Copenhagen laden saliva into an empty water bottle and addresses the truck crew, "Yeah, motherfuckers! Here we go!"

Similar motivational shouts pop up from random trucks in the line. Apparently, I'm not the only one who thinks we're about to drive into something heavy tonight. We are jubilant; a real combat operation is a blessed release from the mind-numbing reality of patrolling the same sector again and again, day after day.

Even better, tonight is our night to clean out the neighborhood. If the enemy *has* been tipped off and we are met with heavy resistance, this will be our opportunity to crush them once and for all.

We're looking forward to greeting all of the insurgent mortar teams, wackos with AKs, trained snipers, and local bomb makers. If they want to make a stand for themselves tonight, they'll have to go all in and be present. Tonight is the perfect venue for terrorist population control, and the excitement in the air is palpable. Everyone is hoping that it's a big one. The more we can kill tonight, the quieter our neighborhoods will be in the coming months. It's time to make a combative political statement.

Even the MPs at the gate, who normally appear tired-looking, sluggish, and stoic, pitch in with the noise as we roll out the gate. They know something big is going on. It's rare for a convoy to roll anywhere in an element bigger than five trucks. A battalion going out? Sure; it must be something big.

The cheering, yee-haws, and shouting stop as we approach the gate, where we assume our usual quiet and professional posture.

Everyone is aware of the danger, but we are also ready to face it. We get to go be infantrymen tonight, guaranteed. That's priceless.

The headlights of each truck in the convoy, twenty sets in all, switch off as we pull out of Mad and into our own well-known traffic circle. We will be running on blackout tonight, with no light whatsoever coming from the trucks. Instead of navigating in a well-lit fashion, drivers and TCs will rely solely on their night vision optics, as will we all, to carry out the duties of the evening.

As we turn onto the main drag I don't know what to think. Fifteen trucks ahead of me, and four behind, I feel impelled toward the nightly task like never before. On the gun, even more freedom has been taken from me. Where to run, how fast to move, and where to take cover are no longer choices of mine. The gun is like a rollercoaster; where the truck goes, I go. I'm at the mercy of it.

I relish the slight cool breeze on the October air. I can feel the winter coming, and I can't wait. Pulling my thoughts away from reflections on the weather, I focus once again on the task at hand.

Pulling security in pattern with the rest of the trucks, I take a field of fire to the nine o' clock of the convoy. Standing in the turret I feel each bump and crack in the road as our Humvee trundles forward at about ten miles per hour.

Nobody starts a conversation; it's going to be a short drive, as the target building is within two miles of our current location.

As well as providing gunners with steady weapons platforms, the slow speed is taken to avoid making any more noise than is absolutely necessary. Our diesel engines emit nothing more than a low hum as we gently idle forward into the dark.

This section of the town is blessedly absent of street lamps, and in a wonderful, courteous nod from the heavens above the moon is not showing itself tonight. The absence of any near light results in almost no lume, and were it not for my nods I would not be able to see more than ten meters in any direction. It's the perfect light level for us; my very favorite kind.

Suddenly, I feel a surge of adrenaline in my body. We told the IA about the op. The whole town doubtless knows. There's a reason why we're rolling a battalion deep. I'm scared, and I'm excited.

Brass is outwardly motivated.

"You guys excited to be headed to the playoffs? I'd call it the Super Bowl, but it's not the last game of the season."

"I don't follow sports too much, Sarge, but I can say, playing every once in a while has to be all right."

"Amen to that, brother."

Radio chatter goes wild as the target building comes into view.

Not fully surrounded by the typical urban maze, the target building stands at the edge of a large dirt wasteland roughly the size of a football field. Empty space stretches toward us like a welcoming mat rolled out from the building, save for random yellow brick piles, automobile wrecks, and smatterings of assorted garbage. Beyond and behind the target building the crazy, claustrophobic maze of Fahad's mulhallas await. The main road we're currently driving on tightly flanks the right side of the building, and the traditional brand of apartment blocks, businesses, and concrete tenements continue down the thoroughfare on the opposite side of the street.

374

The night is dead quiet as we approach the objective, and as our convoy slows, half of it peels away, driving abreast of itself in a wide swath, cutting across the wasteland where the trucks come to a stop roughly fifty meters from the front of the building.

Five more trucks continue on the road ahead, stopping once they reach a flanking position parallel to the target building on the main road.

My group peels off, staying farther behind than the first group and forms a lazy-W position facing to the nine o'clock from our previous direction of travel to the north. It looks like we're pulling rear security from the get-go.

From my position looking west, I can see Forrester in the halted truck just beside mine to the left, manning another fifty and actively scanning his sector.

To my right, also on a MK-19, another D Co paratrooper pulls security to the ten o' clock. I have a special affinity for that truck; Chapps is the acting TC tonight, and apparently, he has seen fit to ensure that the MK-19 on his truck is covering our flank, rather than sitting comfortably back in the line.

In less than thirty seconds we have the target completely surrounded. Alpha wraps around the building to the left while Charlie halts in the street to the right; Bravo forms a crescent front and center, while D Co, behind it all, faces to the nine o' clock, effectively pulling rear-guard as well as completely cutting off the target building from most of western Fahad.

I can see the final part of the movement on the other side of the bullet-proof glass that stands inches from the right side of my face. In a huge gaggle, what must be over a hundred soldiers from the Iraqi army are spreading out, not necessarily taking cover, but definitely standing by pillars of concrete and behind parked vehicles across the main road from the target building.

A minute goes by, then two. I guess we're just scoping it out.

Though I can see many buildings on the horizon, most of them are more than four hundred meters out, and in this darkness they have become the least of my concerns.

The rest of the Delta company gunners rotate their turrets, with every man picking up a field of fire where another truck's field of fire leaves off. We don't pick up sectors towards the rest of our trucks to the north, to mitigate occurrences of flagging. Besides, they can watch out for themselves.

Being in the middle of our own formation, having generally formed a north-south line perpendicular to the crescent formed by the rest of the battalion, I continue to scan the near structures to the nine o' clock while those in the southern most trucks of our formation pick up sectors to the southwest, south, and east. Chapel's truck, just north of mine, picks up his sector where the battalion leaves off, covering a swath of denser urban territory to the northwest.

Nearest to the open field where our gun-line finds itself are a dozen low one-story buildings, shanty huts, and crumbling yellow-brick buildings. Whether they are currently serving as free housing for squatters, storage of sorts, or are just vacant wrecks is impossible for me to tell.

Sergeant Major speaks over the net, "All trucks, stand fast. Standby for dismount in five mics. Just wait for a spell and see how it looks, how copy?"

Four platoon sergeants send up their acknowledgements one by one. It simply wouldn't do to have fifty paratroopers dismount only to get creamed in the near ambush of the century.

Looking to my right, I stare at the looming target structure standing about a hundred meters away. There is no sign of any activity at all from the building. Every window is black. I notice as well, that the power grid is up and running famously around Fahad tonight.

From the small structures to my front, electric light pours out of select windows, and deeper into Fahad the small glows of streetlamps and residential lighting can be seen. That should serve as an alarm bell to everyone. Our target building is the largest structure in the surrounding area, and it also happens to be the only structure without a single light on. Coincidence? I think not.

We have the building surrounded. Charlie can gun down any runners trying to flee from the rear of the building, and any other egress needs to pass directly through the crescent formed by Alpha and Bravo. They're trapped. We can afford to be patient; there is nowhere left for them to run.

The operation has already picked up a decidedly slow pace as we all wait and watch our sectors. Every man searches for a target.

Not being able to help myself, I peel my eyes away from my own lane and scan the windows of the main structure through my nods. I can't see anything move.

Gunners from Alpha and Bravo have begun shining windows one by one with their IR flood lamps. Window by window, illuminated from the outside by our intrusive, invisible light, vacant rooms show the edges of their contents one by one.

Empty window frames, lonely ragged curtains, broken glass, and empty concrete greets us behind the windows, with not a soul in sight.

Could it have been bad intel?

"Hey, Brass, any chance that they knew we were coming here in force tonight, and just took off?"

"Stranger things have happened, Pearce. Wouldn't surprise me at all. I don't expect it's vacant, but it's a real possibility so far."

Nobody speaks. Everybody watches and waits. The only sound present is the low hum of diesel engines and the token pops and beeps coming from the radio in the cab beneath me.

The Sergeant Major speaks again, verifying that CAS will be on sight in less than twenty minutes, and will be able to maintain a presence near us for a maximum of three hours, unless of course they get called away to bigger, more exciting things.

I keep my eyes peeled, watching for movement of any kind in the line of houses to my front. A full ten minutes have passed since the battalion-wide mass excitement promised by the guarantee of a real combat operation.

Not losing a bit of alertness or concentration, I allow myself to relax a bit as some of the adrenaline leaves my body. I verify that my safety round is still seated well in place just below my butterfly trigger and lean back against the rear of the turret. I may very well be here for quite some time; I might as well get comfortable.

"All units, dismount."

That's the call. Soldiers from Alpha, Bravo, and Charlie emerge from the safety of their metal shells and start moving to their pre-determined locations for the operation.

Alpha dismounts are taking a high over-watch position in a tall building only fifty meters or so from the target building. Although only two stories tall, the small structure sits crookedly on an elevated hill. While structurally not as tall as the target, Alpha's new home is eye-level or better with the third floor of the target building. As they move, Chapel's gunner rotates his turret a bit farther to the left, as half of his field of fire has now been taken from him, due to the presence of the boots on the ground.

Charlie is on their way across the street, taking positions of cover amidst the concrete and debris of apartment blocks and store-fronts, falling into place with our gaggle of Iraqi friends, who in turn move farther down the street to the north. Iraqi command was insistent that their people should be the ones making sure that nobody could escape the structure to the rear. That's an eyebrow raiser. Maybe you can buy your way past them for a falafel and some chai.

Bravo Dismounts move quickly to the front of the building, taking positions around the crooked steps leading up to the double doors where they immediately start looking through ground floor windows. In a matter of seconds the battalion dismount is over.

D Co is staying put. Our dismounts will come into play if we need to get anyone out of a hot spot. While the dismounted crews from the other trucks have maintained the same usual equipment standards, D Co soldiers are packing extra medical equipment tonight, complete with more than enough IV bags, plenty of hemostat bandages, tourniquets, and extra Israeli bandages.

"Ya'll dismounts unstrap that ammo and get it ready."

By my feet, I feel the rustling of another D Co trooper and Duke as they loosen the ratchet straps that hold the boxes of .50 caliber ammunition into place. It's a good idea to be proactive in these situations.

After another thirty more seconds of quiet, the fighting starts.

Through my nods and the scratched glass to my right, I can see dozens of muzzle flashes erupt from the top floor of the target building as two handfuls of AK-47s show us how loud they can scream.

Trucks in the Alpha and Bravo gun-lines open up on the building, and the night is quiet no longer. Four fifties, four MK-19s, and two M240Bs open up on the third floor of the building, plunging our quiet field into open war.

Looking again to my sector, I hear a new ruckus and my heart starts pounding. Alpha company dismounts open fire from the roof of their newly acquired building as their own line of trucks unleash hell below them.

Traffic on the net goes haywire with paratroopers accidentally cutting off each other's radio chatter as every TC and dismounted fire-team begin simultaneously calling out enemy positions to battalion command.

From across the street to the east Charlie company and a slew of Iraqis open fire on their side of the structure. While C Co takes cover and returns fire most of the Iraqi army soldiers scatter like a kicked ant hill.

Dozens of them run down alleys to the east where they disappear into the night, while a dozen more run across the street to the front of the building, eager to huddle up with the Bravo dismounts who are newly engaged with targets on the first floor themselves, taking cover behind the brickwork in front of the building while they fire through windows and doorjambs.

Somewhere in the night a man screams in pain.

I concentrate on my field of fire, and remind myself just to watch my lane, but nothing is there. No running men. No gunfire. No movement of any kind. Swinging my turret around and engaging the building would be the biggest no no I could make. It's not generally acceptable to fire heavy weapons right over your buddies' heads, and I can't drop security on my own sector.

I watch and wait, but follow the track of the battle from the other side of the window to my right.

Through my nods the world has become a freakish lightshow of tracers, muzzle flash, and the running IA.

The noise is incredible as over a dozen heavy weapon systems open fire on the enemy, of which there must be more than fifty at present. Hajji has gone cyclic, firing on truck crews with their triggers crunched down at full-throttle.

All around, reports from M-4s can barely be heard against the storm of sound. I can't hear individual rounds being fired. Instead, all the night is a Hellish roar, with the flashes from gunfire so frequent and bright that I can see the silhouettes of enemy fighters on the third floor, as well as the dark outlines of my brothers at the front of the building.

Screaming, howling men are growing in number. I can hear wailing from the target building, and screaming from a dozen wounded Iraqi army soldiers who never made it across the street, each calling out from the dirt road as they try to crawl their way across it. The volume of fire is great, and Charlie cannot move.

I'm worried by not being able to do anything from my position. I'm pissed off, not being able to do anything from my position. I wait for our trucks to move; I wait for orders. I wait helplessly for anything as I look desperately out from my turret, clearly seeing enemy fighters that I'm not allowed to engage.

The fight drags on as soldiers call out from their turrets for new cans of ammunition, or on the ground for coverage during reloads.

I'm watching as fighters die on the third floor, and the battle seems to be going in our favor.

One of the Alpha MK-19s opens up on another group of insurgents on the west side of the building. I cannot see the men, but I can hear their screams as a dozen 40mm HE rounds walk their way across the windows to destroy the bodies of the enemy, as well as their hiding places.

Severed limbs and crumbling masonry fall to the street below, and the heavy gun keeps rocking.

Movement.

I catch a glimpse, not a man, but a shadow, probably a hundred meters away behind a window on the second floor of a building to the west. My lane.

Shutting out the rest of the spectacle that is unfolding itself over my right shoulder, I crank my turret a bit to the right. I'm not the only one.

In the truck to the right side of mine, Chapel's gunner traverses toward the newly suspicious bank of windows, and like me, patiently waits and watches.

A sharp explosion followed by a chorus of new howling and new pain cries out into the darkness, but I keep watching my field of fire.

The constant gunfire shows no signs of letting up, abating, or slowing. With all but D Co engaged, the volume of fire continues on. As the combat escalates with automatic fire from the IA who have not run, our dismounts engaging point targets, our trucks decimating the target building, and a hoard of enemies discharging their AKs, the noise seems to grow even denser.

Smartly foregoing radio communication, not wanting to play a game of telephone through his TC over the net, the D Co soldier to my right, Parker, I think his name is, shouts through the din at my turret.

"Hey, you see movement?"

"Yeah, I got it too!"

Movement doesn't mean the enemy. It could just be curious housewives or children.

"I got a lot more now! Three windows!"

Parker is closer to the windows than I am, and even though I'm looking as intently as I can, I'm not picking out what he is, so I take his word for it while keeping watch and holding my turret steady.

Automatic weapons fire opens up on Chapel's truck from the window farthest from my position.

Angry and excited, I slam the safety round out from underneath my butterfly trigger and discharge some of my own fifty caliber rage.

My right eye goes dark, immediately night-blinded by the flashing of the .50 barrel. With no fancy muzzle break, and no flash suppressor, it's just the way a big nasty heavy machinegun should be.

Protected by the light dampener in my monocular, the vision in my left eye remains clear.

I fire three five round bursts and watch through my adrenaline haze as green flashes of light go out from me and slam their way home, sparking and thudding where the AK flash was just a second before. I'm on target.

In concert with me, Parker goes cyclic on the MK-19, immediately putting the terrible destruction of my own rounds to shame as 40mm grenades dash the enemy firing position to pieces.

The light blooms in my nods are fast and beautiful. Streamers of molten shrapnel, burning explosives, and brick debris fly free from the impact points like miniature fireworks, showering my left eye with their loud displays of streaking green.

After my first bursts I cease fire, watching the other windows and waiting for another flash. World War Three or not, it's still a civilian neighborhood. If we were authorized to drop a five hundred pound bomb on it, we would have moved the trucks away and done it already.

Parker lets his gun go silent and waits with me once more. We're awake. They have our attention. Both of us had fantastic shot groups, and I'd say that we're par for the course this evening.

Adrenaline has my hands shaking. I watch. I wait. I take deep breaths to slow the beating of my heart. Through the new, fresh ringing in my ears Brass calls up to me.

"You get you some, motherfucker? You get you some? Keep watching! That's good shit! Fucking Pearce, man!"

He's much more excited than I am. He's not hanging out the top of the turret like a twisted fairground version of Whack-a-Mole. In my defense, I'm a mole with a fifty. That makes me feel better.

"I sure did; Parker *definitely* did though!"

Staying low in the turret, I gaze over the feed tray of my weapon to my field of fire that looms just over the armored plate that sits forward of the gun, and wait.

There aren't four windows anymore. There are four misshapen holes, slightly wider now than they were before. There's less room for them to hide there now.

Breaking my own fixation from the target windows, I crank my turret a bit back to the left and start scanning my entire sector with gusto.

The fifty caliber echo in my turret was deafening, with the steel to my left and right catching the sound, bouncing it at my head again and again. Though muted and under a shrill buzz, I can hear the battle raging on behind me, not waning for a moment.

Brass calls up again from below.

"You see that? Just left of last time. Second floor. Watch it."

I do; I watch it very closely.

"Roger, got it."

Parker has it too, swiveling his turret directly at the movement.

We're totally focused on it. The trucks to my left should have everything to the rear covered. Go team.

A weapon opens fire on Parker's truck once again, this time from the new position, and our response time is even better this go-round.

"RPK. RPD or some shit!"

The enemy fire is no AK.

Fully automatic, the enemy fire rips into the front of Chapp's vehicle while Parker immediately fires back.

I give three bursts myself and watch as the rounds hit home, but the enemy fire continues unabated, now joined by a friend.

Buzzing, sparking loud and angry, two enemy rounds hit the front plate of my turret and ricochet into the night. I don't use controlled bursts to talk back.

Hammering down on the butterfly, I give a twenty-round burst from the left side of the window to the right, suppressing the best way I know how.

Brass gives me a yeehaw from below as more hot tracers fly just above my turret. Parker opens up to give them what for, but only gives them two, and the unthinkable happens. His MK-19 jumps the pindle.

The loaded weapon, weighing in at more than seventy pounds, thuds heavily as it crashes onto the hood of the Humvee.

Over the sound of my own firing and the zipping and popping of incoming rounds I can hear Parker call down to Chapps. I can't hear the words, but from the panicked, shrill tone of the shouting I know that it can't be anything good. I wish I could hear Chapel's reply, but there's no time to think about that now.

I fire another burst, and then another.

Seeing the awkward and dangerous situation, the rearmost truck in our line pulls forward out of formation as its turret swivels to join our fight.

Having two fifties hammer the target is essential now that one gun is down. Conserving my ammo, I drop my rate of fire back down to five round bursts, and the other truck does the same. We're talking. Gun talk. Him. Me. Him. Me. I don't know how much I've fired, but I'll call for a reload when I need it.

With the new volume of fire from the west, Alpha company dismounts have redirected their fire for the time being, helping us to hammer into the newcomers.

To my right I see Chapps. I see Chapps in the fucking open.

Climbing onto the hood of his sparking Humvee while directly under a heavy volume of enemy fire, Chapel grabs the weapon and hoists it up amidst the hail of tracers that whizz and pop just inches from his body, as he works with Parker to seat the MK-19 onto its pindle once again.

Covering fire. I double my volume, as does the gunner on my left. We're suppressing the shit out of them.

I look to my right once more, and Chapps is already gone, seated safely once again inside his truck.

He's a brave bastard. He's the best NCO I've ever known.

Parker tells us that he's back in the fight, in the good way.

He fires a twenty-round burst of 40mm into the window that previously housed our new fully automatic friends.

After his burst there is a large, noticeably burning hole in the structure. There's not a window anymore. There's not even a wall. He opened up the side of the entire building.

We're not getting shot at anymore.

With not a word over coms, the other .50 truck drives backwards once again, reclaiming it's former position in the line.

I check my ammo and find only three rounds left on the belt, jutting lonely-like from the left side of my feed tray.

"Ammo. I need a can."

My voice sounds breathy and far away. My mouth is dry and my hands are shaking. I feel as if the whole Middle Eastern world is drawing a bead on me now and I feel naked, exposed in the turret from face to belly button, waiting for a sniper's bullet.

I'm also ecstatic. We got us some, and behind us, the getting is still good.

Quickly, I bring the empty can into the vehicle and pass it on, trading it out for one with a more substantial weight.

Through the artificial light of gunfire I can see my weapon good enough with my right eye, and I'm able to load rather smoothly despite the shaking in my fingers.

I rack my bolt to the rear, then loose it, letting it slam forward with a healthy sounding clink.

"Brass, test-fire!"

"Go fucker!"

I fire three rounds into the dark pit that used to house the enemy gunman. I'm up again.

"Good to go."

Immediately, I feel relieved and empowered; for a moment, my stress is gone.

I watch and wait once again.

A voice comes over the net, "CP this is Bravo One-Four, we have established a foothold on the first floor, how copy, over?"

"Roger Bravo. Good copy, over."

"We're holding; Bravo out."

The call is shaky. It's the voice of a man who's just run a thousand meter dash and is high on adrenaline.

The fight at the front of the building has ceased for the time being, and it's clear that command doesn't want them running into the building just yet.

With so many enemy fighters, the structure is bound to be booby-trapped or mined. What's more, this is no longer a capture mission. The battalion has collectively graduated to a search and destroy posture. Why send Bravo into further danger deep in the heart of the structure when we're still killing masses of the enemy from the outside?

Behind me, the battle around the outside of the main target building is starting to slow. No longer a looming cacophony of lead-roaring noise, the battle sounds like a battle again, with gunshots spaced far enough apart that the individual reports of weapons can be heard.

A single shot here, and a burst or two there. It sounds like we have the situation under control.

Radio chatter is flowing more freely now, as the initial calls in the chaos have ceased.

Ammunition reports go up, and Alpha and Bravo are low. Casualty calls go out, and a soldier from Alpha is dead, with two more wounded from Bravo and three additional wounded from Charlie. There are no wounded reported from Delta, although Chapel certainly had his chance.

God must love grizzled, chain-smoking, soldierly biker pals.

CP comes over the net again.

"All units, hold what you've got. Continue to engage targets as you see them. IA elements are assembling to the north side of the target building, roughly two hundred meters from it, be advised."

I call down, "So no shooting the uniformed Hajjis behind the building? Got it."

Nobody laughs at my attempt at humor. It wasn't really humor to begin with. More important shit is happening now anyway.

With a healthy amount of suspicion, calmed breathing, and a slower heart-rate, I continue to scan my sector, doing as I've been told, and as is natural. I've got to find the movement.

And then, quiet. Blessed quiet. The radio pops and beeps in the night, but there is no chatter.

Emergencies are attended to for the time being as the battalion, all engines still running, watches and waits for more contacts.

Nobody speaks. Noise discipline is the rule once again, as the raucous gunfire has stopped.

By the front of the building a wounded IA sits in the dirt and lights the most expensive cigarette of his life.

Three rounds sound off into the night, and the man is likely dead before his body hits the ground. There is no return fire. Nobody saw where it came from.

I watch my lane. I don't think about my life. I don't think about the time stretching out before morning. I just watch my lane.

I whisper, "Hey, anybody got a pinch?"

Somebody does, and the can is handed up to me from an unknown person below. I mash a fresh pinch into my lip and it tastes good, moist, and sweet. It's peach Skoal. As I hand the can of dip back down below I miss Cole, my reliable dipping buddy.

I whisper, "Thanks," and the night continues.

I can see the silhouette of the truck to my right now with my naked eye. A fire is burning in the main structure, casting a sickly orange light that covers the courtyard in an otherworldly glow, faintly revealing us to the night.

I take a moment to look straight above, and I am amazed as always by the volume of stars that I can see through my nods. In every inch of the sky there are a million more stars than are ever present to the naked eye, even on the clearest moonless night.

I watch my lane.

An automatic weapon fires to my rear. No reply.

Looking over my right shoulder, I watch the event unfold from my thick window of bullet-resistant glass. From somewhere, two AKs fire again, but this time Charlie must have seen them from across the road.

A dozen M-4s sharply crack from positions behind concrete pillars and the battle is on again.

One truck fires, then two. Then a whole platoon.

As it initially started, the sound ebbs and grows. The spaces from the reverberations of individual rounds become few and far between. The main orchestral syncopation diminishes, and the wasteland is covered once again by the steady and otherworldly mechanical screaming.

The sound makes my turret shake, vibrating with the anger and hatred of the world. I can feel the bass in my chest, as if I were standing in front of a subwoofer in a dance hall. It's the song of men ripping each other apart, a grungy bass-line of metal, dubstep, and thrash.

The CP brings good tidings over the net.

"Alpha and Charlie, take cover and hunker down tight, break, Bravo mount up. I repeat, Bravo, Break contact and move back to the vehicles."

Bravo sends its acknowledgment, and through my window on the world I can see the Bravo gun-line go cyclic.

Rather than taking metered and measured six to eight round bursts, the Bravo gun-line goes wild, throwing everything they have at the second and third floors, covering the way for the Bravo foot-soldiers as they run across the open field, back to the safety of their armor.

As they run, pockets of IA around them seem to get the general idea of what's going on, so they scatter into the night, leaving handfuls of dead Iraqi soldiers behind on the front steps -- the only sign that they were ever there.

The radio takes a long pause.

CP comes back, "All units mount up, I say again, all units mount up. Break back to the trucks; CAS is inbound to Tally, three mics."

Initial acknowledgements come in rapidly one by one from Alpha, Bravo, and Charlie. Continuing transmissions can be heard across the net, as individual squad and fire-team leaders send up their 'Rogers' and positive confirmation.

Within the space of a minute, new radio calls shower the net declaring that different groups of dismounted paratroopers have made it safely back into their respective vehicles.

Through the screaming of dying Iraqi soldiers and enemy wounded, the shouting of paratroopers from every company can be heard, picking up a triumphant harmony with the drumming of the guns.

Brass can no longer contain himself and shouts, *"Gonna get us a lightshow too, motherfuckers!"*

My heart is racing as I scan my field of fire as the world around me mashes itself into a deeper state of Hell once again, but I feel jubilant. I feel like screaming myself, but I'll hold it in for now and wait for the big show.

We're stuck in, sure, but we have a few different friends in high places, some slightly lower in the sky than others.

One minute passes, then two.

"All units, Tally out, one mic."

One more minute scrapes by in the din.

"All units, Tally-Ho."

I can hear the choppers coming; they're flying in like bats out of Hell. A few seconds more, and archangels are among us.

I can't see the birds until they're right above us. Seeming to take their time, the two Apaches open fire with their chainguns, methodically sweeping every floor of the building, cutting it east to west, and stem to stern.

The choppers are low, and the guns are loud. Breaking protocol, I look to my right again as I stuff my right pinky into my ear to protect my already ringing drum from the continued audio assault.

The sparks are beautiful, and they light up my nods as if all the target building were a stage, and its insurgents, the players.

Gunfire from the trucks does not let up or cease, but it continues on in concert with the birds, creating a compound compression wave of hot leaden death that bodily sweeps its way back and forth throughout the building.

The chainguns stop, and as if on cue, the battalion ceases fire.

Nothing can be heard in the long night save for the whirring blades of the helicopters.

"All units, danger close; it's hellfire time, enjoy the show, CP out."

Streaks of fiery light, small in origin, bloom to life as rockets blast free from launch tubes hovering only sixty feet above and roar toward the objective.

The rockets are bolts of fire that scream through the night, yet they are still slow enough that I can track their movement across the battlefield to the roof of the target building.

They come rapidly, spaced one second apart, and the explosions are deafening.

Gouts of flame spark toward the heavens in plumes, expelling juts of fire and molten brick that shoot up from the target building like geysers.

The structural damage is immediate, and the front of the building sags.

As quickly as they came our friends are gone, and except for the now painful and oppressive ringing in my ears the night is silent.

As I have done on other occasions, while I give my lane my full attention once again, I think about the awesome destructive power than my army wields. I am chilled and awed, and in this moment, I am very proud.

I stare into the dark night as more radio calls are made. Alpha dismounts are black on ammo. The battalion has three flat tires that will be attended to later. The IA are reporting more than thirty dead.

"From what? Standing in the open, yeah?"

"Your guess is as good as mine, man. Lead poisoning, most likely."

I wait for what seems like a full hour, eyes riveted on my field of fire, scanning from left to right, right to left, foreground to background. Looking from pile of rubble to pile of rubble, window to door, then to more windows, I'm relentless in my search for the enemy.

The hunt continues in the trucks to my right, and the rest of the battalion to my four o' clock. Turrets lazily swivel back and forth, each gunner combing the surrounding buildings as well as the now violently burning ruin of the target building for signs of any enemy combatants left still alive.

"All units, this is CP."

The voice of the Sergeant Major sounds urgent.

"A-C130 is reporting a group of armed insurgents numbering over forty strong moving south toward your position from multiple locations roughly two clicks to the north, how copy, over."

All platoon sergeants call back their Rogers and copys.

The battle seems to be on again, but the time frame is limited. With our main objective completed and a handful of wounded soldiers to attend to, command has decided that it's time for the battalion to move back to Mad, but not before our new interlopers have been taken care of.

Everyone sits quietly and listens as instructions are doled out to individual platoon leaders over the net, quickly issuing a warning order and combined operations order to each element of the battalion.

Alpha is picking up rear security, as they are now hazardously low on ammunition, while dismounts from Charlie, having fired the least in the engagement are heading north in the mulhallas to stop the enemy in their tracks. Bravo is returning the Mad early with the battalion's wounded, and Delta will be sitting tight, waiting for the chance to flank the enemy when the fight rips off with Charlie. It figures that they would use us this way; it was in the initial game plan all along.

Leaving our assault positions, the battalion loses its crescent shape, each element slowly driving into the night, emptying from the wasteland in front of the burning building like movie-goers leaving a parking lot at eleven pm on a Friday.

The line of Alpha trucks pick up fields of fire behind us while they slowly trundle to the rear. Beyond Alpha, Bravo turns a corner vanishing from sight, taking the wounded with them as they head back from whence we came.

I'm pulling duty on first truck this time, while Forrester will be right behind me in the second truck on another MK-19. Chapel is in the rear of our convoy, as Parker is low on 40mm.

Charlie company dismounts, with their own trucks running in a line behind them, start briskly jogging north up the road where they disappear into the darkness behind the smoldering wreck of the target building. My group will be heading north two streets over to the west, paralleling their advance.

I'm not familiar with the small side-street we're driving up, and I am continually leery of the three and four-story buildings on both sides of the road. In close quarters like these, I cannot elevate my gun high enough to engage passed the third floor. My M-4 is in the turret beside me, but it provides little comfort. My job is to operate the fifty first and foremost, before anything else. Even before personal safety.

Not driving faster than Charlie Company can walk, we idle up the filthy and deserted streets. Being first, I keep my turret pointed directly ahead, and do as best I can to scan everything in my field of view to the front, left, and right.

From the east, 7.62 automatic weapons fire opens up from two streets over, and Charlie fires back.

As we accelerate, a frantic call comes crashing over the net,

"CP this is Charlie One-Three! We're heavily engaged, Near ambush, we have five, no, seven wounded, over!"

That's our rally call.

I can hear fire from enemy weapons cycling up as our convoy accelerates and takes a hard right turn followed by a sharp left, then another right.

It's a dead end.

The sound of the fight is intensifying, but our road has abruptly ended, blocked by trash and broken down automobiles, with the street itself ending in a narrow alleyway, not wide enough to accommodate a Humvee on any day.

"Charlie One-Three, Break back to the JSS. Repeat, Break Contact. Move to the JSS as fast as you can."

Brass shouts from the TC's seat, "You ready? We've got block 'em! Get this piece of shit turned around!"

The U-turn is a jumbled, chaotic mess, with each truck in the line needing to do four and five point turns to navigate the narrow street, and the whole time the gunfight, just one street over, is diminishing.

"CP, this is Charlie, we have broken contact; we are moving east, but not fast, over!"

"Roger. Delta, sitrep."

James comes across the net, "We are west of the last contact point; we are moving east, time now, over."

"Roger Delta. Stop those bastards, out."

Brass's red light illuminates his tactical map below me as he gives quick directions to Freddy, who is sitting in his default position behind the steering wheel.

I'm exhilarated. I'm lead truck. Over forty armed men. I've never been so scared, or so wildly amped-up in my entire life.

There's a fear to jumping out of an airplane; an undertow of reality that sits in the belly of the metal beneath your feet and clutches at your shoulders through the weight of your parachute. That fear has nothing on this. I'm going to be the bulls-eye. The primary target.

I'm going to get me some.

"Right here, now; take a right."

We're speeding now, taking turns faster than is recommended.

I do my best to keep track of our direction in the winding path we take, but I'm at a loss. It doesn't matter; I just have to keeping looking forward, stand in the turret, and not piss myself.

"Left here, left now, pull forward twenty meters, and fucking stop."

We round the turn, and I recognize this road. It leads north into

390

Tiger square, into the very center of Fahad. Normally a busy market street, it appears to be totally vacant tonight.

Our truck slows to a halt, and facing north, I scan my sector quickly from left to right.

"Watch the roofs, D. Watch for frags from the roofs."

"Roger."

I do look at the roofs, but all I see are the jumbled silhouettes of broken down facades and crumbling bricks, with nary an insurgent in sight.

To my right and left, for over a hundred meters on either side, the road is flanked by parked vehicles and the staple concrete pillars that stand in front of almost every building along the length of the market road. The pillars are good cover, and the enemy has plenty of decent firing positions.

To my front, at the very end of the street, two concrete T-barriers stand. They used to block off the end of the street to through traffic, but someone has moved them, and now they stand wide enough apart to accommodate our trucks. I'd call that a lucky break, but for the time being, I'll be staying put.

James calls our status up, "CP, this is Delta, we are in position, over."

Everything checks out. I just have to sit, and watch, and wait. There's no guesswork about this one. We know they're here. They know we're here.

All of our trucks pick up a lazy-W formation, and the second truck rolls into a position just behind mine to the left.

My heart is hammering, and I'm soaked to the bone with sweat despite the late October chill in the air.

I check to make sure that my turret is clear, traversing smoothly, and that my butterfly trigger is free. I try to swallow, but it's difficult. I would love to take a swig from my canteen, but there is no time for that.

My right leg begins to shake, and I try to steady my breathing, focusing on the task at hand. The world becomes a slow tunnel as I scan from left to right with fear gnawing at my ribs. The stretch of time is endless. I know the fight is coming; the twisted feeling in my gut is intense and cold; there's no running from it. It's inescapable.

I might really die this time.

At the end of the road I see a man dressed in black as he jumps from the cover of one T-Barrier to another.

"You see that, Brass?"

"Sure did, but wait. They fire, then you fire. That's how we gotta do it."

"Roger."

I'm now standing exposed from navel to face in front of forty men who legally get to take their best shot first. God bless America.

Quickly, very quickly, I talk to God.

Protect me tonight. Forgive me. I'm sorry, mom.

More movement from the left side of the ally. I don't see what it was. There's movement on the right.

"Get ready, motherfucker."

I haven't talked to Emily in over two months.

I look up, looking for grenadiers.

Soldiers, move your safety selection levers to the firing position and watch your lanes.

I'm nearly blinded when Hajji filth opens fire on my left side from the cover of a concrete pillar.

No time to think.

I swivel my turret to the left with both hands on my fifty grips. Foregoing the crank, I wedge the turret over with my legs and body weight.

I fire.

The light in my nods is blinding. Two flashes. Now three. Now one from the right.

The world goes away as I depress the butterfly again and again, moving the thumping, flashing menace from one target to the next.

I can't hear a thing. My ears grow dim, and I'm left alone in a world of fear and flashing light, with the shrill ringing in my head laying a shroud over it all.

I see a target running, clearly exposed on the left, and I put three rounds in him. The concrete wall behind him breaks apart, hammered by the force of rounds emerging from his exit wounds, and before his body falls I'm engaging a target on the right hand side of the street.

More flashes. More.

Forrester opens fire behind me, sending a salvo of grenades raking down the pillars on the left. He silences the enemy muzzle flashes and temporarily blinds me.

A man screams into the night. Pain and rage. I shout back.

"Come and get it you dirty bitch!"

There are more flashes from the end of the street, so I continue to lay down on the butterfly.

Controlled bursts.

The enemy is firing wildly now, desperately. Tracers rip passed my turret a bit too high, or a bit too wide.

Stray rounds hit the chicken-plate under my gun, and the sparks threaten to blind me with the brightness of their flashing, but I keep firing.

My gun goes dry.

I depress the butterfly, holding level on the chest of a running man, but nothing happens.

"Can! I need a can!"

I no longer have bullets to hide behind, but I do have the sides of my turret.

Quickly, I swivel the gun forty-five degrees to the right, granting myself a bit of shelter for the reload.

The men are still running. Three now. No, four. Hauling as fast as they can, they're coming to kill me before I can get the gun up.

I feel the fresh can of ammunition in my hands and I think about dropping it, grabbing my M-4, and protecting myself as best I can.

Shunting the idea away, I hoist the new can up, and leaning forward out of the safety of metal and glass, I throw the empty can away into the street. That chore being done, I lift the fresh can toward its place in the now empty bracket.

Moving my shaking hands as fast as they will go, I try to work the can into its seat, but it's got a corner stuck on a diagonal and I need to-

Looking up from my fumbling work, I see that the enemy is right on top of me. A man less than ten meters away pops out of cover and levels his rifle to fire. Then he explodes.

Forrester sends a shower of explosive metal into the pillars, breaking the enemies apart in a shower of blood, fire, and concrete chips.

A chunk of grenade shrapnel or concrete impacts the ammo can just inches in front of my face, ripping it mightily out of my hands where it falls out of reach, bent, inert, and useless onto the hood of the Humvee.

"Can! I need another can!"

I'm dimly aware of my hand stinging and throbbing, but I have no time to look at the damage. I flex it, and it works. That's good enough.

"Jesus Christ, D, don't drop it this time!"

"Yeah."

This time, I get the rounds quickly seated in the tray and pull out the start of the belt. More gunfire hits and pings off my turret, making me flinch. I set into the task at hand.

Lifting the feed-tray cover with my shakings hands, I slap a round under the feeder claw.

Another round hits the right edge of my turret, splattering me with sparks, and I fumble the God-damned rounds again.

I'm going to die here because I'm a stupid fuck who didn't pay enough attention.

I can't see what I'm doing. The fight has made me night-blind in my right eye, and my nods are focused one hundred meters out. My turret is the home of fear, chaos, and darkness, as my hands fumble through protective gloves, feeling for the feeder claw of a weapon I cannot see, all the while with tracers ripping the air around and above me.

Motherfuckers, haven't killed me yet!

I catch the link and slap the feed-tray cover closed, then rack my bolt to the rear and let it go. It gives off the most satisfying clink that I've ever heard.

Two flashes come from the left and I make them go away; a flash comes from the right and I erase it also.

Getting the gun up, all of my fear leaves me. I'm alive. The weapon is up, and somebody has some real hell to pay for playing with my emotions tonight, but the alley goes quiet. Wonderfully quiet. Peacefully, blissfully quiet.

I can't hear a thing. Shocked out, I just breathe and look forward, waiting.

I can see the bodies of a dozen men splayed out on the sidewalks, mostly in pieces thanks to Forrester's explosive work.

Sweat stings my eyes, but I don't remove my hands from my weapon to wipe it. I'm sure my hand is bleeding, but my soul isn't leaking out my face so it doesn't matter.

A minute passes. Or five. Or an hour; there's no way for me to tell. The bells in my head hammer loudly, but I can still make out the thrum-thrum-thrum of the diesel engine underneath me, and I feel its vibrations running up my legs.

Relaxing a moment, I lean forward, lowering my profile in the turret and gazing toward the front as best I can. I've been away for a while.

I'm starting to think again, and I'm tired. I'm fading on adrenaline, fast.

I see movement to the left. I don't have to wait to be shot at this time. I'll get him first.

Using the crank, I swivel the turret a hair to the left, aiming at the center of the street to catch the man on the run if he does. All his friends are dead. He should run. I'd run. He does; he makes a break for it.

I see the man, facial details hidden by darkness and distance as he starts his long run across the road. It's the shortest ten meter dash of his entire life.

Lurching his shoulders forward, he bears his weight down to cant into a full sprint and takes three strides.

I've trapped him.

Aiming where he'll be, when he'll be there, I fire an eight-round burst. It does it.

The first rounds rack his body, lifting him slightly off the ground and distorting his frame. Impacts from the inevitable automatic strays spark on the wall behind him, showering flickering light through the space where his pelvis was. Halfway through the burst one of his legs detaches and smacks against the wall behind him.

He doesn't make it across the street. Most of him made it a little more than halfway; I've got to give him credit for that.

"Delta this is CP. Break back to Mad, repeat, Charlie is in the JSS. Break back to Mad, how copy, over?"

"Roger, CP. That's a good copy."

Slowly, ever so slowly, our convoy starts rolling again.

Thank you God. Thank you, thank you, thank you.

I don't look at the bodies of the broken men that we've laid low. I look ahead to my sector and continue to scan for more targets.

We pass through the T-barriers at the end of the street and continue unopposed, on our quick and merry jaunt back to Mad.

When we pull into the front gate I flip my nods up and away from my face, and the natural bluish light of the early morning hurts my left eye.

"Brass, what the fuck time is it?"

"Round 0630."

"We were out there all fucking night?"

"All God-damned night; you said it."

I'm in a time warp. I thought we were out for an hour, maybe two max. We've been gone almost six. I'm missing time.

I stand up in the turret and stretch as best I can as our tired convoy trundles to the parking area, but my heart is still beating quickly and I have a victorious surge of adrenaline in my veins.

The MPs at the gate clap and shout for us as we drive by. Looking down, I see why.

The hoods of our trucks, and the roofs around our turrets are covered in links and empty shell casings. On other trucks as well as my own, I see cracked glass, and the telling gray bullet marks that have punched away ragged circles in our beige paint. Doubtless, they've been listening to us fight all night long. All of Baghdad doubtless heard the Hellfires; I'm sure I'll be hearing them for the rest of my life.

"You don't mess with the 82nd, do you? Hey up there, do you, Pearce? Yeah, that's right!"

Brass is laughing himself into stitches. He's obviously pumped. I've never seen him more excited.

"All units. Refit and standby."

"What's that, Brass, we ain't done?"

"Naw man. You must've missed the chatter, being as you can't hear for shit now and all. One hour, we're going out again. Still got movement out there."

"Can't be much of it. I think we took out the garbage tonight. That had to be nearly all the trash in the neighborhood."

I smile down at Brass, where he sits craning his southern neck up at me, and add, "Took it out sumthin' fierce!"

More laughter all around.

With the truck stopped, there's only one thing left to do. I have to locate Chapel and have some smoky-break time.

I feel lightheaded and shaky on my feet when my boots hit the ground, like I've been at sea for too long. The slight moment of nausea is gone before I can really feel it, so I shake it off. Dropping my IBA, helmet, and rifle in a neat pile, I walk over to Chapel's truck and easily recognize him in the early dark, with the rays of the sun just about to break over the horizon.

"Bold move Chapps. I saw that. Rightly done; that shit was cool."

"Cool? I guess so. Wish I could see that stupid shit on a highlight real. Oh well, done is done. We got the gun back up."

I don't have anything else to say about it. It was brave. It was heroic, and it was necessary. To Chapel, it's nothing. He does what a Sergeant does, with not a second thought to it.

"Camel Wide?"

He extends the pack to me, and I gladly take two.

"I can use a change every now and again."

Firing up with our Zippos, we stand and puff away at the day's first cigarettes, relishing the smokes themselves, and the break that accompanies them.

The smoke fills my lungs and immediately satisfies me. I'm free for now, for an hour.

"How's Charlie? I couldn't hear the radio too good after, you know."

"Only one dead. The others will be fine. Only six are going to the green zone, the rest will probably RTD in a week or so."

"Good news. When that shit came down over the net, well, you kn-"

Chapel cuts me off, "I hear you man. Got it. Good job out there today."

"Good job for all of us. We fucking smacked the shit out of them."

"Keep your head on straight. Just get ready to go back out there."

"Ready as I'll ever be."

Chapel turns back to his own crew, doubtless to start checking his soldiers gear, direct ammunition resupply, and do a quick PMCS of his truck before it's time to go out again. He's like that. Before he gets absorbed in the task at hand, and before I snuff out my smoke, he turns to me and smiles.

"Hey Pearce, two weeks, brother. You can do anything for two weeks."

Walking back to my truck, there's precious little I have to do to make ready again. Just reload the fucking gun I guess. Take a piss. Eat a brownie. Screw my head on straight, things like that.

Sunlight streams over the walls of Mad as I light my second smoke. Morning prayer music starts to play from loudspeakers in the neighborhood as the stone Iraqi world is bathed in the soft pink light of a new day.

We'll probably be on media blackout again soon.

I take a drag on the new smoke while I think on the words of a wise man.

Two weeks.

Glossary

82ndABN DIV – The 82nd Airborne Division. If you are a bad person, they will come looking for you, and then break your shit off.

AAFES – The Army and Air Force Exchange Service. Basically, this is the organization that sets up post exhanges (PXs) so that all the green plastic army men can buy tobacco.

ACAP – I don't know what the acronym stands for. This is just what you have to do to get out of the army, or in my case, the 82nd ABN DIV.

ACH – Advanced Combat Helmet. A Kevlar variant of the tried and true WWII issue K-pot.

ACOG – Advanced Combat Optical Gunsight.

AK-47 – The original Kalashnikov rifle. Firing a variant of the NATO 7.62 round, this is the preferred rugged, cheap, and reliable battle rifle of the Middle East. They didn't make it though; they can't make anything. It's a fantastic and scary rifle because the Russians made it.

AP – Armor Piercing, such as .50 AP.

Apache – The AH-64 Attack Helicopter. This is the coolest combat helicopter in the American arsenal. It's high-speed, and it can break your shit off.

ARCOM – The Army Commendation Medal.

Article 15 – You must have fucked up. This is the legalese document that sends men and their careers straight to Hell.

ASIP – This is a radio. I know what the letters mean, but I don't know if I'm allowed to tell you, so I won't.

Assault Pack – Smaller than a traditional Alice Pack or rucksack, this is like an elementary school backpack for rugged dudes. You can put shit in there and then carry it around for a while. I never assaulted anything while wearing an Assault Pack. Weird.

Assistan – This isn't a real place. I just like to throw it in when mentioning any of the other Stans, of which there are many.

Asshole – I shouldn't have to tell you what this is. If you don't know, you shouldn't be reading my book in the first place.

AT-4 – (1)   This is the common platoon designator that the army gives to anti-tank or heavy weapons elements sometimes. (2) AT-4 is the nomenclature for the standard US Army issued shoulder-fired anti-tank rocket launcher.   Front Toward Enemy and all that.   See Backblast.

AO – Area of Operations.

AWOL – Absent Without leave.   See Article 15 or Shitbag.

B's – Barracks

Backblast – This is the incredible jet of flame that is expelled from a shoulder-fired rocket launcher.   Spewn out of the ass-end of a launch-tube in a seventy-five degree arc, the flame can reach temperatures in excess of 7,500 degrees Fahrenheight.   Backblast can cook a bitch.

Battle-Rattle – When a soldier has all of his crap on, it can weigh as much as eighty pounds or more, depending on what kind of weapon system(s) he is carrying.   Generally, us infantry types tie down or tape everything into quiet, stable positions attached to our personal gear however we can get it to quietly fit; this also prevents equipment loss; misplacing your keys is a slightly less stressful situation than misplacing an incendiary grenade.   Without fail, a man in a ceramic, plastic, and metal suit, actively carrying a boatload of small metal objects and wielding a long metal stick is not generally a quiet creature, regardless of the measures he has taken to remain quiet.   Hence the term; I don't have to say any more.

Barrett 107 – This rifle is a .50 Caliber beast.

BDA – Battle Damage Assessment.

Blackhawk – The UH-60.   It's a utility helicopter.   It is flown by a guy who uses it to carry other dudes around.

Blaster – See Gatpiece.

BOHICA – Bend Over Here It Comes Again.   See Fucked.

Bradley Fighting Vehicle – The Bradley Fighting Vehicle.

Brainbucket – See ACH.

Buttonhook – A tight, sharp turn taken while on foot, most commonly around an object on ingress or egress, such as a Humvee door or a doorjamb.

Burka – The musty black blankets that Muslims force their women to hide in.

CAS – Close, or Combat Air Support.

Casualty – When I was six years old, I thought that casualty just meant somebody who had died. That's not the case. The term casualty applies both to those simply wounded in combat, as well as those who are killed outright.

CAV - Cavalry

CCO – Close Combat Optic; with no magnification, this is the standard US Army reflex sight.

Choke-Slam – This is the act of lifting another man off the ground by his throat with only one hand, and then promptly and forcefully returning him to the earth.

Clapped Up – This is not a venereal disease. See Fucked.

Clip – Often confused with the proper term magazine, there is no such thing as a clip that you put into a pistol or a rifle. It is more proper to use the term clip in the following contexts: I need to clip my fingernails; he's running at a good clip. Also, there are hair-clips, or a flying bullet may nearly clip you. The age-old confusion between the terms clip and magazine most likely originated from 'stripper-clips,' which used to be used to feed ammunition into some WWII era rifles, as well as still being employed to transport ammunition in an orderly fashion today. See Magazine for further clarification.

CLP – The weapon lubricant that Cleans, Lubricates, and Protects. While CLP is a brand name, the army refers to every type of gun oil as CLP.

Co – Company.

CO – Commanding Officer

Coms – Communications. See ASIP.

CP – Command Post. See Talk.

CQ – Closed Quarters, also known as fire-guard. This is the duty station that requires a soldier to stay awake while everyone else sleeps, so he can guard them. He should be awake when he does this. CQs are normally in radio contact with the CP. See CP.

Cyclic – Or, 'going cyclic,' is the common terminology for, rather than firing an automatic weapon in controlled bursts, just mashing the trigger down and seeing what the thing can *really* do. It's every six-year-old boy's fantasy.

DAPS – Deltoid Armpit... Protector... Something.

Dead Space – Not only a super-awesome survival-horror videogame, this is the term used to refer to space in a tactical environment that cannot be seen, such as when entering and clearing a room, i.e. Go check the dead space behind that sofa.

Dirty Leg – A filthy leg. See Filthy Leg.

D-Fac – Dining Facility, or chow hall. Chow is army talk for food.

Dunderfuck – See Goat Rope.

ECP – Entry Control Point.

EFP – Explosively Formed Projectile. This new-fangled and frightening IED can cut through the thickest tank armor like it's nothing but butter.

EOD – Explosive Ordinance Disposal.

Falafel – A bread-based meat pocket; nobody can ever really be sure what's in there.

Filthy Leg – See Leg.

Five-Fifty Cord – Five-Fifty parachute cord. The actual kind of small rope that is used on real Army Airborne T-10 Charlie parachutes! Infantry types use this cord for everything, as it is very strong. Only about three millimeters in diameter, one strand can hold up to five hundred and fifty pounds of tension, hence the name.

Flagging – (1) This is the unsightly and uncouth practice of accidentally aiming the muzzle of your weapon squarely at one of your buddies. (2) Accidentally presenting your weapon into, or out of an object that makes an enemy aware of your location, even though you cannot see them. i.e. 'Hey buddy, stop flagging your shit around the corner.'

FOB – Forward Operating Base

Fobbit – Somebody who lives on, and never leaves the Fob. See POG.

FRG – Mainly composed of army wives, this stands for Family Readiness Group. They get to bitch about things because the army makes them feel like what they have to say matters. Also, they send deployed infantry types all sorts of rad and delicious junk-food.

FUBAR – Fucked Up Beyond All Repair. See Fucked. Also, go watch Saving Private Ryan; you obviously missed that film.

Fucked – This is really, really bad. You are so screwed.

402

Fuck-O – See Asshole.

Fucked Up – See the definition two lines above this one.

Gat – Pistol.

Gatpiece – Rifle.

Goat Rope – See FUBAR.

Going Cyclic – See Cyclic.

GRUNT – Grunt, or more properly GRU(nt), used to be the common Vietnam Era appellation for Ground Replacement Unit (not trained). In spite of its decidedly negative connotation, this term has been adapted for modern times, and now it is commonly used to refer to any infantryman or other hardy combat-arms foot-soldier. A grunt is a highly combative army dude, and he will break your shit. Grunts are the opposite of POGs. See POG.

GTA – C'mon. You know what this is.

Hajji – The formal term for an Islamic male who has successfully completed the pilgrimage to Mecca.

HE – High Explosive.

Hemmed Up – See Fucked Up.

HESCO – I've never known what the acronym stands for. These are simple cardboard or burlap wire mesh cubes that take up about three cubic feet when they are unfolded. The hollow wire mesh squares are then filled with dirt, and you have yourself a reliable barrier. It's ingenious really. Basically, it's a giant sand-bag cube.

High Crawl – Most often confused with low crawling, this is when an infantryman crawls forward on his elbows while looking straight ahead. That may not seem very high, but the alternative low crawl consists of dragging your face along the ground while pulling yourself forward using nothing but the clawing motions of your fingers and toes. Low crawling sucks. High crawling is better.

High Value Item – Anything that costs a bunch of money that the army gives you and tells you that you are responsible for. If you lose it, they'll fuck you up. See Fucked Up.

Hook and Pile Tape – This is the non-trademark term that the army uses to refer to Velcro.

Hooligans – Sometimes pronounced 'Haligans,' this is a backpack portable set of tools consisting of a bunch of different crowbars and pry-bars. Sometimes they even come with a cute little battering ram, but nobody ever wants to carry that shit around.

IA – Iraqi Army. No comment. See Shitbag.

IBA – Interceptor Body Armor. A hot and musty tactical vest with ceramic plates in the front and back that can stop up to a 7.62 round. But, it can only stop one, as the ceramic will shatter on the first impact, provided that you are lucky enough to get shot in the very center of the ceramic plate; there is a considerable amount of plate-less space on the vest.

IED – Improvised Explosive Device.

Indirect Fire – People try to kill you with this, even though they don't have a line of sight to you. This is how the army commonly refers to mortar and rocket attacks. If you are ever caught in a mortar attack's impact area, trust me, it doesn't seem very indirect at all.

IP – Iraqi Police. No comment. Actually, just read my book. You should understand then.

IR – Infrared. It's science stuff.

J-DAM – This is a big missile, much like a Tomahawk missile. It really, really breaks things.

JSS – Joint Service Station.

KBR – This is a private contracting corporation that works on overseas military posts. They often provide shower and latrine facilities, run dining facilities, and fulfill many of the maintenance roles that are required to keep a FOB operational. See FOB.

K Pot – The American classic. See ACH.

Lazy W – A halted truck formation in which a line of trucks, all still generally facing their original direction of travel, angle themselves outward at 45 degree angles at intervals: left, right, left, and so one.

Leg – A soldier who is not Airborne. See Dirty Leg.

Long Gun – A common term for referring to military or police sniper systems.

Lower-Slaboobistan - There's really no such place; I just make up silly words from time to time.

Loophole – A small cutaway in a wall or other object that allows a soldier to fire his weapon, or observe his surroundings while minimally exposing himself. Loopholes went out of style for architectural planning when castles and other fortresses went out of style. If there is something that can be referred to as a loophole on the modern day battlefield, it is most likely a hole that something busted into the side of something else.

LP – Listening Post.

LT – Lieutenant. There is a surprisingly colorful history associated with the words Lieutenant, and Leftenant. It's wonderfully interesting reading, and I would recommend the short study to anyone.

Lume – A short word for illumination. There are numerical degrees of lume, and the system is most commonly known and used by pilots. I don't know how to use the system; infantrymen just like to say lume all the time. It makes us sound smart.

M-24 – This is the military variant of what used to be a .30-06 rifle, chambered to fire the NATO 7.62 round. This is the basic long gun that is the preferred sniper system for modern American army infantry scouts.

M240-B – My favorite 7.62 machine gun. It's really swell! It's a heavier, meaner version of the old M-60. Think Rambo, and you'll know what I'm talking about.

M-4 – This is the standard 5.56 carbine that they give to cool guys. It's basically a shorter M-16 with a retractable butt stock. It shoots harmless BBs.

Magazine – This is the actual term that people should use to refer to the bullet-filled metal slide that you stuff into a gun to make it happy.

Man-Dress – This is the dress that Arabian men wear. The get-up is never complete without flip-flops, body odor, and urine stains.

M-Bitter – This is a small radio. You put it in your pouch and then you talk to people on it and stuff.

Mer – Shorthand slang for MRE. See MRE.

Mic – Mic, pronounced 'Mike,' is army talk for minute, or mics for minutes.

MK-19 – The Mark 19 is a fully automatic 40mm grenade launching heavy weapon system. You wouldn't like it when it's angry, but it has saved my life before. *Love it, love it.*

MRE - Meal Ready to Eat. These are the standard food simulators provided to soldiers by the US of A.

Mortar – This is a really scary thing that falls out of the sky and then explodes. You never know where they're going to land.

MP – Military Police.

Mulhalla – Short, narrow residential pathways through old Babylon. Normally about four feet wide, these are the basic alleyways that lead to the concrete or brick cubbyholes that people call home. It's important to remember that most of Baghdad was built over a thousand years before the first automobile, so it's not uncommon to find streets that are only three feet wide between residential buildings.

NCO – Non Commissioned Officers, otherwise known as sergeants.

Ne'er do well – People who never do anything well.

NODs – Night Optical Devices, or Night-Vision Optics. It's just more simple to say nods all the time.

Noob – Somebody who is new, especially in the realm of online first-person shooters.

OP – (1) Operation. (2) Observation Post.

PEQ-2/4 – These are infrared toys, that when mated with the M-4 make sci-fi babies happen.

PMCS – Preventative Maintenance Checks and Services. This term is most commonly used in reference to vehicles, and can be heard constantly around Army motor pools.

POG – Personnel Other than Grunt. These are not combat soldiers. Every infantryman is a soldier, but not every soldier is an infantryman. See Fobbit.

PSP – Playstation Portable. This toy is rad, especially if you don't have access to anything else for months and months at a time.

PT – Physical Training.

Poopsterbate – The act of visiting a latrine, and while there, taking a shit and masturbating, but never at the same time. That would be kind of like a blumpkin, and that sort of stuff is just weird and disturbing.

PVT – Private. Enlisted ranks E-1 and E-2 in Army pay-grade talk.

PX – Post Exchange; an AAFES store. See AAFES.

QRF – Quick Reaction Force.

RPG - (1) Really Pretty Girl. (2) Rocket Propelled Grenade. (3) Role Playing Game – Nerdy. (4) Role Playing Game – Kinky.

RTB – Return to Base.

RTD – Return to Duty, often in reference to a casualty who will heal up just fine soon, and then get back to work as if nothing happened.

RTO – Radio Telephone Operator.   The guy who carries the ASIP around and says stuff on it.   See ASIP.

'Same Same' – Most Arabian men love the same same. They'll walk right up to you and ask, 'Mista, Mista, same same?' All the while rubbing their index fingers together in a disgusting manner.   I think you know what I'm trying to say; Iraqi police stations always smell like butt-sex and man vinegar.

Sensitive Items – See High Value Items.

Sitrep – Situation report.

Shitbag – This is the very worst kind of soldier.   They are like bags, only full of shit.   Real shit.

SGT – Sergeant, E-5.

SPC – Specialist, E-4.

SSGT – Staff Sergeant, E-6.

S & T – Supply and Transport.   This is the never-ending Hell where self-respecting infantrymen fear to tread.

SFC – Sergeant First Class, E-7.

Smag – This is a sort of impolite, vulgar, and highly un-recommended way to address a Sergeant Major.   It rhymes with vag. If you wear an army uniform and a Sergeant Major ever hears you use this term, see Fucked.

Smoke – (1)   To inhale burning cigarettes.   (2)   The act of physically punishing another soldier through the beautiful majesty of physical exertion.   (3)   To eat a dick.

SOP – Standard Operating Procedure.

Talk - Command Post.   See CP.

TC – Truck Commander.

Terp – Interpreter, or *'Multhaljim.'*

To Chair – A common Anglicized variant of the French touché.

VBIED – Vehicle Born Improved Explosive Device.   These can be very dangerous indeed, as they are mobile and can be stuffed with literally hundreds of pounds of high-grade explosives.

About the Author

Dallas Pearce was honorably discharged from the U. S. Army after returning home safely from Baghdad, Iraq. He currently lives with his three silly Dachshunds in central Montana, where he has an understandably warm affection for the long, cold winter months. He enjoys fishing, shooting the longbow, playing classical guitar, and writing.

Baghdad at Night is also available for purchase on Amazon.com. Use the amazon.com search bar and enter '*Baghdad at Night* by Dallas Pearce' to locate the Kindle e-book.